A STIFF Wind Blows

Gary McConville

Lagomorph Publishing LLC

All characters in this work of fiction are either a product of the author's imagination or are used fictitiously. Political events noted herein may have been intentionally twisted for 'visual' effect.

Coaching by author of *Lipstick Apology*:
Jennifer Jabaley of Blue Ridge, GA

Beta reader and supplier of heaping doses of adrenaline in early stages:
Elizabeth Ayala of San Mateo, CA

Short page editing by author of Rabbits: Gentle Hearts Valiant Spirits:
Marie Mead of Roswell, GA

Guidance /Editor /Proofreader:
Valerie Mathews of The Exit 271 Studio, Athens, GA

Grammarian and dear family friend:
Heidi Nichols of Durango, CO

Cover art and interior graphics:
Kaj Johnson of runrabbitgraphics.com

Story line edits plus interior and exterior design layout:
Jera Publishing, www.jerapublishing.com

Rough critiquing:
An array of wonderful writers of The Lawrenceville Sci-Fi Writers Critique Group.

A portion of the profits from sale of this book and related merchandise profits selected chapters of the House Rabbit Society based in Richmond, California. For more information on rabbit care, local chapters, and events, please visit: http://www.rabbit.org

For additional information on the alternative Libertarian Party, please visit: https://www.lp.org

The Winds Series by Lagomorph Publishing LLC
Suite 420-328
855 Woodstock Road
Roswell, GA 30075

ISBN 978-1-7320758-0-1

Printed in the United States of America.

I dedicate this novel to Francis Robert McConville, best father and great optimist. Also to Steven Robert McConville, brother and obsessive organizer who made life appear magically easy. Taken from us too soon, we miss you both, terribly.

And my soul mate, Nancy, to whom I frequently bare my inner self. This story was only possible because of you.

Christian

Hope you enjoy...

M Gary

:)

CONTENTS

PART 3: FRIENDS

PART 4: GENESIS

PART 1:
LOST IN A DREAM

CHAPTER 1
A Solitude Gladly Surrendered

Wrought with nightmares and despair, sits a man gazing out a glass portal of the Atlantis's starboard bow. He feels caged inside the darkened room, millions of miles from home. He wallows in self-doubt, hands trembling, like those of someone well beyond his early thirties. Eyes following stars drifting lazily past, his head suddenly twists past the empty vials lining his dresser. "Blasted pill lady," Gregory calls out. "Why's she never around?"

Gazing down, he opens the ivory box on his lap, smiling at the captain's gift. His shaky hands examine the fine craftsmanship of the hand-carved shofar. Holding it to his lips, he recalls scores of masked rebels, perched high atop the many summits overlooking the plateau on Jake's Mountain. There the female choir poised, arms stretched upward, sweet voices harmonizing to the hand-carved woodwinds of their male counterparts, singing songs of distaste for the Empire and its prized starship Atlantis, perched below.

Gregory's heart flutters in memory of Rena's sweet voice, echoing above the others in the dew-kissed, pre-dawn morning.

Our loved ones vanished without a clue.
Property stolen by suits of red and blue.
Oh, the trickery they reek,
in their twisted animal speak.
Nothing worthy they say,
Having heard it all anyway.
Six thousand years of political lies and biblical story.
Six thousand years of your goddamn righteous glory.

Rena's fiery words ... her almighty plan ... the twenty-third of November. All burn through his memory. If only she had not been swallowed up in the darkness. If only I could be with her again. If only I had kept away from that damn dust.

A disturbance interrupts his rebellious thoughts. He drops the shofar inside its protective sleeve in the felt-lined case and slides it across the room. As it finds safe haven under his single bed, his gaze leaves the hallway in favor of the impersonal blackness beyond.

The patter of small feet across his cold vinyl floor draws a rare smile. Without hesitation, five-year-old Ayla climbs into his familiar lap and wraps her arms around his neck. Staring past his long nose, she bats her dark-brown eyes at him. "Tell me a story, Uncle Greg. Something about Mommy."

Gregory brushes the hair from her eyes as he once did with his big sister. "Doesn't your dad—?"

"Every time I ask, Daddy gets real quiet, like he's seen a ghost or something."

"What about—?"

"Oh, him. He always pats my head and sends me off to play. Then he disappears behind that slimy replicator machine." Ayla's lower lip swells. "They never tell me anything about Mommy. They never have time for me."

Watching her squirm in his lap, shaking her shoulder-length blonde hair, a tear gathers on Gregory's cheek. "Those two men really loved her, I can tell you that. Your mom was one special lady."

Ayla wipes her uncle's tear. She reaches deep in her pocket and shoves a graphene bunny in his face. "You can have this. Father made it for me." She watches as Gregory takes it in his hand and grins before setting it on the floor at his feet. "Daddy said they locked you in some crazy place, gave you a Carrot Syndro—"

"Tourette's Syndrome." Gregory pats her on the head. "Now how about that story?"

Ayla buries her head in his lap. "Please! Please!"

"Now, promise you'll stay awake this time, Ayla." Feeling her nod, Gregory begins. "You must understand, sweetie, things were not always like this. Why, your great Grampa James—"

"I remember him."

Gregory chuckles. "I was merely your age when he ... uh ... departed. There have been many changes since his time, none for the better. I remember sitting on *his* lap, listening to *him* carrying on about endless wars over stupid—"

"What are wars, Uncle Greg?"

Gregory scans the room for answers. After a minute, he regains control of his twitching hands. He takes a deep breath and grins at his niece, head buried in his lap. "Well, the world was running out of energy. Everyone wanted what the others had. Countries merged into continents and continents into the seven great empires. The empires became so powerful that anyone questioning them would disappear, never to be heard from again."

Ayla's head rises. She stares into her uncle's similar brown eyes. "Like what happened to you, Uncle Greg? Everyone told me about the Cos, how Mommy had—"

"Hush now. Let me finish." Gregory's hands tremble. He takes several deep breaths. A full yawn devours Ayla's face before she returns it to Gregory's lap. "As I was saying, Ayla, with everyone's quest for energy, there were big changes taking place. Many sacred customs and superstitions gave way to science and research. But all this effort turned up nothing. Even the energy in those Martian rocks—"

"Uncle Greg!" she moans, raising her head along with her voice. "Not that Martian stuff again. I want to hear about—"

"Okay. Okay. As I said, your mom was special. She was one of the special triad that were, like three of a perfect pair. Each one filled me in on the details of what happened after I was … uh … away."

"Like you're telling me now."

Gregory grins. "Your mom was among the Empire's trusted few. But not being much of a … brown-noser, she was never selected to ride in the Empire's fancy starship, like the chosen few. Now Brutus—"

"Was *he* chosen?"

"Patience, my sweet Ayla. I'm getting to that. Now Brutus, he was a childhood bully. With his enormous size, he had bloodied many a kid's nose. Lucky for the rest of us, as he grew older, he learned how to step on fewer toes." Gregory reaches down and pinches her tiny digits.

"Stop!" she yells, curling her feet underneath her.

"Checking if you were paying attention, sweetie." Ayla nods and reburies her head. "Brutus used small favors to climb up the ranks of the trusted few, and with his mechanical skills and fierce loyalty, he soon gained access to the most highly secured areas."

Ayla yawns. "Like the Starship Atlantis?"

"Yes, even the Atlantis. There was no doubt *his* name was on that chosen list. But my tale is not really about those two. It's about my upstairs neighbor, my best friend, Andorf Johnson."

Gregory marvels at Ayla's soft innocence as she sleeps in his lap. His eyes dampen as he turns to gaze out the glass portal. "If only we hadn't disturbed that damn dust. Things would have been way different. Oh, I remember Andorf and that rugby game, like it was yesterday."

CHAPTER 2

Late To The Game

A man's cratered face and glimmering incisor smile recede deep within the shadows of City Park's rundown maintenance hut. Makeup channeling down her cheeks, a desperate woman cries out from the dark recesses. She tugs insistently on the trench coat of the combative man, twenty years her junior. Perhaps the woman seeks an unlicensed pharmaceutical for a dying loved one, or perhaps this is an indiscrete rendezvous for unresolved coin exchange. "You don't understand. I must have it!" she cries out once more.

Shifting winds carry the enticing aroma of freshly brewed java. Andorf detours towards a bleacher packed with cheering rugby fans, dressed in light sweaters, swinging their arms in unison this brisk spring evening. Their stomping feet mask the evil voice calling from below as Andorf scans the source of the caffeinated blend. A chemically-etched hand clamps around his sleeve, drawing him within spitting distance of a polished porcelain smile. The cratered-face man unsnaps his long trench coat open to reveal countless inner pockets stuffed with six-ounce colored vials. The man pops a vial in Andorf's face, spilling an orange powder onto his spotless EasyGlide sneakers. Andorf struggles to free himself, but the man's crusty hand squeezes tighter. Teeth sparkling at each word, the dealer snorts an overplayed line.

"Got whatcha need, buddy. O.M.P., Oxy, Biludes, all cooked up fresh this very morning. Try this Magic Dust ... it'll cure anything that ails you. A mere ten piece, three for a quarter."

Andorf leans away from the dealer's stale breath, but the man's scarred hand refuses to release him. "What happened to the lady back at the hut? You didn't k—kill her did you?"

The stranger snorts through an evil grin. "She was a worthless two-party candidate pleading for my vote. One must distance himself from such unscrupulous rubbish if one expects to maintain a healthy business clientele. As I was saying ..."

Andorf scans his surroundings, plotting an escape. "What if I'm an agent, waiting on my partner?"

The pusher gags and spits blackish phlegm out his splayed lips. "Agent? You ain't no stinkin' agent, buddy. You don't dress like 'em and hell, you don't smell like 'em." The unlicensed pharmacist sniffs at the pair of argyle-socked shoes dangling above. "Now that guy up there, he smells like an agent."

Andorf breaks free of the dealer's grasp. "Well, you look like a pervert, flashing me with your open coat like that. Surely the authorities—"

The dealer laughs. "Authorities? You think them authorities care? They did away with medical care decades ago. Long as no kids get involved, they don't give a damn what I do. And besides, how would fine upstanding citizens like yourself fill their medical needs without unlicensed pharmacists like me?" The pusher reopens both sides of his trench coat. "Come on, buddy. Take yer pick."

At the dealer's deflating prices, Andorf darts off. A bountiful whiff of coffee fragrance sends him hiking to a grassy area behind the bleachers where a trailer-like contraption of recycled parts lies bound together with rusty baling wire. Wary of its stability, Andorf steps away and reads the vendor's name below the 'No Change' sign dangling from conduit above the makeshift counter.

"Hey, Chester, how much for the brew?" Andorf looks around the contraption. "Hello, anyone back there?"

A sun-parched man appears, wearing flimsy octagon glasses and stitched-together clothing scraps of similar pattern to what Andorf is wearing. "My name! How do you know my name?"

Andorf takes another step back, startled by the old man's nearly transparent pointing finger poking in his face at each jittery worn-out word. He finds something jabbingly familiar about the old man, but cannot quite put a finger on it.

"I told ya' before, mister, I ain't selling no drink." The old man pauses, wheezing and laboring for breath. "I don't do that no more, I tell ya'."

Eyeing the sign above, Andorf projects open palms at the old geezer. "Hey! Hey! Calm down, old man. Chester Drawers is your name, isn't it?"

After a glance above, the old man stabilizes himself against the well-scratched acrylic countertop. "Wasn't sure if I knew ya', that's all. Last time someone called me Chester like that, he turned out to be one of those good-for-nothing government agents." The old man rotates his mouth as if chewing his thoughts. "Thirty days in the hole. That's what those mothers stole from me. Thirty damn days. I ain't selling no drink. Ya' got that?"

Andorf gulps, prompting the vendor along with his hands. "Sure, sure, old man."

In crooked stance, Chester catches his breath. Parched mouth troubling for words, he peers suspiciously at Andorf with cross-examining eyes. "Agents and detectives, they're like roaches I tell you. Once they appear, you can't get rid of them."

Andorf scans the rows of mugs dangling from a wire above their heads. "Look old man, I'm in a hurry."

"Sixteen bucks," the vendor says, fumbling with a long hooked stick. He taps one of the mugs, nudging it closer. "The drink is free, I tell you. I ain't selling no drink."

"What? Sixteen bucks? How about a coffee without one of your fancy mugs?"

"Have it your way." The old man grins at Andorf as his spider-veined hand grabs Andorf's hand and flips it over. He grabs a carafe of fresh brew and laughs hard at Andorf's sudden hand jerk, before dancing about, gasping for air. After a good minute, the old man finds his breath.

Andorf points to a mug in dead center. "I'll take that one."

The old man snickers. With his crooked stick, he lowers the souvenir mug onto the counter and pours his steaming brew, half of which finds its way into the mug. "These collector mugs are a real bargain. But like our politicians, they come with a price and are all the same."

Andorf pulls a twenty-piece from deep within his pocket and watches it vanish into a leather pouch hanging around the vendor's neck. Chester follows him around the side of the makeshift trailer to the condiments counter, beneath the 'After Thoughts' sign. He watches Andorf stir in three creamer sticks.

"I used to stir creamer in figure-eight patterns like that … three at a time, just like you." Chester's eyes brighten. He leans into his younger protégé. "Hear me well, son. Detectives will pay you a little visit. Next, come the agents. Looking for another they'll all be … someone who slips through their hands like water. Naybudah mi fond."

Andorf takes a sip from the mug. He winces at the old man. "What'd you say?"

Chester loses his grin. "Tenulian—you haven't learned it yet," he mumbles tight-lipped. "It is nothing, my friend. You will do just fine." Scratching at his bald crown, Chester stares deep into Andorf's identical blue eyes. "Thrice you will cast your eyes upon a friend from a prior dawn." He coughs a few times before regaining wind. "I remember like yesterday. It began with that childhood rival plotting against me, even going as far to use his girlfriend to—"

Sipping his brew, Andorf waves off Chester. Avoiding further eye contact with the old man, he walks off, doubling his pace. He hears Chester grumbling above the cheering fans as he puts distance between himself and the vendor.

"The militia will be here soon. Mark my words, son, they're on their way. And this time when someone tells you to duck, you had better duck."

Andorf bends down and pockets a discarded souvenir stick flag, oblivious to the handful of pumped-up players easing past. Advancing downfield much faster than the game ball, he slows to slurp the tasty blend. He finds his friend Gregory near the home team's goal line, engrossed in the game. He calls out on his approach. "Only *you* would be positioned way out here."

"About time you showed up, Andorf. We're well into the third quarter. You know how I hate to wait."

Andorf mocks his friend's words with loud slurps. Shivering, he pulls his drooping collar over his neck. "A bit chilly this evening."

Gregory pries his eyes from the action long enough for his dark browns to give Andorf a once over. "The old relic gave you a history lesson, didn't he?"

Andorf nods. "That walking imitation of death wheezed so loud, I could barely understand him. Seems he was waging a one-man battle against the Empire."

"I'm already liking the old coot." Gregory chuckles and glances back at the game. "He kinda reminds me of you."

Andorf gazes back at the stands. "What's with all those crazed fans? There must be three hundred of them crammed in those bleachers."

"Isn't it grand? I've never seen so many citizens gathered in public." Gregory looks about, twitching. "Close to the action."

Andorf leaps from the path of flankers in hot pursuit as the game ball whizzes past. The ball carrier is tackled near the sideline. Clutching the ball on his fall to the ground, he refuses to release it. Opponents join the ruck from all directions. Referees call offside with their whistles, but the pileup continues. After an opposing scrumhalf stomps on the carrier's hands, a flanker digs the ball out and spins it off to a teammate.

"Do they always play this rough? There appears to be no rules."

Gregory squints at his downstairs neighbor. "Laws. In rugby they're called laws."

They follow the players downfield until a fuel truck convoy speeding down an adjacent dirt road sends massive dust clouds across the field. Warblers by the dozens, abandon their cozy spots atop the perimeter fence. Fans use sweaters to filter out silt and swat at warblers buzzing past their heads. Play ceases as players and refs stop to cover their faces with their shirts.

Gregory shakes a fist at the passing trucks. "Bastards! Why must they ruin everything? It's all about their damn warship."

"Warship? Don't you mean starship?"

"Warship, starship, what's the damn difference? Look at all the havoc that thing wreaks. Aren't you sick of all those infomercials featuring Fat Max plugging whatever the Canine Empire does for its citizens?"

"Stop that, Gregory. Before they haul your butt off to the Cos."

Gregory grabs Andorf by the shoulders. "We've got to do something, end what those statists have been cramming down our throats." Gregory's eyes twitch. "Hell, you could run for mayor, Andorf. People around here know you. You'd be an easy win. Tell me one person who doesn't like you."

Andorf drops his shirt and stares, stupefied, at Gregory. He throws both hands in the air. "You're delusional, Gregory. You know I have no interest in politics. Besides, who in their right mind would vote for me?"

"Well, you've got my vote and certainly you'd vote for yourself. That's two."

Andorf's hand cradles his chin. "My grandfather *was* a two-term governor of New Mexico but … I don't know. I'd have to awaken with the sun, listening to everyone's bad ideas."

"Bad ideas? Like what?"

"Like me running for mayor."

"Just sleep on it, Andorf. We could stand a few changes around here. Think of all the resources consumed by that black hole up there on Jake's Mountain. Perhaps you could free up a few—"

"I don't like it either, Gregory, but without that shiny starship, most everyone would be out panhandling. I dare you to find anyone whose job isn't nursed by the Atlantis."

Loud cheering draws their eyes back to the field. Refs blow whistles as a fan steals the game ball and runs back to the safety of the bleachers, angry players closing in. At the last minute, he tosses the ball onto the field and blends into the boisterous crowd. Refs flail their arms, calling the pissed-off players from both teams back onto the field.

Gregory blows warm air across his fingers. "As I said before, everyone loves the—"

East Virginia warblers again puncture the evening's stillness. They circle overhead, buzz the fans, and disappear as quickly as they arrived. The crowd quiets. With the exception of the coffee vendor's departing taillights, all eyes and ears are tuned to the darkening sky.

A dull patter of blades whipping the air sends fans onto the field, overwhelming referees and players. A pair of Coyote attack helicopters, engines straining under heavy payload, descends through the clouds. Cold water rains down upon fans as they run to escape the warbirds' sweeping floodlights.

A smaller, more agile two-man Whippet with '600D' stenciled across its fuselage, appears in a central position between the warbirds, as if coordinating the rain dance. The voice of Sergeant Rudy Ginzbug yells out from the Whippet's skid-mounted speakers. "Take that, you moderates. Run! Run for your lives."

Gregory shakes a fist at the wandering copters from the end field's transparent safety. A floodlight suddenly sweeps across him and Andorf, throwing them into the chaos. Andorf grabs his friend's arm and runs down the field past the goal line, weaving a path clear of the sweeping lights. Gregory freezes outside a 36-inch concrete drainpipe protruding from a break in the hillside. "I'm not going in there."

Andorf shoves his friend toward the pipe. "Dammit, Gregory! Hurry!"

With Andorf at his heels, Gregory reluctantly dives inside. A discarded fiber film wraps itself around Andorf's calf. He freezes, Chester's raspy words ringing in his ears. "Duck! Duck I say!"

Gregory crawls from the pipe and leaps after Andorf. The Whippet copter sweeps past, ripping the plastic film away from Andorf's ankle, along with the old man's words. Shots ring out. One bullet zips past Andorf's nose. Another zings by Gregory's ear lobe. Gregory grabs hold of Andorf and drags him deep inside the pipe. Safely inside, Gregory feels the side of his head. "What the hell were you doing out there, Andorf? That last bullet nearly sliced off my ear."

Andorf mumbles. "The old man ... he was warning me."

"Dammit, Andorf! Not those voices again."

"But I heard him, clear as day."

Gregory withdraws deeper inside the damp concrete pipe. "I'd be more concerned about the militia if I were you."

"Shhh. Someone's out there," Andorf whispers, backing into Gregory. They wait, expecting an unfriendly face to leer in at them at any moment. Watching Gregory's shaking leg, Andorf feels his best friend about to crawl out of his skin.

Gregory whispers. "It'll end in a binding flash, no witnesses."

"Hush, Gregory, they'll—"

"I can't breathe." Gregory gasps, worming over Andorf. He lunges for the fresh open air, but stops at the sight of army boots, inches beyond the pipe's opening. Andorf crawls after him. In the dark pipe, he jams his face into Gregory's shoes. An overhead tapping has them covering each other's mouths, pleading that their pulsating hearts will not betray them. The tapping abruptly ceases.

"They were standing right here, Sergeant Ginzbug," a disciplined young voice yells.

From his limited view, they see boots marching off. Gregory slithers out, waving Andorf on before disappearing into the night.

Andorf hesitates. He shimmies halfway out of the pipe and into a pair of muddy boots. As his face suddenly illuminates, he stands, raising both hands to a private and the 9 mm at his head. Smelling powder residue from the barrel, nudging closer, Andorf slowly shifts his weight from one foot to the other. Beads of sweat form on his temples.

"Run, ass-wipe. Give me an excuse." The private turns his head, keeping one eye on his captive. "Sarge! I've got our—"

FWAP!

Andorf stares at the private lying face down at his feet and then at the metal sign wavering above Gregory's head.

"That's what you get for interrupting the game, asshole. Home team was about to score."

Andorf watches his friend raise the sign to finish the job. He grabs the sign on its downswing. "Stop, Gregory. No need to kill the bastard."

Gregory tosses the sign. Grumbling, he kicks at the fallen soldier boy in the ribs. Their faces illuminate at an approaching flashlight flickering side to side. Andorf and Gregory slice tracks through the uncut grass. Within minutes, they have scaled the perimeter fence and sit atop a hill overlooking the game field. Out of breath, hands resting heavy on their knees, Gregory looks squarely at Andorf. "Big plans tonight?"

Andorf staggers to his feet, huffing to catch his breath. "Are you're kidding me? Haven't we had enough excitement for one—?"

The trio of helicopters ascends and zooms off only to be replaced by three others, hovering and sweeping the now barren field with their floodlights. Gregory stands, stretching a cramp from his leg. "The government mouthpiece has arrived. Can't wait to see what the evening news fabricates *this* time."

Andorf snickers. "As usual, late to the game."

The guys walk home in silence. Gregory waves and enters his ground-floor condo. Andorf tromps up the flight of steps and triple locks himself inside the unit directly above Gregory. He moistens a bowl of dehydrated milk-coated cereal and pauses, hypnotized in front of The Eye. For three minutes, he unconsciously drools at the scantily dressed young woman of the 'Ride The Tube' commercial pictured above the scrolling countdown to Starship Atlantis's launch, sixty-four days away. After the train whisks her away through multiple sets of gyrating tubes, Andorf addresses his soggy cereal.

An up-to-the-minute news blurb flashes on the display. "More on left-wing radicals removing bricks from the Lincoln Memorial after this breaking story, live from Liberty Field. A local militia broke up the latest in a series of riots. Seen here, hundreds of drunken protestors rampage through an otherwise peaceful recreational area. Many were found bathing in the nude. Update at eleven."

"What? They weren't drunk! No one was nude!" Andorf swipes an arm, reducing the volume to near-mute level. He chuckles at swears emanating from Gregory's unit directly below.

CHAPTER 3
A Rude Awakening

Between snores, Andorf calls out to the elusive brown-eyed girl in his dreams running beneath a plush canopy of real, analog trees. He slips an arm around her waist. Feeling hot breath on his face, he pulls her closer, rubs her ... prickly face? A deep voice interrupts his dream.

"Cut that out!"

Andorf's eyes pop open to see Gregory's unshaved face, hovering above. "Ahh," he yells on his fall from the couch.

Gregory drops to his knees, again looming inches from Andorf's face. "Are you okay? Did I wake you?"

From the cold vinyl floor, Andorf's half-focused eyes squint at the amber numbers flashing on the ceiling. He staggers to his feet, slips on last night's shirt, and beelines for the bathroom, paying little attention to Gregory tagging right behind. The louder he urinates, the louder Gregory speaks.

"Have you forgotten about today? We're getting you elected."

"How can anyone be so perky this early in the day?" Andorf yawns out, rubbing his eyes with his spare hand. He quits pissing and turns to Gregory, member hanging from his briefs. "Elected? Did I get drunk and do something stupid last night? Tell me it washes off."

"Early? I wouldn't call midday early. So about last night, you said you'd sleep on it. Well, you've slept, haven't you? Hey, check out these signs I made."

Gregory coaxes him into the living room. Andorf follows, rubbing his tired eyes. He squints to read one of his friend's homemade signs. "How will anyone know me without a last name?"

"Johnson wouldn't fit. How many Andorfs can there be, anyway?" Gregory directs his friend to the front window. "Come see. I planted one at the corner."

Andorf peers down at the lawn and back at his friend. "Sign? What sign?"

Gregory dashes out the front door, swearing. He runs up and down the second floor balcony, avoiding cracked cement sections and pointing at the corner. "I planted one right over there just five minutes ago."

Pulling up a pair of self-tightening polyform jeans, Andorf staggers into the kitchen. He extracts a mug from his collection, blows out dust, and eases it into the Brewmeister-5000. Seconds later, he traces Gregory's pace down the front steps, careful not to spill the steaming cup of Early Bird Special. The courtyard's sparse imitation grass tickles his bare feet as he watches Gregory at the street corner argue with a one-inch hole in the ground. Digital trees flicker and buzz at Gregory's neurotic hand motions.

"It was right there, I swear," Gregory yells, kicking at the ground.

Andorf yawns, politely covering his mouth. "Get another. I'll stand here and guard your hole."

Gregory complains his way up the front steps. In no time, he returns with a replacement sign, and with the aid of a large stone, plants it firmly in the same hole. He and Andorf alternate stomps around the base of the shiny metal stake.

Gregory grins. "Let them try and snatch that one."

Walking away, the best friends glance over their shoulders multiple times. One step shy of his front door, the pair stares at the empty hole on the far side of the visually perfect digitalized lawn.

Gregory's nostrils flair "The bastards can't get away with this. I spent all morning working on them. Quick, call the government Records Office, Crimes Division. They'll know what to do. Did I tell you my sister works in the government complex?"

Andorf flashes a dry look. "Only a dozen times. Why are you always trying to hook us up? Is she covered in acne? Has she contracted some incurable disease?"

Gregory darts back through Andorf's door. "No and no. She's smart, independent, has a great job."

Andorf shakes his cup dry in the kitchen sink. "I'll bet she walks with a limp, leans to one side, and is uglier than sin."

"Hey! That's my sister you're talking about. She's drop dead gorgeous and never votes two-party. Problem is she's dating a government mule. You know ... some big ox."

Andorf steadies himself against Gregory, hands trembling, as he relives a painful clip from his childhood.

Gregory points at the wall-mounted comm-box. "Call."

Andorf walks into the kitchen, shaking it off. He taps a sequence of icons on the comm-box and listens to mindless government rhetoric. "Press one for Mandarin, press two for Spanish, press three for ..." He presses zero expecting a live person.

"Invalid option. Press one for Mandarin ..." He waits again until the last option plays. Again, he presses the unspoken zero. After ten rings, a proper oriental voice answers.

"Matte Kudasai."

"Huh?"

"It means 'please wait' in Hotot-speak," Gregory says, ear warming the hand-piece.

Andorf waits through lines of Fat Max Okinawa's pro-government hype sandwiched between iterations of 'Ride The Tube' infomercials and up-to-the-minute countdown until Starship Atlantis's launch, some sixty-three days off. A woman's sharp voice splices in.

"Records office, Crimes Division, may I help you?"

Andorf detects a twang of snooty in her voice. "I'd like to report a theft."

"Voice patterns match you as Andorf Johnson, Dakota Condominiums, unit 201."

"Correct. I would like to—"

"This crime you are reporting, Mister Johnson, are there witnesses?"

Andorf's mouth twists. "Well, not exactly."

Gregory jabs him in the ribs. "Tell her about the stolen signs."

Andorf pushes him aside, nearly disconnecting as his finger slips from the tiny wall-mounted screen.

"Are you sure this actually happened, sir?" the hurried woman asks. "Perhaps the items were merely misplaced."

"Look," Andorf says, winding up. "We placed signs in my yard, and the minute our backs were turned, they were gone … stolen."

"And?"

"And what? Aren't you going to do anything about this?"

Gregory leans into the comm-box. "Yeah, do something about—" Cupping Gregory's mouth with his hand, Andorf pushes him away.

"Tell me, sir. Where did these incidents occur?"

"My front yard, in bright daylight."

"Matte Kudasai."

"Huh?" Andorf taps staccato on the comm-box screen as sequencing infomercials and comm-box instructions replay. He flinches at a loud thunk of a thick, bound book dropping onto a counter and the woman's troubled voice.

"Sir? Are you there?"

"Unfortunately, yes."

"According to Article Four, the Domicile Domain reference, of the recently revised Official Book of Agendas, private property no longer exists."

"What the hell are you talking about?" Andorf yells. "I hold the property deed to this—"

"You may have bought your document, Mister Johnson, but you no longer own the property it represents. Furthermore, if you do not own such property, you certainly have no say in what transpires on such property."

Gregory nuzzles closer to the comm-box. "What?" he yells.

"Have a nice day, Mister Johnson. You also, Mister Gray." *Click!*

The connection breaks. Andorf's reddened face spins to Gregory. "They're not getting away with this Domicile Domain crap."

"So you're running for mayor?"

Andorf rubs his chin. "I don't know about that, but I'm definitely getting to the bottom of this. I'm paying that Records Office a little visit."

"Watch out for that Wretched Wanda. You won't believe the hell she put me through last time I filed architectural drawings."

CHAPTER 4

The Public Records Office

As the public bus rolls up to the David R. Steiner government complex, Andorf replays the raspy words of the old man from the rugby game. "Thrice you will cast your eyes upon a friend from a prior dawn." He steps off the exit ramp, foot feeling for the vibrating ground, but an overhead rattling steals his attention and he trips on a broken segment of poorly maintained sidewalk. Luckily, a passing stranger's kind hand prevents his fall.

"Thank you, sir." Andorf's hand trembles at the sight of a burly man's sparsely bearded face. Childhood memories bite through his conscience as if he was back in yesterdays. He scans, plotting an escape.

The large man scrunches his brow. He speaks quicker than his massive retracting hands. "Andorf Johnson. What the hell are *you* doing here?"

Andorf apprehensively backs away, surprised to see his childhood adversary. He remembers how Brutus had bloodied many a nose back in the day. If it were not for their fathers being close friends, Andorf's nose would have been on his list. Hopefully the bully has since matured. "Brutus Bittner?"

Brutus stares up at the huge pillars supporting the overhead transit system. To Andorf's relief, Brutus chuckles. "Why are you using that antiquated bus transit instead of The Tube?"

Andorf watches the bus merge between sputtering battery-powered motorbikes, and turns to face his former schoolmate, with whom he has not spoken as many words in ten years. "To tell you the truth, big guy, I really don't trust all that ... uh ... mechanical mumbo jumbo spinning around up there."

"But the Tube is fast. It's our future." Brutus's voice elevates to a higher octave. His arms contort as he describes the technical facets and inter-dependent mechanics of The Tube. His exaggerated hand gestures barely contain his enthusiasm. His deep voice successively booms with brief pauses. He nearly forgets to breathe. "And the inner pod spins in one direction while the cylinder spins in the other, creating a vacuum smooth ride. As the infomercials say, it's like arriving before you've departed. It's good for the environment."

Andorf grabs hold of his head with both hands. "All those spheres rotating within spheres, I get dizzy just thinking about it. The last thing I want is to be stuck inside a gigantic vacuum cleaner."

"You're so old school, Andorf. Why, you can travel from one end of the city to the other—"

"I know, I know, before I know I even left." Andorf blinks several times.

"The Tube will eventually go everywhere. They're already expanding to—"

"Outside the perimeter?"

Blood drains from Brutus's face. He flashes Andorf an evil glare. "You know as well as I do that citizens aren't allowed out there. It's not safe. Why, the perimeter wall was built to protect us from mutant creatures feeding on the toxic waste."

Andorf smirks. "Next you'll be blaming the retracting beaches on global warming."

"Why do you think our coastlines are bound by fifty-foot seawalls?" Brutus asks. "We've already lost a quarter of our land mass. Did you know Albuquerque used to be an inland city? My master tells me so."

Andorf steps away, keeping an eye on his former adversary. "Look at you, Brutus. You are enslaved by your loyalty, and to whom, some arrogant master?"

"All men have masters. For some, it's repayment of a selfish act. For others ..." Brutus pauses, gazing upward. "It's a higher power. But for me ..." He throws a hand over his heart. "It's respect for a truly great man whom I deeply admire."

"I don't buy it. How can you respect anyone who enslaves you?"

"I am not a slave. All men need a guiding force."

"And who is this master of whom you speak so highly?"

Brutus bows. "Maxwell Okinawa, from the Hotot Empire."

Picturing an eight-foot snail, Andorf feels the hairs rise on the back of his neck. "Well, things are about to change around here. In fact I'm—"

Brutus snickers. "What, running for mayor?"

Andorf sees no win to the debate. Clearing his throat, he resets his irritation to a more cordial tone. "So Brutus, what have *you* been doing with yourself? I take it you've become some kind of engineering nerd?"

Brutus's large hands proudly gather on his waist. "Unlike you, I've ingested technology. I'm a technical specialist aboard the Atlantis. I've dreamt of that starship since before I could crawl. Now I'm living the dream. Imagine thousands of citizens like you and I traveling beyond the stars on a venerable quest to bring new energy back to Earth. It's technology like The Tube up there that makes it happen."

"Geez, Brutus. I never knew you were into that stuff. All I remember is everyone calling you a big ox."

Brutus snickers. He rolls up his sleeves to expose a pair of beefy, grease-stained arms. "I've discovered that I'm good with my hands."

Andorf turns into the sun, cupping a hand to shade his rolling eyes. "A mechanic. Imagine that."

"I'm more like an engineer, in charge of all the starship's mechanisms. Take the starship's logical deviators. I get migraines worrying about them and other control mechanisms, not to mention the electro-hydraulics. Everything has to be tested and retested before—"

"You sound like that David Kennington guy on the techno channel. You know … that fixit nerd who can repair most anything. The Eye still plays snippets of his old shows after midnight."

"I have no time to watch, but I'll take that as a compliment. The world would grind to a screeching halt without nerds like me. You know it took seven thousand gypsies working day and night to assemble the starship."

"I've never been good with gadgets."

"I remember how everyone teased you about getting things all Andorf'd up."

"And *you* were one of those kids." Andorf snorts, fighting hard to restrain his hands from curling into fists. "I swear, Brutus, if our fathers weren't such good friends—"

Brutus chuckles. "Funny how things turned out. Who would have guessed I'd move up the government ladder, become one of the Empire's trusted few? Like how that clumsy cleaning lady inadvertently discovered a new energy source by knocking the Martian rock sample off the rock collector's bookshelf. We'd never be heading to planet Nero for Genghis if it weren't for her."

"Did they ever find her remains?"

"Are you kidding me? There's a two-mile crater where the subdivision used to be. Say, tough break about your parents' accident. That old salvage yard on Veatrice was a terribly dangerous place."

"I hate that place," Andorf growls. "It left me with a lousy monthly reminder."

"I hear your stipend is a nice one."

"I get by." Andorf taps his wrist. He squints at the dim amber numbers projecting across Brutus's wide chest in the bright daylight. "2 p.m., late for my appointment. Must run."

"Check out both extremist party headquarters if you're ever in Cecal City," Brutus yells. "They're downtown, across the street from one another. You'll find them real eye openers."

"I'll do that." Andorf turns for the Gert Nudel Records Building. "Perhaps we'll run into each other sometime." He turns and dashes without looking back. He hears Brutus's fading voice.

"You can count on it."

*

Inside the Records Office, Andorf follows a ringing past a series of vacant rooms, through a half-shut office door. The drab, sage walls appear untouched since the building's origin some forty years ago. Wedged behind stacks of legal manuals, slouches a woman in her mid-fifties with temporal taps pinching her head. Her soprano humming harmonizes with the piped-in muzak, barely masking the old building's subtle creaks and groans. Andorf assumes by the way she repetitively slides forms between folder leaves, it is either a sleazy romance novel or techno porn that the temporal taps are pumping directly into her cerebrum. The frosted-glass Record's Office door slams shut behind him. Andorf clears his throat several times, but it is his index finger dinging the counter bell that grabs the clerk's attention.

The clerk sits up, snarling rudeness under her breath. She utters mouthfuls of niceties at the inconvenient visitor on her waddle to the front counter. Appearing with a distorted smile longer than her concern, Andorf is glad the wide countertop separates them. The woman stares him down. "What time is your appointment, sir?"

Andorf grimaces at her squeaky, high-pitched voice. "I—I don't have one."

"How can you expect to see anyone without an appointment?" Straight-faced, the clerk removes a single acetate form off a six-inch stack to her right and visually directs him to use the fibrowax scribe to her left. "Fill out Form 'B' completely and drop it in that inbox over there when you are done."

As Andorf reaches for the form, she whips around and ... *whap*! He quickly withdraws his reddening hand. "You need an appointment for that, sir."

"What? I need an appointment to get a form?"

"We run a tight ship here at the Records Office," says the squeaky voice.

"So how do I get one of *those* forms?"

Frustrated by his insistence, the clerk surveys the empty office, swearing like a drunken sailor. Reaching beneath the counter, she slips him one thin 'A' acetate form and one disgusted stare. "Fill this out in its entirety. If there is one blank line, we will just have to wipe it clean and start over. Am I perfectly clear, sir?"

Andorf looks the opaque film over. "It asks for my blood type. Is that really necessary?"

"You never know," she says in a sassy note. "And don't forget your next of kin. You know, just in case."

Andorf looks about the sparse room with but a single desk and a bathroom sign taped over one of many vertical cracks running from floor to ceiling. "Of course, I see how dangerous this place can be."

Before he can raise another question, the clerk is back at her desk, legs propped, temporal taps suckling her brain. She appears to have fallen deep inside a fantasy realm, all thoughts tethered to her Kimball Thinker. Andorf reaches behind the counter and exits the office with a stack of 'A' forms. The moment the door opens, an overpowering aroma draws him down the stairs and into the basement break room. He stands at the java machine, salivating at the thought of a warm cup in his hand.

"Help yourself," says a deep voice of a man seated at a table, face buried behind the daily rag.

Andorf fills a creamer-lined fiber cup. He settles in at the closest table with his stack of 'A' forms, watching the coffee whitener migrating throughout his cup. "Thank you," he says between slurps. He scribes N/A on the many questionable lines of Form 'A'. Casting his chair aside, Andorf dreads facing the nasty records clerk again.

"Don't forget the backside," the stranger says, face unrevealed. "You don't want her rubbing off all your well thought out answers, do ya?"

Andorf plops back into his seat. "You won't believe what I went through with that lady upstairs."

The stranger clears his throat. "Wanton Wanda ain't no lady. Have another cup. You're gonna need it."

Andorf refills his cup and glances back with an appreciative nod, only to find himself alone and the news rag spread across the next table. He completes Form 'A' and after thirteen reluctant steps, reappears at the clerk's front counter. This time, he goes right for the … *ding!*

Wanda waddles to the counter. "Do you have an appointment, sir?"

Flashing an overzealous smile, Andorf drops the film in the empty counter tray.

Slipping one hand under the counter, Wanda appears confused. She scans the sparse room. "Oh my. I'm out of 'A' forms. I must fill out a reorder form." With an eye glued on Andorf, she again feels under the counter. "Now where'd I put my reorder forms?"

In frustration, Andorf grabs one of her fat arms as she turns away. The clerk emits a rabid growl. Her fat head twists around as if to spit pea soup. "You keep those claws to yourself, young man."

Andorf releases her arm and quickly backs away. She lifts his Form 'A' and scrutinizes every line, scouring at his sloppy penmanship. She flips the form over and shakes her head side to side.

Andorf whimpers like a scolded puppy. "What'd I do wrong? Did I—"

"You filled out a 'B' form," she says, pointing at the bottom of the form." She flips the form around to show Andorf. "See right there?

This one says Form 'B' right there on the bottom. See? What you want is Form 'A'."

Andorf rips the form from her fat hands. He compares it to an identical 'A' form. With his designated fibrowax scribe, he strikes out the 'B', writes 'A' next to it, and sporting a shit-eating grin, hands it back to the clerk. "Can I have my appointment *now*?"

For a good minute, the clerk stares at the form. "Oh my!" she yells. "In my twenty years as an assistant to the assistant, this has never happened." She drops the form and grabs hold of the countertop, examining Andorf from head to toe. "I know who you are! You are one of those—those—free thinkers, aren't you? I heard about your kind. Fortunately, there aren't many of you left."

As the clerk appears faint, Andorf fans her with a stack of 'B' forms from the counter, "Look lady—"

Backing away, Wanda's eyes bulge. She covers her mouth. "What has this world come to? First those naked bathers in the park and now this." She takes another moment to size Andorf up before handing him the form. "Bring your form back when it's signed, mister."

Andorf scratches a large X across the bottom and hands it right back. "Can I have my appointment now?"

Wanda examines the acetate sheet, beginning with the first line. She lowers the form to glare at Andorf. "We are having sign problems, I see."

"Finally," he says, under his breath as he nods. "That's right, ma'am. Two signs were stolen from of my yard today. What are you going to do about that?"

The clerk drops the form into an empty inbox and flips through screen after screen of blank appointments projected on the counter surface from below. "Looks like we have an opening this time a week from tomorrow, sir." Andorf's views the vacant calendar. Watching him steam, the clerk scrambles for an answer. "Or, perhaps I could look this up right now." She waddles back to her desk and returns. Andorf clinches his hands at the recognized sound of a thick, bound book dropping onto a counter. Wanda's jittering hands flip through several dozen acetate pages. "Here it is, sir."

Andorf sighs.

"The cyber access code." After several minutes of Wanda hen-pecking the counter surface, a double-sided screen lowers from the ceiling between them. Her hands make busy time tapping here and there on her side of the translucent information panel. From the backside, Andorf follows the indiscernible technical jargon spewing across the screen and the shadows of Wanda's flattening finger taps, cringing at each of her random verbal squeaks. She abruptly pauses with an 'ah-ha' moment."

Andorf grins.

Wanda fingers the displayed line as she reads. "No signage shall be publicly displayed without a twenty-day period following written approval from both registered political parties."

Andorf scratches his head. "What do you mean by *both* registered political parties? This is insane! Why are there only two political parties mentioned?"

"Just a minute, sir." The clerk waddles to her desk and returns with a thin pamphlet of approved political terms. Wetting her index finger, she flips through more slick acetate pages. "I believe definitions are in this first section. Oh yes, right here." She pauses to adjust the high-powered magnifier overlaying the fine print. "It says here that registered political parties are organizations who have filed papers with the government stating political purpose of such organization. The party name must not be offensive, cause confusion, nor be more than one hundred and forty characters. There must be more than five hundred financial contributors. Either party—"

"Again with the two parties," Andorf says, raising his voice. "Are they in cahoots? This whole thing smells of corruption."

Wanda closes the pamphlet. "That's silly, sir. How can there be more than two? Left or right, up or down. It says so right here in this book written by the bi-party election committee."

Andorf feel his blood pressure percolating. He slaps both hands onto the counter. "I want to see your manager."

The clerk frantically feels under the counter for the missing 'A' forms. "Do you have an appointment, sir?"

Andorf begins to yell. "Didn't you hear me? I demand to see your manager."

Wanda's desk-mounted comm-unit sounds. Out of desperation, she returns to her desk, picks up a stack of appointment forms, and throws them onto the counter. "Now, don't tell anyone I did this, sir."

Andorf pounds on the wall, ready to verbally tear into her. Wanda's comm-unit continues to sound. Wanda waddles back to her desk and flips through dust-covered files until a rear office door creaks open. A tall figure appears. An overpowering, thick German voice screams over the background muzak. "What the hell's going on out here, Wanda? Why can't you ever answer your damn comm-unit?"

Andorf expects the worst as a well-dressed man wearing a single monocle steps into the room. A smile grows on his face. "Wilhelm Mattigan!"

"Uh—uh," Wanda says. Confused by the sudden lack of official protocol, she digs through her employee handbook. "You know I don't answer that thing after lunch. I wrote that above my name when I signed my employment contract."

The man's souring face morphs to a large grin. He reaches for Andorf's hand. "Andorf Johnson. Why, I haven't seen you since—"

"We were kids," Andorf says.

"My ole pal. You are the last one I would expect to see here. I assume this is no personal visit?"

Andorf shakes Wilhelm's outstretched hand. "I'm here about signs, stolen right from my front yard. As much run around as I'm getting, you'd think I was running for office."

Wilhelm's grin retracts. His eyes bounce between Andorf and his clerk. "You register for that up on six."

Tethered to her Kimball, Wanda flashes confused looks at the pair. Wilhelm taps Andorf's shoulder and directs him into a corner, away from Wanda's lip-reading eyes.

"So tell me, old friend … what happened with these signs."

Andorf shrugs his shoulders. "My downstairs neighbor had some crazy notion about me running for office. He even posted homemade signs in the yard. You know, the ones on those fat metal stakes?"

Wilhelm nods.

"The minute we turned our backs, someone lifted the sign. My neighbor, Gregory, grabs a second sign and plunks it into the same hole. We had that sucker pounded in really well this time and weren't twenty yards away when guess what?"

"It too went missing?"

"And to make matters worse, the line operator went spouting off about some stupid Domicile Domain law and how I no longer own my property. Would you believe that, Wilhelm? Property that I've bought and paid for, not even my own."

"Whoa there, Andorf. You have no idea what you're up against. Our politicians trumped up that one to line their pockets. They make the rules and only *they* can change them. And you had better believe not a one is in the public interest."

"Then maybe I *should* run for mayor, as my friend Gregory says."

Wilhelm turns white. "You cannot," he whispers, glancing back at Wanda. Wanda's eyes flash away as she slips behind stacks of legal manuals piled high upon her desk. "Check out my worthless clerk over there. Somehow, she's even more incompetent than the one before her. In spite of her excessive carelessness, the attorney general says I cannot even fire her."

Andorf chuckles. "Guess it pays to keep a Lynch pin in your pocket."

Wilhelm glances back at Wanda. "I'll explain over dinner. Meet me at the new bird café in the old section. 8 p.m."

Before Andorf agrees, his friend has retreated into his rear office. On his exit through the frosted door, Andorf grins at Wanda's eyes peeking from between the stacked manuals. On the short bus ride home, he questions Wilhelm's instructions. Like Nixon and the Watergate tapes, the more it replays in his head, the less he remembers.

CHAPTER 5

The Toucan Chew

On his stroll down Tolerance Way, Andorf pronounces the name of each brightly lit marquee which leaps out of the darkness. He pauses at the Toucan Chew and scopes out the joint. A nearby lightning strike drives him inside.

An overdressed maître-d approaches. "May I help you, sir?"

"I'm looking for an old friend—a tall, balding gentleman—wearing a monocle."

"Heavy German accent?"

Following a nod, Andorf is briskly escorted between diners, past busy servers, to an isolated table in the far reaches of the restaurant, where a man sits, arguing in German with three portable radios. Whisking Andorf's escort off with his hands, the man lifts his dark shades. He raises the volumes on the competing talk radios. Catching the maître-d glancing back on a rapid escape, Andorf pulls up a chair.

"Retinal scans," Wilhelm whispers, tapping his sunglasses. "In the blink of an eye, they know your identity." He stops and looks around. "Best we keep this short."

Andorf fidgets in his chair. "Why all the ..."

Wilhelm peers mechanically at the motorized grid lights suspended eight feet above their heads. He leans close and whispers. "Devices are everywhere, watching, listening. Take my word. We are never alone. Eyes, ears … everywhere."

"I get frequently the feeling I'm being tailed by some guy in a black trench coat. But I've gotten used to it."

Wilhelm twitches at the diners staring from distant tables. "If anyone hears what I'm about to tell you, they would lock me away. Hell, they would lock *you* away."

Andorf glances at the motorized lights, now five feet above their heads. "You're scaring me, Wilhelm. What's this all about?"

"The less you know the better you are." Wilhelm scans the room. "Things are never as they appear."

Andorf's nose wiggles. "Things? What things?"

"You say you want to run for office, right?"

"Well, I—"

"You really don't know, do you? What you're up against?"

Andorf shrugs his shoulders. "It's politics. How serious can it be?"

"Let me ask you this, Andorf," Wilhelm says. "The second time your grandfather, Gary, ran for president, who were the two-party candidates?"

"Some arrogant lying woman and a high-dollar thief."

"And who was elected?"

"The thief."

Wilhelm scrutinizes Andorf's face. "Are you sure about that?"

"Of course. Although Arrogance won the popular vote by a comfortable margin, that bi-party Electoral College picked Thief. It was all over the media. Everybody …" Andorf analyzes Wilhelm's soured face. "Now wait a minute, Wilhelm. What are you implying?"

"Smoke and mirrors. As I said, things are *never* as they appear." Wilhelm's anxiety bleeds into Andorf. Each take turns scanning the dining area. "After the election," Wilhelm whispers. "Didn't Arrogance appear more and more like the thief?"

Andorf grins. "Well, yes. They all look the same after a while. Lighting, camera angles, I suppose."

Andorf leans hard against his backrest, lost for words in the company of Wilhelm's cutting glare. Wilhelm leans closer. "Let me give you a clue, my old friend. That wasn't the thief."

"What?" Andorf yells.

Wilhelm hushes Andorf with his hand and waits on his silent nod. "Most everyone is too engraved in just getting by to worry about such details. Sure, there are a few engineering types out there who notice these things, but for the rest of us, we cannot perceive much beyond our physical realm. The government ran studies on this." He stops and holds his water glass up to magnify faces of nearby patrons. "Things are either hot or cold, red or blue. We are always given exactly two choices. We cannot handle more than two. That is why the government takes things away, returns them digitized. Binary, my friend. Only two choices."

"Like picking a favorite team in a ball game." Andorf wads his fists, throwing short punches. "Two teams, duking it out."

"It's no joke, Andorf. In this game, the winner is predetermined. Nominations play only out as a gesture of fairness. In reality, a secret panel of Tox and E-Cons make the decisions. Our vote don't count. Binary generator machines determine the pre-election results."

"That's unfair!" Andorf yells.

Wilhelm whispers. "The process only need a scent of fairness to mask their stench. Party voters blindly ride along the well-greased machines. Then someone like you sticks his nose where it doesn't belong and gets it chopped off." Wilhelm laughs at Andorf's disturbed glare. "Remember the Electoral College, before the suckers were used as target practice?"

"Look, Wilhelm, I only want to—"

"Don't, my friend. It will get you nowhere but an early grave."

"But if we don't—"

"Don't say we." Wilhelm leers at the surrounding tables of patrons who have halved their distance. He pushes away from the table. "Everyone is out for themselves. The Empire relies on this. Alone, the government pretty much ignores you. Even as two, you are not much of a threat, but more than two—they break up the party. They captured a few, perhaps killed one or two. Then the media cranks up their rumor mill, riles everyone up with their lies. Like last night at City Park. I wonder what *really* happened."

Wilhelm's paranoia has Andorf staring at the nearby diners. He leans into Wilhelm and whispers. "It was only a rugby game. I was there with my friend. We saw the militia rounding up citizens by the handfuls.

Wilhelm shudders. "Off to the Cos they went. Oh, the things I have heard about that terrible place. Experiments, modified body parts, last stop before the power cube factory. As for me, I'd rather be shot."

Andorf gulps. "Where the hell is our waiter? I'm starving."

"I ordered him to leave me alone, if he knew what was good for him."

Andorf squinches his nose at Wilhelm. "That explains a lot. But tell me this, what about that creepy newsvendor in the downstairs breakroom?"

"You must have imagined that. Our breakroom is self-serve. Stress will do that, Andorf. Say, you don't use wireless devices, do you? The Empire monitors all communication."

"Sheez, Wilhelm, every first grader knows that."

Wilhelm's eyes bounce off the motorized track lights, twelve inches above. He pulls his sunglasses and pushes further away from the table. "They've been listening. They dim the lights hoping you won't notice." Wilhelm grabs his three radios and darts.

"Hey, slow down," Andorf yells, chasing him between crowded tables, clipping busy waiters. He barges out the front door to find Wilhelm standing at the corner, examining a corner street sign.

Wilhelm pulls on the signpost. "Look at this. The bloody Empire isn't infallible. It misses things once in a while."

Andorf reads the sign. "Tolerance and Livefree. What's this have to do with anything?"

Wilhelm looks about the street, nervously. "Truth is what we are told, my friend. Everyone accepts this." Wilhelm grabs hold of Andorf by the shoulders as if to shake some sense into him. "The Empire controls the media. The Eye pipes truth into everyone's head 24x7. How are you going to get around that? Tell me."

Andorf scratches his head, watching Wilhelm scan the evening sky. "A king once said knowledge is a dirty thing if no one plays by the rules."

Wilhelm drops his voice to a whisper. He stares directly into Andorf's eyes. "They *are* playing by the rules. Their rules. The ones they conceived. It is all there … in the Public Archives' building … open for anyone's viewing. The doors are never locked." Wilhelm looks back and grins at Andorf. "Inside you will find a key. There lies the Book of Agendas. It begins with Article I, 'Controlling the Media.'"

Wilhelm looks nervously at all the bystanders milling about the dark, damp street. "I don't know why I'm telling you this. It is a short ride to the Cos for anyone merely mentioning the book."

Andorf stares bewildered. "An independent or third-party candidate could—"

Wilhelm pulls Andorf away from curious citizens who pause to listen. "Didn't you hear a word I said? How could any independent ever win? The two parties will lie and cheat to keep you off the ballot. Look how many judges in Oklahoma, Pennsylvania, Michigan and what was once Colorado were bought to keep your grandpa off the ballot. It would cost you a small fortune to run. A billion dollars would not be enough. Even that beloved millionaire Bloomberg knew this. He threw in the towel on his presidential bid way back when."

"So why not spill the beans, Wilhelm? You're in the Records—"

"They'd laugh at me, Andorf. Look at the dim-witted clerk they dumped on me. She is as incompetent as the day she was hired, some twenty years ago. Don't you think if I had any authority I would have replaced her by now?"

"But there must be somebody … someone who can bring change."

"For your own sanity, Andorf, I beg you not to pursue this any further. From here on out, watch what you say and to whom you say it, else you'll end up in that Cos." Wilhelm's eyes return to the skies. "They have satellites up there," he whispers. "See that one directly above us. They are reading our lips."

Andorf raises his head to search the dark sky. "I'll check out that book, Wilhelm. Wilhelm?" He scans the immediate proximity and realizes Wilhelm is gone. *Perhaps I will hit the Archives' building. It's right on my way home.*

CHAPTER 6

You Won't Believe What's There!

A good half-mile ahead, the massive monolith shadows its lesser neighbors, growing larger with each step. Andorf digs deep in his soul for the courage he held firmly in his grip only moments ago. Leg muscles cramping, he labors down the gloomy, barren street.

At someone's whistle, he eases into the shadows of the Archives' building, gazing at the moonlit clouds racing over the roofline. Flattening into layered ivy growing on the building's damp stone wall, he feels moist tentacles of thick vines circling his arms, digging into his back, as the building seems to bellow out a warning. He rips away, leaving pieces of his shirt-back behind. Gathering wit, he traces the wall around to hide behind overgrown shrubbery to the left side of the building's front steps. The shrubbery's sharp thorns tear through his pants, cutting into his legs. With no one in sight, he leaps onto the concrete landing and presses hard against the heavy, alien-shaped door. It refuses to budge. With a second hard push, the door creaks open.

Dust streams past, fanning out along the moonlit street. Andorf gazes back at the cracked sidewalk, lines illuminated by the soft glow of digitalized trees. His shirt unpeels from his shoulders like an unstrapped bra. He holds what is left of his shirt loosely over his nose and steps inside an unsavory dark world. With his other hand, he plucks a hardbound book off the floor and swipes a path through the dust-saturated cobwebs. A dust halo glows a cherry red from an exit sign, barely above his head. In eerie stillness, he senses another's presence, watching.

"Hello?" his muffled voice calls out. "Anyone there?"

Andorf jumps at the sensation of something gnawing on his EasyGlides and lands on something not quite solid. His high-pitched shriek harmonizes with that of a long-tailed critter scurrying across the dusty room. His sneakers echo off the high-vaulted ceiling, as he runs for the exit through the billowing dust. Outside, he gasps. He slams the heavy door and heads for the street, dusting off his pants. Air, fresh air never tasted so good.

*

The ground shakes. Approaching the condominium complex, an enormous concrete pillar trembles as a vacuum pod tumbles high speed through a cylindrical tube overhead. Andorf peeks through the ground-floor curtains to see Gregory flipping through architectural holograms. He grabs the back door knob and barges inside to take a seat at the table beside his downstairs neighbor. Gregory raises a brow.

"Where's your shirt? Why are you so filthy, Andorf? Wait—don't tell me—a political fund raiser?"

Andorf sneezes into cupped hands. Gregory flashes a dirty glare as he grabs a fresh hand towel from the bathroom and returns. Andorf blows twice into the towel. Grinning, he displays the thick dark snot on Gregory's finest.

"That's gross, Andorf. Even for you."

Andorf acknowledges with repeated elephant sounds, blowing into the towel. After a moment, he gains enough composure to sniffle. "I was in the government Archives' building."

Gregory shifts in his seat. He scans Andorf's face as if his friend is pulling a fast one. "The Archives? I thought the old library was razed years ago."

"It's still there."

"Yeah, right. You're the last person I'd find in a library."

"You won't believe what's there."

Gregory smiles, sarcastically. "Books?"

Andorf eyes the organized shelves and everything else in Gregory's living room, neatly tucked in defined partitions, museum perfect. Even The Eye's screen is framed dead center on the living room wall. With Gregory seated squarely in his chair, Andorf appears to be the only thing out of place.

"I broke—uh—walked right in the place. I was told I could find answers." Andorf again blows into the towel. After inspecting the thick black goo, he shakes layered dust from his clothes like a wet dog.

"Stop! Don't be doing that in here." Gregory disappears and returns, dragging a coiled-up three-inch-diameter hose. He snaps it into the wall receptacle and the hose comes alive with a loud sucking noise. Andorf raises his arms as the hose shares time between him and his seat cushion. "Hold still," Gregory yells, grabbing hold of Andorf's shoulder.

Andorf stands and slowly rotates. "You've got to see this place, Gregory. It's like something from the twenties."

"You know, you can do hard time for breaking and entering. How'd you get past security?"

"There wasn't any. I just walked right in." Andorf grins. "It was just me and the dust."

"And you brought me samples. How kind." Gregory runs the hose over Andorf's back and then torso, ending at his EasyGlides.

"Missed a spot." Andorf laughs, continuing his slow rotation.

Gregory runs a second pass with the hose. "Quit moving!"

"Seriously, Gregory, you should see this place." Andorf rustles dust from his thick brown hair as Gregory holds the hose near his head. "It's open for anyone to see."

Gregory picks cobwebs off Andorf's filthy pants and sucks them from his hands. "Besides dust and spiders, what else is there?"

"Answers, my friend. You heard what that woman on the comm-box said about us no longer owning our condos. And what about your stolen signs? Aren't you one bit curious how they get away with these things?"

"Perhaps you should take my sister. She has dreams like you, speaks of some guy with glasses like yours." Gregory grabs hold of his chin. "Hmm. If I didn't know any better—"

"Quit brushing her off on me."

Andorf follows Gregory into the bedroom closet, watching his friend curl the hose into a neat coil and shove it onto the top shelf. Both head for the bathroom to wash their hands. "I need your help, buddy. You're the only one I can—hey! Wait!"

Andorf finds Gregory examining his framed collections of rare one-inch squares of bamboo, banana, Bible, and corrugated paper with detailed explanations, each illuminated in natural light by individual soft-glow projectors.

Crossing his fingers behind his back, Andorf ad-libs his best sales pitch. "All kinds of papers, there at the Archives. Most of it was text paper, but there was some of this cloth Bible paper. You know, the stuff with embedded lines running across the pages."

Gregory salivates. "Bible paper?" He steps closer, eyes homing in on the individually illuminated framed one-inch squares.

Andorf reads the detailed description below Gregory's focus. "With decontaminated virgin fibers."

"And you say there were no guards?"

Andorf nods. "Walked right in. It wasn't even locked."

Gregory paces the small kitchen. Andorf follows, mocking his friend's moves behind his back. He stops short. Andorf piles into him. He spins his doubting face to Andorf. "I—I don't know, Andorf. What if we got—"

"Caught? It's a library for heaven sake."

"What if we change our minds? Can we just leave if we change our minds?"

Andorf nods. "Straight away. No questions."

"Well, if the Archives' building is open to everyone, as you say …" Gregory rubs his chin. "I can't see much harm in giving it a little peek, but we can't stay long."

"No, not long," Andorf says. "What about Sunday night?"

A coy smile captures Gregory's face. "Covert operations like this *do* run in my family. Shall I bring my own dust?"

Andorf laughs. "Nah. There's plenty to go around."

"Now I don't want to be puking up that nasty stuff." Gregory eyes his filthy hand towel balled up on his spotless table. "Fit us with decontamination outfits … like those guys wear when they sanitize homes … and don't expect me to do any heavy lifting. I don't do heavy."

"Got it all planned out. I'm bringing breathers, protective gear, and flashlights. Did I tell you … it's really dark in there?"

Gregory looks back at the footsteps terminating at his kitchen door. "I'll bet you led a dust trail all the way here. Anyone could have easily—"

A flash has them dashing for the front window. For ten minutes, they watch torrents flowing down the street and strobing figures rushing to escape the downpour. A second nearby lightning strike pixilates each of the digitized trees dotting the courtyard. Both jump away from the window.

Andorf grins. "A ninety-five percent chance of rain Sunday evening."

Gregory nods. He looks Andorf over. "You look like you haven't slept in a week."

Andorf rubs his tired eyes. "Those dreams I told you about. They have me walking around in a stupor. I saw real analog trees, not simulations like those digital ones outside. My elusive girl was running beneath huge branch canopies. She was with dozens of others, near a fleet of white panel vans."

"You and that mystery girl. Do you even know who she is?"

Andorf drifts into the living room, shaking his head. "I saw her last night—crouching right here in this room—bawling her eyes out." Andorf flails his arms. "Shelves were falling, everything was scattered all over your floor."

Gregory calmly scans his collection of framed, one-inch, hermetically-sealed, individually illuminated paper squares. He squares up one frame and then another. "I wouldn't stand for such a thing."

"Didn't you hear me, Gregory?" Andorf yells. "It's getting worse. I'm too afraid to sleep in my own bed. I'm seeing things that haven't happened. I never dreamt like this before. That elusive girl, why is she haunting me like this?"

Gregory pulls a small level from his pocket and straightens each of his framed, one-inch paper squares. "Go home, Andorf. Get a good night's sleep. That archive dust is fogging up your brain. Tomorrow night, we'll dig up some dirt on the Empire, o'dark-thirty."

CHAPTER 7

The Archives

Hair shower-damp, and belly swelled with liquid dinner, Andorf tosses about, head wedged between familiar creases of his overstuffed couch pillows. A chill runs up his back. He pulls the worn army blanket over his head. He dares himself not to dream but is soon swimming in dreamland.

"I'm not leaving without you," he calls out, jarring himself awake. One eye pops open and then the other, at bright daylight infiltrating his pulled curtains. He slips on a shirt and flies down the front steps. An optical scan unlocks an electric biped from its charging station and ensures a partial charge for the five-mile round trip. He whizzes off, not much faster than he could jog.

Cruising sparse aisles of the surplus mart, he grabs pairs of everything he needs. With reservation, the heavily bearded cashier announces each item he rings them up. "Two infrared illuminators, two infrared mini-goggles, two masks with ten-minute breathers and two four-inch filters." The cashier smiles at the last pairs of ribbed gloves. "You'll love these Crylex gloves, Andorf. They feel like they've been sprayed on. We've had a run on them this week. Dare I say, the last we'll see of *these* guys."

Andorf grins. "Don't you guys ever restock, Zeeshan? You're out of everything."

"It won't help. With government rationing, we cannot keep anything. Take these gloves. They've sat on our shelves for years collecting dust. But now everyone's buying them. And now you are buying my last pairs. I don't know what everyone's doing with them, but something serious is going down."

"Lucky I came in today."

The cashier nods. "Two pairs of auto-wrap, knee-high, rubber boots."

"Are they bite-proof?"

"Snakes?"

Andorf scans the vacant store. He snickers at the yellowing bi-party campaign posters, some dating back to the 1960s, plastered about the store. "Rat infestation."

Zeeshan nods. "With taxes and the latest government surcharges, your bill comes to four twenty-two and fifty."

Andorf leans in for a retinal scan. "I'll be back next week for the hay."

"Better sooner than later, Andorf. We are nearly out of third-cut. No telling when we'll see any more."

*

Andorf finds his downstairs neighbor sprawled across the couch, lazily flipping through historical holograms. Gregory flinches at his Andorf's sudden appearance. "Did you know, two centuries ago your Archives' building was a fancy-shmancy art museum? Yep, the first building in town to install light tunnels."

"And if you don't drop that viewer, you'll never see the place. Say, what's with The Eye over there? Why's it so quiet and what's with it flashing all white like that?"

Looking up, Gregory grins. "You just missed my sister, Serin. She installed new logic chips that blank untruths."

The Eye awakens to an overplayed 'Ride The Tube' commercial. The boys stare hypnotized at the scantily dressed gal hopping from one pod to another before spinning off the screen. The Eye mutes again, picturing only a scrolling countdown to Starship Atlantis's launch, sixty-one days away.

"Check out the molecular straps on these suckers." With a firm tug, Gregory's sneakers wrap snuggly around his ankles. "They're made from the latest poly compound, guaranteed for life."

Andorf spies his own sneakers, looking pristine, except for the green and yellow stains and an occasional small rat bite. He drops a large canvas sack at Gregory's feet and pulls out goodies, one item at a time. "We have our infrared illuminators, infrared mini-goggles, full facial masks with ten-minute breathers, and built-in four-inch exhaust filters, Crylex gloves, and one-size-fits-all bite-proof rubber boots."

Gregory grimaces at the rubber boots. He hurries Andorf out his back door. "Get me out of here, Andorf, before my sanity returns."

Andorf dumps his sack into a tall-wheeled carrier. "If anyone asks, we're just two guys out doing their laundry."

"Look at you, Andorf, with your dark clothes and infrared gear. You've actually planned this thing out." Gregory tags his friend's shoulder. "Mind telling me what the hell went down last night? I hear your shower and then all hell breaks loose up there. It sounded like you and some girl were having a great time. I was about to come upstairs for a little three-way."

Andorf hides his reddening face. "Gregory, stop."

"Hey, some girls are into that stuff, especially ones with brothers. If it was me, I would have shared her with *you*."

Andorf grabs Gregory's arm, stopping him in the middle of the street. "It was my elusive blonde all right, this time wearing a cream-colored wedding dress. She kept telling me 'not now, Andorf.'

And there were helicopter blades pounding and papers swirling about and—"

"Not that. Tell me about the girl. What happened after—"

"I don't know. I awoke on the cold floor." Andorf leaves Gregory with his wild images, daring not to elaborate. Gregory catches up and shakes his head in silence. They hike down darkening streets, gazing up at moon-drenched silhouettes and multi-unit housing transitioning into taller office buildings. Both grin at the faint kiss of raindrops on their faces. A good downpour will cover their tracks.

"All buildings appear to be grabbing for the moon, escaping the Empire's grasp." Gregory's steps quicken as if to catch up with his runaway inner child. His voice revs as he runs ahead. "Is that your Archives' building over there? I'll bet it's spooky dark inside." Gregory's haunting face tantalizes Andorf with eerie vocal intonations. "Bones of the dead will forever haunt our souls. Woo!"

Andorf smirks at Gregory's lighthearted levity and the towering monolith growing larger with each step. "Aren't you at least one little bit afraid? My heart's racing just thinking of the place."

Gregory rubs his hands together. "Mine too. I can't wait to look inside. Come on, don't be a pussy." He races down the walkway and runs up the steps to the Archives' building expecting to dart right inside, but freezes at the sight of fiber boards nailed haphazardly across the doorframe. Gregory tugs on the boards; they refuse to budge.

Andorf stashes the cart behind bushes to the left of the landing and joins his friend for a closer look. He too yanks on the boards in vain.

"Looks like someone was expecting your return, Andorf." Gregory chuckles. "Perhaps they want their dust back. Maybe a crowbar will—Andorf?"

Andorf follows the wall around to the north side of the building. He dares not get tangled again in the tentacles of thick ivy clinging to the building's stone wall. In a flash of passing headlights, he spots burglar bars securing the basement windows. One appears to be half-removed. He kicks and kicks at the rusted bar, and eventually the weak weld breaks loose. He grabs the iron piece and heads back around the building's corner where Gregory is swearing progressively louder, under his breath. He creeps up from behind and ... "Boo!"

Gregory spins about with balled fists, ready to strike. "Dammit, Andorf! Didn't you see that night watchman?"

Andorf peeks from between the branches and then leans into his friend. He takes a whiff. "Been taking a nip, have we?"

Gregory pushes him off with extended arms. "The bastard guard smashed his liquor bottle against the wall above, see?"

"Hey, you're bleeding."

"Like duh."

Andorf shoves the rusty iron bar in Gregory's face. "Look what I found."

"A burglar bar? Hey, you can't be destroying government property like—"

Andorf leaps onto the landing, pries a board loose with his rusty tool, and hands it to Gregory. Then a second and third board, only to wait dumbfounded on Gregory as he stacks them neatly to the right of the landing. "Stop with your OCD."

Gregory huffs. "It'll expedite our exit, I promise. You never did say what we're looking for in there."

"We went through all this, Gregory. Evidence. There's an official agenda book in there. I'm to look for a key." Andorf repositions himself, giving full weight behind the final board. He yanks and yanks, and the board breaks loose with a high shrieking note, landing, rusty nails up on the walkway.

Hearing an approaching whistle, the guys dive behind the thick shrubbery. Andorf reaches for the pry bar until Gregory jerks him back by his shirt seconds before a flashlight sweeps the landing. The white light sweeps across the bushes, inches above their heads and narrows on the exposed doorframe. Gregory grabs hold of his pants leg to steady his trembling hand.

The night watchman trips forward, up the walkway, whistling an intoxicated rendition of the once popular 'Twentieth Century Schizoid Man.' Andorf squeezes his eyes shut. He cracks one eye open to see the guard's stitched pants cuffs as the man stumbles up the steps. The guard's light refocuses upon the many nail holes. His off-key whistling ceases. He stumbles closer, head lurching back at the sight of the fiber boards neatly stacked on the right of the landing. He bends down, grabs Andorf's iron pry bar, and staggers down the steps, one drunken footstep after another. Face contorting, he freezes. He lifts his shoe and stares at the attached board, nails jamming through his sole. In the wavering moonlight, he removes his shoes and inspects the bloody mess. His eyes suddenly cross. He cowls like a cat in heat. Seconds later, he is lying face down on the walkway.

Andorf climbs onto the landing. "At least you didn't have to hit *this one* over the head."

"Hey!" Gregory yells, untangling from the thorny bushes. "If you remember, that militant brat at the rugby game was about to blow your head off. This drunken slob was out making an honest living."

"Let's go. He won't be too happy with us when he comes to." Andorf chases Gregory inside with the canvas bag and shuts the mammoth door behind. He and Gregory blindly feel for their supplies. The Crylex gloves easily slip on, but the rubber boots prove more of a challenge. After strapping on an infrared mini-goggle, each attaches a breather and lowers his mask. Activating the infrared illuminators, an eerie green fogginess encompasses their immediate proximity. With dust raining down like a waterfall, it is as though they are submerged at the bottom of a murky lake.

"Ten minutes of air," Andorf muffles out, setting his timer.

"Now I know how Armstrong felt in his early spacesuit," Gregory says.

Their eyes follow the green glow up the towering books and shelves. Gregory points. "As a prior librarian, I'd say legal manuals would be over there."

Andorf and Gregory zigzag in slow steps between haphazardly stacked document boxes, toward rows of decaying iron shelves, which moan and groan at the weight of legal journals. Andorf salivates at the thought of feeling real paper in his bare hands. Clipping the illuminator onto his mask, he pulls off his gloves and drops to his knees. He grabs at the bound journals only to see them crumble to dust between his gentle fingers. Andorf flails his hands, a warning too late. Gregory pulls at a weathered binder. As the bound volume clears the shelf, its inner pages detach and cascade one after another onto the floor, adding to the dust pile at his feet. Both gawk at the precious word fragments, scrambled together, blowing about the floor like alphabet soup in a Texas dirt devil.

Gregory shakes it off. He directs Andorf to go left while he goes right. After a minute, each pauses to wipe his mask. Gregory looks down at his feet and shrieks at large rats gnawing on his rubber boots. He shakes his legs and sprints for Andorf, bringing with him a whirlwind of trailing dust. In near zero visibility, he strains to see Andorf's masked anger as both wait for the dust to settle.

Their exhaust valves clog, making breathing impossible. Both yank their masks off and take shallow breaths through their shirts while they tap crud from the air filters. Securing their masks tightly over their faces, they again navigate between stacked boxes, frequently pausing to wipe their faceplates. Andorf raises three fingers in front of Gregory's faceplate. Three minutes of breathable air. Gregory nods.

After wiping his mask, Andorf points at a shelf unit on the fringes of illumination. "Found something." Both creep ahead painfully slow, holding illuminators above their heads. Andorf drops to his knees. He tosses his gloves and snatches a shiny key from the lowest shelf. Grasping it between his thumb and index finger, he flashes the key in Gregory's face. "A key."

"*Aqui* means 'h*ere'* in Español."

As Andorf's timepiece sounds, the key falls into the dust soup mix. Within seconds, the key and its shelf impression have vanished. "We're out of air."

He and Gregory drop their masks. Andorf swipes dust from the faded gold words of the bookbinder where the key had sat. Gregory kneels alongside. "Official Agenda," Andorf says, reading the binder.

Gregory gently swipes the binder, revealing a second and third line. "Of the Great Canine Empire." Wiping his brow, he squints at Andorf. "It's true!"

Andorf carefully slides the artifact from the shelf and lays it on the floor. With Gregory holding an illuminator above, Andorf slowly opens the cover. As he turns past the index, Andorf and his best friend marvel at its pristine condition. In spite of yellowed pages, the dark black words staining a viable cloth fabric appears intact. Eyes bulging, even Andorf begins to drool.

Gregory also salivates. He reaches from behind and feels the fabric with his bare hands. "That's real Bible paper, Andorf, made from woven cloth and real analog trees, like the rumors we heard back in grade school."

Andorf returns to the page. "Get a load of this date. This was printed before we were born. It's a relic from our grandparent's day."

Gregory hovers above as Andorf leafs through the delicate pages of finely scripted text and confusing legalese. "In all my years at the library, I've never seen fonts like these. You know how valuable this is?"

Andorf flips another page and pauses. His and Gregory's eyes flashing wide open. There in front of them lies hard proof.

> *Article One – (Media Empowerment) The government reserves the right to limit, restrict and otherwise control any form of media without regard for public or private dissemination, advisement, dispersion or notification thereof to the general populace.*

Eyes tiring at the government rhetoric, Andorf follows the eight-point font down the one page and up the next. Another section of verbiage virtually leaps off the page.

> *Article Four – (Domicile Domain) Confiscation of condemned land, buildings, and other such personal property shall be deemed necessary for the public good and shall be exercised without compensation or retribution of any means.*

"Why those thieving bastards!" Andorf yells, choking on the dust. He flips his shirt and holds it over his nose. Gregory follows suit. "Domicile Domain has been on the books for forty years before it became law. Wait until the media—no! Wait! Article One says the Empire controls the media."

Gregory empties a fiber box. At Andorf's nod, he places the treasured piece between their abandoned masks and gloves.

Andorf rises to his feet and helps Gregory seal the top. "We'll take this back to your place, snap a visual copy."

Gregory stares at him in disbelief. "Why *my* place? This was *your* big idea."

"Who's the pussy now, Gregory?" Rat packs scamper past. Andorf's snickering face pales. Eyes bugging out, he grabs hold of Gregory's arm. "See how fast those suckers were running?"

The floor begins to vibrate, knocking Andorf and Gregory off their feet. Breathing heavily, they pull their shirts over their heads. "I've heard this rumbling before," Gregory says, curling into a fetal position. "It's not a good sound."

"Be absolutely still." Andorf flips off the illuminators. His heart pounds in sync with the helicopter blades beating above. In his dark clothes, he huddles over Gregory as an intense white light bathes the dusty room. Andorf whispers. "This is what happened in that dream."

From his balled-up position underneath, Gregory clamps his hands around Andorf's throat and squeezes. "I'll tell you what you can do with your damn dreams. How could you leave *this* part out? How? How?"

Gasping for air, Andorf pries his friend's hands loose. He spits brown clumps, wipes his mouth. "Calm down, Gregory. I didn't want to scare you."

Gregory sits up to lean against Andorf. "If I'd known about this part, I never would have helped with your little escapade. But you knew that, didn't you? What happens next? Is this the part where we die?"

He suddenly quiets. On the floor nearby there is movement. Gregory's eyes narrow on a rat hobbling past, beady red eyes appearing focused on his legs. Baring its teeth, the lone rat turns and heads straight for his inner thigh.

Gregory backs against Andorf as a razor-thin blue beam descends from an overhead light tube. At first, the beam circles them, snapping at the billowing dust. The beam intensifies, etching a line in the concrete floor. Everything about them begins to hum. The beam heads straight for Gregory's knee and then homes in on the rodent, eleven inches from his crotch. Jittering, the rat emits a high-pitched shriek and ... *ZAP*! The rodent splatters between Gregory's legs, leaving the guys cringing at the smell of scorched guts and fur emanating from Gregory's crotch as the beam retracts upward.

A pack of rats appears, iridescent eyes glowing in the immediate darkness, long toenails clicking on the hard floor. The boldest rat creeps closer, inches at a time. It suddenly darts for Gregory's crotch, but stops to pick at the fried remains of his friend.

Other rats join the feast. Gregory eases back, keeping an eye on the picnic. "Even the rats are turning on one another."

The copter hovers for another minute and then leaves, as suddenly as it appeared, floor rumbling and dusty papers swirling about. Andorf leaps to his feet. "Hurry, Gregory. I think they're landing."

Gregory lies on the floor like a spoiled child. "I—I can't move my legs, Andorf."

"I'm not leaving without you," Andorf says, grabbing the fiber box in one hand and Gregory's arm with the other. He drags his best friend and the fiber box across towards the faint cherry red glow of the exit sign, knocking over countless towering boxes. Dust plumes flower over their heads as Andorf races for the door. He drops Gregory and the box and presses hard against the heavy entry door. It opens. Dust pours from the doorway, soon replaced by the cool evening air. Gregory crawls outside after Andorf to lie alongside on the landing, coughing and coughing. Andorf finds strength to sit on the steps, and spits out a wad of slimy gunk.

"Saliva!" Gregory yells. "They'll match your DNA."

Andorf sucks the dark mucous wad back in his mouth like a spaghetti noodle before it reaches the walkway. Following Gregory's lead, he blows the gunk back onto his filthy shirt. Both stagger to their feet and pat themselves down, trying not to inhale any of the Archives' escaping dust. Andorf pulls the door shut. Gregory loads the fiber box onto the cart, throws their boots in the canvas sack, and places the sack atop the fiber box.

Hovering above the stirring guard, Andorf sees Gregory already halfway to the street with the cart. He runs to catch up and follows Gregory to a dumpster behind a cluster of one-story office buildings. Gregory slides the hatch open and disposes of the canvas bag and its contents.

"Hey!" Andorf yells. "I paid good coin for that—"

"You want to be caught with this stuff, Andorf? They'd haul us off to the Cos without blinking." Gregory takes off for the street, hauling the cart and the fiber box. A second thumping in the night sky has him and Andorf dashing inside the office building's shadows. They flatten against the brick building, watching floodlights sweep over the dumpster, the cart, and then down the street, heading toward the Archives' building.

Exchanging sighs, they sprint down the street. Pulling the cart, Gregory grins at his upstairs neighbor. "Grandpa Gray would be proud. And wait until sis hears about this. She'll be green." He smiles at Andorf, wearing his best salesman face. "You should really meet her. The two of you—"

Andorf grunts. "As if I don't have enough baggage."

They see a pair of flashes illuminate the surrounding buildings. Seconds later, they flinch at the sound of gunshots. Gregory sucks wind through his teeth.

"The night watchman—they killed him."

"Let's get out of here." Andorf takes off running. "The guard may have seen us, ratted on us." Gregory grabs the cart and chases after Andorf, both leaving a trailing dust path behind.

CHAPTER 8
So Good To Be Home

Gregory lifts a corner of his welcome mat. Andorf looks at him as though he has lost his mind. "You can't be hiding your key like this. You never know who will—"

Gregory unlocks the door and tosses him the key. "Here. Next time I'll bother you for the key."

Andorf triple locks the back door while Gregory pillages through the hall closet, where everything has its place. He extracts the imager from its nitrogel wrapper. Andorf grabs a change of clothes from Gregory's drawers. "I'll take a quick one while you set that thing up." He swats at several tiny bugs circling the overhead light fixture. "If you don't get rid of these suckers, they'll end up in my unit."

"I can't get rid of the bastards. For some reason they love my ceilings. I knock them off, stomp on them, flush them away, and within minutes, exterminators are banging at my doors. When they leave, the bugs are back. You'd think they planted new ones.

Andorf heads for the bathroom, swatting at the bugs.

"Don't!" Gregory yells. "The exterminators will come. They'll replace our keyed locks with retinal devices. The Empire will be tracking our every move."

Andorf shrugs. In the shower, he watches the wash water darken and clog up the drain. Kicking the thick clumps aside, he flashes back to early childhood when he and his best friend back then were crawling beneath his house. He smiles at the memory of friends gathering freely in public, when a kid could whistle out the words 'here it' and be surrounded by playmates seconds later. *Bart ... Brett ... Brett Conyers, that's it. Funny how friends wash down time's drain, gone before you know it. I wonder what ever happened to that crazy kid.*

Andorf steps from the steamy bathroom brushing his thick, shoulder-length hair. He opens the door and call out. "I'm not sleeping well. That girl I told you about? She's in my thoughts 24x7, as though I'm finally about to meet her."

"Seriously, Andorf. I'm on the verge of having you committed." Gregory grabs fresh clothes and snarls at Andorf. "Don't go opening our treasure. I'll only be a minute. Hey, what are you doing? Don't swat those things."

With Andorf's bath having depleted the saline thermal mass, Gregory's shower is a brisk one. He springs from the bathroom toweling down a shiver. Dressing, he reviews how Andorf power cabled the imager. He inspects the tripod-mounted lenses aimed at the fiber box from three obtuse angles. At his nod, Andorf releases a slug in the power inductor and recording begins. Their impatient hands poised above the box, Gregory gently removes the cover.

Their jaws drop in disbelief at the alphabet of letters interspersed amongst the gloves, masks and filters. Andorf digs frantically through the dust for some intact piece of their treasure. "Dust. Nothing but dust. After all we went through, we have nothing to show. No one will believe us now."

Gregory grumbles, grabbing at the mix of scrambled words. "I should have known. How could I have been so stupid? As bad as that environment was for us, it was safe haven for those old books. Decades in a controlled environment and we destroyed them in minutes." His hands brush the bottom of the box. He sweeps through the dust, following each seam of the fiber box. He withdraws a filthy hand and squints cross-eyed at the tiny encapsulated chip wedged between his finger nail. He rubs away the dust and examines its markings. "This is bad."

Andorf sweeps his hand along the bottom edge and extracts a second chip. "Found another."

Gregory gazes at both chips side by side. "It's how The Empire tracks their assets. A simple handheld device can locate these RFID tags down to within an inch. They must have been hidden in the binder."

Andorf smirks. "No worries. Surely, their power cubes are dead by now."

"Don't you know how RFID tags work, Andorf? They draw power from a radio signal. The tags can lie dormant for centuries and when the right frequency awakens them, a coded message is transmitted several times before they fall back asleep. Government agents are probably homing in on us right now at this very moment. Gregory dashes for the commode. He starts flushing as if pumping for oil.

Andorf chases him. "Keep at it, Gregory. Put some distance between us."

"You know what my water bill will be like?"

"It's better than being hauled off to the Cos? Say, about that crazy dream … I didn't tell you the half of it."

Gregory stops flushing. He lowers the seat and sits. "I'm about to hate you even more, if that's possible?"

"That turbo-copter was there alright, and so was the part where I dragged your butt out of the Archives'."

Gregory stares him down.

Andorf shamefully nods. "And my elusive girl—" Andorf begins to drool on Gregory's spotless tile floor. "She's got brown eyes and this … this gorgeous nose … even larger than yours."

"Go on. She's beginning to sound like my—"

Gregory's front door pounds as if someone is trying to bust through. There is a second pounding on the kitchen door. Both doorknobs rattle like they are coming apart. Andorf and Gregory crawl for the living room curtains. From either side, they peer into the blackness. They hear a rustling outside the window, see shadows streaking past. They drop to the floor.

Andorf gasps. "The illuminators! We left them back at the—"

"What's it matter?" Gregory shrieks, in a parrot-like voice.

The kitchen doorknob twists as if it were coming off. Same with the living room knob. Andorf and Gregory crawl on all fours for the dark bedroom, dragging the fiber box behind. Gregory hurriedly shoves it into the walk-in closet and joins Andorf, already hiding under his bed.

Gregory's arm twitches like crazy. "How many were there?"

"At least two, maybe four," Andorf says. "Why would they waste their time on nobodies like us?"

Gregory drops his voice to a whisper. "Quiet, Andorf. The Empire has rooms full of people, listening to everyone, everywhere. Anything anyone says is digitized like those bogus trees out there. It's all stored in some spatial database. They have enough evidence to bust down anyone's door anytime they feel like it. They'll pipe in gas. Then they'll—"

"Stop your paranoia, Gregory. So we borrowed a book. What's the big deal?"

Gregory's eyes bulge. "You don't think breaking into the Archives' was a big deal?"

"Well … no … not from a seasoned criminal's point of view."

"I'm afraid of you, Andorf." He grabs his former friend's neck and squeezes hard. "What you've gotten me into?"

Andorf peels back Gregory's hands. "You mean *us*, Gregory. What I have gotten *us* into."

Gregory goes for his neck again, but Andorf blocks his reach. "They'll come for us in the middle of the night … when we're asleep. We're vulnerable when we sleep. They won't even need gas, you'll see. After the experiments, we won't recognize each other, let alone ourselves."

Andorf crawls out from under the bed, distancing himself from Gregory's rage. Gregory crawls out after him, pointing an index finger.

"One of us will disappear, leaving the other wondering. It's crueler that way, you'll see." Gregory points at his back door. "Our neighbors out there, they'll witness the whole thing, but no one will care. In hours, it'll be as if we … never existed."

Andorf snarls. "You know those unlicensed pharmacists sell pills for this."

They hear turbos rev up. They run to the front window, pulling opposite ends of the drapes aside. They see two copters hovering above the courtyard's grassy area before zooming off high above the thinning evening street traffic.

"I'm not kidding, Andorf. One of us will go missing. Those agents will be back, snooping around, harassing the lone survivor. That's how it works. My big sister told me all about it." Steadying himself, both hands atop Andorf's shoulders, Gregory takes a deep breath. He stares directly into Andorf's eyes. "Promise that if it's me they haul off, you'll never quit looking. Promise me, Andorf. Promise you'll never quit looking."

Andorf jerks away. "Alright! I promise! If I don't you'll be hounding me to death."

"And visit the mountaintops at sunrise, sing my name to Rena and the others. Make sure I'm not forgotten."

Andorf runs for the kitchen window. Separating the curtain slats, he scans the backyard. "Later," he says, flying out the back door and up the steps, into his condo. He quickly flips triple deadbolts on each outside door and then peers from behind his drapes into the front courtyard. Gathering his drapes tightly shut, he surveys the living room, comparing it to Gregory's place.

Staring at the rare Patriot poster covering his bricked up fireplace, he snuggles under the warm wool army blanket. Fully dressed, including his EasyGlides, he is ready to dart if anyone breaks in. *Everything resets in the morning. It always does. That is the purpose of sleep. Ah, it is so good to be home.*

PART 2: EPIPHANY

CHAPTER 9
The Awakening

Andorf's brain is more wired than Appalachian Power. He resists sleep, but soon as his heavy head hits the pillow, he is dreaming. He sees the elusive girl of dreams past crouching in the middle of the debris, sobbing her heart out. Then she paces about, yelling at someone not there. "The neighbors—what are they scared of?"

He eyes the back door, plotting an escape. Before he takes one dishonorable step, the girl grabs him by the shoulders, wrapping around him in a full embrace. Her brown eyes stare squarely in his eyes. Never before has he felt such intense feelings.

Breaking sounds jar him awake. Andorf wonders how many times he has dreamt this event. He sits straight up in a cold sweat, spine tingling at the unmistakable sound of a door divorcing its hinges. His eyes flair at faint shadows racing across his living room ceiling.

He leaps to his feet at the thin voice emanating from Gregory's unit directly below and darts out the kitchen door. From the rear balcony, he scans the proximity and the quadrant between the neighboring buildings. He creeps down the back steps, slinks around the side of the building. He finds Gregory's front door not only pried off its hinges but also partially detached from its casing, leaning broken inside its splintered frame. Through one of many cracks, he sees a figure prancing about in Gregory's dark living room. Andorf withdraws behind the safety of the building's sidewall. He dashes around to the back door. Wiping sweat off his temples, he reaches deep inside his front pocket, slips Gregory's spare key in the kitchen door lock, clenching his teeth at each tumbler click. As the door nudges open, a strange power draws him inside, across the creaky kitchen floor.

Andorf peeks into living room and sees a silhouette rummaging through Gregory's scattered possessions. He retracts his head and grabs a kitchen chair, ready to take out at least one of the intruders. Holding his breath, he dashes out, determined to deliver the first blow, but freezes on his third step, chair suspended high above his head. He gawks at the blonde-haired girl. Her damp cheeks disarm him. He lowers the chair and offers her the seat. At first, she is startled, but then smiles at the kind gesture. She rises and then collapses in the chair.

"How could they do this?" she cries, wiping her runny nose with the back of her hand. "They took him in the middle of the night … to that terrible place … where you're never heard from again." She gazes at him, arms twisting about mindlessly. She stands and paces the room. "How can they treat him this way? They neighbors … what are they scared of?"

Andorf recognizes her sweet voice from his dreams. He feels her stopping short of asking the same question about him before her head falls into her waiting hands. He eyes the back door for a viable escape route. Before he takes a dishonorable step, she rises and grabs him by the shoulders, wrapping around him into a full embrace. She presses so hard, he cannot tell her pounding heart from his own. Inhaling her wild mountain flower perfume, he imagines walking past a field of sunflowers, running his fingers through her hair. Her damp face pulls away. His heart melts at the sight her light brown eyes, twinkling behind her tears as they gaze into his own.

"My brother, Greg" she says. "You know him, don't you? You two are …" She loosens her hold as if gathering her thoughts, looking for some clue, any clue of what to make of this somewhat familiar guy.

Andorf clamps his mouth shut, struggling to restrain his thoughts. The harder he tries, the harder it becomes. *It's you, the girl of my dreams.*

The girl pushes him away. "I'm what?"

"You're Gregory's sister, the one he's been trying to pair me with for as long as I can remember."

She glares suspiciously from a safer arm's length. "How's that?"

"Well, uh, Gregory—"

"No! Rewind back to the girl of your dreams."

Andorf's jaw drops. *I never said that! How did she hear what I was thinking?*

She steps closer. "How are you doing this? Your lips aren't moving, but I'm hearing your every word."

Andorf grabs her arm. He drags her toward the broken front door to scrutinize her face. In the bright morning light, he compares her to the elusive girl from his dreams.

She pulls herself free of his loose grip. "What do you mean elusive?"

"I didn't say that either."

"You most certainly did. I heard it plain as day."

Splitting awkward glances between Gregory's sister and the damaged door, Andorf suddenly feels naked. He feels her empathizing with his internal strife. He flashes a little boy smile, too embarrassed to speak, before turning away. "You're reading my thoughts, aren't you? Why didn't Gregory warn me about you?"

Her hand turns his face toward hers. "Don't you think this is a bit unnerving for me also? It's not every day a girl finds anyone open as you appear to be."

Lost for words, Andorf studies the curves of her beautiful face. *Those high cheeks, those brown eyes, that beautiful large—*

The girl looks away for a moment. "Stop that. You're making me self-conscious. You and your open heart are killing me."

"It's just that ..."

"That what?"

Andorf gulps, gazing down at his EasyGlides before staring into her eyes. "You've been in my dreams, for months. There, I've said it."

She stares at him for the longest time.

What's she mean about me being goofy but nice. Andorf tugs at his shirt. "Oh, you mean these? I showered here last night after we—"

Her eyes narrow. "You read my thoughts as well." Taking a deep breath, she smiles, offering an open hand. "I'm Serin, Serin Gray. You must be the friend Greg frequently spoke of."

Andorf sandwiches her hand between his hands. He cracks a warm smile, first in many days. "I'm Andorf. Gregory and I are best friends. What a crazy way for us to meet after all of Gregory's attempts."

Serin chuckles. "It appears he was working us from both ends. You know, for a moment there I thought one of us was about to tuck tail and run."

"Indeed." Still holding her hand, Andorf leads her through the debris pile, past smashed frames, which once held hermetically-sealed, perfectly squared, one-inch paper samples. "I wonder what they were looking for?" Turning his guilty face away, he eyes the walk-in bedroom closet, piled knee-high in debris. He peeks under the bed.

"Why are you not telling me everything, Andorf?"

Andorf directs her to the bed with a nod. "You had better sit down."

Serin complies. She watches him pillage through the mess on the bedroom floor. Andorf leaps for a shelf working loose from its last anchor, catching cascading books along with Serin's grin. Their eyes home in on the many toggling eyes of Gregory's collector feline tick-tocks. Not a one displays the same time, but all of the finely painted eyes move left and right in perfect unison.

"We're being watched," she whispers. "Let's pick this up another time. Please don't do anything about my brother, not until—"

"Tomorrow night? We' can talk over dinner. I've found a new restaurant."

"Don't tell me. The one on LiveFree with the crazy bird name? The Tall Macaw, the Hungry Parrot, the—"

"Toucan Chew."

She smirks at the sexual innuendo contrasting Andorf's naivety. "I've heard the food is phenomenal."

"I've been there once but wouldn't know." Andorf says, under his breath. He gives Gregory's place a last look-over. Though craving her affection, he cannot wait to be alone again with his own thoughts. "Seven?"

Serin jumps up. Slipping on her backpack, she follows him through the living room debris field. "I'll come hungry. You can tell me all about that fiber box you were searching for."

One foot out the front door, Andorf freezes to examine Gregory's damaged door. "You should really have this looked at." With a light touch, the door falls off the frame, ending his graceful escape. He catches Serin wiping her eyes, watching him transcend the front steps, gazing as if unsure what to make of her brother's best friend. "Now to see about Gregory."

CHAPTER 10
Never Alone

The office manager storms past. Sporting blazing red locks and an Irish temper, he hurdles around Serin's hexagonal wall, projecting his typical bulldog glare. "What the hell's the matter now, Gray? Last week the integrator passed POC with flying colors."

Serin lifts her eyes. "We've picked up extraneous bits from somewhere upstream. I'm working out the linking errors."

"Now it's got excessive links? Bit errors?" he yells, storming out the trans-paned glass door. "McGuire! Where's McGuire?"

The busy body in the next hex pokes her head over their common four-foot wall. Her overpowering soapy fragrance clings to her like an indelible film from soft water baths. Her half-baked smile and painted-over eyes barely mask the fiftyish woman's bloodshot eyes. "What's real here? Come on, girl. Spit it out."

Serin tears and sniffles through a prepared grin. "My kid brother. He's gone missing."

The coworker hands her a fresh tissue. "On his way to the Cos, no doubt. If the man's got him, sweetie, there ain't nothin' you can do about it."

Serin cringes. "I know but—"

"You have to go on living your life without him. Several boyfriends of mine came up missing like that. Yep. You jes haveta move on," she says in a musical tone.

Serin nods, wiping her runny nose with the tissue.

"I can tell you more, but I don't wanna scare ya'." The woman looks Serin over from head to toe. "What's really botherin' you, girl. It's man problems, ain't it?"

"Well, there's this new guy—"

The woman wipes at Serin's eyes with her own tissue and frets at the missing trail of facial war paint on the spent tissue. "Go on, sweetie. I'm listenin'."

"He's kind of goofy but genuine, if you know what I mean. I think he's the guy I was telling you about from my dreams. The one I couldn't get him out of my head, no matter how hard I tried."

The woman snorts. "I've been in love a few times. Yeah, I remember those things. I'm only in my forties, you know. Now if he turns out to be another one of those losers, I'm really gonna be disappointed."

"You should see the way his nose wiggles when he gets all nervous. Let me show you." Serin takes a small device resembling a relic jPhone from her backpack. She drags an index finger across one corner of the simulcon and holds it near her cornea until it clicks. Her coworker crowds in for a closer look. The pixel image refines to smaller and smaller pixels until Andorf's face appears on the small screen.

Salivating, the coworker reaches over the four-foot separator wall and takes the device from Serin's hands. "Why he *does* look cute with that shaggy hair of his and those wire-rimmed glasses hanging off the tip of his narrow nose like that. You know he looks like that guy from the aviator band my grandparents used to play, Jeffer-something. Back in the 70s, when that garb you're wearing was in fashion the first time. Here, I'd better give this back to you before you have *me* daydreaming. So, I take it that big brute you were seeing is now available?"

Serin grins. "No, not really. But I've got a dinner date with the new guy."

The woman lunges over the wall, grabbing for Serin's throat beyond reach. "Honey, you can't be doing that stuff. Triads are unethical and most likely illegal. There's a man shortage out there and you're hoggin' all the good ones."

"Each has his strong points. Why can't I keep both?"

"Damn, you're greedy. I've been looking for a good man for years and here you are stringing em' along like charms. I certainly hope you're not looking for a third."

Serin laughs. "Can't a girl have what makes her happy? What's so wrong with that?"

"It's immoral I tell ya. It's usually one guy or gal, if you swing that way." The busy body retracts behind the wall. "Young love, I remember those days."

*

Andorf grins at the rattraps, each bearing the mug of a two-party candidate from elections past, decorating the store windows. As if by habit, he enters a side door, ducking at missing items that once bumped his head. The empty surplus store appears like a thrift shop at closing.

"I like your humor, Zeeshan."

A bearded man in his late twenties bearing a Pakistani accent even thicker than the stains on his coveralls surfaces from behind the counter. "I had to do something, my friend. They were the only thing in the store not selling. The ones in the windows and the few propping the doors are about all I have left."

"Where's Mike? He was holding some—"

"With nothing left to sell, I had to let him go. I can no longer pay him."

Andorf scans the sparse aisles. He edges closer to the clerk. "Everything is disappearing, Zeeshan. Even my best friend, Gregory, came up missing this morning."

"No! No! No! This cannot be, Andorf. Why Mister Gregory was in here just a few days ago, buying up the last of my blank signs." Zeeshan winces. "If the government has gotten hold of him, there's nothing you can do."

"But, I've got to do something. Gregory's my—"

"Don't waste your time." Zeeshan scans the vacant store. Mouth curling, he leans into Andorf. "The Empire swallows up things like a black hole, my friend, and the Tox are draining your wallet while the E-Cons are busy raping you in your own bedroom." Again, he looks around. "I hear you're looking for Colorado Gold."

Andorf watches the spinning icons interact across the countertop and Zeeshan's nimble fingers dancing across the surface. "How about a few new words in Urdu while we wait?"

"No more lessons, Andorf. My head hurts when you speak them."

"Then tell me about Islamabad."

Zeeshan's hand balls into a fist. It slams down hard on the counter. "And you wonder why so many westerners lose their heads in my land. I am a Christian from Karachi. I swear, Andorf, if you were not my friend—"

"Not funny, Zeeshan."

Both take deep breaths. Soon a short inventory list appears on the countertop. "Ah, the gods are smiling once again." Zeeshan scans the list. His joy regresses to regret. "You must settle on Topeka Timothy. That is if the rats have left us any."

Despite his towering six-and-a-half-foot frame, Zeeshan easily slips past Andorf to maneuver the twisting maze of empty shelves. Andorf follows the sound of creaking floorboards, catching up with Zeeshan at the rear door. Zeeshan pries a rattrap from beneath the rear door and shoves it into one of his many pockets. The battered screen-door bangs shut as they step outside. Zeeshan turns around to focus on the building's rusty tin roof. "Rust eats up my surplus store and there's not a bucket of paint between here and Cecal City. Believe me, I have looked. And there is not an ounce of tar to be found anywhere. Every time it rains, I run with buckets. What do I do now? All my buckets have been sold."

Amidst the blazing afternoon heat, they tromp across a quarter mile of overgrown pasture full of stickers toward a weathered barn, shirts sweat-glued to their backs. Crickets rub out monotonous tunes, eerily pausing briefly between choruses. They step around evaporated mud puddles, overstep over-powering smells of whatnots scurrying beneath them. Nearing the dilapidated barn, a thick fog of insects swoops down, baring razor-sharp teeth. Zeeshan flings the rickety tin door aside. "Hurry, Andorf! Hurry!"

Andorf runs inside, Zeeshan close behind. A swift yank on a dangling cord dimly illuminates the musty barn. Zeeshan grabs an open-frame cart and directs Andorf around several decaying artifacts scattered about the dirt floor. The squeaking wheels bounce over surface roots and come to rest against a section of rusted-out siding. Each stiff breeze lifts and vibrates randomly nailed roofing scraps above.

Andorf spots six greying hay bales on the ground. He sifts through the musty, picked-over bales and shake dust. "This stuff isn't fit for a horse."

Zeeshan removes the best of the six bales. "You should take this one, my friend. I can hold the others one, maybe two days, but no more."

Andorf throws his hands up and then nods. "Why is everything suddenly in short supply?"

At Andorf's grave look, Zeeshan loads the bale onto the cart "It's all about Starship Atlantis's launch in two months, Andorf. Things never used to be like this. Take those bugs out there. They have plenty of good carcasses to gnaw on. But no, like the government, they lick our sweat, suck our blood. And they no longer make those cute buzzing sounds. They follow my few remaining customers and me. It began the day after that orgy in City Park. I heard all about it on the Twisted News."

Andorf cringes. "Just spray them."

"Don't you think I've tried that? Everything dies except those flying teeth."

Zeeshan yanks the cord and follows Andorf with the cart. At the rickety outside door, they scan for insects before darting across the overgrown pasture. The squeaky cartwheels keep grasshoppers at bay, but not the swarming carnivores. Andorf swats at the descending cloud as they near the store. After a few misses, he sends a handful of the critters pinging off the store's corrugated siding. He and Zeeshan pause outside the back door, sifting through the leaves and rocks, grabbing hopelessly at tiny sparkles of light.

With a pair of tweezers from his coverall pockets, Zeeshan extracts a tiny insect spinning amongst the leaves. He holds it in Andorf's face. "Got one!"

Andorf stares cross-eyed. "What the hell *is* that?"

"Follow me, Andorf. My back office magnifier never lies." Zeeshan inserts the specimen into the machine. Both walk closer, squinting at the magnified object projected onto a large calibrated screen. They turn and home in on the slide. "Definitely man-made."

In a bright flash and puff of black smoke, they become temporarily blinded. Rubbing their eyes, Andorf and Zeeshan exchange glazed looks. "Our specimen self-destructed," Andorf yells. He dashes out of the back office and through the side door, Zeeshan chasing after.

"Wait, Andorf! Are you not curious about what comes next?"

Andorf's voice flutters. "I don't want to know, Zeeshan. Some things are best left unknown."

Zeeshan straps the bale onto the back of Andorf's rented motorbike. "Forty bucks, my friend. Supply and demand and taxes and government surcharge."

Andorf grabs Zeeshan by his collar. At Zeeshan's death stare, he drops his hands. "But I need a bale every other month. Help me out here, Zeeshan. This damn biped only holds one bale. I barely made it here on one charge."

Zeeshan steps back, wincing at Andorf, as if rethinking their friendship. "We'll settle up next week when you return for more hay. Best you get home, while the sun is high and the bath water still warm."

CHAPTER 11
Brett

"BOMBS EXPLODE outside Two Party Square Government Complex downtown late this morning. Dozens of bystanders were injured, but no fatalities have been reported in this latest round of terrorist activity. Thus far, no group has claimed responsibility. With elections around the corner, this latest incident wears the fabric of the right-wing political group calling themselves the Bogus Boat People."

Cleaning up for his big date, Andorf ignores the drama unfolding on The Eye in the next room. He sucks down a warm brew and flies out the front door. His expedience terminates at the dinner line winding across the sidewalk and around the corner of the Corner Cafe. He notes a wiry man of late twenties, scribing on a pocket tablet near the front of the line.

Andorf traverses the long line to rounds of verbal threats. "Brett? Is that you?"

Brett peers above his stressed grin. "Andorf, ole buddy. How you been? Why I haven't seen you since—"

Andorf steps closer. "Grade school. I'm getting by, living off a government stipend. The hours are great, but the pay sucks."

Brett snorts.

"I can't believe it's you. I was thinking about you the other day. Are you married or … you know?"

"Nah. I'm way too busy covering political scandals for a real life. I'm hoping to snag a meal, if I can ever get in this joint. So what about you, Andorf? Which lucky girl finally nailed you down?"

Andorf smirks. "No one yet. But who knows, I'm meeting someone special for dinner at seven."

"By your grin, I suspect she's more than special." Brett squints, aiming his self-focusing binocular implants through the café windows. "It's nearly seven now. You'd better not keep her waiting."

Andorf inspects the press pass clipped to Brett's shirt as they inch forward with the line. "I need to ask you about my neighbor, Gregory. He disappeared … yesterday … in the middle of the night. It's like no one cares."

Bewilderment precedes Brett's long chilling glare. "You're kidding me, aren't ya? Number one, he's most likely been taken to the Cos. Number two, to get any information you've got to kiss some serious political party ass." Brett's own distasteful words spur him to rip open a pouch and shove a wad of gum powder in his mouth.

"But they're the bastards I'm fighting. Surely, someone in the media like yourself—"

Tagging one foot in line like a base runner, Brett stretches uncomfortably close to whisper. "Don't you know both radicalized parties own the media? Believe me, I know. They'll totally ignore you unless—" After several unfriendly jabs, Brett fills the preceding gap in line.

Andorf tags along, despite the mob's hostile voices. "Unless what?"

Hecklers leap past Brett, pushing him a few pegs backwards. Growling, Brett turns back to Andorf. "Try breaking the law or violating some bloody Empire agenda. You'll either get arrested or elected. Either way, you'll make the media spotlight for a few days." Brett pauses to spit out a wad of gum. "You know the difference between politicians and criminals?"

Andorf hunches his shoulders, as do others in line behind them.

"Our taxes feed both, but only the politicians walk the streets. Like big-wig banker execs, they screw up and it's us taxpayers who pay their fines."

Andorf's lips purse. "I was wondering how much of that stuff was true. It's is all over The Eye."

"Creative journalism we call it. It livens things up a tad. You wouldn't want a bunch of stale news out there, would ya?"

"What if I join the debates as an independent? I could—"

Brett laughs hard, as do the others in line. "The Commission on Debates is composed of Tox and E-Cons. They would never allow anyone to speak publicly without being in their clique. There hasn't been free speech since the turn of the century. Look how the government persecuted that Tisdale woman back in Georgia thirty years ago for merely recording an E-Con rally—and that was before they confiscated our guns."

"What if I speak with this commission? Someone has to—"

"Won't do you any good, I tell you. The E-Cons are still smarting from when Ross Perot grabbed up twenty percent of their votes. Now you need fifteen percent in a straw poll and guess who tallies the results?"

Andorf's psyche drops to his knees. "So you're telling me I can't get into the debates without this fifteen percent, and I can't get this bogus fifteen percent unless I get media coverage which both parties control?"

Brett grins. "Alas the futility. Without a fat bankroll, pocket politicians and crooked judge, they will laugh you off the ballots. Whatever you do, it'll never be enough. You'll go broke fighting them. You can't win. Would you believe they spend a half-billion dollars of our taxes on their conventions every four years? A half-billion of taxpayer money. How you gonna fight that?"

"Dirty bastards!"

"It's how the game's played." Brett stares directly at Andorf. "Look, I'm as pissed as you, probably more so. But media pays me well to keep my trap shut so forget everything I'm telling you." Brett sees people in line running a hand across their mouths as if zipping their mouths. He edges closer to Andorf. "Did you hear about the Hotot Empire?"

Andorf scans the western sky, as do others standing in line. "Have they attacked us again?"

Brett's voice drops to a whisper. With one foot on third base, he steps from the line. "Don't tell anyone but the Hotot Empire is crumbling. That's right. The Asian regime is eroding from the inside out. It's losing the iron grip on their citizens. All hell is breaking loose over there. And to think, it all started with some guy in Ankara named Big Turk. Would you believe that?"

Andorf's jaw drops, as does everyone within a news-hungry earshot of Brett.

Again, Brett whispers, this time directly in Andorf's ear. "I was there when the feed buzzed through. Some fool punched it down an unscrambled channel, and for brief seconds, it flashed up on everyone's screens. The higher-ups shooed us out of the room, shut everything down. Can't have anything like this getting out. It would spread panic throughout our Canine Empire, give citizens ideas. Like the E-Cons, our bosses denied everything, threatened our lives if we divulged one single word."

"I could see how this revolutionary stuff could catch on."

Brett grins. "Like the plague." The cafe door swings open, and Brett darts inside. He pauses to look down at Andorf. "Here, this time, next Friday. I know someone who may help find your friend."

Andorf's eyes narrow on his childhood friend before he walks off. Why Brett? Why now? He recalls the coffee vendor's warning, of running into three old acquaintances. *Brutus, Wilhelm, and now Brett. I have bad feelings about this. It was great seeing Brett again, but what's he hiding?*

CHAPTER 12
Dinner Date

Late as usual, Andorf strolls beneath the brightly lit marquee of the Toucan Chew. A hand grabs his arm and drags him inside, through the busy restaurant, and to a table in the rear, a good twenty feet from the nearest table. Glancing at the zone lighting glowing eight feet above, he takes a seat.

"I was beginning to think you stood me up," Serin yells over the ambiance.

Andorf yells back. "I ran into an old friend."

Serin inspects his face over her second glass of Vegi-Complete. "I thought you wanted to be with *me*."

Her sweet honeysuckle perfume inflames his nostrils. Heart fluttering, he examines her shoulder-length blonde hair framing her shoulders. Between her high cheekbones and irresistible brown eyes, he feels setup. With little chance of noticing anything below the neckline of her low-cut lavender peasant blouse, each time he looks away, her beauty reels him in like a yoyo. He squirms in his seat, feeling that the evening's cards have been stacked against him. "I did—I do."

Serin blushes at Andorf's clumsy inspection. "You know … to discuss what to do about my brother. Tell me you didn't do anything. I told you not to—" Her stomach growls. Then a second time, much louder. She gazes around at inattentive diners nearby and laughs. "We'd better order, before I turn cannibalistic."

Andorf cringes at her words. Waiters ignore his hand waves until Serin whips an arm over her head. One magically appears. He punches a reset code on his belt and dashes off. Serin taps on a vivid 3-D display photo and then swivels the screen toward Andorf. "I'm having mushroom chiati."

Andorf stumbles at the many unappealing choices. After difficult moments, he taps the screen, matching Serin's relentless table tapping. He swings the screen aside and brushes an outstretched hand against hers before taking hold of it, pleased by her lack of resistance. "Look, I didn't mean to be so callous back at Gregory's place. I was expecting a burglar, not his sister."

Serin scans Andorf's troubled face and the hand enveloping hers. After an uncomfortable silence, she cracks a smile. "I already have a boyfriend, Andorf."

Andorf's runaway euphoria derails. He swallows at raging disappointment, trying his best to smile. "And now you have another."

Serin massages his hand, volleying a more genuine smile, "I really like you Andorf but …"

Andorf gulps, expecting the rules, the conditions, the bomb.

"I'm not the innocent girl you think I am. You see …" She focuses on Andorf's eyes, as if to scan his thoughts, so available on their first meeting.

Andorf in turn, strains to read her thoughts while scanning for an exit.

"Don't go," she says, clamping down hard on his hand. "It's just with Greg missing, my life has becoming really c ..."

At Serin's hand freeze, Andorf frets about her speaking of commitment or one of the other dreaded 'c' words, none in his favor. Again, he feels the dealer has dealt him a losing hand. He treads lightly through her verbal minefield. Voice stuttering, he turns away, not to lose his slippery footing. "Uh, I didn't know you were so close."

Serin breathes deep. Her eyes scan their cupped hands and Andorf's pained face. "I don't know who to trust anymore, Andorf, let alone have time for a relationship. I can tell your heart is bigger than Jake's Mountain but ..." She turns away, as if cautious to say more. She glares back at him in nail-biting silence, obviously trying to contain her thoughts. Both stare into the other's eyes.

Andorf feels thoughts not his own, dragging him back to Gregory's condo. He sees most everything Gregory owned spread through his living room. He looks up to see tears gathering at the corners of Serin's gorgeous brown eyes. His voice softens. "Too big for my own good? You forget I can hear your thoughts."

She sniffles. "So about Greg, where'd you see him last? Have you any idea where he might be?"

Wiping Serin's eyes with his napkin, Andorf wonders how he feels this close to a girl he just met and why he visualizes romantic scenarios set from Serin's perspective. He drifts back to his last moments with Gregory.

"Andorf! Andorf!" Serin yells, undocking from his absent hand. "Where were you just now? You had a lost little boy look."

"Gregory's condo. There we were, hunched over his image catcher when ..."

"Rewind," Serin says. "You're leaving things out."

Andorf breathes deep. "We found the government agenda book. It was dark and nasty so we packed the dated evidence in a fiber box and brought it back here—I mean Gregory's place. We were about to—"

Serin throws a hand over her mouth. Andorf's thoughts become her own. "Oh my God, Andorf. I see the fabled Official Book of Agendas. It actually exists. You were holding it right there in your hands. I can almost feel the—"

Andorf swallows hard. "And it crumbled into nothingness."

Noticing how diners at surrounding tables are staring at them, Serin leans into Andorf. Her voice drops to a whisper. "I saw a fiber box, Greg all pumped up. Wait! Why is he scared like that?"

Andorf glances at the suspended motorized lighting barely above their heads and the patrons at neighboring tables leaning toward them. He directs Serin to an empty table, hidden in a dark corner, far from the other diners. He waits for her to drop her backpack onto the floor and settle into her seat. "You don't understand. Copters were hovering above, their sweeping blue lasers burning at our feet. We were scared, scared like the pack of—"

"Rats! I see hundreds of them," Serin yells, kicking her feet.

Andorf places both hand atop Serin's arm. After a few minutes, she calms down. "You don't understand. We couldn't see. We couldn't breathe. Dust was—"

"Everywhere, whipping like tornados," Serin says, following his hands.

Their waiter appears from nowhere with a chilled glass of Veggie-Complete. He lingers, discretely grimacing at the motorized lighting, suspended eight feet above Andorf and Serin's heads at their new table. "Your dinners will be out shortly, madam, sir."

Serin dismisses him with whisking hands. She scoots close enough to sit in Andorf's lap. "The Tube reported a murdered guard that night ... at the Archives' building ... before it was set ablaze."

Andorf smirks. "Since when is there truth in anything that fast-food media feeds us?"

Serin quiets. Her face pales. "Wait! That was you two at the—"

Andorf slaps a hand across her mouth. "We were merely borrowing a book." At Serin's nod, he drops his hand. "We packed the artifact in a fiber box and brought it back to Gregory's place. When we opened up the box to record the evidence, all those finely printed words, exquisite paper pages, had crumbled to dust. And to make matters worse, we found RF tags mixed in with the remains." Andorf's pulse revs. "We heard a rustling outside in the bushes, doorknobs twisting like they were about to snap off."

Andorf drops a hand over his pounding heart. He pauses to gather his fleeting wit. Serin coaxes him to continue with her hands.

"Gregory—he stashed the fiber box in the closet," he whispers. "We hid under his bed."

"The ones outside," Serin whispers. "Did you get a good look at them? Were they agents?"

"It all happened so fast. We barely caught the tail lights of two government turbo speeders zooming off." Covering his own mouth, Andorf gazes past Serin. "Our trail of dust led them straight to us. It was supposed to rain last night, wash away our trail. And those RF tags, we never had a chance."

Serin eyes all the untouched plates at surrounding tables, the loaded sporks frozen at patron's mouths at tables slid closer. She cups her both hands over Andorf's ear. "You can't blame disorganization on the weather. You must think these things out down to the last detail, have contingency plans. I cannot believe you didn't know about asset tags. They're everywhere." Serin chuckles. "There may even be few of them implanted beneath your skin right now. I hear the Empire considers its their citizens as property."

Lowering his head in shame, Andorf's eyes widen at the site of Crylex gloves stuffed into Serin's open backpack. Serin follows his eyes and stuffs them further inside. "As you were saying—"

"It all began with those stupid yard signs. Gregory had some crazy notion about me running for office, mayor in fact. He scribed my name on a few signs and planted them at the corner. Each time we turned our backs, a sign went missing."

"That's so like him."

"When I tried to register the theft, I got slapped around by a nasty records bitch. Luckily, my old friend, Wilhelm stepped in to intervene. He's the one who told me about the Archives, open to anyone's viewing."

"It's all available in the government database. Greg knew that. All he had to do was … Wait! Did you say Wilhelm, as in Wilhelm Mattigan?"

Andorf nods.

"There are reasons a government dreg remains on the ground office for years. I wouldn't put much credence in anything he said. I'll bet that swine set you up."

"No, not Wilhelm."

"So back at Greg's place, what happened after the agents flew off?"

Andorf shakes his head, reliving the scene. "We were both scared. I got the hell out of there. I heard Gregory locking up as I tore up the back steps."

"What? You just left him there?"

Andorf watches Serin steam. "Things always reset in the morning. But yesterday was different. I awoke to voices, breaking things. I ran downstairs and grabbed a weapon. That's when I found you balled up on Gregory's floor."

Serin grimaces at Andorf. "You mean that chair? The one you were holding over your head? I thought you were offering me a seat."

He looks at her sheepishly "I could have been. I—I don't remember."

"When you left Gregory's, I scoured the place. There was no sign of your fiber box. The agents must have scarfed up whatever they didn't break."

"Even Gregory."

Serin sighs. "An accomplice to an unmentionable crime. I guess I really can't blame you. Greg is an adult. He knew what he was getting into."

"I have to find him. He made me promise." Andorf gulps. "There may be someone who can help. I'll know more next week."

"Andorf! I told you not to—"

"For the love of Clark Solomon, Serin, I'll never again turn my back on a good friend. I'm not sitting around while whoever does whatever to him. It's been thirty-six hours. For all we know ..."

They notice how quiet the restaurant has become. From an arms-length away, diners quickly turn away while retaining eye contact. Andorf points out the zone lighting nearly clipping their heads. "Perhaps meeting here wasn't such a good idea."

Delivering their dinners, the server catches the pair without appetites. Andorf grabs the waiter's portable receptor and scans his retina to pay the bill. The man takes one look at the device and pulls Andorf aside to whisper in his ear.

"Sir, Your base amount has cleared but there is little room for …" He clears his throat loudly, offering Andorf an open palm.

"I'll settle up when you return with our to-go boxes." Andorf smirks while the waiter promptly disappears with their untouched plates.

Serin raises brow. "Problems?"

Andorf returns to the table, blushing a few shades darker than chartreuse. He digs deep in his pockets for coin. "He recommended I dress more appropriately on my next visit, as if I'd ever return to this dump."

With bagged meals in hand, the couple exchange awkward farewells. Andorf watches Serin's fading silhouette with a nagging feeling of seeing her again much sooner than expected. Splashing a shallow puddle dry, he shakes a fist at the cloudy evening sky. "Now you rain!"

CHAPTER 13

The Initials

The next morning, Andorf feels sucker-punched about Wilhelm. In the cooler, it is Serin's dinner he discovers. One peek and he locks the front door, not wasting any time heading for the Records Office. Heart wrenching at the sight of the troublesome clerk, squirming in her seat, has him regretting his finger dinging the counter bell.

Wanda waddles gracelessly to the front counter, cursing at him beneath her breath. "Do you have an appointment, sir?"

"Where's Wilhelm?" He says, leaning over the counter, sneering at her. "I know he's back there."

"Wilhelm?" she asks. "There's no one here by that name."

"There most certainly is," he yells, pointing behind her at the hidden office. "Wilhelm. Wilhelm Mattigan. He's back there! Call him! We'll get this all straightened out."

"I told you there's no one here named Wilhelm, sir. Perhaps I can look his name up." Chanting Wilhelm's name repeatedly, the fat clerk fat thumbs through screen after screen on the sub-counter display.

Andorf darts past. He ducks into the unlocked office where statistical charts cascade from an over-trimmed, mahogany desk onto the floor. Holding out a crucifix letter opener between them, a stocky well-dressed man leaps to his feet. "Who are you? What are you doing in my office? No one comes in here without an appointment."

Andorf charges ahead. "I should ask you the same. What are you doing in *Wilhelm's* office?"

The aging man swings his crucifix at Andorf. "Look mister, we're out of the free starship maps. Whomever this Wilhelm is, he certainly does not work here. Perhaps you are confused. Like politicians, these government offices all look alike."

"I think not. I clearly remember that dimwit clerk out there." Andorf takes a step back, relaxing his stance. "You must know Wilhelm, Wilhelm Mattigan. A strong German accent? Wears a monocle?"

Doing a double-take, the office manager tosses his makeshift dagger onto a stack of acetates on his desk. "I've been in government nearly twenty years, mister, and I don't recall anyone fitting that description. You can verify that with Wanda out there, but you'll need an appointment." The manager rummages through acetates atop his desk. "I know I've got one of those Form A's around here somewhere."

Keeping an eye on the man, Andorf backs out the door. He immediately hears Wanda's irritating giggle and sees her squirming sensually in her seat as she swipes yet another e-page on her eReader. As the glass door shuts behind, his thoughts revert to friends, who seemingly slipped from existence. *First Gregory, now Wilhelm. Who is next?* Andorf's eyes roll back. His heart flutters. His breath shortens. He runs outside. *Oh my god! No, not …*

*

Andorf slips Gregory's key in the back door, but it refuses to turn. He trots around front and admires the fine millwork on the freshly hung door. An inviting window beckons. Pushing the window screen aside, he snakes inside. Gagging at the caustic sanitizing fumes, he pulls his shirt over his nose and darts between vacant, sterilized rooms, calling for Serin.

With all signs of Gregory meticulously removed, he exits the front door, coughing roughly. He jogs up the stairs. He feels the presence of another growing with each step and fate's hand drawing him closer. At the honeysuckle fragrance tickling his nostrils, his heart pounds like there is no tomorrow. There in the entryway, sits Serin, atop an enormous faded tan suitcase, rubbing her irritated eyes. She lifts her face long enough to smile.

"I came home and found my place ransacked. Without Greg, I've got nowhere to go."

"But how'd you—"

"My brother, Greg, remember?"

Even in her distressed state, Serin is overwhelmingly gorgeous. Restraining his desire, Andorf helps her to her feet. Their eyes lock as she offers a passionate smile. He leans in to kiss her moist lips and ...

"Wait!" she yells, pushing him off with both hands.

Andorf fumbles for his keys, confused. The moment the door opens, Serin darts inside, leaving him to deal with her heavy suitcase. "Way to go," he mumbles, wrestling the manly suitcase inside. Judging by its many scratches, Serin had manhandled the luggage upstairs by herself. Panting, he drops it just inside the door.

Serin returns from the dark bathroom, drying her hands. "Thanks. I was hoping you'd get that."

He projects both arms. "Look, outside, I didn't mean to—"

As the words leave his mouth, Serin backs him against the wall, wraps her hands around his head, and plants a wet one on his lips. She retracts, leaving him leaning against the wall with a dazed grin, realizing his life will never be the same. Eyes still shut, he stutters. "But I thought—"

"Just finishing what you started outside. Your place seems much smaller than Greg's."

"I don't know what her game is, but I could definitely get used to this," he mumbles to himself. He opens his eyes to see her digging through his bedroom. He glances down at the large tan suitcase. "Hey, what's 'B.B.' stand for?"

"I borrowed it from a friend," Serin yells. "Someone who occasionally sleeps over."

Andorf scrutinizes the engraving. He shakes off the shiver of a crazy notion. "Did you bring my dinner from last night?"

She looks at him and laughs. "It was tasty but a bit immature."

Dragging her luggage into the bedroom, he catches her outline dashing for the bathroom. Moments later, she steps out, wearing a petrified face. "I got a good look this time, with the lights on. I'm afraid to touch anything in there. There are mushrooms growing out of the carpet."

"Management knocks fifty bucks off my monthly maintenance fee. They've had a dehumidifier backordered for two years."

An item on the hallway shelf catches Serin's eye. She reaches to examine. "This silly flag. Greg has one just like it."

Andorf grabs the stick flag from her hand and carefully returns it within its dust outline. "You mean like the one he *used to* have. I stopped by his condo on the way up. There's no trace of him anywhere. It's like he's been …"

"Deleted." Serin sucks wind through her teeth. She whips an identical stick flag from her backpack and places it next to the other. "There, now you have two."

Andorf grins at the twin flags. "They were handing them out at the rugby game last week."

"You mean where Greg goes to gawk at the girls?"

"I really didn't notice."

Serin runs her fingers through his thick brown locks. She takes his hand and pulls him into the bedroom. Sitting beside him on the bed, she grins at his enlarging eyes as she seductively unbuttons her blouse, one deliberate button at a time.

Andorf yanks his polo shirt over his head, wondering how far this will go. She answers his thoughts by tossing her blouse onto the floor. His hands freeze, poised at her firm breasts. *What? No bra?*

"I don't need one with Heffner exercises. Well lover, what are you waiting for?"

His hands cup her inviting B-size breasts. Their tongues explore each other's necks. Breathing heavily, she undoes his belt. Andorf unsnaps her jeans and with the help of Serin's wiggles, slides them down to her ankles, before she kicks them off. *Where have you been all my life, Serin Gray?*

She cannot remove his pants fast enough as they assume horizontal positions alongside each other. "I was thinking the same thing, Andorf Johnson."

He grabs her underwear and the passion play abruptly halts. "What's with the men's briefs?"

"Don't stop. I'll explain later," she whispers, tossing them onto the floor.

Andorf blindly reaches between her legs and happily discovers her hairy slippery parting. With a devilish grin, he retracts his hand, takes a whiff, and jumps into action. Tossing about, they explore each other's secrets. Their lovemaking continues throughout the afternoon and well into the evening, heightening at pounding walls and incomprehensible neighborly verbiage.

*

Serin cracks an eye half-open to sunbeams breaking the dusty air and Andorf snoozing alongside. His outstretched hand lazily brushes her face. She kicks one foot, then the other. "Quit licking my feet. I'm really not into that."

"Huh, what?" Andorf says, in yawn.

Her eyes widen. Pulling both legs into a fetal position, she shakes Andorf with both hands. "If you're up here, who's—"

A flume of white fur floats lazily past her nose. From below, a six-pound Chinchilla rabbit leaps onto Andorf's pillow and finds Andorf's face a comfy seat. Andorf spits out a fur ball. "That would be Binky."

As Andorf stretches, Binky leaps off the bed and runs back and forth across the bedroom floor, wildly kicking his rear paws in the air on each pass. Serin sits up, amazed by the rabbit's theatrics.

"What's he doing now?"

Andorf cracks an unfocused eye. "Binkies. He does them whenever he gets really excited, like when he's just awakened the dead."

"He's precious, Andorf. How long have you had him?"

"Five years next month. I rescued him as a baby. We've been through a lot together."

"Why a rabbit? How long do they live?"

"Eight to twelve years with proper diet. Andorf rolls onto his back and rubs his eyes. "Dogs need to go out all the time and cats are roommates who despise you but need a place to crash. Binky is quiet, litter box trained, and his poos don't stink."

Andorf reaches for Serin as she stretches out of the covers, revealing her naked curves. Standing barefoot on the cold floor, she slips the nearest shirt over her shoulders and beelines for the bathroom. Andorf watches through the open door. In the finger-stained mirror, she glares at Andorf's old polo shirt she wears. Failing the sniff test, his shirt gets tossed onto the tiled bathroom floor.

Andorf lies watching her feminine outline traversing back and forth, grabbing clothes from her suitcase. Wearing only briefs, she bends down, stirs him awake with an embracing kiss. He cups her dangling breasts seconds before she darts off, slipping on a blouse. "Some of us have jobs."

Sensing morning activity, the kitchen Brewmaster5000 fires up. Andorf stumbles into the kitchen and pours two cups of his finest java. At the sound of his china cabinet drawer sliding open, he dashes into the dining area to catch Serin's finger-tracing the intricate engravings of his family silverware. "There must be twenty settings in here," she says. "This stuff is worth a small fortune."

Andorf sneaks from behind and rescues the tarnished pieces from her hands. He promptly returns each piece to its proper felt-lined slot in the drawer and reaches around her to slide the drawer shut. "My inheritance is precious. Our family kept them out of government hands for ten generations." He leaves Serin rifling through his china cabinet filled with his prized collection of ceramic mugs. Stepping from the shower, he pokes his head out the door in time to see her blowing kisses from the front door.

"Meet me in the city park before sunset ... near the fountain. There's something we need to discuss. Bye, Binky."

With a towel wrapped around his waist and a damp razor in his hand, Andorf stares at Serin's tan luggage with the 'B.B.' engraving at the bedroom door. *Tonight I'm getting down to the bottom of this. I am asking her about those initials.*

CHAPTER 14

Aliens Among Us

Andorf throws on khakis, a collared shirt, and secures his EasyGlides. His fingers dance through the cooler, grabbing at chilled hydrator straws. He grabs the last braisonberry groat and jogs down the front steps, dragging an inflated brush through his thick, shoulder-length hair. One touch of a button and the brush shrivels to the size of a small pocketknife, destined for his pocket.

He devours the groat as the Cecal City bus arrives. Escalating steps whisk him aboard and after a retinal scan, Andorf takes a seat several rows behind the driver. He peels off the hydrator tops and slams down the drink, imagining how things will play out. *I'll start right at the top, be shuffled from room to room. I'll greet overzealous mulls wanting to shake my hand. Advice will flow as freely as Friday night draft at Hannigans.*

He settles in for the two-hour ride to Cecal City, a mere twenty minutes for those affording the high-priced ticket. He peers enviously out at the turbo speeders zooming past in the seven-mile-per-minute lane. Random passengers voice displeasure at the banana-colored taxis buzzing overhead even faster.

"Their faces distort, going so fast."

"They have more money than time."

One pothole after the other make the Capital bus shudder as if it will break apart. Cracks form down the center aisle. Passengers grab hold of whatever they can reach. The cracks widen and merge. Spreading backwards, a massive crack consumes two empty rows of seats behind Andorf. A window vibrates out of its frame and smashes on the roadway.

The driver winces in the rear view with no sign of slowing. "No worries. I'll borrow one of those at the terminal." He veers into a better-paved lane sending an aging woman flying out the gaping window hole. "No worries. I'll fill her seat at my next stop."

*

Andorf exits the bus peering at words chiseled into the Literals' headquarters: 'TOXIDIANS OF THE GREAT CANINE EMPIRE.' He steps around the seventy-two flickering holo-plaques representing the state count reported on The Eye that morning. The simulated well-manicured lawn casts his EasyGlides a bluish green.

A few spins through the single rotating door lands Andorf on a steel-blue terrazzo floor in the atrium facing a circular desk where a mockery of the infamous Blue Boy painting hangs above. The selected president's face replaces the face of that proud lad and a rolled up list of the remaining five commandments replaces his blue coat on the left. Twin attendants behind the marble counter dash about in smartly pressed navy blue blazers, baby blue bowties, and polished crybaby cuff links.

Andorf smirks at the twin's identical faces. "I'm here to see number one."

Blank faces address him in utter silence, eyes bulging as if spooked.

Leaning against the counter, Andorf glares at the pair. "You guys understand me?"

The twins huddle together, sharing glances with the stranger. They jump into a canned speech, describing the fine features of the

Toxidian headquarters. One stutters the beginning of sentences. The other completes his words. Tiring at their routine, Andorf spots an exit behind the counter and jumps around it, but the twins intercept and block his path. He casually strolls around the other side of the counter, but they block this attempt as well. Andorf clears his throat. "I've got a dying aunt who …"

Arms crossed, the twins shake their heads.

"Interested in a Gatlinburg timeshare just a few states down route?"

Again, the twins block his path. Andorf taps his wrist. "Either of you have the time?"

While the twins fixate on their own timepieces, Andorf struts calmly around the pair. A narrow passage ends at a large rusty door and an even larger soldier projecting that 'what'd you say about my mother?' look blocks his path. Every bit of the 300-pound soldier glares with low regard, shaking his head side-to-side as he stares right through Andorf.

Andorf smiles at the soldier. "I'm here to see numero uno."

The private first class grunts, shaking his head above folded arms.

Andorf taps the private's robust left shoulder. "Say, Gomer, what if I told you I have a cousin in the Marines?"

The private's eyes narrow as if wanting a piece of Andorf. His fingers tighten around the handle of his loaded .44 pistol.

Lowering his head, Andorf steps back. He probes the soldier's mind, seeking some soft pocket of compassion. After a moment, he grins at the private, reads the name on his uniform. "I see you've been working it, Sergeant Graham Parker, been squeezing out the spark."

The private smirks. He begins to speak, but Andorf cuts him off.

"Don't look at me like that. As your m … senator, it's my job to know your name. And yes, I called you Sergeant. You are well on your way." Andorf flashes an ID too fast for eyes. "Senator Johnson says so."

The soldier's stone cold scowl morphs into a jolly grin, spreading across his face like a glass pane cracking from stray pebble impact. He suddenly bursts into a loud chuckle. "Well Jiminy Cricket. Why didn't you just say so, Senator Johnson? Go right ahead. I believe they're expecting you. Don't be late."

Andorf slithers past in disbelief as Private Parker holds the door open. He hears the guard's fading laughter through the rusty steel door. "A senator, how about that. I was speaking with a senator."

Andorf follows a Spanish-tiled floor a distance to its termination. Facing a door on either side, he recalls his location. He goes for the knob to his left. With a slight touch, the golden door swings open to an awaiting crowd. A stick-thin man is the first to scrutinize Andorf's perfectly vertical stance.

"Welcome, friend. I'm Linton, assistant to the assistant to the … well, never mind that. Come on in."

Passing beneath blazing overhead lights, Andorf squints at Linton and his likewise left-leaning coworkers. "Nice to meet you, Linton. I'm Andorf Johnson."

Linton walks around Andorf's extended hand and tiptoes past an aged mahogany door. "What's it matter? What's it matter?" pours out the partially closed door.

Pulling the office door shut, Linton squinches at the sharp, bird-like voice. "Ignore that. Just some washed up remnants of an old goat." He grins forcefully at his new arrival. "Say, you wouldn't you be in the market for parrot, would you?"

Andorf shakes his head.

Linton's beady eyes home in on Andorf. "So tell me, Andrew, why are you really here?"

"See, Linton, I've got this friend who—"

Linton grabs his arm and leads him past an open office where endless duplicators regurgitate acetate forms in duplicate and where workers by the thousands, shuffle forms, date stamping each and every form. "Useless jobs for equally useless citizens, all at the expense of overburdened taxpayers like yourself. Same business model all the way to the top affords tax raises every year."

Andorf spots a woman leaning against the water cooler, dressed in all blue, criticizing them with her eyes as they stroll past. Linton stops Andorf at the scaled replica of the infamous twelve-mile Reid Footbridge suspended over the Sagebrush Desert. Dusting the candy-blue buttons marking every scaled mile, he blurbs about the never-ending, two-year project.

Linton boasts a smile of success, voice swelling in pride. "Isn't it grand, Andrew? Our teams are always uncovering ways to finance projects like this without taxpayers ever noticing."

Like a child, Andorf presses five of the thirteen buttons. "You mean funneling money?"

Office workers drop their acetate forms and quietly stare. Linton kindly grabs hold of Andorf's arm, leading him away from the display. Rubbing his pointy chin, Linton looks over Andorf and his troubling, perfectly vertical stance. "Level with me, Andrew. Are you another one of those E-Cuniculons who snuck past GI Joe back there?"

Andorf raises his voice, "I assure you, Linton, I *am not* one of those denying right-wing bastards. Now about my friend—"

Linton takes a deep breath. "Good! I would hate to think our security lacks merit."

Andorf can no longer hold back his curiosity. He head-points back at the entry door. "I've been meaning to ask you. Why does your hallway end like that, with two doors?"

"You were forced to make a decision, were you not? Your appearance verified that you chose the correct door."

"Yes, but—" Again, the room quiets. Andorf feels a thousand eyes staring at him. Andorf changes his thought at Linton's scorning look. "Now Linton … about my best friend … the one who suddenly …"

Linton's tight facial lines relax. His eyes uncross. He leads Andorf away from the busy office eyes. "Unlike those bloody E-Cons, we believe in all the social freedoms. You know … freedom of speech, freedom to marry anyone you like, things like that."

Andorf halts. "And by anyone, do you mean any *one* person or any person?"

A comical grin consumes Linton's narrow face. He slugs Andorf's right arm. "You are toying with me, Andrew, mixing words like that. You are trying to confuse me, aren't you?"

"Then what about financial freedoms? How much of my income do I get to keep? Right now taxes are eating up most of my …"

Linton's eyes expand. "Oh, Andrew, again you tease me. Taxes and finances are way too complicated for *any* citizen to understand. Let the binary generators figure all that stuff out."

Andorf hesitantly taps Linton's meek shoulder. "So let me get this straight. By electing a Tox, or shall I say a Tax candidate, we get personal freedom, somewhat, but lose our financial freedom?"

Linton's tight face wrinkles. "Think of it as unloading a financial burden, Andy. There are no free lunches. We must pay for social freedom." He steps aside as if to rationalize Andorf's concern, which appears to be nagging him like a thorn in his side. "And best you drop the slang. Never use that filthy Tox word. We are Toxidians." Linton takes a moment, clears his throat. "You must tell me, Andrew, what really brings you here today? Be honest with me."

Andorf stares into Linton's beady little eyes. He takes a deep breath. "Like I've been trying to tell you, Linton, I've been trying to find my best friend, the one who disappeared suddenly in the middle of the night. He's the one who wanted me to run for m … senator. Now if I could get myself elected—"

"But we have a perfectly fine senator," Linton yells. He directs Andorf into a quiet corner. "Has he gotten caught up in another one of his scandals? We closed down that foundation long ago. We no longer accept gifts from foreign powers. Now if they'd like to donate a few dozen cases of their fine wines, who are we to—?"

"No. None of that, Linton. Nothing I'm aware of at the moment."

Linton looks puzzled. "Has our senator been maimed, killed?" Andorf shrugs his shoulders. He feels Linton's thin hand pinching at his elbow. "No! Don't tell me he's terminally ill." Linton gazes back at the office with the closed mahogany door. "He can't be washed up. We're not through with him yet."

"I really haven't—"

"What other reasons would there be to replace a perfectly good senator? It cannot be those silly term limits. We threw those things out years ago."

With thoughts of grabbing Linton by his flimsy shoulders, Andorf looks squarely in his face, "What if he quits?"

Turning pale, Linton scratches his head like a rash. ""Highly unlikely. But if he gets poisoned … you know, accidentally like from day old food, a replacement senator would be elected. That is until one can be selected by a secret council." He smiles awkwardly at Andorf. "Enough of that, Andrew. Come join us for lunch. Like our candidates' idea, it's always stale leftovers."

Weaving between Linton's whiny pleas, Andorf jogs for the exit. He pulls open the golden door to find GI Joe greeting him like a doorman, too willing to assist. Sweating at the hefty private first-class, Andorf says the first thing that comes to mind. "Why is Linton always leaning to deceive?"

"If you don't like the party," says the doorman, wedging himself into the corner, "YOU can always leave." The grinning soldier twists the right doorknob and Andorf is swiftly sucked outside. The door locks shut, leaving Andorf squinting at the mid-day sun, bearing down on him. Engaging street noises suddenly sound more benign than Linton's wiry little voice. The aroma of smoked veggie sausages migrating from across the busy lunch hour street teases him closer.

Andorf finds himself standing amongst a crowd of twenty citizens at the curb, watching an endless stream of trucks, buses, and turbo speeders rushing past. A petite, white-haired woman gazes up at him. "It'll be my dinnertime before we cross."

The other pedestrians mumble in agreement until one tanker truck riding the curb blows past, nearly clipping the group. The elderly woman bursts into a rant, teaching everyone curse words in Romanian.

Andorf also yells out, shaking a fist at the trailing dirt plumes. "Give us a damn break!"

Traffic abruptly ceases. Andorf nearly gets whiplash, watching the eighty-year-old woman fly. He and nineteen others chase after the aging woman. Safely across six-lane Dos Cacas Grande, Andorf bows to the crowd's claps and parting cheers, masked by traffic speeding past once again.

Andorf grins at the sound of the familiar wheezy chuckling and finds the old coffee vendor behind his trailer-like contraption bound together by bailing wire and recycled parts, hunched over, trying to catch his breath. "Nice trick there, son. First traffic break on Dos Cacas all day." The old man gasps between troubled words. His voice drops to a raspy murmur. "Yes, I'm beginning to remember. This is where he tosses me a twenty and tells me to keep the change … right before he visits the—"

Shrugging him off, Andorf extracts a juice drink from the ice-packed cooler at his feet. He takes a deep whiff. "How much for the sausage, Chester?"

"Sold out. Next best thing is my steak dog. It's like eating a cow and a dog in the same bite. Here, this one's got your name on it." Chester hands him the cellophane-wrapped tubular sandwich.

Andorf unwraps the sandwich, so ready to bite down. "So there's real beef in this thing?"

Chester throws dirty looks. "When's the last time you've had anything real?" He reaches for the sandwich, but finds it halfway down Andorf's throat. "Fifteen bucks, for the drink and sandwich."

Andorf flips a twenty piece into the bucket clipped onto the vendor's motorbike below the 'No Change' sign. "Keep the change."

Chester nods, wiping his brow. "Where ya' heading this warm afternoon, son?" He grins as if knowing the answer to his question.

Andorf tips his head to the right. "The E-Con headquarters, over there," he says, speaking through his last chew. "Figured I'd check them both out in one day."

The old man sneers. "Both the same they are. The minute you turn your back, that two-headed snake will bite your butt."

Andorf walks off, feeling he has yet to hear the last from the old geezer. He looks behind and sees only a discarded cellophane wrapper. A stiff wind blows the film high into the air before it swoops down and wraps itself around his ankle. He hears the old man's raspy worn-out voice calling out.

"You won't find it there either, son."

Peeling the wrapper from his leg, Andorf jogs up the wide marble steps leading to the E-Cuniculon headquarters. A recycle barrel at the door nearly swallows his hand, accepting his donation. The bin's mechanical innards churn away, digesting the cellophane in swift jerks. Its hatch swings to one side as it burps.

Andorf enters the mammoth sandstone structure's twelve-foot glass door and examines the dozens of yellowing E-Cuniculon photos dotting a long inner wall speckled between colorized caricatures of Toxidian politicians in compromising positions. The sketches are so intriguing, he misses the clicking power stilettos and the slinky young lady pressed into them.

"I find them rather odd," a sweet southern voice says, twanging in slight echo.

Andorf's jaw drops at the site of the attractive redhead in a free-flowing maroon strapless chiffon dress, approaching with a warm southern smile. Batting inflated eyelashes at her next victim, she latches onto his arm. "You're not so bad looking yourself, sweetie. I'm Victoria," she says, cozying uncomfortably closer.

"I'm Andorf, at least I was the last time I checked."

Without acknowledging his name, she walks him past the photos. "These yellowing pictures were rescued from the Archives. Oh, what an awful dusty place that was. Did you hear some boys broke in the place, burned it to the ground."

Andorf's heart races, reliving the events leading up his last moments with Gregory. "Burned the place?"

Spotting goosebumps running the length of Andorf's arms, the southern charmer casts a quizzical look. "You're not like the others. May I ask what brings you around, mister Andorf?"

Andorf sighs, inhaling her peppermint perfume. He tries to portray a genuine smile. "I'm here about my missing—"

Victoria licks her lips seductively. Her eyes flash below Andorf's waist. "I suspect it's nothing you can do without," she whispers, breath warming Andorf's ear in a twangy southern drawl.

Andorf does his best to stay focused, think of Serin and her missing brother, Gregory, his best friend. "A ... a missing person," he mumbles.

Victoria steps away. "I believe you're in the wrong place. Perhaps you should try the lost and found."

Andorf thinks about his wild card, what worked with GI Joe. "Maybe I'll have more luck as your senator, replace that riffraff—"

Victoria chuckles. "Senator?" She looks Andorf over as if selecting a side of imitation beef. "Well, we can't have our next senator going around looking like that, now can we?" She reaches deep inside her handbag and finds a standard E-Cuniculon-issued, crimson-red necktie. In seconds, her nimble fingers attach the neck noose and secure it with a shiny, Canine-flagged pin. She steps back to examine her handy work. "There. You look more proper, even in those grass-stained sneakers of yours."

"Thank you, Vic ..." He looks and realizes Victoria has walked away.

The intercom across the lobby blasts. "What now, Victoria?"

"There's someone here I think you should see."

"Send him away. I'm in the middle of my—"

"But he's wearing a red tie, sir."

"If I spoke with every wacko wearing a red tie, I'd be—"

"It's crimson, sir, with dancing mastodons. And he's sporting a Canine-flagged pin."

"Mastodons? Well why didn't you say so, Victoria. Send him right in."

Victoria grabs Andorf's arm and leads him through a series of winding hallways. She poses him in front of a brightly illuminated door and walks away, chuckling to herself. Listening to camera motors zooming in on him from all angles, Andorf watches her puffy dress swooshing side to side, smiling at the fading stiletto clicks. He stares at the bright-red door for a good moment. "I'm doing this for you, Gregory."

The door squeaks open on its own accord, revealing a paneled room reeking of oiled leather and stale sausages. Andorf scans all the framed photos of right-leaning E-Cuniculon presidents dating back to Abraham Lincoln encompassing the conservatively sized office, wondering if this time he has bitten off more than he can chew. A high-back leather chair swivels around to reveal a large man stuffing his face with a crisp pork sausage. Scars road-mapping the man's cherried face hint of a checkered past. Juice squirts everywhere as he takes a loud chomp.

"Step inside, boy," the abrasive voice grunts between tasty bites. Looking Andorf over, he chuckles at the crimson-red tie with dancing mastodons. "My grandniece tells me you'd like to become our next senator."

"Well, you see, I've got this friend—"

The party boss crams another sausage between his fat grease-dripping lips. "It takes more than a game show host to be selected." The large man rolls his eyes. "Well, maybe that wasn't such a good example. So tell me, boy, what makes you think you can beat our current deadbeat senator? Have you any idea how tough it is to beat an incumbent? Has he contracted some incurable disease? Got any dirt on him?" Impatiently waiting, he wipes the grease dripping down his chin with his own identical red mastodon tie.

Andorf hides his distaste for the grease pooling on the over-polished executive desk. He avoids focusing on the man's mileage-worn face. "Well, no, not yet. But I'm ready to get in there and shake things up."

Face glowing brighter than either of their crimson-red mastodon ties, the obese man belches. “I take it you’re one of those hotshot kids. You expect to take back our country, reverse the fifty-year tide.”

Andorf is stunned by the man’s bluntness. He is speechless. He feels the weight of the man’s dispassionate eyes fixed firmly upon him.

The man rises from his high-back chair. “Can I be honest with you, boy? Foreigners are running Capitol Hill. They are the ones running the Empire, not good ole red-blooded citizens, like you and me. We took our eyes off the ball by fighting those self-righteous Dash and the Asians moved right into our west coast states, claimed them part of their Hotot Empire. Reason why Alberta, Idaho, and Nevada are no longer part of our Canine Empire. Before we knew it, millions of foreigners were receiving welfare benefits. They overloaded our overspent welfare system, never paid taxes, never learned our language. That’s an invasion I say and now *we’re* the minority.”

Andorf scans the parade of four-ounce, foreign liquor bottles lining the oversized desk like battle reenactments. “But we’re all from other countries. We’re all Heinz 57s, beans in the same sauce.”

The man’s fiery eyes stare Andorf down. “I don’t mean to be rude, boy, but riffraff runs rabid throughout our District of Cecal.” He casts a huge hand at Andorf. “Richard Rococo. I go by Rocky, but for some odd reason, everyone around here calls me Half Pint.”

Not since grade school has Andorf felt so intimidated. He swallows hard at Rocky’s tight handshake. He pulls his hand away, rubbing blood back into it. “I’m Andorf—Andorf Johnson.”

Andorf grimaces at Rocky spitting in a ceramic coffee mug. The party boss bursts into laughter. “You really had me going with that senator bit, boy. Look at the way you dress. How can anyone take you seriously?” He smacks Andorf hard in the dead center of his back and returns to his chair. He leans back and grins. “But you’ve piqued my interest. So go ahead, boy. Tell me about your big plans.”

“Well for starters, Rocky, I’ll pave all the roads. Those tanker trucks create a real mess. And I’ll replace everyone in that worthless

Records Office. Have you ever been there? I cannot believe we pay their salaries. But right now, Rocky, I just need to find my—"

"Sounds like you're venting personal vendettas." Rocky's right hand gestures in rotational motions. "I admire your enthusiasm, but not to disappoint you, the wheels of government turn very s-l-o-w. You've got to quit taking everything so seriously. Make personal demands."

"Yeah, yeah. Now about my friend—"

Rocky reaches upward as if expecting some divine intervention. "The more people fear you, the more powerful you become and the more favors you can pocket. The more favors you pocket, the more powerful you become. People must fear you. That's how things get done in today's government."

Andorf's jaw drops. "So all those rumors of bribes—private deals—and widespread corruptions, they're all true?"

"Call it what you'd like, boy. It matters not what any citizen says. It's all about gaining people's trust. That's what really matters, isn't it? After you are elected, screw the voters. With a handle on the elections, you can get elected with only twenty-two percent of the vote? Just keep your opponent from getting his fifty. It all washes out in the expensive runoff election. Now that's what I call a republic."

Andorf grabs hold of his chin. He begins to pace Rocky's small, grease-stained office. He squints at Rocky's desk portrait with his collection of government issued roadsters. "You know, Rocky. I could use one of those fancy government turbo speeders, the one that cruise the seven-mile-a-minute lanes." Andorf finds himself drooling on Rocky's well-polished shoes. "When do I get my speeder? Can I get a red one?"

Rocky grins. "Now you're getting it, boy. In order to gain anything, someone must lose something. That's how government works." He clears his throat loudly, neck crackling as his head tips further to the right. "But before we get you that vehicle, boy, tell me one thing. Why the E-Cuniculons? Except for that pretty red tie, you don't appear to be one of us."

Andorf freezes. "Well that's just it, Rocky. I'm not of *either* party. I'm thinking if I start out as an E-Con, I can switch to an independent when I'm …"

Rocky scratches his chin. "Like that go-getter back in twenty twelve and sixteen? He was too honest, never stood a chance. Andorf Johnson—hmm. Say, you're not related to that Gary Johnson character, are you?"

Andorf's face swells with pride. "My grandfather, last great man of the century. He proposed fiscal responsibility *and* social freedom—you know—both at the same time."

Rocky peels himself off his sticky seat. He leaps at Andorf, blocking his path. "You're way too honest for politics, boy. You'll never sign our non-conversion pledge."

"Why all the furgonious censorship? Don't you E-Cons even believe in what used to be the first amendment?"

Rocky grunts. He parades Andorf around the small office, pointing out framed pictures of past E-Con presidents. "Of course we believe in that freedom of speech garbage. You're allowed to say anything we want you to say. That *is* what you mean, isn't it, boy?"

Andorf freezes. "But it's not free speech when your wallets control the media."

"Everything costs something. There ain't no free lunch." A wad of grease drips from Rocky's jaw onto Andorf's grass-stained EasyGlides as he throws his right arm around Andorf. "And speaking about money, boy, how much you got?"

Andorf pulls himself free. "What? So now you're robbing me?"

Rocky chuckles like a man grabbing a big stick to beat a small dog. "Who's backing you, boy? Surely, someone's backing you. How can you get anywhere in government without big bucks?"

"You mean ownership? That's what I'm talking about, Rocky. Why must I be bought and paid for by rich clowns who control my every move?"

Rocky laughs hard. "Not every move, son. They don't follow you into the bathroom—well not until you become the president. Then they direct which way to wipe."

"Well, I'm not forfeiting my morals to be another crooked politician. You watch me, Rocky. I'm going places."

"I cannot agree with you more." Rocky grabs Andorf by the shoulders and in one swift move, shoves him out an emergence exit.

One again, Andorf is outside, shading his eyes from the bright sunlight. "What about my friend?" he yells, stumbling away from the great sandstone building. As he gathers his bearings at the corner of Fifth and Drucker, a raspy old voice calls out to him.

"Payoffs, persuasion, pretentious psychobabble," Chester says in his typical rant. He checks Andorf over for damage. "Didn't I tell you E-Cons and Tox were one and the same? Both leave you wanting more parties than two."

Andorf raises a brow. "I have to admit, Chester, if I had listened to you I wouldn't have wasted my *whole* day."

"So what'd you think of Linton and that grumpy Rocky character?" Chester takes a moment to catch his breath. "I slightly remember them from our … I mean, my younger days."

Andorf grimaces. "I couldn't get a read on either one of them. It's as though they weren't—"

"Human!" Chester casts Andorf a horrid look. "Wait till you meet the beast. The one who spews purple goo," he says, grumbling in weak breath. "You'd better hurry, son. Your woman hates to wait and you're—"

"Late," Andorf says, projecting his timepiece display against the old man's chest. He hears the old man's words as he takes off, jogging for the bus stop. From his window seat on the public bus, he studies the sun cowering behind the tall buildings, pondering the day's events. He worries about Serin, alone at the park, waiting. His thoughts flash back to the old man's last words. *What did he mean by sharing her with another?*

CHAPTER 15
A Paradigm Twist

A sense of heightening monophobia hits Andorf as he rounds the six-foot cherry hedges framing the park's open gate. He spots Serin crisscrossing the redbrick fountain as if fighting a losing battle with the advancing fingers of encroaching darkness.

"Lose the noose, mister. You look like a thieving E-Con."

Andorf yanks the red tie and wads it into a ball in his pocket. "It's not mine, Serin, I swear. You've been through my closets. You know I don't own any ties." He homes in to steal a kiss, but Serin angrily backs away.

"We Grays hate to wait. You know this about Greg."

Andorf taps his timepiece and reads the projected numbers on her chest. Grumbling, he fumbles his words. "There used to be real analog trees in this park. I remember reading it a while back … in some book stuffed in a corner of the school library." He whispers, studying her reaction. "An overlooked book they hadn't renewed."

Serin takes his hand, leads him along the paved walkway. "Ah, the banned books. This says worlds about you." Smirking, she glances at Andorf's stained EasyGlides. "Dad said a man's life is worn on his shoes. Except for the food grease, green and orange stains, and the interesting chew marks here and there, I'd say you've led a pretty clean life."

"Still, you really don't know that much about me."

"Are you forgetting where I work, Mister Johnson? I know your grandfather ran a thriving handyman business and became a popular two-term governor of New Mexico. He had a damn good run as third-party presidential candidate back in 2012 despite the E-Con's media blackout, and again with Bill Weld in 2016. Did you know he and Grandpa Jim were running mates on his first go at it? Perhaps we were meant to be together."

"Judge Gray was your grandpa?" Andorf grins. "I visited the party headquarters today? Yup, both in one day."

Serin releases his hand. "No, Andorf. Tell me you didn't."

"I thought if I could infiltrate the ranks I could find where they've taken Gregory, maybe even negotiate a release. I can be a tough negotiator. I had that Rocky character thinking I wanted a fancy red—"

"Half-Pint? The E-Con party boss? Andorf, I told you to give it up, that I'd handle this."

Andorf stops Serin with both hands. "For the love of Clark Solomon, Serin, I'm never again turning my back on a good friend, not for any woman, even a sister."

Serin pulls away. "I don't know who this Solomon guy was, but things like this have to be done gingerly, planned out to the finest detail. The government watches. It knows everything."

Andorf nods. He leads Serin between fields of huge sunflowers. Running his fingers through her hair, he fails to notice the bowing seed heads following them as they walk past. "So, you seem to know all about me. Tell me something about Serin Gray."

"Well, you already know Greg. He absolutely hates when anyone but me calls him that. He'd fight even you, if you—"

"Serin. What're you hiding?"

"Nothing really. There's not much to tell. I work in a bland government office, led a dull life until you happened along. I'm terribly glad you did, I was desperately bored."

Andorf stops and stares deep into her eyes, attempting to peel away layers to her inner thoughts. He sees a desk behind a hexagonal four-foot wall, drawers stuffed with wires and black-box gizmos. He feels the weight of a huge, tan suitcase and hears it banging against step after step as he lugs it up a flight of outside stairs. He focuses on the engraved initials. B.B.

"Stop that, Andorf. You'll find out soon enough why we're here."

"Can you blame me? First Gregory disappears, then an old friend, and now you appear from nowhere. What the hell am I to think?"

"Serin walks ahead, shrugging her shoulders. They say things happen in threes."

Giving chase, Andorf mumbles to himself. "I have dark feelings about this."

Serin takes his hand and leads him deeper into the park, pausing to look at the weatherworn statue of The Working Man Repairing Tomorrow. Bearing a stuffed tool pouch on his hip, the Working Man grips a 76 mm wrench in one hand while reaching upward with the other, face gazing in wonder at what lies beyond the stars.

"That'll be us one day," a deep voice says, from the far side of the statue.

Serin drops Andorf's hand. She runs to the front side of the statue. Rounding the statue, Andorf sees a large burly man in stained coveralls and Serin's hands pawing all over him. Andorf's pulse revs in jealously and the thought of imminent confrontation. He smacks the side of his head. *I told her I would be okay with her second boyfriend. That jolly laugh. Wait, who is that guy? No! Not him! Anyone but Brutus.*

"In fifty days, that'll be us reaching for the stars," Brutus says, slowing his speech. At Serin's contorted face, he turns his head to Andorf's glaring eyes. "What the hell is *he* doing here?" he yells, pointing at his former adversary.

Serin's eyes pong between the guys. "I thought you two were old friends," she says, sheepishly.

Brutus snorts. "We went to school together, but we were never—"

"No, not friends," Andorf says, eyes narrowing on his competition.

Serin focuses on one and then the other as her lovers exchange verbal daggers. After many anxious breaths, she grabs their hands and leads them to sit on a concrete bench, leaving barely enough space for them to join her on either side. Each guy begrudgingly sits, arms folded, each glaring around Serin at the other. Serin grins. "Nice evening, don't you think?"

Between the awkward silence and the muffled swearing, Serin is the only firewall between the two simmering pressure cookers. While Brutus would easily win a fistfight, Andorf would leave Brutus feeling otherwise.

"Let's go for a walk." With Serin tugging on their arms, the guys slowly rise to their feet, each throwing soured faces at Serin holding the other's hand. She looks at Brutus. Then Andorf. "Promise me you won't hurt each other."

Andorf snarls. "No problem here."

"Ouch," Brutus yells, at her tightening grip. "But—"

"No buts, mister. You both must get along. I won't have it any other way."

Brutus snaps a fist at Andorf. "What do you see in that little wimp?"

"His humor, Brutus. Seems you could stand more of that."

Andorf pokes his head around Serin. "If you weren't such a bully, big guy, perhaps you'd have a few friends. Ouch!" Andorf jerks his hand loose from Serin's tightening grip. "What could you possible see in *him*?"

Serin smiles. "Next to that Mister Fix-It on The Eye, Brutus happens to be the world's biggest nerd and he's good with his hands. So you see, you each have what the other lacks. I'd say, together, we make a complete triad."

Brutus and Andorf glare at each other in total disgust. "Are you having sex with him?" They ask in unison, storming off in different directions, arms thrown over their heads.

"It's bad enough sharing you, but with him?" Andorf yells.

Brutus stops to sneer at Andorf. "It's hard enough being a couple—as in two."

Serin tips her head at the pair. Her sweet voice sings out to them:

> "There you both stand,
> Your anger growin.'
> Why I would want you both,
> You're not quite knowin.'
> You bicker like brothers,
> Tho you are both my lovers.
> And someday there may be others.
> So why can't you just let things be?
> Why can't we come together as three?"

With the rivals ignoring her desperate pleas, Serin calls out to each of them. "Brutus, what happened to your open mind? Andorf, you told me you were okay with this. It's both or neither, guys."

Brutus stops and turns to Andorf. "She's been with me longer," he yells, offering a balled hand.

Andorf stops with a balled hand as well. "She likes me better," he yells back.

Serin cries out, flashing them apprehensive grins. She runs after Andorf. "Go speak with Brutus. You're supposed to be this great negotiator. If you love me, you'll do this."

Again, Andorf envisions Serin sitting on the huge, tan suitcase in his breezeway. He focuses on the engraved initials and everything clarifies. 'BB'—Brutus Bittner. Planning his words, he grits his teeth. He takes baby steps toward Brutus before breaking into a jog, calling out to him. "Hey! Imagine us finally friends."

Growling, Brutus does an about face. "We're not friends. We've never been friends. If our fathers weren't best buds I would have—"

Andorf grins. "But we grew up together. That's got to account for something."

Brutus growls louder, teeth crunching together in the middle.

"What about Serin. Are you willing to lose her over this? It's not as if I'm stealing her away from you. Think of it as time-sharing."

At the mention of Serin, Brutus's eyes soften. Gazing at her in the distance with her arms folded, he drops a hefty arm over Andorf's shoulder. "You've just met her. You don't have a clue. Serin gets under your skin—like an itch you can't scratch. I fall asleep dreaming of her. I wake up dreaming of her. All day long, she's all I ever think about. And now she's been having visions, scary ones. You should run, Andorf, while you still have a chance."

"Ah, you're just trying to get rid of me." Andorf takes a deep breath. He flashes Serin a mechanical grin. "Too late, she's been terrorizing my thoughts and dreams for months."

Brutus glances back at Serin. "Then for Serin's sake, we had better make this look good."

Andorf nods. "At least while she's watching. Eyes on Serin, he reaches up grabs Brutus's shoulder on their slow walk back. "You've got to tell me one thing, big guy, does Serin always get her way?"

"Always."

Andorf forces a smile. "How about we grab lunch sometime?"

Brutus grins. "Lunch? You *are* trying to be my friend. Just don't consider this a date. I don't—"

"Not on your life."

Grinning hard at Serin, Brutus leans into Andorf. "Long as you know, I still don't like you."

"Believe me, the feeling is mutual."

CHAPTER 16

Let's Not Tell

Troubled in thought, Andorf darts between rooms, rummaging through his things. He leers at Serin as she trails behind, picking up after him. "Rough day at the office?"

"Your other boyfriend—"

Serin grabs Andorf's waist as he zooms past, halting him at the hallway shelf where a third stick flag has recently been placed between the other two. "It's been four weeks. I thought you two were getting along."

"There we were having a fine lunch, Brutus and I, when he regurgitates everything you two shared before I came along. He made it quite clear I'm your second fiddle."

Serin futilely brushes hair from Andorf's eyes. "The big guy is pulling your strings. Come on. Let's take a walk, before it gets dark. I've got something to tell you."

Andorf jerks away. "Last time we entered the park as a couple, we exited as three. Wait, don't tell me. We're breaking up."

"Andorf, stop that nonsense. I have no intention of leaving either one of you."

Andorf fumbles for his keys amongst a handful of change. "It's something I did, isn't it? Binky, are you recording this?"

Serin's unexpected rib jab sends keys and loose coins flying and Andorf and Serin crawling after them on their hands and knees. Binky awakens to a sharp red beam piercing the front window. He hops along nipping at the coherent spot as it traces the interior walls. Oblivious to the sweeping beam, Andorf grabs his keys and pushes Serin outside.

"Listen to Binky in there," Serin says. "Does he always go nuts every time you leave?"

Andorf grins. On their ten-minute walk, he explains how lucky Binky was that a rescue group had found him after someone had dumped him outside and that rabbits are the third most abandoned pet after dogs and cats. They pass between rows and rows of sunflowers proudly basking in the sunlight. Focusing on the military training exercises in the distance, they overlook the sparkling seed heads turning to face them as they walk past. Andorf grimaces at the barking militants.

"Why are those bastards always here? It's not *their* park. I'll bet it's all about that damn starship. Do they think someone's going to—" Andorf's complaint morphs into laughter. "Steal the damn thing?"

Nearing the park's highest ridge, they step over the brick border and onto the ledge's loose gravel, giving them little room to steady their feet beyond the engraving of Lovers Leap. Serin peers off the sharp drop off and in seconds, loses balance on the shifting gravel. Sliding feet first off the ledge, she grabs hold of Andorf's ankles, taking him with her on the painful ride. Heads held high, they sail off the cliff head on their butts. Andorf counts the seconds they are airborne, before pain strikes with hundreds of sharp branches jabbing at them from everywhere, like amateur acupuncturists. Faces scratched, clothes ripped, bleeding from multiple cuts and abrasions, they cover their heads from the waves of stones pelting them from the steep cliff face above.

Breathing the musty smell of freshly uncovered soil, Andorf unwinds from the shrubbery. His feet gather to dance across loose stones. He gazes back at Serin, still wedged in the outcropping at the cliff edge. "You look terrible, Serin. You're bleeding in places your clothes used to cover. You think you're hurting now? Just wait till you stand up."

Serin peers below at the sheer drop-off and the bush roots working themselves free from the soil. "I don't know whether to laugh or cry."

With every step to stabilize footing on the ridge above, Andorf sends handfuls of rocks raining down upon Serin. Gazing up at the vertical rise, he edges around the dirt ledge, hugging the large protruding rocks. His feet slide off the slippery stones, leaving him clinging to rootlets protruding from the washed-out rock face. One by one, the tiny rootlets snap off in his hands. He peers down at Serin and the widening crack in the soil fanning out from the failing root base.

Serin spits dirt as she untangles from the many twigs poking through her clothes. She rolls out from the bush's grasp and onto the narrow ledge seconds before the bush rips loose and tumbles into the valley. Like dealing with government, she finds little ground to stand on. She leans on her toes, away from the crumbling ledge, gasping at the soil eroding beneath her heels. After several failed attempts, Andorf reaches down and pulls her beside him, against the damp vertical dirt wall. She too grabs hold of the tiny rootlets as the narrow ledge beneath breaks free and disappears. "How can this get any worse?"

"I think we're about to find out," Andorf whispers, dodging falling stones, many a foot in diameter.

They hear a shuffling above mixed with snapping water bottles and military orders to disperse. A white light shines in their eyes, blinding them. Andorf squints at the young cadet's face. The cadet hushes him with a finger at his lips before disappearing.

Shifting her weight, Serin wiggles a six-inch stone loose by Andorf's left knee. Andorf secures one foot into the void. Following Serin's lead, he digs another stone loose and fits his toe in that void, raising himself six inches higher, but the overhead ledge still looms far beyond his grasp. He unseats more and more stones, progressing upwards inches at a time. Clinging to larger, more secured roots, he feels Serin grabbing at his legs and then his waist, coming to a questionable hold with her head at his rump. Bearing Serin's full weight halts further ascent. Andorf manages to flip one hand onto the cement cliff edging. Then the other.

Serin grabs hold of his belt and scales up his back. Andorf's pants loosen and slip below his hips. With his fingers slipping from the slick concrete above, he looks back at her in horror, "I don't know how much longer I can—"

He feels shoes pressing hard on both hands. Andorf squints in agony at every nub of the soldier's rubber boots grinding into the back of his hands. Hands throbbing, his face contorts, knowing Serin cannot cling to his back much longer. He bites his lower lip, holding back the screams. Unable to feel his swollen hands, Andorf shuts his eyes. "Go, Serin, go."

Serin crawls up Andorf's back and over his shoulders to safety. With the dirt hitting in his face, Andorf takes a deep breath, relieved by the absence of her weight. Pain races down his weakened muscles. He struggles to pull himself over the rock ledge. Serin locks her hands around his wrists. Pulling her head over the ledge, Andorf slips further and further down the rock face, kicking at the absence of footing in the vertical wall. He pulls Serin's shoulders over the edge. She loses grip of one sweaty wrist.

"Serin, let go," Andorf yells in feeble voice.

"Never my love." Serin clamps her other hand onto his other wrist, locking her fingers. She feels her chest slipping over the ledge.

His short time with Serin flashes before his eyes. How they met in Gregory's condo. Serin sitting atop the tan suitcase with that desperate look on her face. How he failed Gregory when—

He feels Serin releasing his wrist as long fingers wrap around both of his forearms. The lanky young cadet inches backwards, dragging him up and over the sharp rocky ledge. Within seconds, he lays face down, legs dangling off the ledge, with Serin standing over him, struggling to find breath.

Serin strains to make out the young man's face. "Thank you. I thought we were—"

Andorf gasps. "Goners."

The cadet chuckles in a much older voice. The tall man peels off a facemask and tosses it beside his discarded army grubs. He flashes a Cheshire smile as the evening absorbs him. Collecting discarded hydrators, Serin pours the remains into hers and Andorf's parched mouths. In a sudden burst of energy, she brushes Andorf's face with the back of her hand. "Come on lover, race you home." Serin grins back at his dazed smile. "Yes, I did call it home. But don't forget about Brutus. You must make room for him also."

A chill lazes up his spine as Andorf staggers slowly to his feet. He forces every muscle to move. "I'm not quite there yet, but I *am* trying."

"I expect better than that, lover. There'll come a day soon when we'll all be living together."

*

The pair arrive home to find Brutus perched on the lower steps, scowling at the site of them approaching, hand in hand. His voice elevates. "We must talk."

Andorf limps past, swollen hands futilely digging into his pants pocket as he labors up the front steps. To Brutus's dismay, Serin reaches deep inside Andorf's pants and grabs his keys. She unlocks the door and darts inside.

Brutus follows Andorf inside. His jaw drops at first sight of Serin's torn and bloodied clothes. Swearing at the top of his lungs, he backs Andorf through the living room and slams him against the kitchen wall, raising a fist. "You did this to her? I'm going to—"

Andorf struggles to work free of Brutus's hold. He balls his swollen hands into fists the best he can. Brutus swings his head aside, averting the weak blow.

Serin wedges between the childhood rivals. "Look at Andorf, you fool. Can't you see he's injured?"

Andorf shoves away from Brutus, dropping his fists at Brutus's loosened grip. "Damn right! We slid off that cliff at City Park."

Brutus gulps. "You man Lover's Leap? Why, no one could survive that such a fall."

Following Serin's direction, Andorf takes a seat at the kitchen table. "Just when the local Nazi militia dropped in for a friendly visit."

"Nazi, my ass," Serin says. "If that young cadet hadn't come along when he did, we'd both be lying on the bottom of that ravine."

"He wasn't a cadet, Serin. You saw him peel off that uniform. He was wearing something underneath that made him blend into the night," she says, dashing off.

Brutus's head nearly twists off, following the volleys as the pair spin their tale. He lowers the overhead light to get a closer look at their deep cuts and scratches and blood oozing from everywhere. His eyes widen at the sight of Andorf's engorged hands, approaching the size of his own. "Look, Andorf ... I didn't mean—"

Serin returns, cleaned up and in fresh clothes, holding a well-used tube of goop. She squeezes between her guys. "Now let me see those hands, sweetie." Serin morphs into Nurse Serin, squirting dabs of emerald green goop laced with orange powder onto Andorf's hands.

Andorf rolls his eyes as she rigorously massages the cream into his aching hands. "Ahh. Where'd you get that orange stuff? It looks like—"

"A fruit guy outside the Records Office," Serin says. "He's out there most every day. The jumpy guy with etched hands sold me an expensive cantaloupe with this cream stuffed way up inside."

Brutus drops into a seat at the table. "We have one of those guys in the shipyard. I've always wondered how he made a living selling only fruit. Hmm. Forty percent Magic Dust," he says, reading the squeeze bottle's spiraling ingredient label.

Andorf's ears perk. "I've heard of Magic Dust. An unlicensed pharmacist was pushing that stuff at the rugby game last month, the one I went to with Gregory."

Serin wipes her hands on a towel and steps around Andorf to sit on Brutus's lap. She rubs his pouting cheeks and leans closer to stroke his long thinning locks. "So what's all the fuss, baby? What troubling you?"

Andorf and Serin exchange awkward glances as the gravity of what Brutus wants to say surfaces. Both know better than to interrupt Brutus, well in deep thought. Andorf squirms in his seat, expecting more bad news. Serin settles into Brutus's lap and waits. She falls from Brutus's lap as he slams a heavy fist onto the table, ending a painful pause that lasted far too long.

"I don't know if this triad experiment is working out. I like Andorf okay, but I get so jealous seeing you together, I just want to—"

"Me also," Andorf says, watching Serin take a seat between them. 'I'm tired of being the middleman. It feels—"

"Awkward." Brutus nods. "Like I'm—"

"Breaking the law." Andorf peers jealously at Brutus, also nodding.

Voice rising in stance, Serin kicks her chair into the table. "Look at you two, so close you complete each other's words. You think only of yourselves. What the hell's going to happen when there's another?"

Andorf gulps. He feels his blood about to boil. "Who?"

Brutus stands, pointing at his rival. "I've barely gotten used to *him*. Now you're telling me there's another?"

Andorf also jumps to his feet, confused. "Yeah, who is this other guy?"

Serin grins. She begins to sing, prancing around her lovers. "A child is coming."

"What?" Andorf yells.

"I said a child is coming."

Mouth puckering, Brutus scowls at Andorf. "I knew this would happen. You should have been more careful, Andorf."

Andorf begins to sweat. "It wasn't me, I swear."

Scratching her itchy belly, Serin steps between them, before the blows begin. "You can't lie about this, guys. It was one or the other of you, if not both."

Brutus rubs at his forehead. "Well, there was that one time."

"Oops!" Andorf says, recalling his own slip up.

Brutus's eyes cross. He begins to pace the living room. "What about the bean counters? They'll be sniffing around, expecting a baby's name?"

Serin places their hands on her belly, smiling at one, then the other. "Or tracing the lines of *her* hands."

Andorf squints. "Or his eyes with an optical scan."

Serin scans the small room. "What about her personal freedoms? Right now, they're looking pretty grim."

Brutus grins. "Let's not mention anything about him."

"Her," Serin says.

Andorf confused looks at the pair. "But what kind of life would that be? He'd be living the life of a gypsy."

"She," Serin says.

Brutus throws a hand at Andorf. "Hey, I was raised as a gypsy. Look how I turned out to be."

"Now that explains it all." Andorf chuckles. "From the minute you began to crawl."

Serin lands between them. "Stop it boys. Your child is coming."

"He'll be his own man," Brutus says. "If I have anything to say about it."

"And *she'll* have the cutest attire, so free of the Empire's desire." Serin opens her eyes to see her lovers slapping each other on their backs, laughing like old friends. She watches the pair pacing about the living room, arguing baby names. "Hey, you two. Don't you think *I* had anything to do with this?"

Shaking off the guy's newfound adoration for each other, she plops onto the couch, air fingering through channels on The Eye, gagging at Fat Max Okinawa's rhetoric on each channel, picturing above the scrolling countdown to Starship Atlantis's launch, some 22 days away. She pauses at a breaking news story. A swift finger swipe raises the volume loud enough to drown out the boys' camaraderie with another nameless reporter earning his mark in the world through exaggerated sensationalism.

"Explosives were stolen from construction sites a second time in as many months," the reporter announces. "Suspects include a radicalized right-wing group calling themselves The Bogus Boat People."

Brutus quiets and joins Serin on the couch. She drapes an arm around his shoulder, watching Andorf take a seat at her feet. She nudges Andorf with a soft toe jab. "I hope you haven't joined up with any of those terrorists, Andorf."

Brutus nudges Andorf with his own foot. "You've been known to do some crazy shit."

Thinking of his old friend, Brett, Andorf grins.

CHAPTER 17
The Triad

In the tiny rear office of a quaint countryside chapel, one block off Speedway, elderly preacher Bonnie attends to the nervous bride, so thrilled to be wedding her favored renegade niece. Serin smiles at her aunt. "Are you okay with this, Aunt Bonnie? In a traditional church, the three of us would be cast as deviates."

"My dear, those right-wing bastards and their antiquated ideals nearly put me out of the marrying business." The preacher looks over Serin's notes. "Just you worry about *your* lines. I'll be fine. Say, what's with that brother of yours? Surely, Greggy would be here by now."

Serin takes hold of her aunt's shoulder. "You haven't heard? Greg disappeared six weeks ago."

Bonnie's knees weaken. If not for Serin's grasp, she would have collapsed. She brushes off Serin and takes a seat. "My God! That was the time of the Archives' murder. I saw it on the Twisted News. A pair of thugs knifed a night watchman." She frowns at Sara. "If the agents have him, there's nothing we can do. He's on his way to the Cos."

Serin grimaces. "That's what everyone tells us, but Andorf and I haven't given up. We still have a few leads."

"Don't waste your time, child. There's nothing you can do short of breaking him out of the wretched place."

*

Walking around the chapel for the front entrance, Brutus jabs Andorf in the ribs. "It's not too late to back out."

Andorf smirks, stepping beyond the span of Brutus's playful hands. "And let you have all the fun? I don't think so."

"But you appear to be drowning, Poo. I'm giving you an easy—"

"How about if I go in there alone, big guy, and *you* wait out here for *me*?"

"Cold day in hell."

Andorf tugs on his borrowed tie. He pulls open one of the chapel's double-doors. Brutus opens the other. Programmed organ notes greet them from speakers high above. Eyeing the roomful of gypsy friends, Brutus takes the left aisle, Andorf the right. Steps pacing with the music, each keeping somber eyes on the other. They rejoin center stage at the base of the preacher's altar to face each other, exchanging awkward looks. Fidgety time passes to a variety of jovial tunes.

The preacher holding a door for her niece and the chapel brightens. Chatter drops to whispers. The grooms fixate on their bride as she steps inside, hair ruffling in the gentle breeze. Dressed in a white lace gown, adorned with carnations flowing graciously to the floor, Serin pauses to adjust her garment. Andorf's thoughts flash back to the elusive girl from dreams past, wearing that same white lace dress and intricately embroidered headband. *Here I am marrying my best friend's sister and Gregory is ...*

"Not now, Andorf. This is my *day."* Serin's words ring clear in his head. He looks up to see Serin shaking her head at him before turning away. Locking arms with her aunt, she begins the procession, advancing slowly down the center aisle in lock step with the organ's sweet tones.

"How's she do it? She's always in my thoughts," Andorf says, mumbling.

"Join the club, Poo," Brutus whispers, out the side of his mouth.

Alongside her aunt, Serin smiles at her grooms dressed in identical tan khakis, flowered shirts, and jubilant grins. She arrives at the pulpit, taking a place between her grooms while Preacher Bonnie settles into her comfortable spot behind her protective, slightly raised pulpit. Shuffling scripts and prepared opening lines, she clears her throat, sips water from a concealed flask. "It makes me proud to be finally marrying off my great niece, Serin." The preacher's eyes roll upward, following her hands. "Oh, how long I have waited for this day."

Serin blushes at the audience's laughter as her aunt opens the marked pages of her well-worn family cloth. Her eyes pong from one groom to the other. Both grin back at Serin.

Preacher Bonnie clears her throat and rattles off well-rehearsed lines about uniting the triad in the presence of the Lord, three sacred hearts finding each other, and love enduring the sands of time. Before Andorf knows it, he and Brutus are wearing Serin's rings and Serin is wearing both of their rings, snuggled side by side.

Preacher Bonnie smiles. "Kiss your bride, gentlemen. Hurry, before she changes her mind."

Without hesitation, Serin stretches to kiss Brutus and then Andorf. The threesome examines their ringed fingers while the preacher's simulated organ music plays. They follow Bonnie into her back office. After signing the fiber forms, Preacher Bonnie separates the pages with moistened fingers.

"Let's see … one copy gets filed and—"

Serin grabs the forms from her aunt's hand. Rolling them up, she shoves all three copies into her backpack.

Preacher Bonnie balks. "Niece or no niece, I could get in big trouble for this."

Serin calms the preacher with a hug. "Our little secret."

The preacher turns her back as they change clothes. "I hope the ceremony went well."

"You were great, Aunt Bonnie," Andorf says.

Aunt Bonnie turns and whispers in Serin's ear. "I must know, child. Which one?"

Serin smiles at her new husbands. "Andorf and I are hoping for a girl, but Brutus—"

"No, I mean the father. Which one's the father?" At Serin's lost look, Aunt Bonnie squeezes her arm. "Perhaps one from each, twins." Serin cringes.

Brutus dashes outside, half-dressed when he hears three beeps of a gyro-taxi's horn. Serin and Andorf run out the back door, also buttoning up. They climb in the rear of the gyro-taxi and wait for Brutus to force himself through the small rear passenger door. Soon they are peering at the gridlocked street traffic some thirty feet below, listening to traffic buzzing overhead in the lesser traveled commercial lanes. Their cab suddenly veers away from the caravan of similar banana-colored taxis and drops for a three-point landing beneath the Harigados Fine Dinery's fanning canopy.

After prying himself out the rear door, Brutus flips a coin at the cabbie. The silver-dollar-sized fifty-dollar piece twinkles under the bright canopy lights, spiraling toward the cabbie's expecting hand. "Be back in an hour," Brutus yells. The cabbie revs up his gyros and leaves in a thick cloud of blue smoke.

An over-dressed maître-d directs them through brass entry doors and promptly disappears, leaving Andorf and Brutus sitting crammed together, watching Serin pace about the tiny inlet of overstuffed seats, fuming about having to wait.

Brutus slips off and in moments returns with an elder gentleman in tow, shiny coins jingling in his hand. "Seems I still have a few connections around here."

The waiter directs the threesome to a table, activates the scrolling panoramic menu screens, and retreats. Serin studies the overwhelming selections. Andorf shakes his head, lost at everything flashing on the table in front of him. Brutus grins, as if already knowing what he wants. He flags a passing waiter, displays his wedding ring. "We're celebrating our wedding tonight, the three of us."

"May I take your drink orders, madam, sirs?" says the waiter, unimpressed.

"A round of melonritas," Brutus says, surrounded by nods.

The waiter grins politely. "Very well, folks. Enter your selections whenever ready."

As he turns away, Serin grabs the waiter's arm. She tips her head toward Brutus. "Better make *his* a double, if you know what I mean."

With a nod, the waiter vanishes. Serin and Brutus enter their choices and stare Andorf down. "Just pick something, Andorf," Serin yells. "Anything."

"It's all good," Brutus says.

Under watchful eyes, Andorf finally taps his order. He grins at Brutus. "So, Serin actually learned Asia-speak? I heard the Hotots find it insulting when foreigners speaks their tongue." Andorf laughs and looks at Serin. "Which Hotot are you trying to piss off? No, don't tell me, not—"

Brutus grimaces at Serin's souring face. "It can only be Max."

Andorf lifts a brow. "That overgrown slug on The Tube ads? I take it she knows his royal eminence."

"Indeed," says Brutus. "And best you keep the two hot heads away from each other."

Serin growls. "Watch it, Bittner."

Brutus reaches too late for Serin's retreating arm. "All I'm saying is that Max had better keep his distance if he knows what's good for him, that's all." He cringes at Serin's folded arms. "And he hates it when someone messes up the fine dialect of his native tongue."

Serin's mouth tightens. "Then I'll say it all wrong next time I see the slimy worm."

"Every Hotot I've heard sounded like they've got a mouth full of rice." Andorf grins at their approaching Asian server. "No insult intended."

The waiter leaves three mugs carved from miniature watermelons on their table before departing. Brutus makes loud slurps with his straw, peering over his double-sized mug at Serin. "What I meant was—"

Serin removes her straw and gulps down a good third her melonrita. She drops the mug onto the table with a loud *thunk*. "How you can work for that stinkin' beast?"

Brutus lowers his head. "Max is my master. He highly respects me."

Eyes narrowing, Serin slugs Brutus's shoulder. "Quit calling him that. He's your boss. Only a fool takes credence in anything that gibberish-ranting tongue says."

"Riddle-speak he does," Andorf says, feeling left out of the Max-jab.

Brutus clears his throat. "He's got a lot on his mind. What, with the starship launch in fourteen days ..."

"Still, that doesn't give him—"

Throwing up both hands, Andorf leaps from his chair. "Why's everything's about that damn starship, perched high on that mountain plateau like the Empire's crown jewel?" He tips his head, raising suspicious brow at the pair. "Now wait a minute. The Eye's scrolling messages say the launch date is noon on Monday, *fifteen* days. Now you say fourteen days. What the hell's going on?"

Serin grins at Brutus before turning to Andorf. She grabs his forearm, coaxing him to sit down with a voice sweet as honey. "Soon. It'll all be over real soon."

Andorf sneers at her and Brutus. "Whenever it happens, it won't be soon enough. I wish the Atlantis to just go away."

Serin's eyes narrow on Brutus. "I heard some bozo talked Andorf into visiting the bi-party headquarters. Both of them in one day. If he takes any more two-party crap, he'll end up bent over their laps."

"Wanting more parties than two," Andorf says.

Brutus snickers, choking on his laugh. "Now what decrep would do something so cruel?"

"Dammit, Brutus. You know how damn gullible he is."

"It was merely a suggestion. How'd I know he'd actually go through with it?"

Following their volleys, Andorf folds his arms into his chest. "Wait a minute, guys. I *am* capable of making my own decisions." At reprimanding glares, he drops his arms and stares silently at his melon mug. After a few slurps, his eyes glaze. "Where are we all going to live?"

"They watch my place like a hawk," Brutus says. "The *last* thing I need is to raise suspicions."

Serin eyes Andorf. "My place isn't safe either and I'm already living with you, Andorf."

Andorf sighs. "Was this yet another pre-decided vote? You've both seen my place. It's barely large enough for the two, let alone three."

Spotting the approaching server, Brutus pushes away from the table. "It's settled then. We'll stop by the church to get my bags."

An entree cart rolls up to their table. Placing a warm plate in front of Serin, the server bows. "You will be enjoying our teriyaki salmon with sweet potato soufflé, madam." Turning to Andorf, the server graciously places a covered plate onto the table. Escaping steam follows the path of the removed cover. "And for you, the child's fish bars with candied totted taters. I assume you do not want the turbo-speeder toy?"

With condescending looks volleying between him and his plate, Andorf grabs the toy speeder and waves the server on. He lifts his eyes to a smirking audience. "What? It's the only picture I recognized."

A foghorn announces the arrival of an enormous, clay cruise ship filled with varieties of sushi and sashimi. As the ship docks portside, Brutus fills the upper pools with soy sauce and reorients the massive ship, without spilling one drop or any of the fishy passengers. He salivates as the first chopstick passenger nears his widening mouth.

Serin fumbles with her chopsticks and drops them onto the table. "If the Hotos are so civilized, why do they eat with these fiber sticks? You'd think they'd at least sharpen them as spears."

The husbands wisely exchange their sticks in favor of carbene sporks. Between bites, they crack jokes, each racier than the last.

Grinning at how well her men are getting along at the moment, Serin taps a questionable gizmo against the order pad. Nervously awaiting payment approval, she collects lemon seeds from her garnish.

Jaw dropping, the server discretely leans closer. "The GMO police will arrest you for having real seeds."

Serin places the seeds between the folds of a napkin and tucks it into her backpack. "Let them frisk me. I'm not giving up my stash."

*

Back at the chapel, Brutus struggles to lift three heavy bags into the trunk. He squeezes into the cab and it drops a few inches. The extra weight mandates a slow, frustrating ride through the city streets. The cabbie's angry mug thrusts into Brutus's face before turning away.

After many stops, they arrive at Andorf's condo. The cabbie waits at the rear hatch, watching Brutus unload his oversized bags. He drags the smallest of three bags, following Brutus across the grassy courtyard, and leaves it at the first step, refusing to proceed any further. Brutus flips more than coin in the cabbie's direction.

From the balcony, the triad watches the taxi zoom away up to the taxi level, gagging migrating mallards in its wake of blue smoke. Serin and Andorf leave Brutus to deal with his luggage. Serin beelines for the bathroom. Andorf kicks off his EasyGlides as Brutus digs into one of his bags. Brutus extracts a small plastic box, forms a loop antenna with a twelve-inch strip of bare wire, and attaches it to the small black box. Andorf follows him from room to room watching Brutus swipe his hand in rotating motions.

Serin reappears, zipping her pants. She pulls Andorf aside and whispers. "He's scanning for bugs."

Andorf scowls. "Your brother may have had a bug problem, but I can assure you, my place is clean. I had an exterminator—"

"Listening devices, silly. You know, hidden transmitters. You wouldn't believe how many of the suckers Brutus found in my place." Serin's visually scans the living room. "The Empire has many ears."

Brutus pauses. He hushes them with an index finger to his lips.

Andorf's eyes bounce between the others. "So it's like a game?"

"If only it were so." Serin grabs Andorf's forearm and leads him outside. "The Canine Empire monitors its citizens. They collect, dissect, cleanse, and twist our every word. They have recordings of us saying whatever they'd like."

"Like Headbook posts?"

"Worse. Citizens accept *this* media-ized slander as gospel and even believe the impossible. We must remain absolutely quiet until every room has been swept clean."

Andorf nods. He follows Serin back inside to catch Brutus running from the bathroom, holding what appears to be a drowned fly in a pair of tweezers. Salivating in technology, Brutus presents the dripping specimen.

"This here is the latest in boutique spyware devices. I've heard rumors about these suckers, but have never seen one—not until now. See those tiny wings?"

Serin and Andorf stare cross-eyed at the nearly invisible device. Andorf squints. "Barely."

"They're not actually wings. The tiniest air movement can vibrate them enough to transmit anything it hears over two miles. And see those beady eyes? They activate the device at the slightest lighting change. Pretty neat stuff, huh? Someone thinks you two are important enough to earn this little pup."

Andorf gulps "So, all this time, the Empire's been listening to me?"

"They're after *me*." Serin scans the ceiling for similar devices. "Has anyone visited here recently?"

Andorf scratches his head. "Only the exterminators."

Brutus grimaces. "It's exterminators and repair guys who create diversions and plant these things behind your back."

Serin slaps a hand over her mouth. "You were with me in Greg's place. I was crying so loud we didn't hear them up here."

Andorf's jaw drops. "So you're telling me Gregory's abduction was merely a—"

"Distraction," Serin says.

"That they stole my best friend only to spy on me?"

"Us."

"But, how could they possibly know you'd be staying here, Serin?"

Brutus looks away, holding the specimen to the overhead light. "This one is sleeping, but as soon as it dries out—"

"What?" Andorf yells. "What happens then? Does it explode in a puff of smoke like the one at the—"

Raising a brow, Brutus turns to Andorf. "Wait! What'd you say about something exploding?"

Animating his flailing hands, Andorf replays his afternoon with the nervous surplus storeowner. "And when Zeeshan snapped the bug onto the magnifier, it didn't look like an insect at all. It went poof in a bright flash and was gone. Now what kind of bug would explode like that?"

Brutus gulps. "Early spy-bot models self-destructed like that. I'll bet that's what it was. They couldn't hear well so they flew in swarms. Many microphones spread over a large area hear like a much large one. But they had a severe limitation. Their tiny photovoltaic eyes only allowed flight in direct sunlight."

"That's why they didn't follow us inside the barn." Andorf plops down hard into his indented spot on the sofa. Moments later, Binky jumps into his lap. Binky nuzzles into Andorf's chest to receive alternating stokes on his puffy cheeks and the bridge of his nose. "Binkers, I've been wondering where you were hiding, buddy."

Brutus sneezes at the fluffs of fur floating past. "Hey! Where'd that thing come from? How'd he get in here?"

Serin grins. "Easy, big guy. Binky is Andorf's pet rabbit. He's litter box trained and sleeps most of the day."

Brutus smirks. "Just like you, Poo. Funny you've not mentioned him until now."

Binky leaps from Andorf's lap and runs back and forth across the living room, kicking his hind feet high into the air. Serin offers a pet, but Brutus, sitting alongside Andorf, scares him under the couch.

"Ouch!" Brutus yells, lifting his legs high in the air. "Your little rat just bit me."

Serin chuckles. "Perhaps he's checking out his next meal."

Andorf reaches under the couch to pet Binky. "Relax. You're barely bleeding. You should see what it's like when he chomps down with his molars."

At Brutus's heavy foot stomp, Binky scrambles for the hay-packed kitchen table litterbox. "He'll be *my* next meal if he's not careful. I don't know if he'll work out as a fourth resident."

Serin clears her throat. She brushes the hair from Brutus's eyes. "This was Binky's home long before us, just like *we* were together before Andorf came along."

Andorf snorts. "And he's not the fourth resident, you are. I advise you not to go around barefoot for a few days, until he gets to know you. Did I tell you Binky has a thing for people's feet?"

Serin grins as if remembering *her* introduction to Binky, how he kept licking her feet. "See how his ears are turned in another direction? He appears to be looking at us while his ears are focusing over there. That's where his attention lies."

Brutus grunts. "Where does the rat sleep? Surely that furry rat won't be sharing our bed?"

Andorf leads the others into his small bedroom. He looks at the cozy bed where he and Serin barely fit. "The big question, is where are *we* sleeping tonight?"

Serin plunks down in the middle of the mattress. Unbuttoning her blouse, she winks coyly at them over her shoulder. "Sleep? Who expects to get any sleep tonight?"

CHAPTER 18
Enlightenment

Andorf gawks at the overwhelming quantity of debris that has been piling around him over the past eight days. Brutus's mattress alone swallows half the bedroom acreage, but at least it hides six bales of hay. He wades through stacks of Brutus-mess. "I hear there's a game sphere hiding somewhere."

Brutus lifts his eyes from the hand-held bug detector long enough to grin. "It won't be much fun on that two-dimensional Eye over there and good luck finding it."

Andorf dims the lights. He closes blinds, and pulls drapes shut. Standing on a chair, he twists a painted-over dimple in the ceiling, dropping a video emitter rod. He moves about, lowering three additional emitters in a square pattern, sending colored beams dancing wildly about the center of the living room. A vivid half-scale genie appears.

Serin appears with an eight-sided sphere in her hands and fixates on the projected 3D jolly green wizard scratching his head. She unrolls her hand. "Looking for this?"

The triad gathers around the wizard, sitting on the floor outside the well-defined perimeter. Serin pokes a finger through one of the beams. After a few seconds, the image re-stabilizes. "You hid the emitters well. I never would've guessed."

"Spent weeks getting them properly aligned," Andorf says. "I can't have exterminators walking off with them." He points at the crisp, ultra-high definition clouds circling in the holographic sky. "No fuzzy images or jagged edges like you see at the pubs."

Brutus leaves and returns with accessories. He rotates the game sphere, and alien-like creatures with photon pistols replace the genie. "On *this* side we have Psycho, a three-dimensional shoot-em up game with interactive characters. Wireless armbands control your movements and the head buds read our thoughts, extracting random pieces of each player's experiences, making each game different."

A buzzing sound in the bedroom has Serin breaking multiple beams, darting for a communication glove. The jittering images drop to the floor, trying to re-sync with the light sources. Andorf rotates the octa-sphere and the hologram blurs, morphing into a medieval chess game. "So there's eight games on this thing?"

"Seven," Brutus says. "With the blank side up, it powers off."

"Hey, what's this one called Sumatra?"

Brutus grins. "Serin's favorite, but she's never played it in 3D."

Words of a secret rendezvous spills from the bedroom in Serin's voice. There are moments of silence before she emits a blood-curdling scream. She appears in the living room holding a bright orange device in one hand and a frazzled power cord dangling from the other. "Look what *your* rabbit did to my hair dehydrator!"

Andorf cringes, surveying the damage. "Oops. Did I tell you Binky chews things? Good thing it wasn't plugged in."

"Andorf!"

"Look around. Notice anything below knee-level without protective wrap? I—I'll buy you a new one."

Serin scans the kitchen and living room furniture. "I 've been meaning to ask you about that ribby-looking stuff."

Brutus feels the lamp table legs. "It's everywhere."

Andorf grins apologetically at Serin's growls. "You can't really blame Binkers. Lagomorphs are chewers."

"It's about time you got rid of that ancient contraption," Brutus says. "Who uses anything with power cords? Inductive power has been—"

Serin lowers both hands onto her hips. "*You* try holding one of those heavy things for … oh, that's right, guys don't use these things."

Brutus winks at her. "You shouldn't really have that thing. What if they … hey, what's that sound?"

Binky hops past, nudging the game sphere with his nose. He stops to chin it a few times before pushing it across the living room floor like a puck.

Serin chuckles. "Looks like you've also got hockey on that thing."

Brutus grabs the octa-sphere on Binky's route under the sofa. "Funny! Very funny. What's with that chinning thing?"

Andorf chuckles. "He was claiming it as his own. Did I tell you Binky does that?"

Brutus scratches his chin. "Who would've guessed a rabbit would be so playful."

Andorf reaches under the couch to pet Binky. "Pets are only as playful as you allow them to be. Locking them in cages all day—"

Serin as she breaks into tears and runs off. He turns to follow, but Brutus lassos him by the belt loops. Andorf's eyes narrow at Brutus.

"She's heard from Gregory, hasn't she? Tell me he's not locked away in that crazy place."

"The Cos?" Brutus looks away. "I can't say."

Andorf feels Brutus's guilt. Heart racing, he walks around Brutus's distant stare. "So he *is* locked up at the Cos. You can't block it from your thoughts. Are you forgetting I can—"

Brutus walks off, grumbling. "All I can say is that things are happening behind the scenes."

Andorf follows. "Scenes? What things? What do you mean?"

"Believe me, Andorf, the less you know the better."

With both hands, Andorf grabs hold of Brutus's shoulders to spin him about. "Why's everyone telling me to quit looking for Gregory?

He's my best friend. He made me promise to never give up, never quit looking for him."

"Get the guy out of your head, Andorf. When Serin wants you to know, she'll tell you. Just leave it at that."

"She's blocked all thoughts of him. But you, you know where he is, don't you? She's told you, hasn't she?"

"You know as much as I, Poo. Serin wants it this way."

A loud wail pours from the bedroom door. Andorf takes steps, but again Brutus lassos him.

"I wouldn't if I were you. The last thing we need is a lover throwing up barricades. An ex-girlfriend did that frequently and believe me, it ain't pretty. Give Serin time to simmer. She'll be back to her regular self in short time." For a brief moment, Brutus appears lost in thought. "Just be glad Vickie's father isn't running you off with a bat."

"Vickie?"

Brutus winks at Andorf. "Nothing—a bad memory."

Serin reappears in the kitchen. "I'll be scarce the next few days. Try to keep out of trouble, boys, especially you, Andorf."

"Why? Where are you—"

A large hand clamps over Andorf's mouth. Brutus shakes his head, warning Andorf not to go there. He drops his hand to a distant rumbling. They dash for opposite ends of the living room curtain and peer at streams of flickering lights, cracking the evening sky.

"By their tight formation, floodlights sweeping side to side—" Brutus releases the curtain. "I'd say they're definitely looking for someone."

Andorf remains watching a pair of lights break formation. "Well, whoever they're after, they're heading this way."

In the blink of an eye, the front courtyard is bathed in light. Andorf drops the curtain as floodlights sweep past the windows. The floor begins to resonant to the beat of copter blades. The guys dart back and forth, checking door and window locks as Binky hops frantically from room to room, searching for anything not vibrating.

Brutus catches his game sphere falling from Andorf's trophy shelf along with other breakables. Andorf races about, rescuing dancing table lamps. Binky and the guys cross paths multiple times amidst smashing picture glass.

"Serin, come help!" Andorf yells.

"Serin?" Brutus yells.

A red laser beam finds a path inside. Hands filled, the guys take shelter against living room walls. Eyes bugged out, they watch Binky hopping past, nipping at the swift well-focused beam taking multiple sweeps across the living room walls.

"Who the hell are they're looking for?" Andorf whispers. Blood suddenly drains from his face, recalling the old man's words. "Someone who slips through their hands like water."

Andorf darts for the bathroom, Brutus the bedroom. Grimacing at everything crashing around them, they converge in the hallway wearing horrified faces.

Andorf stares at Brutus, eyes glazing over. "She's gone!"

Brutus stumbles for words. "Look, uh, I'm sure she's—"

"Running," Andorf says. "I feel her heart racing. I see her running, ducking into shadows. She feels me in her thoughts. She's blocking me. No, Serin! Don't!"

Brutus's jaw drops. "Where is she? Who's she with?"

Andorf shakes his head. "She cut me off. I lost her."

A second red beam traces the living room walls. They scramble for the kitchen to lean against opposite sides of the back door. Breathing hard, eyes narrowing on Brutus, Andorf cannot get the words out fast enough. "Why do I get this nagging feeling you're not telling me everything?"

A turbo-copter zooms past, saturating the kitchen in white light. They hear a second copter relinquishing its position directly above before both copters break off, sweeping the courtyard one last time on their retreat.

Andorf uncovers his ears. He grabs Brutus's shoulders and rustles him with all his might. "What the hell's going on here, Brutus? Why are they after our Serin?"

Brutus avoids eye contact. He staggers out the sliding door onto the back balcony to watch the departing copters becoming one with the evening sky. Andorf catches him leaning against the rail, hands cupped tightly over his face. For the first time in his life, Andorf witnesses Brutus wearing damp cheeks.

Andorf places a kinder hand on Brutus's shoulder. "It's time, big guy. Time to fess up."

Brutus faces Andorf, wiping his eyes. "I—I don't know where to start." He hushes Andorf with a lone finger. Brushing himself and Andorf off, he directs Andorf inside, away from the sliding glass door. "Serin *did* find her brother," he whispers. "If she doesn't get caught, we'll see her in a few days. What just happened may have been a diversion. She's quite good at moving about without detection."

Andorf trails him across the living room. "I don't follow you."

Brutus pulls the drapes tight. He pulls Andorf away from the curtain and whispers in his ear. "I shouldn't tell you this but … she's one of the Tri-Omegas, the resistance."

"What?" Andorf falls back a few steps.

"Shhh!"

"But I thought you did a full sweep last night." Andorf whispers, twisting his head up at the ceiling.

"That was last night. The Empire has insect-like devices that latch onto clothing. You become vulnerable each time you step outside."

"I don't understand. You and Serin work for the government. You both have perfect covers."

Brutus sneers. "The Empire watches everyone. If only I had a Kofferman Wobbulator. I could zap those—"

The vibrating back wall sends them diving for the floor. A lone copter buzzes a low pass through the back courtyard, Its floodlight infiltrate the kitchen windows before moving on.

"Media," Brutus whispers. "As usual, late to the game."

Rising to his feet, Andorf stares down at Brutus. "Things have been bugging me about Serin. When a woman moves in, she always takes over the place. Our Serin hasn't done that. And her men's briefs, what that all about?"

"Serin maintains a ZFP, zero-feminine footprint as part of her evasion tactics. Think what it would be like if the agents came snooping around and found panties. It'd be a dead giveaway. With the exception of that enticing perfume, she wears no makeup, no jewelry, not even a bra. But you know, every time I ask her what it's called, she says 'In Your Dreams'.

Andorf scratches his head. "What about that massive hair dryer?"

"Your rabbit resolved that issue. Thank you, Binky."

"But we've got to warn her."

Brutus throws up a hand. "Even if we knew where she was, we'd be leading them right to her. We have to go about like nothing happened."

"What about that red laser beam? The one they used at the Archives' was blue."

"The latest in chromatograph technology. In three scans, the red beam can not only decipher your DNA, but can tell what you've had for lunch. Now the blue laser is what they use once they've found their prey. It can slice off a man's finger, right down to a smoking nub."

Andorf appears squeamish. He grabs Brutus's arm. "I've got something to show you. We must go now, while we still can."

Brutus follows at a distance, listening to Andorf detail recent dreams of government suits lurking in shadows, watching his every move. Andorf iterates how they drag him into the dark recesses of the landing and how he breaks free long enough to slip his key into the front door before hairy arms slip under his armpits from behind and press him hard against the door, leaving him gazing helplessly at his dangling keys.

The dinner line at the Corner Café packs tight, disallowing passage. "Watch this," Andorf says. He squinches his face and people in line shift, allowing them safe passage to the other side. Andorf grins at Brutus as he turns and exits through the crowd, leaving Brutus to face the rowdy crowd. Brutus hikes past scorning faces, around the corner, and through the street to rejoin Andorf, destined to listen to his chuckling during the five-minute walk home.

"They were toying with you, Andorf. I see this all the time."

"What would you think if I crossed Dos Cacas Grande at lunch-time? I willed the traffic to stop and they did. The moment I hit the curb, traffic once again came barreling past. In fact, a whole line of us made it safely across, even a greying old lady."

"Daytime traffic? Yeah, good luck with that." Brutus scratches at his chin. "Hey, maybe I should start calling you Moses or that Chinese brother who could swallow the sea. What was his name?"

"Ha ha. Very funny."

"Let's say you *do* have this mind control thing going on, Andorf. What can you do with it? Can you have someone come fix me dinner? I'm starving."

"I'm afraid it doesn't work like that, big guy."

Brutus takes a misstep, nearly tripping for no apparent reason. "You willed me to do that, didn't you? I know you did."

"Very funny, Brutus." Andorf pauses. He looks about in a full three-sixty. "Brutus?"

CHAPTER 19
Uninvited Guests

Outside his condo and suddenly alone, Andorf cringes at the thought of eyes watching his every move. He subconsciously sidesteps the four-man Brown Beagle helicopter perched across the courtyard and jogs up the front stairs. He steps onto the landing, nostrils burning at the putrid stench of cheap government cologne. Hands grab hold and pull him into the dark recesses. Andorf manages to drag the tall man dressed in a dark suit into the lit breezeway before the man's lanky arms slip under his armpits from behind, locking them around his neck.

"What do you want? I have nothing of value," Andorf yells, twisting and turning to break loose. At the sight of Andorf's narrowing eyes, a shorter chubby man, also wearing a dark suit, retraces his steps.

The tall man tightens his grip. "Tell us what we want and we might leave you alone."

Shorty scans Andorf's eyes with a handheld identifier device. "Says here you are Andorf Johnson, unemployed, previous owner of this condo. Oh, by the way, this is being recorded. Everything and anything can and will be used against you. Blah blah blah."

"Yes, but I'm the *current* owner!" Andorf yells.

"Haven't you been watching The Eye, kid," spouts the tallest of the pair. "The Empire owns all property now. Eminent Domicile took care of that. And as for you, you think we give a damn? We care about you less than a politician."

Andorf looks dumbfounded. "How is that even possible?"

"We're detectives. We know things." The tall man suddenly releases Andorf. "Looks like we mistook you for someone else."

The chubby man reaches into his government issued jacket and removes another fancy gadget. One finger stroke across the pixon recorder and Serin's image appears amidst the breezeway's dusty air. "Do you know the present whereabouts of this pretty lady? We take it you know Miss Serin Gray?"

Andorf looks the men over. Keeping one eye on them, he takes a slow stroll around the fuzzy holographic replication, inspecting it from different angles before pausing to squint at the tall man's eyes. "And who wants to know?"

The pair throw open hands at Andorf, displaying badges embedded in their palms and retracting them the moment Andorf reaches to touch. "Detective Souder from Records," the tall one says. "This here's my partner, Detective Kannady. I take it you are Serin's husband?"

"One of them," Andorf says, stretching the first word.

The detectives exchange foul glances. Stepping closer, Souder's head tips a few of the curious neighbors gathering around them. "Mind if we discuss this inside?"

Andorf smiles sarcastically at the previously unseen neighbors. He unlocks his front door and leads the detectives inside. "And which government office are you guys from?"

Kannady darts in and gives the living room a good looking over.

Souder places a hand on Andorf's shoulder and parades him around the living room, while Kannady covertly slips into the bedroom. "It seems this—" Souder clears his throat. "This wife of yours has been socializing with known suspects whose intent is to destabilize our Canine Empire."

Andorf spots Kannady probing around the bedroom. He sees him reaching into a pocket, trying to hide his actions. At first, its appears to be an act of thievery. But as Andorf watches, he sees him hiding things.

Souder unclips a wallet-sized device from his belt. He extends the handle and sweeps the living room, side to side. Rainbow outlines magically appear everywhere he sweeps. "Yep, your Serin Gray is all over this place. I'd say she's been here most recently."

The device flickers and hums to a hash of green and amber lines racing across the living room floor. Andorf picks at the pieces of colors scattered across the lamp, appearing as if the lamp was shattered.

"There was a scuffle her on the floor, like two people wrestling," Souder says. "I can make out someone's leg atop your precious table lamp." Souder slaps the gizmo against his palm. "Damn thing keeps jumping chapters ahead. It's been in the shop twice for this."

As Souder re-clips the device, Andorf turns away, heading for the bedroom. Souder grabs his arm.

"Now back to this Serin Gray of yours. According to eyewitnesses, whose identities I cannot divulge, she has been associating with well-known underground collaborates whose identities I also cannot divulge."

"Sounds like trumped-up garbage to me." Andorf swallows hard, attempting to remain calm. After a deep breath, he grins. "So tell me, Mister Souder, if that's really your name … has this group you call collaborates actually been caught breaking any of your laws, or are they *merely* suspected of doing whatever you think they may or may not be doing?"

"Yes, indeed. Many have been caught performing questionable acts, of which I'm not at liberty to describe."

"So let me get this straight. These citizens you call suspects, who you won't identify, haven't actually been caught doing anything wrong. Do I have that right?"

Souder grins. "Once they become suspects, we haul them in for questioning. Oh, they'll be photographed, retinas scanned, faces touched up, bruises painted over, you know, for the holographs. After a night or two in jail, one of their accomplices usually springs them."

"And those accomplices are added to your suspect lists."

"You're a fast learner, kid."

"Imagine that," Andorf says. "All this time, I thought we lived in a free country."

"It may be free for you being unemployed, but the rest of us are paying your bills."

Andorf spots Kannady advance to his kitchen and begin to rummage through the cooler. He grins at Souder. "And what makes my Serin so interesting? She works high up in your Records Office, on one of the upper floors."

Popping a few skinless grapes in his mouth, Kannady rejoins his partner in the living room. He winks indiscreetly at Souder.

Souder slides a hand onto Andorf's shoulder. "We've been observing Serin Gray for some time. We believe she's been pocketing electronic components from the tech lab. Have you noticed any suspicious activities on her part?"

"What about these suspects she hangs with?" Kannady says, wiping cheese from his slobbering lips. "As you admitted earlier, she *does* have another husband. How well do you know *the other* husband? Are you sure there is *just one* other?"

Andorf looks at Souder, then Kannady. "Are you guys actually detectives? You're from that 'Beat The Reaper' game show, aren't you? Which one of you has the hidden camera?"

Souder snorts. Beady eyes narrowing, he pulls Andorf aside. "Ever hear of the Cease Over-Marriage Act? COMA is the law in twenty-six states."

Kannady chuckles "Why, your wife has violated the law in more states than there are E-Con candidates."

Andorf's blood begins to boil. "How's the government come up with this crap? How could you possibly enforce such a stupid thing?

Seventy-two is today's state count, isn't it? What about the forty-six other states?"

"It's the people," Souder says. "Hard working, right-leaning preservatives, imposing social intolerance on the public. How much more patriotic can you get? Remember those campaigns, the ones that saturated the media last March?"

"You're telling me that was real?" Andorf yells. "I thought it was another trick to sell media-watch."

Souder snarls. "You're darn tooting it was real. The S.O.B.s frightened everyone so badly with exaggeration that it became law."

"It even scared citizens in the other six empires into enacting similar laws," Kannady says.

Souder grins at Andorf. "The media went to town with that one. It's amazing what you can accomplish by lining politician's pockets. So you see, COMA protects good citizens like you and me."

Andorf steps away, jaw dropped. "I don't see any harm in—"

Souder grabs Andorf's arm. "What happens when this other guy your wife is married to finds a second wife? Then *she* finds another husband and so on. This crazy multiple-marriage fad could quickly get out of hand." Both detectives pale at the thought.

Kannady's face turns green, as if he swallowed a live crab. "Why, it could turn into a chain, threatening the very sanctity of marriage."

Andorf walks away from the pair. "Don't you guys have anything better to do than to come around harassing me with these obnoxious questions?"

Souder pauses at the improvised bookcase alongside the old bricked up fireplace. Focusing on the bead of sweat accumulating at Andorf's brow, he runs a finger over the overfilled shelves. "You can tell quite a bit about a man by the holo-books he reads."

Andorf gulps as Souder's fingers trace over his forbidden copy of 'The Inconvenient Government.' Souder skips over the family Bible and pulls one of Serin's technical manuals from the shelf. He opens the book-frame in the middle and squints at the complex schematic holograms. "What the hell is a pulse modulated remote control ten-meter transmitter?"

Andorf clears his throat. "It's not complicated once you understand the underlying mathematical concepts."

The detective blows past images of balloon-supported antennas and lengthy transformational formulas. Slamming the holo-book shut, Souder reads the binder. "Who's this Gene Lewis W5LE guy? He sounds like a real ham."

Andorf bites his tongue. "So I've heard."

Souder lays the book-frame face down and steps away. "So you're one of those brainy college grads. I bet you're wondering just how I came to be a detective."

Andorf chuckles. "F's in grade school?"

Souder's hands go straight for Andorf's collar. His partner scowls and he backs off. He picks up the Lewis manual again and smacks it against his palm. "I ought to haul you in for questioning, see how you hold up to agents working you over."

Andorf grins at Souder, facetiously. "If you lock me up, who will you guys harass?"

Souder tosses the book onto the shelf and scratches at his balding crown. He takes hold of Andorf's arm and parades him about the living room. "It's a good thing I like you, kid."

Kannady chimes in. "Yeah, good thing."

The detectives freeze at the full-size poster covering the bricked-up fireplace. They zero in on the patriot dragging an E-Cuniculon and his Toxidian counterpart off by their collars to an outside trash receptacle.

Andorf grins. "Pretty neat drawing, don't you think?"

"It's anti-government," Souder says, snarling at Andorf. "You may think that's *real* funny whiz kid, but it doesn't belong there."

Kannady points at the poster. "Look, Souder, those circus animals look like our political mascots."

Similar to the depiction in the patriot poster, Andorf grabs the pair by their collars, drags them across the living room, and tosses them out the partially opened front door into the trashy neighbor collective. "Why don't you two get a life and stay the hell out of mine?"

Unlike Souder, Kannady is cushioned by the swarming crowd. "But we're not done here."

Souder lands on his butt. "We'll be back, next time it'll be agents."

"Do what you must. But you're crazy if you think I'm swallowing any of your crap. And you know where you can stick your C.O.M.A.!" To neighbor's cheers, Andorf slams the front door. From the front window, he watches his uninvited guests untangle themselves from the jubilant crowd and hike down the steps. Above the disbursing neighbor's continuing cheer, he hears four doors shutting followed by the whine of a turbocharged engine. He watches two copters hover and then zoom off into the night.

CHAPTER 20

The Eye

Brutus plows through the back door. His large trembling hands hurriedly latch the triple deadbolts. Between deep breaths, he frantically yells at Andorf. "What the hell was that? Were they here about Serin? Were they asking about me?"

Andorf holds an index finger to his lips and leads Brutus and his swelling face into the bedroom where Binky is hopping about, sniffing at this and that. Andorf inspects each nudged item and extracts tiny stick-on devices. Brutus snatches the pieces from Andorf's hands and after a flushing sound, returns from the bathroom wiping his brow.

Binky darts across their feet heading for the kitchen. Andorf produces a carrot and holds it inches above Binky's head. Binky latches onto the nub and dashes under the sofa.

Brutus sweats profusely. "Those dicks were looking for Serin, weren't they? What'd you tell them? Come on, Poo. Spit it out."

"Well … they said she was mingling … or was it associating with suspects."

"Did they say she was mingling or associating? It's important."

"Socializing, that's it. And they got real interested in her *other* husband."

Brutus slaps his damp forehead. Throwing serious eye at Andorf, he steadies himself against the kitchen wall. "They came to arrest her. Did you tell them I was living here? Did they call me by name?"

"No, none of that. Your name never came up. But I'll tell you this, they were absolutely crazed about her having two husbands. They kept referring to you as the "other husband," asking how well I knew you, where you were. They were ticked about Serin violating stupid COMA laws in twenty-six states. Oh yeah … they told me I no longer own this place, that it was confiscated by the imposed Eminent Domicile laws."

"Bastards!"

"They looked the place over pretty good, but when the tall one fingered through my books, especially this one. I was sweating."

"Why? What have you got stashed?"

"Spare keys and my now worthless deed. Only someone seeking spiritual guidance would ever look there."

Brutus smiles at Andorf's family Bible. "Or someone who reads Shakespeare."

"That Souder guy went through one of Serin's technical manuals, asking stupid questions. He wasn't exactly what you'd call an intellectual."

Brutus grabs hold of Andorf's arm. "Wait! Not Souder, as in Kannady and Souder? A tall thin man and his short pudgy sidekick?"

"You know the clowns?"

Brutus's eyes refocus after a good minute. He begins to pace the living room floor. "The agency sends in the detectives, muddy the waters four days before the agents arrive."

Andorf carefully peels the bottom and sides of the full-size patriot poster. He rolls it up to reveal a hollowed out opening behind. Grinning at Brutus, he brushes loose mortar aside with his hands. "Here's where I stash Binky's food pellets. I chiseled out a few bricks, nearly large enough to hide someone."

Brutus quickly backs away. “No, not me. I’d never fit in that small space.”

Andorf releases the poster and stares at Brutus in disbelief. “What’s the matter, big guy? Don’t tell me you’re … claustrophobic?”

“I—I just don’t like tight places, that’s all.”

Andorf raises an index finger. “Bet I can name one exception.”

Brutus grabs hold of Andorf’s shoulders. He stares into his eyes. “Our ruthless queen, we must protect her at all costs.”

Andorf nods. “I’ll pull a few more bricks, open it up a bit. She can hide in there.”

“And replace that damn Libertarian poster with something less controversial, like Raquel Welch.”

Andorf grimaces. “Everyone’s seen Shawshank Redemption. That’d be the first place they’d look.”

“Then pick out a starship poster at the Six-Ten. The government keeps files on everything it finds distasteful and exterminator complaints and now Souder and Kannady.”

Andorf presses insistently on the poster’s curling edges to no avail. “Then I hope they all go blind looking at all the files.”

Brutus whips a roll of special tape from his oversized pants pocket. “Magnatape. I won’t go anywhere without the stuff.” He rips a piece off and sings the popular infomercial jingle, “With a strip this long …”

Andorf harmonizes. “Problem’s all gone.”

With a brief chuckle, Brutus secures the curling poster edges. “They’ll never suspect a thing when they return.”

“Return? Jeez Brutus, you’re giving me the willies.”

“Oh, your uninvited guests will be back alright, only next time it’ll be the big time agents.” Brutus spots Andorf admiring the patriot poster. He takes a breath. “Ah, yes. I see what happened. The detectives criticized your poster and you grabbed them by their collars and threw them out.”

Andorf grins. “Every man has limits.”

"Mark your calendar, Andorf. They'll be back in four days ... agents next time with all sorts of techno gadgets. Another four days and Ginzbug will come busting through that door with his militia." Brutus turns and mumbles a bit too loud. "We're cutting this too damn close."

"Didn't you heard what I said about Eminent Domicile? The government confiscated my property. They can waltz right in here anytime they'd like, just like what they did to Gregory."

"But you let those detectives in. I was outside watching."

"It was cheaper than replacing someone else's door. But I won't take this crap any longer. I won't be bullied by these morons. First, I'm dealing with these idiots in the Records Office and now lamebrain detectives. How'd we end up with elephants and jackasses running our government?"

"Watch your tongue, Andorf, or it'll be *your* butt they haul off next to the Cos. The government works on strict four-day schedules. They'll be back in four days."

Grabbing his chin, Andorf stares at Brutus. "That'll be November 19th and four days after that, the 23rd, one day before the starship launches. We have a week to find a place. In the meantime, we've got to warn Serin."

"We've been through this, Poo. We can't find Serin. We'd lead them straight to her. Damn! I knew it was only a matter of time before they'd catch on. From here on out, we mustn't be seen in public together. The last thing I need is for them to be watching *me*."

Andorf runs into the kitchen. He tugs and tugs on the kitchen junk drawer, but it refuses to open beyond a few inches. Brutus pushes him aside. He slips a hefty finger in the drawer and with a firm tug, pops the drawer off its tracks. Andorf's eyes widen at the sight of black boxes filled with electronic parts taking residence in his receipt drawer. Brutus blocks his reaching hand. "What the hell are these? They weren't in there last week."

Brutus growls, again pushing Andorf aside. "Hey, don't touch those."

"But what are they for? What are they doing in my junk drawer?"

"Leave them alone, I tell you. They're Serin's."

Andorf glances at the black boxes and then at Brutus. "So it's true ... what those detectives said about Serin lifting electronic parts." He reaches past Brutus, grabs one of the black boxes, and examines its connectors. "This one looks like one of gizmos dad used to build, only his—"

"Put that back!" Brutus grabs the ten-meter transmitter from Andorf's hands and returns it to the junk drawer.

"Where'd she learn about this stuff? It's not anything they taught us back in our counter subversive general education."

"Serin's great uncle was some ham radio guy, back when that stuff was legal. He was always building contraptions from scrap parts and selling them on the side. You know, before the government confiscated the analog airwaves and digitized everything."

Andorf grins. "My dad had cabinets full of those stripy-colored things. He also had the knack."

"Sharona on that. Leave her things alone and pray no one else opens that drawer. It'll be the end of you." Brutus slips the drawer back on its wobbly track and shoves it snug against the stop.

Andorf draws a blank expression. He begins to ask, but keeps it bottled up inside until he can no longer keep it inside. "Where'd Serin go? Time to spill the beans, big guy."

Brutus swallows. He leans into Andorf. "She found her brother."

"Gregory's locked away in the Cos, isn't he? She's been out there visiting him, hasn't she? That's why all the secretive comms and why she disappears to for days at a time."

Brutus turns away. "Quit asking, Poo. I can't say anymore."

Andorf follows Brutus's eyes until a flashing light catches his attention. He runs into the living room, pointing at The Eye's glowing green light. "Did you see that, Brutus? Come take a look."

Brutus sits with him in front of The Eye. "That's a power light, standard on every Eye unit."

“But notice the size of the black spot on the right side.”

They home in on the hypnotic half-inch black spot, daring themselves not to blink. They stare and stare. For a split second, the black spot disappears. Both flinch when the spot reappears on the left side of the green light.

Brutus jumps to his feet. “It blinked like—“

“An eye,” Andorf says. “It’s really an eye. It’s been watching us all this time.”

“Good thing Serin disabled the antenna the day she moved in.”

“So it’s blind? It can’t see us?”

“Oh, it can still see us all right, but without an antenna, the transmitted signal is too weak to go beyond a few feet. I’ll bet those repair techs go nuts with their fancy test gear. Everything looks fine in here, but outside in their surveillance trucks … nothing.”

Andorf grabs at Brutus’s shoulders with both hands. “You and Serin suckered me into this little espionage game of yours, but you won’t tell me anything. What am I to think? Huh?”

“I can’t tell you anymore. If the authorities snarf you up, they’ll torture it out of you. I wouldn’t put my worst enemy through that.” He grins at Andorf. “I’m not saying you’re my …”

Andorf nods. “You’re not the only one feeling claustrophobic. I’m gaining compassion for those political gangs.”

“This ain’t the same thing, Poo. Much civilian blood stains their gangster hands.”

Andorf takes steps for the back door. He hears Brutus calling out as the back door slams behind. “You can’t leave now, Poo. It’s not safe out there.”

PART 3: FRIENDS

CHAPTER 21
Within Shadows

Andorf descends the back steps to the sound of triple deadbolts engaging on his back door. With Brutus's warning ringing fresh in his ears, he feels eyes watching from everywhere. An odor of stale alcohol engulfs him as he scans the trash-filled void beneath the dark lower steps. His neck hairs rise at the feeling of someone lurking in the shadows. A screen door creaks open. A voice deep in Nordic slant calls out.

"Hey, mister. Mister Andy der."

Andorf makes out an outline of man cautiously remaining within the breezeway's shadows. He spooks at the hand reaching out and trips, landing one knee on the rough cement floor. From between short stacks of bricks resembling those he had chiseled from his own fireplace, he gazes up at the stranger's troubled face.

"Oh, mister Andy. Are you OK?" a wrinkled man says, offering his sun-stained hand. "I hope you not hurt. My wife ... what she does wid doze things."

Andorf climbs to his feet. Leaning against stacked moving boxes, he brushes dust and mortar chunks from his clothes. An eerie familiarity about his new downstairs neighbor sets in. "Have we met?"

"I don't dink so. I heard doze udders, in deh courtyard. Dey all call you Andy. I hope—"

"It's okay. I've been called worse. Wait, what others?"

"Das what I must speak wid you about. Doze strange men in dark suits. Deh ones who smell so bad. Dey ask about you … and dat young lady."

"The detectives? What'd you tell them?"

With rotating hand motions, the man beckons Andorf closer. "Mister Andy, I must tell you. Dat woman up der. Up der wid you and dat, dat big man."

Andorf laughs at the man's hand descriptions of Serin and Brutus. "Yah … I mean yes?"

"Doze men, dey ask many questions. Dey ask about dat lady of yours. Dey talk with neighbors. Dey tell everyone how dangerous she is, how we should call dem next time we see her. Dat pretty lady of yours, in trouble she is?"

Andorf shakes his head. Swallowing in near panic, he tries to rationalize what this man is saying, from a foreigner's perspective.

The man chugs a drink from his whisky bottle before staring at Andorf with sorrow-filled eyes. "I don't believe dem, not one bit. I tell dem dey are wrong, she is sweet girl. Dey don't want to hear dis. Dey make doze ugly government faces. Dey keep telling me she is much trouble. Dey talk to all deh neighbors. Here, see? Dey give us deez cards."

Andorf squints at the card's six-point font and looks back at his strange downstairs neighbor. "Was one a tall stocky man, the other short and pudgy?"

"Oh, no, mister Andy. Doze guys went upstairs." The man pauses for a moment, scratching at his week-old beard. "Deez two guys were skinny, wearing doze government suits. You gotta suspect anyone wearing dat cheap cologne. Dey gave me deh creeps, doze guys, standing outside watching everyone like dat. Dey look like thieves in der black suits."

Andorf's hands impatiently encourage the man to say more.

"Well, I thought doze men went away so I went about my doings. Den I look outside and der dey are wid some lady. Long yellow hair she had. Dey was raising such a holler. Daz when I see dem walking off wid deh girl, her arms tied wid doz binders. Dey left in dat whirly flying machine."

"Serin," Andorf says, slapping a hand over his mouth. He lightly touches the old man's shoulder. "Did you get a good look at her?"

"It was dark, hard to see from behind dis door. She looked like dat lady of yours."

"What about your wife? Did she—"

"My wife pretty, but not like dat lady of yours. She old like me." The man hesitates for a moment. "One more ding I must say, Andy. Dat big man up der—"

"Brutus? What about him?"

"Yah, Brutus. Datz him. Careful around him you be." He raises a pointed finger at Andorf. "I see bullies like dat. Throw you under da bus dey will. I see others like him do just dat. Why do you dink I walk with dis bad back like I do? I watch my back around him, mister Andy, I would. Doze bullies, dey never change, you know."

"No, no. Brutus is not like that. He's a nice guy, when you get to know him. But tell me, what's with all the bricks? Why are they piled up outside like that?"

"My little helper … she much stronger den me. You know, wid my back, I not carry much. Say, Andy, do you need any bricks?"

"Not right now, thank you."

"People talk about dat guy, Andy … deh one who lived here before me. Dey say he was taken away, middle of deh night. Daz is deh way dey do it. You sleep in your bed and you wake up somewhere else, yah."

"What else did you hear about my friend, the one who used to live here?"

"Daz all I know, Andy. Dat was before we came. We were on der list. When dis place open up we moved, same day. Hard to find a place you know. You must move right in. As undocumented citizens, we send our kids to school for free. Medical care is free, we get a monthly deposit in our accounts, and we pay no taxes. How great is dis country?"

Andorf shrugs his shoulders. "You appear to be from the Flemish Empire, Danish or Norwegian perhaps?" He reaches to shakes the man's hand. "My name is actually Andorf."

The old man vigorously shakes Andorf's hand. "Good to meet you, Andy. Name here is Svensson, but call me Sven. You deh first actual American I meet in dis building."

Answering the call of his growling stomach, Andorf waves goodbye. He turns past trash accumulating beneath the back steps, mumbling under his breath. "Sven. Hmm. He resembles someone I used to know."

CHAPTER 22

New Friends

Toting a full belly and a caffeinated grin, Andorf jogs down the Corner Café's steps. Staring ahead at the long line, he once again bumps into his childhood friend, Brett, spilling much of Brett's precious Jamaican Roast.

Brett growls, looking up at Andorf. "You know how long I waited in line for this? Hey, where'd you come from? How long you been standing there?"

Andorf scowls. "What do you mean? I've been here every night looking for you. You knew someone who can help find my friend."

Flashing a caustic gaze, Brett chokes down the last of his drink. "That was months ago. Things have changed." Brett's face goes blank. He grabs Andorf's arm and leads him away from the inquisitive dinner crowd. "Look, this really isn't a good time."

"But my friend," Andorf says. "The one who disappeared—"

"Like I said—"

"You once told me there wasn't anything one blood brother wouldn't do for the other."

"Geez, Andorf, we were stupid kids back then. Things are different now."

"Please, Brett. I'm begging you."

Barely dusk, the fading sky surrenders to impending darkness. Sparsely placed streetlights randomly fire purple and then dull orange, hinting of a once brighter day. Brett leads him around a sharp bend, where the intrepid three-lane California Street necks down barely two and well-lit single floor office façades merge into the evening's blackness. Andorf peers at the corner street sign with reservations. "Are we heading for Darktown?" he asks, in a shuddering voice.

Brett grabs Andorf by the shoulders, pulling Andorf's face but inches from his own. "You'll keep your trap shut when we get there, if you know what's good for you. This is serious stuff here, Andorf. These guys don't mess around." He squeezes hard on Andorf's shoulders. "Before we go any further, tell me, are you in or not?"

Tasting Jamaican Roast in Brett's breath, Andorf pulls away to straighten his shirt. "I'm in, I think. Yeah, I'm in. Let's do this."

Brett takes off, running at a slow trot. He calls back to Andorf. "All right then. Don't get your panties in a wad."

"So, what am I in on? What are we doing?"

"If you want to find your friend, keep up and be quiet."

Struggling to keep up, Andorf grills Brett about everything from media chase copters to that slinky gal on The Tube ads. "Fabrication," Brett repeats many times. He stops beneath the moonlit clouds to lean against a signpost, rubbing his sore ankles.

A waning moon breaking the clouds reveals the first two letters of the California Street sign on one side and the first four letters of Veatrice on the other. Andorf gawks at the two words becoming one. He begins to shake uncontrollably as the word CAVEAT leaps out. He peers across the way, at the barbed-wire topped walls sparkling in the damp evening air. Resurfacing childhood scars stab at him like daggers. Andorf wants to run, hide, but his feet are fixed, as if nailed to the ground.

"I spent the last of my childhood behind those walls, running amongst shards of metal debris. Dad was always in hot pursuit, determined to retrieve whatever critical part I mindlessly snatched in my grubby little hands. Mom chased after us, warning of the dangers. Oh, it was so much fun having him all to myself, even for those brief moments. I gave Dad plenty of exercise, and he expanded my vocabulary of choice words."

Brett chuckles. "I can see your folks being scrapyard dogs."

Andorf snarls at his old friend. "They were much more than that. Dad built all sorts of gizmos from that worthless junk. A few even ended up as control circuits in three starship prototypes."

Brett's face swells. "So your dad had the knack. I hear the Starship Atlantis was built on gypsy sweat, seven thousand gypsies in fact. They have strange ways—collecting things discarded—things of the dead. Your buddy, Brutus, is one of them, isn't he?"

"Wait! How do you know Brutus?"

"You're forgetting that investigative research is my job. You know, turning false into fact. I even know things The Empire has yet to discover." Brett begins to salivate. "Say, are the prototypes back there? Can we—"

"Are you kidding me? The damn thing was disassembled years ago. Piece by piece it was reassembled up on Jake's Mountain. In the back is where ..." Andorf pales, choking out the words. "Some idiot dropped O2 tanks in the boiler without removing the valves. After the debris cleared, everyone scrambled to get that damn furnace back online." Andorf's voice raises and then cracks. "They didn't give a damn about my parents. They were expendable ... like gypsies."

"Ahh! You're better off, my friend," Brett says. "*My folks* were caught hoarding illegal silverware and hauled off to the Cos in the middle of the night. No doubt, they were milled down as essential ingredients in the power cell factories next door. That's what they do with the older citizens, the ones they can't rehabilitate at the Cos."

Andorf's face reddens. Fists shaking, he begins to yell. "How can you be so detached? Why, my blood boils looking at that salvage yard. I wish I could blow it up along with that damn starship."

Brett walks off snickering. "You may get your chance, buddy boy. You'd better come along if you want to find that friend of yours."

"No! Wait! I'd never! That would seal humanity's fate, return us to the dark ages."

"Wishes have crazy ways of becoming true." Brett calls out, ten paces beyond, "You had better catch up. You wouldn't want to be caught alone in the low-rent district."

Following Brett, Andorf slips in and out of moon shadows on the narrowing pavement, feeling terribly alone. Dead-animal odors are everywhere. Houses are dimly lit by appearing and disappearing window silhouettes. With bats flickering low overhead, Andorf for once is too scared to speak. He looks about and notices he *is* alone.

"Brett?" he whispers, scanning the surrounding brush. A branch on his right moves to one side. He steps cautiously through the shrubbery, vines scratching his exposed arms. He feels his socks soaking up water seeping through the green, yellow, and grease-stained EasyGlides. His feet sink into the muck. With each step through the soggy marsh bed, his sneakers squish and spelunk as he forces his steps, one shoe at a time. Swatting at buzzes about his face, he hears brush moving directly behind. He spins around so ready to wring someone's neck, but Brett is not there. Feeling a gnawing on one ankle and a tentacle growth wrapping the other ankle, Andorf tears a path through the stickery thicket, not stopping until he clears the thick brush. He looks down to see a slimy creature unwrap from his ankles and slither through the tall weeds for the thick protective cover of the marsh. He bends down to squeeze the water from his sneakers. Behind him, a twig snaps.

"Boo!" Brett yells, in his ear.

Andorf takes a wide swipe. "I'm going to kill you."

Laughing aloud, Brett judiciously steps back. "Guess I was wrong about you, Andorf. You're braver than I thought." He takes off, running through knee-high weeds growing out of the once-paved road, with Andorf closing in with his squishing EasyGlides. Lights suddenly appear from the darkness, like an oasis of humanity. Brett slows to a stop, as does Andorf to glance at curtained lights of a poorly maintained housing cluster.

"Remember, don't say anything," Brett says. "Let me do the talking."

Andorf grins. "You know me."

"Dummy up, Andorf. These guys mean business." Brett roughs his hair and then goes for Andorf's hair, but is pushed away. "And whatever you do, don't stare at Holder. Gang boss wasted the last guy who did that."

Andorf spots something dangling from Brett's rear pocket. Both freeze at the muffled thunk it makes hitting the ground. Andorf reaches for the shiny object in the weeds. "Is that a—"

"Careful, buddy boy. It's loaded." Brett grabs the pistol from Andorf's hands and leads him through the uniform rows of dilapidated duplexes, past colored bedsheet curtains and pieces of children's toys, scattered about neglected lawns.

Andorf gags at the stale odor of boiling gruel and poke salad spilling from nearly every opened window. Like Brett, he raises his arms above the stinging, waist-high grass blades. He stumbles on the crumbling walkway leading up to the narrow porch of the darkest duplex, isolated far behind the other units. Chipped brick steps terminate at an eye-level peephole jammed through a splintered door beneath a five-watt bulb dangling overhead on exposed wires, swinging and occasionally sparking in the slight breeze.

Brett steps onto the narrow porch, cupping Andorf's gaping mouth with his hand. "Something big is about to go down. Play it cool."

After several of Brett's distinct knocks, Andorf pivots on his heels. "Maybe we should—"

Brett kicks the door open. Brushing fallen cockroaches from his shirt, Andorf follows Brett inside a dark, smoke-filled room where odors of the unbathed attack them. Adjusting to the darkness, Andorf eyes the four pistols jammed in his and Brett's faces with four angry mugs standing behind them.

"Why the warm welcome?" Brett says, flashing open palms. Andorf does likewise, watching Brett's piece transfer into questionable hands. A wily hand smacks Brett's face. *Whack!*

"You dumb ass media stiff," the gang boss yells. "What the hell were you thinking?"

Brett's sweaty hand rubs feeling back into his face. "I bring a new recruit and you treat me this way, Holder? Why, Andorf here hates the Empire like—"

Holder looks Andorf over. "I don't give a rat's ass if you went to school with this stooge. How the hell ya' know he's not another Jose Thursday?"

"He's a straight up guy, Holder, I swear."

The creepiest of the thugs, a Frankenstein wannabe laughs, nudging Andorf dead center of his back. "What kind of name is Andorf?"

"You're supposed to be down at that damn studio, spying for us," Holder yells. "You got no time for friends, Conyers."

A second thug thumps Brett in the back of his head with his gun. "Yeah, gang boss's right."

As Brett fumbles for an acceptable response, Andorf pushes pistols aside with his hands. "That's right, guys. I hate those mothers all right. They can all burn in hell."

Holder and the others release Brett to focus on Andorf's brash tactics. Shoving his face in Andorf's, Holder's voice mellows to a pious chuckle. "So you hate those mothers, do ya?"

Andorf knows he must conjure up something believable and quick. He backs away from Holder's liquid rotgut stench. He begins to pace the confined area between the sofa and stuffed chairs. "You see, I've been working on the inside. Yeah, that's it. I've been scoping out the Records Office, analyzing their operation, their vulnerabilities."

"Go on." At Holder's grin, the thugs close in on Andorf.

"I've been rubbing noses with detectives, obtaining valuable information."

"Like what, Mac? Oh yeah, get used to being called Mac."

With his life in question and the thugs surrounding him, Andorf pulls out the stops. "Like starship maps, guard schedules—"

One thug laughs, chorused by the others. "Like we can't get that stuff at any Six-Ten store."

Andorf cozies into the nearest chair. He envisions Wretched Wanda, back at the Records Office with so much information at her fingertips. "But I know where they keep personal bank records and passkeys too." The gang sobers. "All without an appointment," he quickly adds.

Jaws drop. The room becomes deathly quiet. Then like popcorn, the thugs begin to laugh.

Holder grins, scanning his gang. "Well how about that, boys? Mac here is a one-man crime spree." Eyes narrowing, he jabs an index finger into Andorf's cheek. "You sit right there, Mac." He points at the bulkiest amongst his group. "Pinky, keep an eye on him."

At Holder's head tilt, Brett and the remaining thugs head for the back bedroom, leaving Andorf alone with Pinky's seething stare. Wondering if he will be walking out alive, Andorf's eyes drift from Pinky's evil grin, to the fingers massaging every crevice of his pistol, to the door where he entered moments earlier. He flinches at Holder's random outbursts and the stucco wall flexing behind.

Pinky breaks the awkward silence. "You had us going for a minute with that 'without an appointment' bit. I knew better. You know, identity theft is serious stuff. You can do serious time. Now if I were to blow you away, hah. Worst case would be a few years of lying around the slammer, watching The Eye, getting fat on free meals."

"You'd have it better than most servicemen."

Massaging his pistol, Pinky smiles. "Why I never enlisted."

The bedroom door flies open and two thugs toss Brett onto the floor. Eyes bruised, nose bleeding, he crawls to lie at Andorf's feet.

Pinky snickers. "Boss must really like ya'. Else you'd be leaving in a body bag."

Andorf leans forward, but Pinky, cocking his pistol, changes his mind. "Settle down there, Mac. I'd put a cap in ya', but that'd disturb Holder. Gang boss gets angry when I do that."

Andorf eases back into the uncomfortable chair, gawking at Brett. He slowly lowers his head toward Brett and whispers. "We're in deep shit, aren't we?"

Groaning in pain, Brett mumbles out the corner of his bruised mouth. "Holder's only making a point. He's mad about me bringing you."

"Did your parents used to beat you? You're in denial, Brett, like those thieving E-Cons. Next you'll be telling me there's no such thing as acid rain or global warming."

Brett waves him off. "Holder's only playing around. Like Pinky said, if he wanted to kill me, I'd be already dead."

Pinky snickers. "That's for sure."

Andorf grimaces. "You should see yourself. Your face, it's all bloody. And your shirt—"

Brett curls his mouth into a grin. "You don't look so hot either, Andorf. That marsh did a number on you."

Pinky's jaw drops, scanning Andorf's scratched arms and bloody pants leg. "You guys were in the marsh? At night?"

Brett and Andorf nod.

Pinky tosses Andorf his headrest towel. The bedroom door creaks opens. Holder reappears with three clinging leeches. "So, Mac, we may have some use for you after all. Consider yourself the latest member of the Bogus Boat People."

Andorf cannot tell if Holder is yelling or speaking in a normal raunchy voice. Gulping at the gang's name, he instinctively rises.

"Sit you back down, Mac. The boys and I have a few details to work out.

"Boss, these guys were in Willow Marsh tonight, the one with underground caverns connecting with the lagoon outside the perimeter. Go ahead, Mac. Show them where one of those slithering mutated creatures got ya'." Andorf draws up his pant legs. All but Holder gasps at the chew marks on Andorf's legs.

Holder chuckles. "So we have a couple brave ones here. I think you'll like what we have planned for the two of you." He exchanges smirks with the thugs and bends to whisper in Pinky's ear. The gang converges around a foldup metal card table in the next room. Holder takes a deep swig from a whisky bottle, pours four shots, and slams the empty bottle onto the table. "A round for our newest pal."

The thugs drain their shots and slam them onto the table, mimicking Holder.

"Best you be back here Friday, 9:00 p.m. sharp, Mac," Holder yells. "A minute late and we'll hunt you down. And wear black, like you're attending your momma's funeral."

Andorf nods at the gang's snickers. "What about Brett?"

Holder spits on the floor. "Get the hell out of here. Pinky, see him out."

Andorf trips over Brett and hurries out the front door. Tall grass slice his arms like sharp palm fronds. Hearing the door slam and Pinky's large feet skipping down the broken brick steps, he zigzags to make himself a more difficult target.

"Good thing I like ya'," Pinky yells out. "Even though you believe in those acid rain and round world conspiracies. Spilling the beans would be the last thing you ever do. Ya' know that, don't ya? We got our eyes on ya', Mac."

With Pinky on his tail, Andorf has no intent of stopping until he is in the clear. He spots Speedway's late night traffic zooming past in the distance as the evening events play in his head like an endless loop. *What if I don't show up? They don't know where I live. They've got Brett. They'll worm it out of him. My God. They'll come after Brutus. Five against one, he won't stand a chance. If only Brutus were here. No, I can't get him involved. This must end here.*

Andorf flags down a public bus, and in spite of the nagging feeling of being tracked, pays with a retinal scan. He examines the run schedule taped above the optical scanner and grins at the driver's foot pressing down on the accelerator pedal. Watching his pre-Holder world zoom past, each road bump reminds him of life's struggles. At the wedding chapel zipping past, he longs for Serin's warm embrace and flowery perfume. The bus swerves around the line of diners spilling into the street outside the Corner Café. Andorf yanks on the pull-cord until the bus slows to a stop, directly across from his condominium complex. Stepping onto the curb, he feels the run-in with Holder was but a warmup for the remaining late-evening drama.

CHAPTER 23

Round Two

Andorf tightens the Velcro straps on his EasyGlides. Stomach in knots, he jogs across the less-travelled, residential end of Speedway, through the courtyard and up his front steps. Gagging at the stench of cheap government cologne, he hurriedly slips a key into the front door. His hand reaches for the knob and … hairy arms slip under his armpits from behind. Andorf is face-slammed into the wall, casting his glasses onto the concrete floor. He squinches helplessly at his dangling keys.

"This time you're answering questions, boy," a deep voice growls. "Where the hell is Serin Gray?"

A thinner, dark-suited agent slinks around the corner, shaking her thin, tight hips. The maiden licks her pencil lips, snarling at Andorf. "Serin Gray cannot be far away. I can taste her scent."

Andorf feels the bitch licking away at his inner thoughts. He focuses on the Corner Cafe with its long dinner line. He flinches at her thoughts of hybrid humans overtaking the city and her retracting, serpent-like tongue.

At her nod, the man releases Andorf to retrieve his glasses. Through cracked lenses, Andorf sees the pudgy man kicking the front door open and his female partner turning away to speak into the two-way radio imbedded in her wrist. “Agent Pinscher here with Agent Dinmont at the target location. We’re going in.”

In spite of Andorf’s feeble attempts to block the man, Dinmont barges past, phasor pistol primed and ready. “But you guys are a day early. You’re not supposed to be here until—”

“So we’re twenty minutes early,” says Dinmont. “Sue me.”

“You won’t find anyone. No one’s in there,” Andorf yells. He follows the agents inside, but falls quiet at Pinscher’s phasor pressing firmly against his skull. Pinscher directs him toward the bedroom, where Dinmont is meticulously sweeping his bedroom with a motley collection of hand-held devices. Andorf edges past, into the walk-in closet. Both agents squeeze around him to grab at clothes.

Andorf backs out and sits atop a waist-high mattress, kicking his sneaker heels on the underlying hay bales, grinning at the pair. “If someone else lived here, where are all their shoes?”

Exiting, Dinmont scans the bare bedroom walls. “We know you don’t live here alone, boy.” After searching the dresser drawers and finding disappointment instead of dainty lingerie, he heads for the bathroom, snarling at Andorf. In the closet, Pinscher relieves one of Serin’s blouses from its hanger.

Andorf smirks. “It’s a tight fit.”

Pinscher throws Andorf a disgusted look and directs him toward the bathroom in time to catch Dinmont poised and ready to grab the shower curtain.

“No!” Andorf yells. His fearful face morphs to a facetious grin. “That’s where I hide the Dead Kennedys.”

Again, Andorf finds a phasor pistol trained upon him. With Pinscher covering Andorf, Dinmont returns to the bathtub, weapon poised. He slides the curtain aside to an empty tub and sighs, nearly as loud as Andorf. Dinmont kicks angrily at the twenty-five gallon stainless steel drum under the sink stenciled ‘I.Y.D.’ The agents grab at everything not nailed down. Pinscher squirts shampoo bottles into the sink and tosses them onto the floor. Dinmont sniffs towels and rifles through the medicine cabinet.

Andorf finally understands what Brutus meant by Serin's zero-feminine footprint. He clears his throat loudly and snickers at the frustrated agents. "If a woman lived here, wouldn't you find makeup and eyeliner and war paint all over the place? How about lipstick or earrings or mascara-stained grout? And where's all the toilet rolls and those ..." Andorf pauses, glancing at Pinscher. "Sani-plugs?"

Dinmont cringes. Pinscher tosses an empty tooth cream bottle at him.

"And what about bras hanging everywhere? Have you guys found any of that stuff, huh?" Andorf steps into the living room to kick off his damp EasyGlides. He paces the living room, watching the agents destroy his bathroom. He lifts his bare foot to keep from landing on a mortar chunk at the base of the patriot poster and, eyeing the agents, discretely kicks the two-inch chunk under the couch, awakening Binky.

Andorf's skin suddenly gains goosebumps at the feeling of being watched. He turns and stares at the poster. Eyes drawn to the mysterious slits cut into the patriot's pupils. He steps closer and flinches at the pair of eyes on the other side, gazing back at him. Andorf glances at the frustrated agents and back at the poster, but this time no eyes greet him.

The agents charge into his kitchen. They begin stripping the pantry shelves. "Quit that," Andorf yells, running after them. "Enough is enough!"

Pincher turns to Andorf in snake-like reflexes. Andorf freezes in his tracks. Dinmont stuffs his head inside the cooler. "Hey, what kind of guy has no brew?"

"One who doesn't drink," Andorf says.

"And look at all this yogurt and legume spread and Serbian Pule cheese. You know how long it takes the labs, I mean farms, to grow this stuff? Why, this cheese alone ..."

Andorf's turns a horrid face aside. *Serin's fancy cheese.*

"Enough of the damn cheese, Dinmont. Get your butt in here. Show this stooge the evidence." Pinscher's eyes widen as if reading Andorf's thoughts. Hands out, she rushes him. Grabbing Andorf's neck, she drives his face into the face of the patriot poster. Andorf flinches at the blinking eyes, staring inches away. "Where the hell is Serin Grey?" Pinscher yells.

Darting from the kitchen, Dinmont steps on Binky's lifelike stuffed rat. The toy as it squeaks 'momma'. Dinmont reaches into his pocket and tosses a small plastic box at Andorf's feet. The cover flies off, spilling out handfuls of color-striped resistors, capacitors, and miniature black balls with silver fingers extending in all directions like an annual spider convention. "We found those in her office desk. Care to explain?"

Andorf shrugs his shoulders. "She makes jewelry. My birthday is—"

Dinmont grabs his cuffs and twists Andorf's arm behind his back. Pinscher squeezes Andorf's face with one hand and stares deep inside his bright blue eyes. "This Serin Gray, she engulfs you. I see it in your face."

Dinmont struggles to keep hold of Andorf's jerking wrist. "We know she has two husbands. That *was* what you told Detective Souder, wasn't it? Perhaps she stays with that other husband, gets it on with him right there on that couch in your absence. I'll bet she and that other guy are doing the nasty right now, at this very moment."

Pinscher's sinister eyes narrow on Andorf as she jabs her lips into his. Andorf feels her serpent tongue rubbing the insides of his cheeks. Shivering, he feels her licking away at his thoughts. Andorf struggles to pull away but finds her hands attached firmly around his cranium. He focuses on the evening's meetup with Holder and then cringes at Pinscher's forked tongue retracting between her pencil lips as she backs away. He cannot spit hard enough to extricate her foul, cold-blooded taste from his mouth.

Pinscher snorts, turning to Dinmont. "This one's not as innocent as he appears."

Dinmont grins. "Perhaps we'll have better luck with the other husband."

Feeling his head ready to explode, Andorf's eyes roll back as he forces himself into a trance. He probes Dinmont's mind and then Pinscher's. After a minute, he grins fiendishly at Pinscher. "I know your most dreaded fear, the thing that haunts both your dreams."

Both agents laugh. Dinmont tightens his grip on Andorf. "You can't scare us. We're the government."

Andorf growls at the agent's chuckles, head twisting about, trying to break free. He purses his lips and whistles 'here it,' as the neighborhood kids did back in the day to gather up the troops. He whistles long and hard.

"Hold still, boy," Dinmont yells, struggling with Andorf's hands. Pinscher manages to slap a cuff around one of Andorf's wrists, but Andorf flails his other hand away, determined to stay free. Then she pauses, staring cross-eyed at the floating white fur ball hopping past. "Oww," she screams, releasing Andorf to grab her bleeding leg "What the hell just bit me?"

"Ye-ow!" Dinmont yells, grabbing his own leg.

Andorf chuckles. "Two can play this game," he mumbles, recalling his last night with Gregory back at the Archives' and the pack of rats scurrying past. Reliving the fear of the large rat with iridescent red eyes homing in on Gregory's crotch, he focuses on Pinscher. With Pinscher twitching, he focuses on Dinmont, visualizing animations of Binky's toy rat. "Momma," he chants.

Dinmont's face pales. "We've been bitten by rats," he yells, leading Pinscher on a hop around the living room floor. "You have one serious rat infestation, boy."

Andorf grins at the dancing agents. "Did I mention that they carry all sorts of diseases, ones that make you really sick? Now Ruthy is a shriveled up prune, but she can still deliver a healthy bite. Now Kimmy over there ..."

Both agents turn ghastly white. “The bastard’s named his rats,” Pinscher yells.

“Like pets,” Dinmont yells back.

Andorf struts about the living room, arms out-stretched like a zombie. “And they have diseases you’ll never recover from. I once had a neighbor bitten by a rat.”

Dinmont freezes. His voice deepens. “What happened to *him*?”

“You didn’t hear? It was all over The Eye. There was nothing they could do. The poison spread for weeks. It was so painful that *she* took her own life. A hanging, I believe.”

With Andorf holding the front door open, Pinscher grabs her partner’s arms and drags him outside. “Did you see the size of those things? They were the size of cats.”

In the breezeway, Dinmont looks Pinscher over. “But we missed the kitchen drawers.”

Pinscher’s eyes widen. “Are you kidding me, Dandie? Look at my leg. You won’t catch me back in there—not with a dozen exterminators. Let Ginzbug deal with them. Oh my God! My leg’s gone numb. I can’t feel my toes.”

“Hold still,” Dinmont says. “Let me have a look.”

Pinscher gulps at the trails of blood leading back to Andorf’s front door. She reluctantly rolls up her slacks and shies away from the unmarked yellow vial Dinmont pulls from his pocket after he vigorously shakes it and pops the stained, plastic cap.

“What the hell’s that orange powder?”

He grabs Pinscher’s leg and holds the vial above her wound. “Hold still, it’s Magic Dust. I bought it from a fruit vendor at the shop. It’ll sting at first, so be ready.”

With Pinscher gritting her teeth, Dinmont sprinkles the powder onto her wound. She breathes hard and fast as her leg and face turn cherry red. She stumbles away, howling. “It burns like fire!”

"It's cleaning out the wound." Dinmont repeats the process on his own wound, uttering niceties Andorf had not heard since childhood. After several minutes, Dinmont breathes normal again.

"So who's the drug peddler?" Pinscher says. "Why haven't we busted him?"

"How can you nab a guy for selling fruit? And besides, the unlicensed pharmacist provides a valuable service."

Pinscher snarls. "You give me great confidence, Dandie. Why's my mouth taste like old socks?"

"One of many known side effects," Dinmont mumbles, dropping the vial into his pocket.

From his doorway, Andorf leers at the odd couple on the landing. "Ready for round two?" he whispers. Recalling a movie scene where political rats are roaming the streets in the District of Cecal, he focuses on Pinscher.

Pinscher squirms. She raises her head to see Andorf chuckling from behind his cracked door. "He's about to let them all loose," she screams, running down the front steps.

Dinmont hobbles after her, pausing mid-way down, inches shy of Pinscher's projected finger. "Not a word of this to anyone, Dandie. My last partner ended up taking a walk off our thirtieth floor roof."

As Andorf double locks the door, Binky hops around him in circles, flipping binkies high in the air. He races past the box of the electronic parts to stand at the cooler impatiently on his rear paws. Like many times before, Andorf opens the cooler, Binky nudges the crisper drawer open, grabs a carrot, and dashes under the sofa. This time Binky kicks a two-inch mortar chunk across the living room floor like a hockey puck.

Andorf picks up the piece and strolls closer to the patriot poster. He pokes his finger into the patriot poster's empty eyeholes. Examining the poster, he spots curling around the edges. With a few gentle tugs, the poster peels away, revealing a hollowed-out area large enough for someone to pass and a utility ladder leading down below. He imagines his Flemish neighbor. *Sven—*

CHAPTER 24
Serin Returns

Unpeeling from a delivery jumpsuit, Serin unrolls her long hair from beneath the matching cap. She discards her backpack and sees Binky hopping here and there, chinning things, and Brutus trailing behind. Brutus pauses long enough to smile. "The furry guy knows where the exterminators planted their bugs."

"Of course, silly," Serin says. "He watched the bastards plant the damn things."

"How'd the drop go at the Cos?"

"I left the package in some brush, beneath a canopy of the trees. I hope Greg—"

Brutus's eyes widen. "Trees? You mean real analog trees?"

Serin nods. "They were just as Andorf described from his dreams … so thick, they blocked the moonlight. It was easy to hide from the sky's snooping eyes."

"Speaking of Andorf, he's been creating waves with the authorities." Brutus parades her around, detailing Andorf's dealings with the detectives, the agents and his mind tricks with the café dinner line. "People allowed him to break line multiple times, but they wouldn't let me pass. And that day he visited the bi-party—"

"Don't remind me," Serin says.

"Yeah, but listen to this. He actually stopped lunchtime traffic on Dos Cacas Grande's so he could cross. It was like a parting of the tides. And look how he manhandled the detectives and had Binky attack those agents."

Serin's eyes flash back at the patriot poster. "I was wondering about the blood stains at the door."

"Binky also has the magic. Too bad they won't be around when—"

"Careful with Andorf," Serin says. "I've been sensing an apprehension about our living arrangements."

"As long as he sees us as a family unit he won't be a problem. It's your mind snapping that bothers me. I see the way you two converse without words. I get the feeling you won't need me, that one day you'll run off with *him*."

Serin pulls Brutus close, hugging him as she rolls her eyes. She playfully nibbles on his ear lobe. "You needn't worry, baby. Nothing's changed between you and I."

Pulse racing, Brutus jerks away. "Stop! You know how that turns me on."

"We're at a critical impasse. Keep Andorf your main concern."

"I have Malcom keeping tabs on him. My fellow gypsies are keeping busy. Launch is three days off and still you worry"

"I stopped by the office on my way here. My desk has been cleaned out and everyone's been replaced, even my boss. I can't tell if anyone's still intercepting the Empire's signals. I don't know who is left, whom to trust. And now you tell me nags and dicks have been snooping around. Of course, I'm worrying. Our domestic arrangements are on borrowed time. Oh yeah, what about Fat Max?"

Brutus grumbles. "Don't call him that. He's an honored man in the Canine Empire."

Serin's voice rises. "How can you respect such a slithering beast? Why, if I'm ever within spitting distance—"

Brutus shuffles his feet. "Everyone's running scared. Maximillian no longer speaks, but I'm sure if he suspects anything … my few remaining informants would have noticed."

"You'd better be right. My clan is also thinning. You never know who'll disappear next."

Binky scampers past with a small wire hanging from his mouth. On all fours, Serin pries his jaws open and extracts the wire while Brutus follows the debris trail to the remains of a chewed up spy device. Binky burrows himself under the sofa, staring back at them.

"A bug, or what's left of one," Brutus says.

"I hope they aren't toxic. Andorf would never forgive us."

"Ah, he's fine," Brutus says. "You see the way Andorf babies him. Most citizens don't eat as well as Binky. Hey, look at his ears. They're pointing straight up like antennas."

Serin leaps for the front window. Brutus joins her, pulling the curtain aside. Brutus salivates at the cute butt swaying back and forth outside. "It's our delivery gal. Small wonder she still comes around. She must need it badly."

Serin slugs him and storms off.

Brutus runs after her. "I meant her job. The detectives scooped her up thinking she was you." He gathers a clump of hay and tosses it into Binky's litter box under the kitchen table. Binky lifts his chin and darts across the living room, landing directly in the middle of the litter box.

Serin grins. "If I didn't know any better I'd say you're quite fond of that little rascal."

"Making sure he's got enough to eat, that's all. Hey, did you see him wink at me just now?"

"So, tell me more about Andorf and these agents."

"From what Andorf said, Binky did a real number on them, especially that Pinscher bitch. They tore the place apart looking for traces of you. Their search ended at the cooler with your—"

"Pule cheese." Serin's eyes widen. Her horrid face turns to Brutus. "Wait! Did you say Pinscher, as in Dinmont and Pinscher of the Dirty Dogs?"

Brutus nods. "Next come Sergeant Rudy Ginzbug and his militia. Four days, five max."

"We must expedite our plans."

*

The front door gently closes. Hiding black clothes, Andorf sneaks past Serin and Brutus. He returns from the bedroom, senses overwhelmed by the rare aroma of a home cooked meal. "You're back," he yells, racing into the kitchen. He lifts Serin off her feet with a bear hug, kissing her madly about her neck. Andorf plays with her hair as if reading Braille, pausing at Brutus's cutting glare. "Whatever it is, you sure smell good. I mean—"

Serin giggles. "I see you're hungry, but not for food. I should stay away more often." She unwraps herself from Andorf's claws. "Dessert comes later. Go sit down and eat."

Andorf loads a plate and plops down at the table. "I met the Swedish guy downstairs. I think he's been spying on us." He takes bites and speaks between chews. "The man moved into Gregory's unit say too quickly. He may be a government spy. We still have a week to find another place, don't we?"

Serin and Brutus exchanges quick glances. Brutus places a hand on Andorf's sagging shoulder. He winks at Serin. "Four days max. But don't worry, we're a family now. We'll pool our resources."

Rubbing her itchy belly, Serin kisses Andorf's cheek. "An expanding family."

Brutus eyes Andorf's crystallized potato. "Hey, you gonna eat that?"

Serin slaps Brutus's reaching hand. "You've already had your dinner, you big ox."

Brutus laughs. "That's what Andorf called me back in the day."

Andorf chokes on the sour memory. He cannot swallow fast enough to say his piece. "And I remember everyone's petrified faces when we would argue. They had no idea our fathers were best friends."

"I remember everyone calling you Poo."

"And you're still calling me that." Andorf flings a pea into Brutus's open mouth. And another. Brutus swallows both.

Serin breakings into laughter, Andorf flings a pea at her unprepared mouth. The guy's chuckling dwindles as they notice the twinkle in Serin's brown eyes. Sporting a devilish grin, Serin heads for the bedroom, coyly peering back over her shoulders. Andorf and Brutus watch her slowly peel the peasant blouse off her shoulders, in alternating shoulder swings before her index finger beckons them into the bedroom. Twirling her briefs, she laughs at her husbands, hopping after her, each with one leg hanging out of his pants. To the downstairs neighbor pounding on their ceiling, she wiggles out of her jeans and jumps into bed. "Time to learn more words in Svedish, boys."

CHAPTER 25
Dark Friday

Friday is the darkest night in Andorf's recent memory. The few people on the streets take notice as only someone with criminal intent would be dressed all in black, some sixty-three and a half hours before the starship launch. "Sheez, you'd think I'd killed someone," he mumbles at the citizens staring intensely.

Andorf takes the sharp left onto California, past the staggered office facades lining the corner. He shivers at the chorus of critters noisily rubbing out their nightly songs. Although he regrets running into Brett, he would gladly welcome his sharp tongue and childish pranks. He reminds himself repeatedly how Holder and his goons await at the end of the road. If early, he would appear anxious, late and ... he would rather not ponder the consequences.

The old salvage yard passes without notice, as does the marsh and the houses with their appearing and disappearing window silhouettes. Waist-high overgrowth scratches his arms on the approach to the last darkened housing unit. He cracks open the door, enters the pitch-black room, neck hairs rising at the dominance of busy voices. Having second thoughts, he reaches back at the doorknob, but Pinky's hefty hand clamps onto his shoulder. The grip tightens. How he hates Pinky's laugh.

Pinky ushers him through a series of hanging blankets and into a small area off the kitchen. In the semi-lit room, Andorf sees Holder hunched over a metal foldup card table, encircled by the remaining thugs and uncorked glass jugs at their feet, bubbling out caustic phosphate fumes. Past his burning nose and itchy, watering eyes, he sees modules, wires, and power cells heaped in piles amongst most likely stolen assemblies, scattered about the table. He recognizes many of the pieces from his childhood days in the junkyard, a few of which he actually held as a child in his grubby little hands.

Watching Pinky wedge into an empty seat, Andorf feels surrounded by interrogating faces, especially that souring face of the bulkiest man, whose scars run from every corner of his face, pulling together at his nose.

"What's *his* problem?" Andorf says, scanning the room for his missing friend, so as not to stare at the ugly man's face.

Pinky chuckles. "You mean Smiley over there? He claimed first crack at you if you didn't show. I'd say you royally pissed him off." Smiley snarls at Andorf and returns to his assembly.

Viewing his timepiece, Holder acknowledges Andorf with a nod. For a good while, Andorf watches shaky hands attach odd pieces in well-rehearsed movement.

Smiley drops his assembly, snarling at Andorf. "What the hell are you staring at, Mac?"

Andorf squints at the modules in everyone's hands. "Looks like six-stage timers and multiphase sequencers. Why, you guys are making b …" Andorf gulps. "Bombs."

The room quiets. Everyone's fingers go limp. Andorf spots ten bloodshot eyes staring at him and his naivety, knowing he crossed the line. *No fast moves. Must not trigger an itchy finger.*

Face hardening, Holder casts his chair aside. He presents Andorf with clenched fists, inches from his sweat-dripping face. Andorf gags at Holder's liquored breath and his mouthful of rotting brown teeth. Cackling like a hyena, the gang boss grins at his thugs. "Let's get rid of this stuff, boys, before it goes off." He passes a fiber box around the table and one by one, the thugs gently place their assemblies inside. The boys disappear with their bubbling jugs while Holder stashes the box beneath a false floor under the kitchen sink.

Clicking teeth, Holder wets his lips. "Seems your pal's running a bit late, Mac. But don't worry, we'll be catching up with him shortly, won't we boys?" He pours a round of black tequila for the bobbing heads, leaving Andorf dry. The thugs grab their jiggers and with gang boss chugging the bottle, they toss down their shots. Holder slams down the bottle and spits the worm onto Andorf's green, yellow, and grease-stained EasyGlides. He gazes at the anxious faces.

"Viva le Mac!" reverberates throughout the room, as four jiggers slam down hard on the table. Andorf takes a round of back slaps and flinches at Smiley's fist pounding.

"I'll get you," Smiley grunts, before joining his fellows, waiting at the front door.

"Follow us, Mac," Holder says, voice dry and hoarse. "We got urgent business."

Time accelerates as Holder hustles them outside. Andorf pauses on the porch, listening to shoes clomping loudly down the block steps and the gang laughing among themselves behind their dark shades.

"Whatcha waitin' on Mac?" Holder yells.

Only Pinky stands waiting on Andorf. "Come on, Mac. Last one out grabs the door."

Andorf reaches behind and closes the door. Pinky kindly shuffles him into the herd. Smiley falls back and nails the back of Andorf's head with his open palm. "Didn't your mama learn ya' about doors, Mac?"

Andorf turns and lurches at Smiley, going for his throat. Squeezing hard, Smiley gasps for air. At Holder's nod, Andorf releases his grip, leaving Smiley bringing up the rear, coughing. Spotting Smiley's finger jabbing Andorf's back, Pinky body-slams Smiley away from Andorf. Andorf keeps his distance, walking with Holder as the large men exchange words.

Holder leads the group across a silent street, between rows of dilapidated storage units. He stops in an unlit alley. With gang boss alongside Andorf, the thugs drop their sunglasses and grab hold of Andorf's shoulder. Holder turns to face Andorf.

"There's this detective who's been tailing us."

"Lurking in shadows," Pinky says.

Andorf gulps. "Watching."

"See. I told you he'd be good at this." Holder grins at his gang. "The dick is around the corner over there, sleeping it off. Ya' got one shot, Mac. Make it count."

Strong arms ferry Andorf around the corner. Eyes barely dilated, he makes out the outline of a lone man sitting atop a box. Holder pulls a white cloth from his front pocket and gently unfolds it, revealing a snub-nose .38. With gloved hands, he loads a single round into a chamber, spins it into place, screws on a crude silencer, and presents it to Andorf.

Andorf looks at the gang and grabs the ivory handle of the classic .38 in his shaking hand. He points it at the darkened figure some twenty feet beyond.

"What if I miss?" he whispers, turning back to the five pistols trained on his head.

Pinky chuckles. "Grandma Moses couldn't miss him from here."

Smiley jams his pistol into the back of Andorf's head. "Let me take him out, boss. I'm begging ya'."

Holder grins at Andorf. "If you don't do it now, Mac, it'll be *you* wearing the lead suit."

"Do it now," Pinky whispers.

Andorf points left of the figure. His index finger squeezes the trigger ever so slowly. The pistol jerks his unsteady hand. After the bullet ricochets off a brick building behind the victim, Holder pries the warm pistol from Andorf's trembling fingers and tosses it into the bushes behind them. "Didn't know you had it in you, Mac. It went clear through the bastard."

With everyone chuckling, Andorf stands in disbelief. Smiley snorts and then spits on Andorf before walking off. "Damn! I thought it'd be you swallowing lead."

A pair of arms drag Andorf closer, to examine the dead detective. Eyes dilated, Andorf fixates on the man, hooded with a black plastic bag over his head, arms tied behind his back. He finds something familiar about the dead man, leaning to the left like a Toxidian. Holder reaches from behind and lifts the bag away. Pinky whips out a worn-out flashlight. He taps it several times and hands the flashlight to Andorf.

"Take a close look," Holder says. "I've got a feeling you may know the guy."

Keeping pistols drawn on Andorf, the thugs back away, snickering. Andorf holds the flashlight with its fading glow to the victim's head. His face contorts in disbelief as he steps closer.

"Brett? I shot Brett?"

The gang walks off, leaving Andorf alone in his remorse. Smiley lags behind. He cocks his pistol and aims it at Andorf. "Ya' just gonna leave the dope here? If you want I could—"

"Leave him be. His prints are all over the gun." Holder head nods his gang to move on.

Andorf grabs Brett's shoulder as he falls to one side. "Brett … this is all a dream. Wake up!" Seeing a real-life dead person for the first time, Andorf touches Brett's cold, lifeless face. Andorf backs away from his childhood friend, stumbling over his own feet. "How can you be dead? I pointed the gun way over there. I—I swear I didn't do this."

Exiting the buildings' shadows, the gang members are aglow in light of large office windows. Pinky calls back to Andorf. "I wouldn't be hanging around, if I were you, Mac."

Andorf freezes at the dark sky lighting up in flashes and the two sharp pops echoing off the surrounding walls. He sees another flash, hears three additional echoes. He runs toward the street as far as the building's shadow allows. Clinging to the storage building's edge, he gazes at Holder and his thugs lying on the asphalt, breathing in the unmistakable smell of spent gunpowder. He hears Holder's hoarse voice.

"I'll get you Mac, you and your little bunny."

Holder's cackling laugh fades into the dark. From the corner of his eye, Andorf spots a thin man in a dark trench coat. The man withdraws deep into the shadows and disappears around the far corner of the building.

Haunted by the man's Cheshire smile, he leans hard against the building, heart clawing at his throat, straining to catch his breath. He peers again at the five bodies and then back at Brett. *Brett! My God, why Brett? What have I done?*

Andorf's brain cranks into overdrive. He begins to step toward Brett but stops himself. He looks around and then, in the blink of an eye, beats a path away from the double crime scenes, doing his best to keep within shadows. He runs toward Speedway, takes the first left, down an unmarked road. Andorf stops to catch his breath under the shell of a cannibalized street lamp, gathering his bearings. He sees a lone silhouette leering out a window across the street, watching. *How dare this guy judge me? He knows nothing about me.* A porchlight appears, illuminating the corner street sign. *Oh, it is Noah's Way.*

The sounds of Speedway grab Andorf's attention. He takes off jogging for the flickering traffic lights ahead, planning his escape. He reaches deep inside his pocket and finds a large coin. *I'll hop a public bus, pay cash. There will be no optical scan records. I'll be gone before the cops and media arrive. I'll be home, fast asleep, before it hits 11:00 p.m. news.*

*

10:00 p.m. and Speedway is another sleepy drag running outward from near center of town like a motorbike spoke. Andorf hides from occasional blinding headlights whizzing past, finding refuge behind untrimmed shrubbery. He suddenly finds himself bathed in shades of green as strobing yellow and blue lights of police turbo-cruisers scream past. Whipping around the corner on two wheels, the 700-horsepower electro-turbos rev, speeding down Broad Street toward the crime scene.

Andorf spots approaching oblong headlights and jumps into the street, waving his arms. The public bus barrels towards him.. He leaps out of the way, cursing like mad, and the bus whizzes past, without stopping. Then the bus's airbrakes squeal. Running down the street, he smells the carbon trace of frictionless brakes. The double bus doors fly open and the front ramp uncoils outward invitingly like a dog's tongue. Andorf darts up the ramp, flashing a shiny ten piece between his fingers, but freezes at the driver's outstretched palms.

The driver points at the 'No Cash After Dark' sign taped above the optical scanner. Eyeing Andorf for a moment, he grabs the coin, drops it in his shirt pocket, and throws his head back for Andorf to take a seat.

Curling his nose at the foul air, Andorf takes a seat three rows behind the driver. He catches the driver's eyes in the rear-view mirror sharing time between him and the road as the empty bus zooms off. The driver laughs heartily, like someone leaving work for the day.

"Your lucky day, kid. I'm heading for the garage."

"But you stopped. The door opened."

The driver's stomach emits loud intestinal gurgling noises. "Broke wind, that's all. We get fined if the bus don't smell minty fresh."

Andorf grins at the driver's collection of dangling air fresheners. The steady purring of the bus's electro-drives and gentle swaying rocks him to sleep. His drooping head leans against the seat in front. He awakens to an imagined poke in his ribs and cups his eyes against the window in time to see the Corner Café line zooming past. He tugs on the pull rope to no avail. The bus suddenly jerks to a stop. Andorf grabs hold of the hand indentations and exits down the bus ramp, listening to the driver cursing out someone he nearly hit. Feet barely planted on firm ground, a familiar voice call out.

"I'm glad you woke up this time. You're ten minutes late."

Andorf grimaces at the old man. "Chester? How'd you know where I live? Where are you doing here at this late hour?"

"Well, I couldn't leave without saying goodbye." Chester grins, wheezing. "I see my ride coming. Got a date with a young blonde. But worry you not, Andorf. I'll see you in another sixty ..." He takes a breath from his disposable oxygen assist. "Oh yes, I almost forgot. When your wife asks you how many more times, you tell her this ... until you won't lose her."

Andorf looks aside, but only Chester's discarded oxygen module remains. Seeing flashing blue and yellow lights in the distance, he runs across the barren end of Speedway. Within seconds, strobing green light bathes his condominium courtyard. He turns and sees officers at their electro-turbo speeders arresting some unfortunate old man across the street. Turning back toward his condo, Andorf finds each step a progressive challenge. He feels dizzy, faint. Everything goes black.

CHAPTER 26

Behind Andorf's Back

Serin nudges Brutus. "I see Poo never made it home. I wonder what trouble he's gotten in now."

Brutus groans. "I hate living this charade. I can't wait until—"

"Patience, sweetie. You think I like living like a sardine? Until now, he's provided a good front. Who'd ever suspect our innocent Andorf?"

Brutus scowls at the eyes winking at him from beneath the sofa. "I'd swear that rabbit knows what we're saying. Have you seen him and Andorf playing? And the way Binky attacked those agents on Andorf's command. It's as if they're mind-linked. I wouldn't be surprised if it's Binky who rats us out."

"I'm more worried about Andorf's recent shenanigans."

"He's been roaming around that pretty head of yours, hasn't he?"

"No, not lately. I've been careful."

Brutus rubs her growing belly. "I remember last time you said that."

Snarling, Serin yanks his hand from her mid-section. "Andorf *has not* been reading my thoughts. Don't you think I'd know?"

Brutus smirks. "It's time we cut him loose."

"Make it look like—"

At a scuffling outside, the pair dash for the front curtains, each pulling back a corner to view lights flashing below. Brutus mumbles. "An accident, second this week."

Serin steps away, leaving him gawking at the cuties gathering outside. "Brutus! Are you listening to me?"

He drops the curtain. "No one will suspect a thing. They guy won't know what hit him."

"Remember, no witnesses."

"I cannot risk being seen with Andorf but I've got my best guy on him. If he gets any more out of control, Malcomb will reel him in."

"So, who's this Malcomb? Is he any good?"

Brutus grins. "Are you kidding me? There's no one better. He's tall, thin, and always wears a dark overcoat. He's known as The Shadow."

"I sense Andorf's increased paranoia. He hides it well but I know it must be driving him crazy."

"Until things change, we'll stick with plan A." Brutus snickers. "I can't wait to have you all to myself again."

Serin bats her eyes at Brutus. "Your jealousy turns me on, big guy. How about one last time in Andorf's place?"

Brutus scoops her in his massive arms, but trips enroute to the bedroom, sending them tumbling onto the floor, locked in a steamy embrace. Serin squawks at each button Brutus pops from her blouse as they thrash about the floor. Serin manages to unsnap her jeans before they too fall victim to Brutus's clumsy hands. Both kick feet, wiggling from their pants. Andorf's table ceramic lamp crashes to the floor, shattering in countless pieces.

Serin's head periscopes to survey the damage. Squinting at the kitchen clock's red glare, she unpeels from Brutus' arms. She gives him a quick kiss, staggers to her feet, and pulls up her jeans, dashing for the bedroom. "I'm so late, big guy."

Brutus reaches for her from the floor. "But, baby ..."

Serin slips on work shoes. Tucking her hair under the matching cap, she runs out the back door, blowing Brutus a kiss.

"Always to be continued," Brutus says, jumping to his feet. He sweeps up broken lamp shards and discards them in the garbage bin, but not before slicing his feet. He wipes his bleeding feet with Serin's blouse and tosses it in the garbage. After roughing his hair, he runs outside, chasing after Serin.

*

Andorf awakens in a fetal position beneath his steps. Glaring at late morning sun and accumulated trash, he wonders how he ended up beneath the 'Rent Me' sign. Shaking off bugs and debris, he staggers up the steps, destined for a long hot shower.

He pulls open the kitchen cooler while towel-drying his hair, and gawks at the yogurt, legume spread and Pule cheese. Speckles embedded in the cheese merge into Katakana characters and then an eight-foot snail with sunken eyes. "What's that girl trying to tell me?" he mumbles, staring at the grim cooler selection.

In the next room, The Eye regurgitates its daily rhetoric. Today's fabrication centers around an interview with a chunky middle-aged man in an all too familiar crime scene, pictured above the scrolling countdown to Starship Atlantis's launch, fifty-one hours away. Andorf steps closer to watch.

"And there we were walking along, minding our business when ..."

The overly zealous reporter extends the microphone. "Last night? 10 p.m.?"

"That's what I said. We were just walking along." The man points at the chalk outline on the sidewalk across the way. "Over there, with my wife when ..."

"Go ahead, sir. Tell us what you saw."

The man shakes dramatically. As if on cue, he leans into the camera, dropping a hand over his heart. "Those five thugs came from nowhere. I thought we were goners. That's when that Brad fella jumped in front to protect us."

Andorf shakes a fist, yelling at the government issued Eye. "Where do they find such actors?"

A robust woman wrestles her way into the interview. Snatching the reporter's microphone, she bounces her husband aside and smiles glamorously into the camera. "Harold would not be here today if it were not for that brave young man. He took the bullet meant for my husband." With sprayed-on tears, she gazes directly at the camera. "We'd both be goners if it wasn't for that Bert guy."

Andorf chuckles over his friend's mispronounced name. "Oh, she *is* good. A tad over dramatic, but—"

The reporter pries his microphone from the woman and points it at her husband's flagging hands. "The cops dropped those sons of bitches," Harold says, snapping his fingers. "Just like that."

The camera pans back to the reporter pulling back a corner of the bloodstained tarp, revealing five corpses piled like mackerels beginning with Pinky on bottom to Holder on top. All grins, the reporter kneels to stay inside the picture. "That's right, folks. The right-wing political gang, a.k.a. the Bogus Boat People, is no more. All members, shot dead last night in what appears to be a botched armed robbery. As these witnesses report, Brad Conners, an innocent bystander, was fatally wounded protecting this husband and wife."

The wife's touching testimonial replays to a background of violins. "He took the bullet meant for my husband."

Pressing an earpiece, the reporter smiles at the camera. "Just in. Bo Conrad, a visiting executive producer from our headquarters in Atlanta, gunned down in cold blood last night by the Bogus Boat Gang. I'm Jorge Anderman of the Twisted News Network. Now back to our regularly scheduled infomercial, already in progress."

"Executive, my ass." Andorf yells at The Eye. He pans the living room, looking for something to toss. "Wait! Where's my table lamp? Why's the sofa way over there?"

He winces at black spot on The Eye's black spot green bulb following him about the room. Face paling, he turns his away. *Holder was wearing gloves. He set me up. Only* my *prints were on that gun. The cops must have it by now.*

Andorf mindlessly tosses a handful of pellets into Binky's overflowing dish. He grabs the chunk of moldy cheese and opens the trash lid. "What's this?" he says, extracting Serin's blouse. Examining the fresh bloodstains, he envisions agents and detectives. The blouse falls from his hands. "Serin—they've killed her," he screams. "I'll run up Jake's Mountain, tell Brutus and ... Wait! What if it was Brutus?"

Andorf's pulse runs rampant as his thoughts. He runs outside, down the front steps in a panic. He dashes across the street to the tune of squealing tires and swerving traffic. *I never trusted Brutus. The way he criticized Serin during the wedding dinner, him planting those bugs in my condo, he's always scheming behind someone's back. Now Brett, he had no family, no one at home depending upon him. I feel bad, but it was either him or me. He would have done the same in my place. Right? Yes, of course he would.*

Andorf's confidence builds. He approaches the Corner Café with the feeling of being tailed. He squeezes through the static crowd waiting outside, jogs up the steps, and takes the last vacant stool at the far end of the counter only to wait and wait, peering over his shoulder. Only after he uprights his coffee cup does a waitress blaze past at whiplashing speed, filling his cup on the fly.

A scan of the room finds everyone fixated on their partially obstructed views of The Eye. Andorf stirs three creamer sticks in the cup in figure-eight patterns and watches them dissolve. He leans forward and fixates on the buxom young lady on The Eye, stretching out of her trikini as she points out a massive overhead cylinder. "How about a ride?" she asks in a sweet, succulent voice, exposing even more skin. She slinks into one of the sleek travel pods, suggestively whisking her hands to one side.

"The vacuum pod sucks you along with such rapid speed, it's like arriving even before you've left," she says stretching the fourth word while smiling between puffy blushed cheeks. "Enjoy the executive way to travel. Come groove The Tube." The pod briskly speeds her through a translucent cylinder, leaving only her innocent giggle behind.

Parked in front of Andorf with a half-full carafe, a plump waitress fixates on The Eye, hips gyrating, hands rhythmically massaging his warm cup. "Those spinning gizmos make me hotter than—"

Andorf pries the waitress's sweaty hands free, extracting her from the trance. She shakes dandruff from her bunned hair, pulls a cloth napkin from her back pocket, and wipes Andorf's drooling lips.

"Why that poor girl. She can't afford any decent clothes so she rides that thing all day in her underwear. We've got a running bet how many more times she can afford to ride that thing."

Andorf winces at the waitress. "But she's only a model on some infomercial."

The waitress wipes again at Andorf's drooling lips. Beneath thick layers of face caulk, her tongue clicks at Andorf. "I don't care what you call her, sugar, it just ain't right." Without dropping her eyes, she spills another splash in his cup and shuffles off to annoy another customer as chatter resumes and diners return to their meals.

Andorf stirs three more creamer sticks in his drink and grizzles at the image of a bearded man behind octagonal glasses fading into his drink. Pondering about Serin, Brutus, and the whereabouts of their dwindling belongings, he futilely wipes at the server's greasy paw prints. He raises the cup to his lips but pauses at The Eye's tail-end coverage of last night's murders.

The frazzled reporter authentically chokes up. "Gang violence took one of our own last night. Our beloved Bryan O'Cannon leaves behind a wife and three young children. A trust fund has been—"

Andorf drops his cup on the counter. "Get his name straight you bastard. It's Brett Conyers!" He lowers his voice, grimacing at the curious faces. "I went to school with the guy," he mumbles.

The waitress swipes a hand, lowering The Eye's volume to but a whisper. She lifts Andorf's cup to wipe up his spill and cozy up to her latest source of gossip. "That's all you're going to hear about for the next week, sweetie. Say, did you really know that Bryan guy? I knew there was more to you than those stinky stained sneakers of yours. So what'll ya' have, sweetie?"

She tops off Andorf's drink and stares into his deep blues, painted nails tapping staccato on the counter. Feeling her beady eyes undressing him, Andorf points at the nearest placard and its daily specials. "Can I get this with three eggs over sleazy and buttered saffron toast on the side?"

Andorf blinks and his warm meal appears in front of him. He shovels in breakfast, mind drifting to the latest victim of the media's advancing the story. He chews on Brett's description of what he called 'creative journalism'. Taking last bites, he feels another's presence, staring at him from behind. Glancing around, he spots a tall thin man in a dark trench coat at the nearest booth, eyes slipping below a newsprint.

Clear as day, Andorf hears the stranger's snippy accusations about what went down last night. His heart skips. Trembling hands tightening around the coffee cup, he imagines using it as a viable weapon. His thoughts clarify. *The man from the break room ... he was at the murder scene. He shot Holder and the others. He's the one who's been tailing me.*

Andorf spins about to see only a crinkled newsprint spread across the next table. He flags his waitress. "Who sat at that table, over there, behind me?"

"Only you in here, sugar," she says, collecting the discarded newsprint without concern. She lifts an arm and gazes at her timepiece. "We're slow now, but just you wait. The lunch line is gathering outside. In ten minutes, we'll be jam packed until closing. Say, are you okay, sugar? You're looking a tad granular."

Scratching his head, Andorf pans the empty room. "Fine, just fine. How long have I been here?"

"Long enough to throw down a few veggie squares, toast and eggs. Now I've seen slow eaters and honey, you ain't one of em'."

Andorf empties the last of his last coin on the counter. In the counter mirror, he spots a foggy shadow of a man in a black trench coat slithering past. Flying after the stranger, Andorf leaves his stool spinning. Cupping eyes, he looks both directions. He runs to Speedway and then to the corner facing California Street without luck. *That trench-coated man … how could he slip past like that?*

CHAPTER 27
Who the Hell is Mac?

Andorf takes a slap on his cheek. "Forget what I said in the marsh," he cries out, turning his cheek. "I didn't mean to do it, I swear."

"Wake up, Andorf," barks a deep baritone voice.

"Get up, you bum. I'm hungry," a softer inviting voice says.

Heart racing, Andorf cracks swollen eyes. "Serin, you're alive! I thought—"

Brutus laughs. "Where ya' been, Mac?"

"Yeah, where ya' been, Mac?" Serin says, mocking Brutus's deep voice.

Brutus helps Andorf sit up on the bed. "Am I supposed to be this Pinky or the Smiley character?"

Serin grabs Andorf's shoulder. "Where were you last night? There was another gang related shooting. It's all over The Eye. Where were you last night?"

"I ran into an old friend, lost track of time." Andorf rubs sleepy eyes at the suspicious pair.

The mattress sags at Brutus's shifting weight. "Remember your pal from grade school? Donner? Conner?"

Andorf fakes a yawn. "Conyers."

Brutus nods. "Yeah, that's him. Conyers, Brett Conyers. He was gunned down last night by that right-wing faction, the Bogus Boat People."

Serin's mouth sours. "First the left-wing radicals destroy all the historical sites and now this. I wish the left and right extremists would just go ahead and kill each other off."

"And castrate those behind the Eminent Domicile scam," Andorf yells. "How could five suckers in the Extreme Court legalized theft without anyone lifting a finger to stop them? Why do we elect such imbeciles?"

Serin sits beside Brutus. "Keep talking like that, Andorf and they'll lock you away. Look what happened to my brother. All he did was, as you said, borrow a book." Serin pulls at Andorf's shirt. "And what's with the black clothes?" She lowers her voice a couple octaves. "Been to a funeral, Mac?"

"Quit calling me that. I'm taking a shower to wash off today." Andorf staggers off to the bathroom. Not bothering to close the door, he waits inside the bathroom, listening to Serin and Brutus cleaning up the remaining evidence of their brief morning escapade.

"I can't believe the lump didn't even notice," Brutus says.

"Don't forget to tell him about—"

Andorf returns wearing an oversized towel wrapped around his waist. He reaches down at a ceramic fragment. Holding the sliver between his thumb and index finger, he shoves it in Brutus's face. "Know anything about this? Someone broke my table lamp. They even moved my sofa. See these floor indents?" Brutus turns but Andorf snaps his head around to squint in Brutus's face.

Brutus gulps. "Hmm. Usually the exterminators are more careful." He takes the sliver from Andorf's hand and stares cross-eyed at it in the overhead light before handing it back. He then runs his hands around the sofa cushions and produces a bug. After waving it in Andorf's face, Brutus throws an index finger over his lips, dashes into the bathroom, and flushes, while covertly dropping the decoy in his pocket.

Andorf looks confused. "Hey, didn't you—"

Serin emerges from the bedroom, spinning around in her new sports shoes. She frowns at Andorf, still wrapped in his towel. "Are we going out?"

Andorf turns, returning a rude hand gesture. Serin peels off his towel and … *SNAP!* She nails Andorf with a direct strike on his butt cheek with the towel. "Ouch!" he yells, running for the bathroom, sporting a bright red mark.

"Are you forgetting I had a brother?" Serin yells. "Hurry up I'm starving."

Andorf reappears wearing only pants. "You've found Gregory? Is he at the—"

"I told you to leave that up to me, but for now …" Serin glances at Brutus and then back at Andorf. "We've found a much larger place."

Brutus's eyes widen. "One with a much better view."

Andorf spots Binky's kitchen litter box overflowing with hay. He calls for his best friend but no one comes to greet him. He scours every inch of the condo, looking in favorite hiding spots, calling out for his furry pal.

"Here we go," Brutus mumbles.

Serin's eyes narrow at Brutus. "You didn't tell him? I changed shoes so you could—"

Brutus rolls his eyes. "He'd figure it out, sooner or later."

"Coward!"

"The exterminators let him out!" Andorf yells, running out the front door. His shouts echo between the condominiums. "Binkers? Anyone seen Binkers?"

At Andorf running up the front steps, Brutus calls out the back door. "Binkers? Binkers? Where are you, buddy?"

Andorf returns, tears streaming down his cherry red face. "Last time he was hiding in the bushes alongside the steps, scared to death something would eat him. He's not out there. He's nowhere!"

Brutus eyes Andorf. "Bastards!"

Serin comforts Andorf with a warm embrace. "I'm sure a neighbor took him in."

"That's right, Poo," Brutus says. "They just don't know where he belongs."

Serin smiles awkwardly. "We'll ask around in the morning, won't we Brutus?" Brutus nods.

Feeling abandoned, Andorf pulls his hands off his face, revealing a lost little boy. He stares at Sara and then Brutus. "Binkers can't be gone. He's my best friend. We moved here together, six years ago. We can't move now. He'd be left behind."

Brutus stares off in defiance. "It'll be okay, Poo. As Serin says, we'll find him."

Serin cradles Andorf's head. She gazes deep inside his liquid blue eyes. "Remember how funny our neighbors acted when Greg disappeared? People do funny things when they don't know what to do."

Brutus chuckles. "Like voting bi-party out of fear."

"But we've got to find him," Andorf cries. "Tell me he's not gone!"

Rifling through her backpack, Serin slips on Crylex gloves. She takes her time massaging a thick tan cream into Andorf's bare shoulders. "Things will be different in the morning. I promise."

Andorf's eyes roll to one side. Brutus catches him as he collapses against Serin. Carefully avoiding his shoulders, he lays Andorf gently across the mattress. Rubbing both hands together, Brutus frowns at Serin. "You shouldn't even be here, Serin. Ginzbug and his militia could bust through that door at any moment. You know this better than anyone. We're at Defcon One."

"If I hadn't come back, Andorf would never have forgiven me."

"What's Defcon One?" Andorf struggles to lift his head before passing out.

Brutus reads the fine print on tan cream rub. “Hey, this stuff can trigger severe hallucinations. It says here ...”

“Nothing Poo can’t handle.” Serin smiles at Andorf. “Sweet dreams, lover.”

PART 4: GENESIS

CHAPTER 28

November 23rd

Andorf awakens to the feel of cold vinyl floor flooring. Not quite himself, he staggers for the dresser, foggy eyes glancing about the sparse bedroom. He pulls each drawer open and finds them empty. In the closet, no clothes. Rubbing his sore shoulders, he stumbles into the kitchen, where every cabinet, cupboard, and pantry shelf has been stripped of contents. Even his junk drawer lies in the middle of the floor, empty.

"My family silverware!" he yells, yanking open each drawer in the dining cabinet. My family heritage … gone!" He collapses on the living room sofa, peering up at the gaping holes in his living room ceiling where his holograph projectors once hid. "Of course the S.O.B.s grabbed those."

With a burst of energy, he stumbles back to the bedroom, kicking at hay scraps on the floor in place of the bales upon which the missing mattresses sat. Grabbing hold of his spinning head, he spots his finest clothes, neatly folded atop his washed EasyGlides on the dresser. *All the signs were there. Serin not decorating … Brutus never unpacking … why didn't I listen?*

Andorf dresses. He runs outside, freezes at the top steps. *Wait! It could not have been them. They would not have taken* my *stuff.* He runs inside, punches a sequence of numbers on the comm-box, and hears the dreaded monotone voice enunciating foreign language choices. After two infomercials sandwiching an up-to-the-minute launch countdown, an elderly woman answers.

"Crimes division, this is Muriel. How may I help you?"

"A theft! I need to report a theft."

The woman laughs. "Theft is no longer a crime. Perhaps you've only misplaced—"

Frustrated by her tone, Andorf taps on the wall, trying to maintain composure. "You don't understand, lady," he yells. "Everything—everything is gone. They've cleaned us out."

"Us?" the detached voice asks.

"I live with two others. Their stuff is gone too." Andorf pants. "When are you sending an agent or at least some derelict detective?"

"We're short-staffed this week, sir. What, with the noon launch, twenty-four hours from now—"

"Why is it when I don't need them, agents are swarming like angry yellow jackets? My taxes are paying their fat …" He hears a lull in her voice. "What is it you're holding back? What aren't you telling me? Wait! That muffled voice, who's that guy telling you what to say?"

"Sir, if you feel it necessary, you can drop by the criminal investigations office. Fill out a missing property report, if you'd like. We're open until five." *Click!*

Andorf takes a last look around at the heavy furniture and dashes out the door, leaving it wide open. "I'll show them what they can do with their missing property report," he yells, flying down the back steps. On the last step, he trips and lands, bad knee on the breezeway floor. He gazes back at the man sprawled out, lying face down across the bottom step, appearing deader than a politician's promise.

"Sven! Who would do this to you?" Andorf crawls closer. He places two fingers across Sven's neck. With his own heart pounding so hard, he cannot find a pulse. Andorf stumbles through the grassy rear courtyard, shielding his face from the blazing noonday sun. His eyes pan the many silhouettes accumulating at open doors and windows in the surrounding condos.

"Who saw this happen?" he yells. "This old man was once afraid like you. He deserves more than this." Catching his breath, he scans the neighboring stranger's eyes blinking from behind the safety of their windows and cracked screen doors. "Next time it'll be one of you. You know that, don't you? You *all* know that."

Dropping his head, Andorf steps over Sven and limps up the steps, pulling himself by the handrails. He lifts the comm-box's hand piece to repeat the report process. After two infomercials, that same detached voice regretfully appears on the line.

"Crimes division, this is Muriel. How may I help you?"

"My neighbor … he's been murdered."

"Are you the one who performed this unkind deed?" Muriel asks, voice peppered in sarcasm. "Sir? Sir? Are you there?"

About to explode, Andorf throws a palm against his throbbing forehead. "Look lady, he was lying face down at the bottom of my staircase. I tripped over him when—"

"So you knocked Sven out?"

"No! No! You don't understand. The man was dead when I found him. I checked his pulse and—Wait! How do you know his name? I didn't—"

"We know everything about the Dakota Condominiums, including you, Andorf Johnson of unit 201, from your bushy brown hair to your freshly washed EasyGlides."

Keeping one hand on the connection, Andorf pounds the wall. "Didn't you hear what I said? The man is dead."

"Oh my, did you say dead? Where is the body now?"

"I told you, lady, at the bottom of my steps." Andorf raises a fist, ready to pound the comm-box. "Is all this really necessary? Can't you just—"

"Following protocol, sir. Now, if you'll come down and fill out a …"

Andorf trembles. His face flushes with heat. "Damaged property report? We're talking about a real person here, an old man, my friend."

"You're either reading my thoughts or you've done this before. You must know anything that generates taxes is property of the Empire. Your friend was—?"

"Paying taxes? I guess. He was buying things."

"I didn't say that, sir. But yes, paying taxes. If so, he is government property. Is the body still there?"

Andorf darts out the back door, leaving the hand piece dangling. He walks the length of the breezeway, leaning over the railing, finding no sign of his dead neighbor. He jogs down the steps, through the Sven's open screen door, and inside his dark kitchen. Hearing sounds of an intruder, he grabs a portable hydrator as an easy weapon. Taking deliberate steps, he eases around the corner. He hardens his grip on the hydrator, ready to pounce.

A voice moans from inside. "Who's Der?"

Lowering his weapon, Andorf sighs at Sven's voice. "It's me, Andorf."

"Der's no Andorf here. Whatever you're selling ..."

"No, Sven. Andorf, your upstairs neighbor."

A commode flushes and Sven staggers out, touch drying his dripping face with a small hand towel. He squints at Andorf. "Excuse me you must, Andy. I not see visitors dis time of day."

"Why it's well after noon, Sven. I saw you lying on the steps and—"

Sven grasps his ears with both hands. "Loud not, Andy. My head ... she pounds ... as if someone hit me with da brick. I like you to stand in one place der, not move around fast like dat."

"But I'm standing still. You look terrible. What happened? Who assaulted you?"

Sven rubs his head, feeling every square inch. "No bumps up der, Andy. I know not what happened. Last ding I remember I was ..." Sven leans to one side and then dashes off. Unpleasant sounds spill out the bathroom, followed by a long flush.

Andorf collects the dead liquor bottles scattered about the dark living room. Sven reappears, touch drying his flushed face on a hand towel.

"I like you checking on me dis way, Andy, but okay I am. Need you not worry about me, my friend. I must have hit da bottle a wee too much. Funny ting doe. I not remember drinking last night." Sven flips on a dim table lamp. Shading his eyes, he looks the room over. "See? Ders no glasses. I not drink from da bottle, you know. Dat would not be right. No."

Andorf touches Sven's shoulder. "My pet rabbit of six years has gone missing. You may have seen him. Binky is white with—"

"People are hungry, my friend. They eat other people's pets when dey get loose."

Andorf takes a deep breath. Speaking calmly and deliberately, he explains first how Binky disappeared and then how he awoke and found all his possessions stolen, including his bed. "Only The Eye and larger furniture remains. They even swiped Binky's hay, five bales."

"Oh Andy no! Dey cannot get away wit dis."

"Did you hear anything, see anyone, Sven? I suspect it occurred last night." Andorf rubs his sore shoulders. "I slept hard, like I was drugged."

"I remember someone. Dey were kicking me in da head."

"Oh, that must have been me, Sven. You see I was—"

Sven staggers back a step. "But why, Andy? I thought dat we were friends."

"I didn't see you lying across the steps. After I tripped on you, I thought you were dead."

Sven grabs his ears. "Stop dat yelling, Andy. Oh, dis terrible headache I got. I only wish I were dead."

"I stood in the courtyard, called for help, but our worthless neighbors wouldn't answer. I saw the bastards hiding, watching me from their—"

Sven waves a pointed finger at Andorf. "Speak not of dem like dat, Andy. Before, strangers we were. Like dem I was, before we became friends. Speak you not dat way, Andy. For all you know, dey too come from de old country."

Andorf pats his friend's shoulder. "Go take care of yourself, Sven. I've got business downtown after I search for Binky."

Sven grins as much as his pained face allows. "You be careful out der, Andy. I have feeling you not be back. I not see you no more."

Andorf grins at Sven but finds himself alone. With ill sounds emanating from the bathroom, he lets himself out the screen door. "I've got the same feeling, my friend."

CHAPTER 29

Can't Slow Down

Speedway, the longest straight road through town, begins at City Hall. It widens and narrows multiple times before disappearing through the perimeter wall outside of town. Unknown to most citizens, Speedway continues as a barely paved, two-lane service road through the restricted area, terminating at the TSP fueling depot. Even fewer know of the hidden dirt-road turnoff outside the perimeter, a stone's throw from the road's final bend.

A white panel van eases off the pavement onto the desolate dirt road, slowing to circumnavigate large potholes and the occasional malformed creature crawling from the lagoon. The lone driver stops to assist a young woman, stumbling in a tall patch of weeds along the roadside. The moment he hops from the driver's door, two men appear from nowhere. He takes wild swings at both men but his head is bagged from behind by the young woman. Strong arms toss him through the van's rear doors, gagged, hands and feet tied. The van then zooms off down the virtually unknown dirt road.

The dash-mounted two-way breaks squelch long enough to warn of suspicious activity. The hostage leans against a sidewall, working his bindings, cursing himself for stopping.

The woman pulls the burlap sack off the captive's head. She tightens the rag stuffed between her captive's lips. "What's that? Not tight enough you say?"

The captive gnaws at the rag in his mouth, struggling to speak.

"Serin Gray? Yep, that's me. Make yourself comfortable. I've got work to do."

The captive's eyes enlarge, watching Serin releases her long blonde hair from her cap and immodestly change into a darker shirt, flashing him a side view of her breasts. She sits on the van's wheel well, peering out the filthy, rear window, feet propped atop the captive. She attaches a hand-drawn map to a penlight-lit clipboard and grabs hold of the spare tire as the van swerves. The hostage rolls around the floor groaning. Serin calls through the open sliding window behind the front seats. "I hear the Empire dumps all sorts of toxic waste along this road, Riley."

The divider window behind the front seats slides further open. A pimple-faced young man, resembling a teen-aged kid, pokes his head through the small opening. At Serin's wink, Riley speaks in an eerie voice. "There have been recent sightings of mutated creatures crawling from the lagoon out there."

From the driver's seat, Riley's big brother, Francis, chuckles. "Can you imagine what would happen if the monsters broke through the perimeter wall, how many citizens they'd devour?"

Serin kicks at the captive's shoes. "Quit squirming or we'll toss you outside."

The captive quiets, settling his back against the opposite wheel well and suddenly accepting security beneath Serin's feet. Serin finds it impossible to scribble on the maps as the van encounters a series of hard bumps. She yells out to the driver.

"Must you hit every blasted pothole, Francis? Are you trying to kill us back here?"

The captive groans in agreement.

Francis backs off the pedal. The van begins to slow.

"Hey! What are you doing?" Serin yells. "We've got a tight schedule. You can't slow down." With the van speeding off, Serin leans back to rehash scenarios, replay the many well-rehearsed dry runs in her head as the van swerves to avoid another rut. "What have I missed? What am I forgetting?" she mumbles, wondering how many of her co-conspirators remain, how many are actually trailing behind.

CHAPTER 30
Now You Tell Me

Andorf forfeits two thirds of his seat on the public bus to a rotund, middle-aged man. Above the man's snoring, he hears everyone's thoughts. One passenger complains of a sloppy brother eating her out of house and home, while another thinks about how he and his husband rarely agree on much other than their distaste for Max and the belligerent Canine Empire. Andorf wonders how he can suddenly hear everyone's thoughts, first the woman on the comm-box and now everyday citizens sitting around him.

The bus finally rolls to a stop at the government complex. The driver flashes envious looks at Andorf's swift exit. With afternoon warmth reflecting off the sidewalk, Andorf welcomes the gentle breeze at his back. He pauses at the kiosk map before charging off for the Investigations Building. Skipping the offline elevator, he jogs the steps, traverses the long corridors of each floor, peers through darkened office windows for any sign of life. He jogs past the fourth floor's engineering labs, heading for the sole light shining from the last office like a ray of sunshine. He pries the heavy metal door open and squint past the brilliant overhead krypton radiators at starship blueprints plastered across every square inch of wall space, drafting table, and most of the floor space. He spots a man shuffling between prints, holding up one and then another in front of his unshaved face. The man's bulky fingers drag shadows across the translucent prints as if transposing text from one print to another. Snaking his way through the paper maze, Andorf stamps indelible footprints on the blueprints, which have taken up residence on the floor. The door shuts with a *BANG!*

Brutus slams his oversized print onto the table. "I told you to leave me alone." With a thumb holding his place on the drawing, he lifts an eye at the intruder. "Oh, you've arrived."

Andorf scans the plethora of rolled fibers. "Brutus? What are *you* doing here? What's with all these drawings?"

Grinning at Andorf dressed in his finest clothes, Brutus studies Andorf's puzzled face. "I'm assigning last minute passengers for the launch. What's got a bug up your—"

Andorf flailing arms sends prints flying of the tables. "We've been robbed! Everything's gone! Even our clothes!"

Grumbling, Brutus returns to his drawing, hiding behind the print.

Andorf yanks the print away from Brutus's face. "Didn't you hear me, you big ox?" Andorf, gasps between phrases. "Every bit of my family silverware ... gone. That's ten complete settings, passed down through seven generations of Johnsons. Have you any idea what that stuff was worth? And I can't even report it. Why, I'd be thrown in jail."

Brutus ignores him, dragging a finger over the print. Each time he turns his back holding up a print, Andorf jumps between him and the print. "And they swiped all of Serin's gizmos from my junk drawer. They even dug my hologram projectors from of the ceiling. Everything is gone, I tell you. Everything!"

Brutus lowers his print and grins. "And I suppose you made calls and they sent you here to engineering."

"Well, to the Investigation Office. All the lights were off so that's how I ended up here." Andorf grabs his arm. "Don't you care, Brutus? Your stuff is gone too."

Brutus stares at Andorf's beet-red face for a moment. "Calm down, Poo, before you trip a breaker. Everything's taken care of. The authorities have our stuff. We'll have it all back in the morning."

"What? How?"

Brutus returns to the print. "You were snoring this morning. Serin and I didn't want to wake you."

"You mean it was all gone when you guys woke up? Why didn't the authorities blow you off like they did me? How could you—"

"Connections, Poo." Brutus lays the print down. "Don't you think I have contacts working this close to Max?"

"Well, yeah. But what about Serin? Something crazy is going on with her. She's been blocking my thoughts, hiding things."

Brutus grabs Andorf's sleeve and leads him out of the room. He scans the vacant hallway, opens the stairway door, and peeks up and down the dark steps before turning back to Andorf. "You're being paranoid."

"I'm being safe, Brutus. If you haven't noticed, everything and everyone's been disappearing. First Gregory. Then two old friends. And now Binkers and all our stuff." Andorf pauses to catch his breath. "I don't want to be next."

Brutus throws an arm around Andorf's shoulder. "Look, I've known Serin way longer than you. Nothing's going on, I tell you."

"She has another lover, doesn't she? Remember her vows? She left out all the forsaking others part. Her Aunt Bonnie was in on this, wasn't she?"

Brutus chuckles. "Stop it, Poo. You're getting all bent over nothing. Leave me alone and let me get back to my drawings."

"I'm fed up with everyone spoon-feeding me lies. The government does it, my friends do it, and Serin does it. The only ones who have been straight with me were Gregory and Binky."

"And look what happened to them," Brutus mumbles.

Scrutinizing Brutus's calm demeanor, Andorf feels Brutus holding back. "And you've been so damn honest. Why the hell should I believe anything you say?"

Brutus grins. "Look, Poo—"

"Well, I'm heading up Jake's Mountain. Those damn agents aboard the Atlantis will take me seriously. They'll tell me what happened to my best friend even if I have to kill every last one of them."

Brutus's ears perk. He grabs Andorf's shirtsleeve. "You'll never get past gate security. Let me gather a few things." Brutus stuffs his marked-up drawings. Barreling out the door, he nearly flattens Andorf.

Andorf chases him through the emergency exit door, voice echoing throughout the stairwell on his descent. "Slow down, big guy. I know you need to be there to watch the Starship launching, but geez, Brutus. That's not until noon tomorrow."

Andorf squeezes out the ground floor exit, trailing Brutus like a shadow. At the charging station, he sweeps his eyes past the optical scanner, unsure of his dwindling balance. Brutus flashes a chilling glare before ripping wires loose from under the seat of one biped and zooming off without payment.

Andorf extracts a biped from the thermal charger and rides after Brutus. "Hey! You can't go around stealing things like that."

Brutus comes alongside Andorf and rips a blue-striped wire loose from beneath his seat. "There. The Empire is now deaf as a bi-party candidate after an election. They won't be tracking us anymore."

"But are you no longer afraid to be seen with me in public?"

Shrugging his shoulders, Brutus leads Andorf toward the street. "In a matter of hours, it won't matter. Let me clue you in about Serin."

"Don't tell me. She's on her way to the Cos to release her brother."

"I didn't say that. You must be reading my mind."

"I woke up this morning reading *everyone's* mind and I'm seeing things that aren't there. It's as though someone's flipped a switch in my brain."

Brutus buzzes toward the road, cursing at his stolen bike. "These damn toys. Why can't they use larger batteries? The undersized power modules they use always need charging. I'm running late. I've got guard duty at the starship and Max is due before dark with his elite guards."

With Brutus's girth, Andorf easily catches up. Following behind, Andorf edges the side of the road. "You know as well as I do that The Empire doesn't want us exploring outside the perimeter. They built the wall for *our* safety."

Brutus scowls. "That's what they want you to believe. Have you ever wondered what's really out there?"

"Trees, real wooden analog trees, plenty of them. I saw them in my dreams. I told Serin about them." Andorf shivers. "I see her on a long dirt road, lagoon on either side of her. I see a guard shack and a dull building with a loading dock where citizens are being held against their will. There are buildings filled with chemical drums and people strapped to gurneys. And I see rows of monotonous machines, stamping out battery cases and human parts stacked ceiling-high in labeled bins."

Brutus cringes. "The Cos and the adjacent power cell factories, where they dispose of the moderate voters." He circles back and grabs hold of Andorf's bike. "Stop this, Poo. You're giving me the creeps. Next, you'll be reading thoughts of the dead." He takes a deep breath. "Serin wouldn't be heading to the Cos right now if it weren't for you and Gregory busting into that Archives' building. Have you ever thought about that? You asked me where she goes. She visits with her brother at the Cos, for days at a time."

Andorf nods. "Ah, that's why I see her riding in the back of a van with three others. But how's she—"

"Serin and her renegade friends hijack a panel van or supply truck." Brutus gazes down at his watch. "That should have happened an hour ago. She's done this so many times, she could find her way to the Cos blindfolded."

"So she's heading there to get Gregory? Hell, she might as well bust down the doors, let *everyone* out."

Brutus grins. He buzzes off at a slow pace. "She's been planning this for months."

Andorf follows. "Damn, Brutus. Aren't you worried about her getting caught?"

"I'm more concerned about you. What the hell were you two doing at the Archives' that night?"

Andorf pulls up alongside Brutus. "A childhood friend at the Records Office suggested I—"

Brutus grabs Andorf's bike, slowing him to a stop. "Don't tell me … Wilhelm Mattigan."

"Oh, so now you're reading *my* thoughts now?"

"I'll bet he met you alone at a restaurant, spoke as one friend warning another. When you nibbled, he gave you a little friendly advice. Then he turns you in. Take a page from the Field Agent's Scout Guide."

"You mean his paranoia was—"

"An act. They sucker you in with that common-man analogy and before you know it, you're being rear ended by a right or left-winged extremist."

Andorf shudders at the roar behind him. Before he can turn, a whoosh and gust of wind sweeps him and Brutus off the road. Partially-combusted hydrocarbons and sand grit scratches their faces, leaves them gasping for air along the side of the road as the tanker truck storms past. Andorf shakes an angry fist, screams at the top of his lungs. "Why are they going so fast? What the hell does TSP stand for?"

Brutus spits pieces of grime from his mouth. "Don't you remember basic science? Tri-Sodium-Phosphate, a major ingredient of rocket fuel."

Andorf grins half-heartedly. "I took science alright, *political* science."

"Like we need more statists brainwashing gullible citizens."

Andorf sours at the thought. "Then what about Max? Serin hates how he manipulates you."

Brutus smirks. "It's nothing like that, Poo. You know how she despises him. Why if those two were ever in the same room …"

Andorf recalls his own tense moments with Holder, dead gang boss of the now defunct Bogus Boat People. He spots a Veatrice street sign, and he veers sharply left. “Got an errand to run, big guy. I’ll catch up with you at the starship.”

“You best appear before sunset,” Brutus yells. “That’s when you know who arrives.”

“Things are about to get interesting, big guy,” Andorf yells out. For the last time, he hears Brutus’s thoughts as clear as day.

If you only knew, Poo. If you only knew.

CHAPTER 31
Unfinished Business

Andorf buzzes through the rundown slum-division. The under-powered biped sputters up to the steps of the Bogus Boat People's last known address, prior to their current residence in the city morgue. He jogs up the chipped brick steps, feeling the gang's evil presence oozing from every crack and crevice of the familiar hideout. Recalling it was *he* who last closed the door, he twists the rusty doorknob. Locked?

Except for the unreachable gap beneath the high bathroom window, the place is sealed tight. The next yard is filled with abandoned toy furniture. Andorf works a sun-faded play bench free from overgrown weeds and drags it beneath the window. With the toy bench flexing under his adult weight, he shoves the groaning window through its warped tracks and snakes inside. A filthy tub's faucet releases a steady drip. His first step sends him sliding across the vinyl floor, slick with grime and mold.

Andorf exits the bathroom, thoughts a jumbled mass of knives and butterflies. Grabbing the bedroom doorknob, he senses Holder's presence, hears him yelling through the door. He shivers at flexing walls and the bare knob warming his palm. The door creaks open to chunks of stucco stubbornly clinging onto bare aluminum studs like abandoned family pictures. Soiled clothing lies heaped atop sleeping bags, scattered about the trash-ridden floor. Holder's voice yells louder and louder, but it is Brett's whimpering cry that drives him from the vacant bedroom.

In the dining area, spent liquor bottles line a cratered metal card table. Foam meal boxes riddle the floor below. A steady kitchen drip harmonizes with the drip in the bathtub, adding music to the otherwise gloomy world. Andorf's eyes are drawn to the card table. He envisions the gang's feverish hands working the bomb assemblies, recalls them jubilantly slamming their shot glasses, feels Smiley's fist pounding his back.

The bombs. Were they planning to assassinate a public figure? Innocent bystanders? I would not put anything past those ruthless thugs.

He removes the false floor beneath the sink, grabs hold of the fiber box. He scans the box filled with bomb makings. Tossing the fiber box onto the table, Holder's voice echoes in his head. "Get rid of this stuff, boys, before it—"

He sees a blinding flash. Everything goes white—

Ears ringing, eyes burning, Andorf feels himself in another place, far from the gang's hideout. Concrete blocks crash around him, interrupting the muffled eerie calm. Coughing, laboring hard for breath under the weight of a fallen ceiling, he watches dust plumes spiraling high into the bright afternoon sky. Andorf is suddenly outside and in big trouble.

Twisting his head in restricted moves, he gawks at all the detached arms and legs intertwined within a towering heap of bricks and metal conduit. Survivors work themselves from the collapsed office building and stumble past with shocked faces, ignoring him and the cries emanating deep from within the rubble.

Two right-leaning men appear from nowhere and sift through the mess, careful not to soil their neatly pressed red suits. "Over here," Andorf gasps, struggling to free his hands. He tries to wave, but cannot feel his hands.

A rescuer looks about, chanting repeatedly. "I didn't do it."

The second man casts his hands at the other. "Don't look at me. I was with you in the E-Cuniculon headquarter, across the street."

Andorf strains. His fingers desperately inch forward. If only I can ... Hey! Look at me, over here."

The men grab at a woman's hand protruding from the debris. They pull and pull until her torso becomes exposed. Their faces grimace, as does Andorf, at the sight of her crushed head. The rescuers shake their heads and move on, leaving her mangled corpse behind. Their voices diminish as they work their way around to the far side of the debris pile.

Andorf stares at the woman lying atop the debris in her ripped, blue pantsuit. He imagines her without the gashes and filth smeared across her broken face. He shudders, recalling her leaning against the water cooler back at the Toxidian headquarters, verbally criticizing him and the assistant to the assistant, Linton.

He cricks his neck and strains. His outstretched fingertips brush something familiar. He strains, stretching his arm to its limit. He feels ... the box, the fiber—

WHAM! Andorf finds himself back at the gang's dark hideout, leaning against the cratered metal card table, holding a corner of the fiber box full of bomb assemblies between his thumb and index finger. He lets go and jumps away, sending shot glasses clattering onto the floor. "What the hell just happen?"

Andorf kicks a path through ankle-high trash, as if on a mission, searching for something beyond the fringes of his grasp. He again hears Holder and his sinister laugh. "Go ahead, Mac. I dare ya'. You'll never find it."

He spots pocketsize notepads buried in the debris at his feet. In the faint light, flips through crinkled pages trying to make sense of the childlike sketches and scribblings. He tosses the notebooks onto the counter. One lands, pages open. A drawing jumps out, daring a second look. Viewing the notepad at the acute angle, chicken scratches morph into drawings of left-leaning stick figures and a street labeled Dos Cacas Grande.

Andorf's heart races. He paces the tiny kitchen in tight circles, kicking up trash. *They* were *planning to blow up the Tox headquarters, kill all those Literals. What would that accomplish?*

Flipping more pages, he finds maps, many depicting TSP trucks like the ones that blew him and Brutus off the road. Tri-Sodium-Phosphate, rocket fuel as Brutus called it. Many have references to populous buildings, remote locations outside the perimeter, large chemical storage tanks. One map extends well beyond the perimeter, with TSP trucks heading in both directions. Andorf's fingers follow the sketch onto the next page, from the perimeter wall, through outskirts of town down Logan Street, and to the base of Jake's Mountain.

"Here's where Logan Street takes that sharp right off Speedway, past offices buildings and narrows behind the Last Stab Diner at the base of Jake's Mountain." Andorf's trembling fingers flip through additional pages of winding mountain roads, terminating at a large parking area with short runs off the backside and a large red 'X' overlaying a sketch of the starship.

Andorf's jaw drops. "No! They were planning to blow up Starship Atlantis. Good thing Holder and his thugs are no longer around. It'll be okay."

His ears perk. Playful voices ratcheting up outside attract him to the back door. With a broken jigger glass, he scratches areas of a painted-over kitchen window to see tots dragging their toy bench and their mothers egging them on from the next yard. Andorf gazes at the bomb assemblies with all their protruding wires. *I've practically invited those kids here. They'll be sneaking inside here, snooping around. I have to get rid of this stuff, all of it.*

In the bedroom closet, Andorf finds an old woman's coat, bearing more cobwebs than fashion. He wraps each assembly between layers of foam meal boxes and eases them into the many large coat pockets. He runs outside and fretting at the sun slipping behind Jake's Mountain, rides off for the long sputtering ride to Jake's Mountain, barely faster than one can walk.

*

Speedway is unusually busy for an early Sunday evening. Andorf takes the bike and dashes across the road. Pushing dangling wires deep inside the coat, he slips it over his shoulders. Behind him, a TSP tanker truck clips the curb. He and others jump from the truck's path and force their way inside the crowded, Last Stab Diner, where life-sized statues of Ron Howard and Henry Winkler greet them. Andorf steps toward the last remaining stool at the counter, but a man abruptly takes the seat. The pudgy, middle-age man frown at Andorf's narrowing eyes and slides off the stool, offering it to Andorf.

Taking the seat, Andorf nods at the man. He fancies the chromed plasti-ware framing old-fashioned Melanese plates and the mustard, ketchup, straws, and creamer sticks flanking laminated menus. Recalling his run-in with the strange man in the black trench coat in the Corner Cafe, he grins at the wall-mounted mirror behind the counter before thumbing through inviting pictures on the huge, plasticized menu.

A greasy waitress edges around the counter, a wad of drool dripping from the corner of her red-painted lips and cheeks. "Ya' gonna order anything from that menu or will ya' be feeling it up all evening?"

Lost in the many selections, Andorf avoids her prying eyes. "A minute ma'am."

"Suit yourself, mister. You still have a couple of hours. Kitchen closes at nine. Can I take your coat?"

"No!" Andorf pulls the coat higher over his shoulders. "Are you still serving breakfast?"

"Honey, we serve everything on that there menu, until 9 p.m."

Andorf drops the menu in its vertical sleeve. "I'll have a couple of eggs over sleazy, millet toast, and strong coffee. Lots of it. I feel a long night coming on."

Before disappearing, the waitress looks Andorf over, dressed in sneakers, his Sunday finest, and the old lady's coat. She returns with a full cup and vanishes as quickly, leaving him staring a hole in his dark steamy cup. Stirring in three creamer sticks, he sees citizens in a graveled area running for their lives as the image blends into the creamy drink.

His second cup bears an aging, bearded reflection of himself behind octagon glasses. The image appears to be warning him as it shrivels into a cloud of dissolving creamer sticks. A third cup reveals his wife, Serin, sitting on the floor in a pool of blood, wallowing in pain.

Andorf pours cup after cup, but images refuse to appear. He envisions Brutus atop Jake's Mountain. He sees him blocking the starship's entry gate and stepping aside to let him board. He thinks about gathering up officials, strapping them down with explosives. *They'll listen to me then, tell me—*

The floor rumbles beneath his feet. The street-side glass picture window quivers. He spins his stool around to catch a glimpse of a TSP tanker convoy navigating around the corner. Tires lap the sidewalk as each truck down shifts around the sharp turn, inches shy of the front entrance. Brakes squeal, tires bounce, and exhaust blows from their vertical stacks. After the turn, engines rev for the narrow winding pass up Jake's Mountain, a few blocks ahead.

The waitress pauses in front of Andorf to watch the TSP trucks roar past. She whips a rag from her rear pocket and follows rolling coffee trails on the counter, fuming words dirtier than the thick black smoke spewing from the trucks. "One of those suckers will take that corner too sharp and ..."

Andorf flinches at the waitress slapping her hands too close to his face.

"Kablooee! You'll see the fireball all the way back to City Park. It'll be all over The Eye. We'll get our five minutes. Yep, me and the Fonz. Just you wait and see." She storms off, talking to herself. "I'll be more famous than Fat Max Okinawa. Everyone will know my name."

"The story won't be about you," Andorf says, calling out to deaf ears and a turned back. "They won't even get your name straight." He stares past his expecting plate. *What's to become of me? Perhaps my destiny lies somewhere up there on Jake's Mountain.*

CHAPTER 32
Serin's Plan

Miles outside the perimeter hang two dreaded signs. 'C.H. COSMOS SANITARIUM' one reads. 'EMPIRE POWER CUBE FACTORY' reads the other. A panel van with three renegades and their captured driver stops, inches shy of the barbwire gate. The under-dash, two-way radio jabbers warnings of suspected subversive activity and then mutes. Riley projects his head through the opening between the front seats to see Serin tracing her fingers across a hand-drawn map.

"Shimmy under the fence here, where the rain water washes out the soil. All power and alarm wires terminate in this box on the back wall of the guard shack. You'll need to pry off the cover."

Riley produces a mini-crowbar. "No problem. I'll just attach the remote trigger while I'm yanking—"

"No," Serin yells. "I'll attach them upon our exit. If anyone sets it off with their two-ways, we'd be sitting ducks. So leave the wires dangling, Riley. Don't attach *anything*, hear me?" Serin waits on his nod.

Francis chuckles from the driver's seat. "I can see the militia running around like rabid hogs."

Serin grins. "By that time we should be back inside the perimeter, blending into evening traffic."

"That's if your little remote works," Francis says.

Riley fidgets, hand gripping the passenger door release. "So I'm in the complex, the alarm's been disabled, and I've got the gate open …"

Serin nods. "Flash an 'O' on your infrared when the gate's open."

"Three longs, got it. What about the guards?"

"If they've eaten dinner, they should be napping at their posts. The gate's open in five or we abort. You'll find an overcharged motorbike with extra batteries hidden in the bushes, half a mile down on your right. It'll get you back to the paved road. After that—"

"You're on your own, little brother." Francis bends his head toward Serin. "So let me get this straight. While the drugs your brother drops into everyone's dinner puts them to sleep, we sneak inside the Cos, load the vans with our friends, and get the hell out, all in less than …" Francis scans his timepiece. "Forty-five minutes?"

"Piece of cake, broheim."

Serin smiles at Riley's youthful innocence. "If anyone awakens …"

Riley winks and attaching a silencer to his piece, slips out the door, pockets heavy with tools. He reappears at the driver's door before turning away. "Serin's well known for her visions. Be easy on her, bro." Dressed in dark clothes, Riley is easily consumed by the night.

Serin extracts a pistol from beneath the driver's seat, screws on a cylinder, and points it at the captive. His eyes bulge and … *PSST!* He leans, slumped against the spare tire. She grins at Francis. "Nothing like a healthy dose of oxythorazine to start out a Sunday evening. And one more thing, Francis … the sliding door's entry code is NOMOREWAR, all one word. It locks down after three tries. At 8 p.m. sharp, the passcode reverts, and the sliding dock door slams shut. No one gets in or out. The rescue goes on with or without me."

Francis raises brow. "8 p.m., NOMOREWAR, one word, got it."

Serin pulls a jeweled box from beneath the passenger seat. She holds it up to the sliding window. "It's important that the captain gets this."

Francis grabs at the treasure, but Serin slides it back under the seat. "What's in the box, contraband?"

"Francis, promise me."

"Okay, okay. I'll personally see that the captain gets your little box. You needn't worry."

"So Francis, who are you guys here to rescue?"

"Riley suspects our parents are in the Cos. They disappeared several years ago and—"

"Parents? They'll be too old to tag along. You should know that."

Francis gulps. "But we can't leave them in in that terrible place. The horror stories we've heard about the Cos. The horrid conditions ... the experiments ... genetic modifications ... not to mention the power cell factory next door."

Serin feels him shriveling inside. She glances at the shiny gold ring decorating his left hand. "I take it you and Riley have wives?"

"Leigh and Kaylis. They'll be waiting for us, bags packed, at the Jason Street turnoff. We'll go right by there. Riley said we could—"

Serin becomes deathly quiet. She appears cold, trance-like. Francis drops his infrared glasses, runs around the van, and climbs through the back door. A chill runs the length of his arms the instant he grabs hold of her quivering shoulders. He feels her frosty breath on his face as she leans into him.

Eyes withdrawn, she whispers through chattering teeth. "A stranger awaits, old and wise. He'll say things ... things we must know."

"Stop that, Serin! You're scaring me." Francis pulls her into a light embrace. His whole body begins to shake. He flinches at something streaking past the windshield. The passenger door suddenly flies open, and Riley leaps inside. Emptying tools from his pockets, Riley gazes through the sliding window, frowning at Serin and his big brother locked in an embrace.

"No wonder you missed my signal, bro. While you two were getting all mushy, I disabled the cameras, the sensors, and the guard's comm-unit. Oh, nothing important. Hey, she's married you know—pregnant too."

Francis releases Serin to rub his frostbitten hands together. "I know you warned me, but Serin's having some sort of meltdown."

Riley reaches through the window and snaps fingers in Serin's face. He grins at Serin's sudden blink. "Why the air tank back there? Are we making bombs now?"

Serin glances at the brothers as if nothing happened. "Hush, someone may hear. It's helium gas."

Riley continues emptying pockets. "Not a chance. It's spooky quiet out there. Both guards in the shack are passed out, snoring away. I was hoping to use my piece. See, I've got the silencer—"

"Put that away, Riley." Serin pushes the pistol out of her face. "What about the alarm box? Did you leave the wires intact?"

Riley grins through the small window. "Everything went like clockwork. Hey, wait! What happen to our friend back there? Serin, did you—"

"Of course not, he's only tranquilized. Francis, get us the hell out of here."

Francis leaps out the rear door and hurriedly climbs into the driver's seat. Driving down the gravel road toward the Cos in a slow creep, he tosses a rag, snickering at his kid brother. "I'll bet Kaylis gets real cozy with that greased face tonight."

"Guys. Guys," Serin whispers. "Keep your voices down. All-knowing Rica hears everything."

The brothers gulp. "Rica?" they harmonize. Riley drops his voice. "Up until a few days ago, I've been erasing the recordings. That when they cleared your desk, replaced everyone. What happened?"

Serin shrugs her shoulders. "And yet the queen bee knows. Keep that gun handy, Riley. You may still get your chance."

Francis drives past rows of drab, white factories, where monotonous sounds of machinery stamping out power cell cases split the air with precision. The piercing sound masks the sound of van tires crunching on the long, gravel path. The nauseating stench of electrified carbon, aluminum chromate, and partially hydrogenated human flesh seeps from every open window.

The trio covers their noses and falls silent. Francis pulls their panel van beneath a large grove of trees, twenty yards from the Cos. A convoy of similar fifteen panel vans, driven by spouses and siblings of those captive in the Cos, arrive one by one. Serin hops out to greet the dozens of citizens encircling her under the trees. She scans all the scared faces.

Riley checks his timepiece. "Seven-thirty."

"You heard, Riley. We have thirty minutes. Anyone left inside when that dock door slams shut at 8 p.m. takes residence at the Cos."

Everyone's eyes shift to the darkening evening sky. A distant rumbling grows louder with each rapid breath. In seconds, a squadron of copters is above, sweeping floodlights across the graveled areas around them, unprotected by the large tree canopies. Swirling dust limiting their vision, all scramble for their vans. They huddle together, covering their ears from piercing sounds of copters hovering just above the trees.

Serin feels her heart amongst dozens of others, pounding and empty voices of her comrades, yearning to scream above the madness of beating copter blades. Leaning against the van's vibrating wall, she tries to focus on their collective minds, but cannot calm their inner voices desiring to cry out. Serin, like her rebel companions, wants to jump outside, out from beneath the protective cover of the magnificent trees, but so many inside the Cos, including her brother, Greg, are counting on her. She braces against van's wall as it rocks side to side. For the first time in her life, she feels trapped, helpless, at the mercy of The Empire's military.

The group stares blankly at one another as their panel van becomes bathed in an eerie ruby red glow. Serin raises herself off the floor and peers outside at the red beams breaking through spots in the plush tree canopy. She shivers at thoughts of everyone's identities being discovered within seconds of skin contact.

"They are searching for human DNA," she whispers to those packed around her like sardines. "If any of those beams cut a path across anyone's flesh—"

A red spot enters the windshield. Everyone packs in tight as their faces become aglow in ruby red watching the tight beam sweep back and forth across the front seats. Francis and Riley breath hard, pressed under the dashboard. The red spot exits the driver's side window, but the brothers remain frozen. Serin lifts her head to see a black trace line etched across the entire windshield and seats. "Riley, Francis ... you guys okay up there?"

"That was close," Riley whispers.

"Too close," Francis says. "If it wasn't for that humming as it pierced the tree branches it would have nailed us."

"Stay put! It's returning." Serin drops to the floor, wedged between her fellow renegades. The brothers clamor for their spots under the dash as the van's interior is again bathed in brilliant ruby red. The beam burns a secondary lines in the windshield glass and retracts.

After what seemed like hours, the copters retreat. Everyone piles out the doors, rubbing at their ears. Never having seen real analog trees, many comrades feel the deep impressions of the tree trunks, like not comprehending the plush trees are real. Serin grins, peering up at the wonderful overhead branches that hid them from the copters. She latches onto Francis and runs toward their panel van. She turns and she calls out. "Riley, gather the troops and head for the dock door."

Riley claps and yells at the wandering crowd. At first, they pay him no mind until he bangs on the nearest panel van. "You heard Serin, everyone. Let's get this done."

Francis pulls up to the Cos, backing the van against the loading dock. While Serin rolls the captive onto the concrete platform, Francis races for the wall-mounted access panel at the large sliding door. At the sound of compatriot feet running across the pavement, he crosses his fingers and then taps the sequence of key presses. He pauses, finger hovering above the last key. Feeling the weight of dozens of eyes amassing around him, he taps the ACCEPT key.

All glance at the overhead access lamp, still glowing blood red. Knowing he has but three tries, Francis presses CLEAR and starts over. His trembling fingers press the nine buttons, followed by the ACCEPT key. The light remains a deep red. He reaches for one last try.

Serin pushes him aside. She recites each character with firm key presses. All breathe deep as she reaches for the ACCEPT key. Sweat dripping down her face, she presses the button. Nothing. She presses harder and …

Still nothing. The overhead lamp remains a blood red. Serin thinks of her brother, Greg, incarcerated inside and begins to tear. Everyone stands in disbelief. With heavy hearts, they stagger off, heads dropped, moaning and cursing. The crowd is suddenly aglow in emerald green light. With a thunk, the mechanical brake releases and an overhead motor engages, driving the heavy metal door squeaking along a corroded track.

Riley charges between rows of opaque vinyl strips dangling above the opening. He scans his timepiece. "Seven forty-three."

Serin pulls two men from the crowd and sends them off to circle the building. She then gestures the others inside, to go separate ways, find their people. She steps through the dangling vinyl strips to find Riley waiting. "What about your folks? Aren't you—"

"If they are here in the Cos, Francis will find them." Riley takes off jogging down the hallway working one side, poking his head into each room and calling for Gregory. Serin keeps up, working the other side, stepping around sleeping guards, nurses, orderlies, and uninformed inmates cluttering the floor.

Serin hears a wheezing. Rounding the next corner, she sees a feeble, old man struggling with a walker. Under flickering lights, he appears flush and frail, pallid skin clinging tight around thinning bones. The old man's stick thin arms reach out for her. The old man's voice bursts in gasps. "Sehr—Aaron—Serin."

Serin feels his life evaporating at every expended syllable. She shivers as he nears, his feeble steps painful to watch.

The old man's parched, quivering lips fumble for words, words not to be wasted, words that need to be spoken. "Serin," he says, with what little wind he can muster. "Alas, I found you—made good my promise." He looks away and coughs. Holding onto his walker with one hand, he grabs her elbow with his barely stronger hand.

Frigid waves radiate up Serin's arm. She wants to run from the dying man's bluish face, hide from the deep-welled eyes behind his beard and scratched-up octagon glasses.

Wheezing with fading strength, he pulls her closer. "Hear me well, precious one," he says. "Find here, my friend, Gregory." He coughs a breath in her face and latches onto her elbow, squeezing a bit harder. He gasps, struggling for wind. "Seven you bear witness … shall perish … this very eve."

Serin reads the old man's nametag. "Chester," she says, watching the old man's strength spiraling away faster than an unclogged drain. "Seven people? This evening? What are you saying?"

Struggling for wind, Chester pauses, unable to regain speech. He finds an oxygen mask in the shallows of his walker and slaps it across his vein-riddled face. He stares at Serin's stomach and pulls the mask to one side. "Little ones there … you'll never meet."

Riley's timepiece sounds *seven fifty-three.* Riley pulls on Serin's arm, dragging her away from the old man and his spell. "Why are you listening to that crazy old fool, Serin?"

The old man projects a lost little boy look at Serin. "Never love another I will," he says, laboring at last breaths.

As Riley pulls her around the next corner, Serin throws open arms back at the old man "Sorry, Chester, but neither of us has much time." She and Riley resume their quest, alternately calling out, probing in rooms. "Greg? Greg? Has anyone seen Gregory Gray?"

Riley freezes. "Serin, I heard—"

Serin bolts around the next corner and flies into her brother's arms, knocking the bags from his hands. "Greg! It's so good to hold you again."

"Geez, sis. Don't squeeze the life out of me."

Riley rounds the corner to find Serin wiping her damp face on Gregory's shirt. "Remember me? We've come to—"

"Rescue me? I'm all packed, ready to go."

Riley grabs Gregory's bag and leads their way through the swelling crowd of rescuers, patients, and their belongings. Serin's timepiece wails in perfect synchronicity with his own, He spots his brother, Francis, behind the mob, parents in tow.

"Seven fifty-five," Serin yells. "How do we get everyone out that door in five minutes?"

Everyone instantly quiets to raised voices outside, barking militia-style commands. Serin and Riley peek outside to see three guards hovering above the bloodied bodies of their scouts lying on the gravel entry, ten yards beyond the loading dock.

Serin recalls the old man's warning of the seven who would perish. "That's two."

A guard points out their fifteen delivery vans parked under the trees. A second guard spots the captive lying on the loading dock. Pistols drawn, the guards rush the open dock door. Serin and Riley withdraw their heads from behind the slats. Boots clomp up the loading dock steps and everyone freezes. The crowd lined up behind Serin and Riley begins to scream out in fear.

Riley steps outside and *ZIP! ZIP! ZIP!* Drops the three guards at close range. He strolls back inside, blowing smoke from his pistol, grinning cockily at his horrified comrades. "Guess they missed the dinner bell."

With Riley's gunshots still echoing, the crowd rushes past Serin and Riley and through the dangling vinyl strips. Riley grabs hold of Serin as the torrent crowd sweeps them outside, onto the loading dock. She stares at the dead guards sprawled across the loading dock and the two scouts lying face down in the gravel entryway. "And three more makes five," she mumbles.

Intertwined amongst the sleeping guards, an orderly twitches. Her eyes flash open to patients and rescuers running past, bags in hand. She pulls a 20cc syringe from her red and blue smock and staggers to her feet. She flings the uncapped emergency syringe, pointy end out, at one citizen and then the next, but in her semi-drugged state from a dinner half-eaten, everyone easily steps clear of her swath. She fumbles down the hall, aiming for a wall-mounted panic button.

Serin feels a sudden burst of energy from someone she once knew. She peers between vinyl slats and sees Chester, lying motionless beneath the wall-mounted panic button and an orderly lying beneath him with a spent needle sticking out of her rump. Chester's final words, same heard in the wedding vows, ring in her head. She lurches to reach the faint shell of a man she loves though Riley maintains his steadfast grip.

"Andorf," she yells out.

Riley shakes her by the shoulders. He takes her face in both hands. "How could he be your Andorf, Serin? He's just some crazy old man."

Serin winces at Riley. "But that *was* Andorf. I'd bet my life on it. Much older, but Chester is him. He came back to me, from the future. How else would he know this would happen. His death now makes the count six." She stares at Riley. "There is still a seventh."

The overhead door relay thunks and they are bathed in blood red light. The heavy dock door shudders on its mal-aligned overhead track. "Mom! Dad!" Riley screams, watching Francis coax their waddling parents closer toward the narrowing gap, dragging their lifelong belongings. He releases Serin and rushes the door as the heavy dock door edges closer to the locking frame. He wedges his shoes lengthwise between the door and the frame. The door jams against the heels of both shoes. The overhead motor hums louder, vibrating against its mount arm. Riley feels his toes squeezing hard-pressed into the shoe.

They begin to buckle. He slips his feet out and yells to his parents. "Leave the bags! Hurry!"

The father shakes his head at the narrow space. He kisses his older son on the lips and shoves him between the door and the frame. Turned sideways, Francis squeezes through the narrowing eight-inch gap.

The fortified simulated shoe leather peels apart and both shoes flatten into the reinforced steel frame. Riley claws at the secured door with both hands.

Serin grabs Riley's waist, pulling him off the door. "Stop, Riley! You'll set off alarms."

"But Mom, Dad … they were so close."

Francis directs his barefoot brother toward the panel van. "We did our best, bro. Mom and Dad never would have made it out."

Serin scans the mass exodus of screaming people across through the gravel drive and her brother, Greg, waiting in the back of the panel van at the loading dock. Stepping over the dead guards stretched across the loading dock, she climbs in the rear of the van. The door shuts and the van speeds off, brothers watching with damp eyes, the last nugget of their childhood being left behind. Francis drops a hand on Riley's shoulder. "At least we know they are still alive, got to say goodbye." He nails the pedal.

Serin takes hold of a back door. She peers through the window at the trailing dust and her fallen scouts. "How will their families ever forgive me?"

Fifteen panel vans fly past the white factories. Their overloaded tires do little to mask the eerie grinding of battery casings. All speed through the guard gate. One van pauses just beyond. Riley grabs at the passenger door release.

"Riley, stay. I've got this." Serin leaps out the back door. With a small bag in hand, she pokes her head through the driver's window. "Wait fifty yards up ahead. First sign of trouble, you guys get the hell out of here." Serin grins at her comrades stuffed in the rear as the van pulls off.

Serin stuffs a penlight in her mouth and identifies wires Riley left dangling. She clips on two of three remote trigger wires and freezes at the click of a trigger directly behind her ear. She spits out the penlight and raises her hands, stuttering words in hopes of masking the van's tires rolling over the gravel drive. "I was only—"

"Keep those hands raised, little lady. I see what you were doing," a guard yells. "Move again and I'll drop you like glass." The guard drags her by the forearms. He shoves her inside the dark guard shack. "Who were you trying to break out?"

Serin gulps, knowing the last van has followed instructions and left without her. She thinks about the motorbike stashed up the road, her chances of escape. As the guard fiddles with the light switch, she squints at the name on his starched, white shirt. Forcing thoughts of Chester, she bursts into tears. "You see, Jimmy, it's my mother. She's sick with the—"

Jimmy shines his light on Serin's face. He takes a long hard look. "You kind of look like that Serin gal everyone's talking about." He slaps one cuff onto her wrist and the other around the door-side handrail. A firm tug confirms her captivity. He plops into a roll-around chair, and with a few swipes across his hand-held imager, 3-D facial images appear atop his desk. The room flickers with colors as he scrolls through the most wanted list, pausing at each female holograph. "Not that one. Nope. Not that one." One image stands out. His expression sharpens. He turns and shines his flashlight on Serin. Voice animated, Jimmy leaps to his feet. "So it *is* you … the infamous Serin Gray. There's a warrant out there for your arrest."

"That girl doesn't even look like me," Serin says, squinting at the projection as she fidgets with her binding, sliding it up and down the handrail. "Look, Jimmy—"

Keeping an eye on her, he leans across the desk and presses buttons on the wall-mounted comm-unit. "Hello, Central? This is—" Jimmy taps the comm-box and tries again. He shoves his face into Serin's. "You think you're pretty clever boogering things up out there, don't ya? Well, you and your brother belong in that crazy home along with the rest of them third-party voters. That's right. We expected you would come for your brother tonight. Did you ever think we were using him as bait?"

Serin throws a soured look.

Jimmy toe-jabs his snoring partner, sprawled across the floor. "Wake up Joe. We've got a live one here. Joe? Joe?"

Rolling onto his back, Joe relinquishes several loud nasal grunts. Jimmy runs out the door and shines his flashlight on the alarm panel box. He grabs at the jumbled wiring mess. "Yeow! This thing's live!" He runs back into the shack. His charred fingers reach for his partner's handheld radio but back off. Again, he kicks at Joe. "Joe! Hey, Joe! You've got to wake up." He throws Serin disgusted looks. "There'll be hell to pay for this, little lady. You can be sure of that."

The second guard begins to stir. Serin knows she must act fast. "I won't be worth much to you after they haul me off, Jimmy. They'll lock you and your buddy in that sanitarium just for knowing about me. Think about it."

Jimmy dashes back outside, cursing about not having his own two-way. Hearing dancing footsteps, Serin cowers at the light suddenly shining in her face. She drops to her knees, covering her head from an expected blow. "I didn't cut those wires, I swear."

A barefoot, pimple-faced man holds the flashlight to his face. "Serin, it's me. I couldn't leave our leader behind, could I?"

"Riley, grab his keys. Hurry!"

The cuffs release and Serin flies out the door, Riley at her heels. They hover above the limp guard. "Please tell me you didn't kill him."

Riley bends down and checks the guard's pulse. "I can tell you one thing, he'll be waking up with one nasty headache."

Serin grabs at the panel box. "Shine your light over here," she says, fumbling with the wires. "Come on, Riley. Shine the—" Serin turns her head. She freezes at the sight of a 45-revolver barrel pressing against Riley's temple and the pissed guard with the name Joe on his starched shirt, cocking the trigger.

"How'd you two escape from that loony bin over there?" Joe yells. "Don't you know it's not safe out here? There's a dangerous lady running around out here."

"So I've heard," Serin mumbles.

Spotting Jimmy, face in the dirt, Joe's hands go straight for his cuffs. He snaps them around Serin and Riley's wrists and hustles them into the guard shack, securing them to the handrail with his partner's second pair. He leans across the desk to press buttons on the comm-unit. "Central? Hello, Central?"

Riley grins at his handiwork.

Joe flashes snide glares at the captive pair. "Unlike Jimmy, I passed the phonetics test." He whips a small two-way from his belt pack. "Central! This is Joe, guard shack one." The radio squelch burps after releasing the button. <PHIST>

"Go ahead Joe. This is Central." <PHIST>

Joe pauses at the sight of something flashing past the door. A hand grabs hold of his flashlight, but Joe refuses to release it. He drops the radio and takes a swing at the intruder, knocking him squarely in the jaw. The man staggers about. As Joe steps back, recoiling his arm to deliver the knockout blow, Serin kicks his leg out from under him, sending him toppling onto the floor. A head blow from his flashlight and Joe is again out for the count.

Gregory stands, rubbing his jaw. "I was wondering what was taking you guys."

The squelch breaks on Joe's handheld. "This is Central, are you there, Joe." <PHIST>

Riley tugs on his cuff. "Say something, buddy, before they send in the troops."

Gregory picks up the two-way. He holds the radio away from his mouth and awkwardly keys the mic button. "Uh, Central, this is Joe," he says in his deepest voice <PHIST>

"You sound different, Joe. Everything alright out there?" <PHIST>

"Central, I dropped the radio in my water bucket. I was uh ... testing it out. Over." <PHIST>

"Word has it our target is heading your way. You and Jimmy stay sharp out there." <PHIST>

"Roger that, central." <PHIST>

"Central out." <PHIST>

"Joe out." <PHIST>

"Get us out of these things," Serin yells.

Gregory unclips Joe's keys and opens the cuffs. After a peck on her brother's cheek, Serin darts out the door. The guys train flashlights on the panel box while she attaches the last wire and uncoils a thirty-three foot wire. Serin plugs one end into the dangling black box and runs the other end up the flagpole. Then she jogs back and snaps in a one-inch power cube.

"How much range does that sucker have?" Gregory asks.

Serin leads them, running for the van. "We're about to find out."

At slamming doors, Francis peels out. Serin wedges herself amongst the many others on the floor, so glad her brother and Riley violated her orders. Scanning the many lost faces, she takes a deep breath. Never has she felt as close to this many strangers.

"Let us remember our fallen comrades who sacrificed their lives this evening. Though I barely knew those two brave men, we would not be sitting here now if it were not for their selfless acts. May they and their families forever remain in our hearts."

A grave silence settles. Everyone's long faces appear to be digesting the price of their newfound freedom. With Serin contemplating their next conflict, wondering who will become the evening's seventh victim, each swerve and pothole is a blunt reminder that they are far from safety.

CHAPTER 33

A Common Destiny

The trailing van a hundred feet shy of the paved road. Serin leaps from the rear door with a second black box. The group of fifteen gathers around her.

Francis smirks. "It's a good ten miles," Francis says, from the driver's seat. "You'll never trigger that alarm from here with that tiny transmitter."

Serin smirks. "It's only nine miles, flying straight over the lagoon and I'm about to tip the odds in our favor."

With Riley's help, she pulls a large balloon and rubber hose from behind the helium tank. Eyes widen at the inflating weather balloon. At Serin's nod, Riley tightens the valve and ties the balloon's neck in a knot. Serin secures a thin bare wire around the neck and after several easy tugs, releases the six-foot balloon.

"That balloon is way overfilled. It'll burst soon as—" Francis pauses at Serin's glare.

Riley feeds the wire from a spool until the line pulls taut against a terminating insulator on the reel. Serin wraps a few feet of the bare wire on the reel side of the insulator and then around the van's rear door handle multiple times. She pulls a cable from her pocket, plugs one end into the black box, and attaches the pair of alligator clips to either side of the insulator. Sporting a wide grin, Serin snaps a one-inch power cube in the black box and flips a small toggle on the black box. Advancing a knob, an L.E.D. glows atop the black box transmitter, dim at first, then blinding bright. "Resonance."

Francis scratches his head. "Huh?"

Riley grins at his older, low-tech brother. "Maximum power into the high antenna."

The black box is unclipped and tossed along the roadside. Riley's firm tug snaps the hair-thin wire, sending the balloon on its way. The balloon, like those watching, seeks freedom, climbing higher and higher in the prevailing winds. Everyone back inside, the panel van turns onto the pavement and merges into Speedway's tanker truck traffic.

"Jason Street, here we come," Riley says. "I can't wait to tell Kaylis about this." At Serin's estranged look, he turns a sour gaze to Francis. "You didn't mention to Serin about picking up our wives?"

"I started to, Riley, but she—"

"Guys, guys, it's alright," Serin says. "The Logan Street turnoff is on our way, but there's not much room back here."

Tailgating a tanker, they sneak through the closing perimeter barricade gate. After a few minutes, they happen upon a similar van broken down on the side of the road. Francis and Riley remove the gas cylinder and spare tire as a handful of renegade friends appear from the shrubbery and squeeze inside the van with their luggage.

Back on the pavement, the panel van handles poorly on overloaded tires. They soon take a right, ease onto Jason Street. An immediate left takes them into an alley behind a row of office buildings. The van's doors fly open to a squadron of turbo-copters thundering overhead, heading in the direction they came. Everyone leaps for cover from the mayhem unfolding a scant twenty yards away on Speedway. Around the corner, a block away on Speedway, they see countless cars weaving through threads of heavy traffic, lights strobing, and sirens screaming.

Serin grins at Francis. "Looks like they got our message."

Francis returns her grin. "I shall never doubt you again, wise one."

The brother's wives, Leigh and Kaylis, appear from behind a dumpster. "Over here!"

After brief moments of affection, Francis and Riley assist them inside and strap four large bags onto the roof. Leigh force-fits between the front seats while Kaylis wedges in back behind Serin. Back on Jason Street, they parallel the busier four-lane Speedway, on a direct route for Jake's Mountain. Both roads jam with traffic, all heading toward the mountain, forces Francis's heavy foot to slow the van to a crawl.

Serin plays out impending events in her head, wondering how this van and the now fourteen other vans will make it through the gauntlet that surely awaits them. She thinks about Chester's warning, wondering who his seventh victim might be. She feels contagious discomfort infecting the tightly packed van and half-heartedly grins at her comrades. "I know things haven't gone as expected, everyone. Don't expect any different from here out."

"What's she mean?" Kaylis appears overly frightened, scanning the sad faces, darting from one to the next. "Why won't anyone answer me?" she yells, turning to the ringleader. "Serin? Are you Serin?"

Serin nods. She gestures Kaylis closer and places a comforting arm around her. "There was a shootout at the Cos tonight. We left two companions behind."

Kaylis's face swells. She backs away and stares at Serin. Her voice sharpens. She bursts into tears. "Leigh and I were waiting in that dark alley for … almost forever. We heard sirens. You were late and we—"

Serin rolls her eyes behind the drama queen's back. "I know dear."

Through the small sliding window, Kaylis's eyes flash at her husband in the passenger seat. She begins to yell. "Why are we stopping, Francis?"

Riley points out the line of taxis and TSP fuel trucks blocking the road ahead. "Calm down, honey. The roads are all jammed. It appears everyone and their mother is heading up Jake's Mountain tonight."

Serin reaches through the sliding glass window and taps the driver's shoulder. "Do what you can, Francis. We've got a starship to catch."

*

Ignoring his jittering hands, Andorf pours yet another cup of coffee from the bottomless carafe at the Last Stab Diner. The closing waitress breezes past. “Last call, mister. The kitchen closes in fifteen.”

Andorf focuses on the antiquated analog clock above the counter. “Eight Forty-Five, damn,” he yells, feet clamoring for the floor. He slips the coat higher over his shoulder and dashes for the door, leaving his last twenty-piece spinning on the counter.

“Watch out for those TSP tankers,” the waitress yells. “Next one’s due right about …” She taps her timepiece a few times. “Now!”

Andorf opens the door to dozens of government street vehicles flying down from Jake’s Mountain. Sirens blazing, they whip past the door, around the corner, and onto Speedway. Hair blown in his face, he presses hard against the diner’s glass picture window, watching vehicles nearly clip the toes of frightened pedestrians who are also hugging the diner’s wall for dear life. In orchestrated moves, TSP tanker trucks buzz past in the opposite direction, turbos winding, and tires screeching, heading up the mountain, forcing the militia to take wider swings onto Speedway. In the wake of rubber and dust, Andorf reaches for a woman holding two young children to pull them from harm’s way, but the diner’s glass door flies open and a fat hand yanks him inside. Rag dangling from her hand, the waitress looks him over for injuries.

“Hell if I’m losing a good tipper like you to those idiots. Best you stay inside, mister.”

Andorf pants, racing the waitress to the marginally safer side of the picture window. Waves of turbo-copters stuffed with news hogs trim the roof thunder past like swarming flies on a fresh pile. “What the hell’s going on?”

“I wouldn’t be surprised if they were heading for that crazy place. You know, the Cos.”

Andorf's ears perk. His heart races with thoughts of Serin and her plans. He leaps out the door and jolts to a stop, heart throbbing at the absence of the mother and her children. Shaking his head, he tosses the flattened biped aside for a long walk up the mountain.

Traffic is backed up on Logan Street as far as Andorf can see and inching ahead on Jake's Mountain Road at the sharp left where it dumps into Speedway for the steep incline up the mountain. At the sound of approaching exhaust resonators, he projects a thumb, hoping to snag a ride. Standing well off the road, in an ivy thicket, he sees no brake lights on the trucks crawling past, downshifting for the steep grade.

Andorf hops aboard the next truck, climbing up the rear ladder, well beyond the driver's mirrored view. He stuffs the coat in a service tube and wedges himself, feet pressed against the aluminum roof ladder. Despite his severe caffeine overdose, exhaust fumes and the slow bumpy ride up Jake's Mountain, gently rock him to sleep. His head jerks back with each snore. Barrages of army vehicles squeezing past down the narrow mountain pass, lights flashing and horns blaring, fail to awaken him, but his face slamming against the truck jars him awake as it jolts to a stop.

He slithers around the rear ladder, glances past the driver's cab and then yanks his head back at the armed guard checking driver's papers, one truck ahead. The tanker lurches forward, leaving him dangling from the ladder while the driver finds second gear. Andorf regains footing and leaps off the passenger side. Landing in a patch of sticker thickets, he panics at the sight of his coat, stuffed with enough explosive to take out this side of Jake's Mountain, cruising past in the service tube. He runs through the overgrowth, chasing the narrow two-lane asphalt. Emerging in the parking area behind the inspector stand, he grabs the coat as the truck creeps past.

He tucks dangling wires deeper inside the large pockets and freezes at the awesome sight of the mammoth starship across the parking lot. Berthed horizontally upon three sets of paralleled railcars, the Starship Atlantis appears much larger than any picture he had ever seen. Its shimmering skin appears so out of place on this mountain plateau, sitting piggybacked atop the long string of specially equipped flatbed railcars. His heart flutters at the thought of the ten passenger decks and the grand views from as many observation rooms. His hands tingle at thought of touching—

Badges flash at Andorf from everywhere. Hands frisk him with nasty comments about his old lady's coat. He covertly pushes the bomb makings deeper into the coat pockets, hoping the soldier will not notice the protruding wires. Hands rip the coat from his shoulders and cast it aside to pat him, largely on the chest, back, and legs. One soldier grabs hold of the coat, eyes narrowing on wires dangling from one of the large pockets.

Andorf's thoughts return to the Archives' with the wide-opened mouth of the rat charging Gregory's crotch. The soldier shivers. He tosses the coat at Andorf and steps away, head nudging him onward.

"Take the coat. You can pass."

Andorf slips the coat over his shoulders.

"Move along," another soldier yells, patting him on the butt. "You're obviously not smuggling any pets. It's the next security check you should be worried about. Hope you're not allergic to latex."

CHAPTER 34
Tightly Wound Springs

Makeshift tents pack large areas of the huge parking lot atop Jake's Mountain. Savory fragrances warming over open fires are as diverse as those who freely offer tastes to wandering strangers and the variety of pets meandering between tents, begging for tasty morsels. Opinions seasoned with distaste for the Canine Empire buzz about. Subjects from Max up to the queen bee herself, Emerica Khan, are all fair game.

Passage through the carnival-like crowd proves a challenge for truck drivers who joined the festivities, virtually shutting down the winding mountain pass with their abandoned tankers. They exchange uniforms and truck paraphernalia for tasty morsels and drink to quench their parched throats.

At the far end of the lot, Starship Atlantis's polished skin reflects the countdown time until liftoff. The thirty-foot magenta numbers commands everyone's attention. Fourteen hours, twenty-nine minutes, and twenty seconds. Nineteen seconds. Eighteen seconds. One must muster inner strength not to stare. Fifteen seconds. Fourteen seconds. Thirteen …

The titanium-reinforced soles of Brutus's boots announce his every step down the starship's long metal ramp toward the day guards huddled on the pavement around the lower gate. The guards, waiting on evening replacements, ignore him with mindless jabbering and stale jokes. Max and his fashionable entourage are unusually late.

Floodlights randomly sweep across Brutus, guards, and the growing crowd of anxious citizens. Swallowing at percolating fears, he glances at the hypnotic sign, stressing over Serin, the plan, and its maddening details. *And where the hell is Andorf? Serin will hold me accountable if–*

Soldiers running down the ramp force him and the day guards to one side. “Out of my way,” the corporal yells, leading his pack.

“Hey, leave that alone,” one private yells at the curious citizens clawing their speeders.

The crowd covers their ears from the piercing turbine noise as the turbo speeders rise above their heads and zoom down the winding mountain road. The speeders leave everyone gagging and picking dirt from their facial orifices.

Near the inspector stand, a ripple in the crowd hints of an approaching vehicle. The day guards cease their jabbering long enough to focus on the event. Citizens strain to see though the highly mirrored windows of the vertically stretched limo easing through the rambunctious crowd. A woman stretched across the hood, clinging onto the wipers, unrolls a painted tongue at the chauffer. The chauffer drops his window and yells in a frustrated voice.

“If it weren’t for the paperwork, bitch, I’d gun it right now.”

The female hood ornament slides off and disappears into the crowd as the limo creeps to a stop a few yards shy of the entry gate. Six elite guards in black blazers pile out, sporting blackened sunglasses and even darker attitudes. Toting pistols smartly holstered at their hips, they wait on their distinguished leader.

The limo leans from side to side, muffled grunts emanating from within. Citizens back away as the complete rear door of the limo swings open. The limo rises as humongous legs gingerly feel for the asphalt and a mammoth beast extracts himself from the vehicle. The crowd gasps, eyes following the grossly overweight man rising to a towering eight-foot stature. Until this moment, few citizens have had the honor of Max Okinawa's presence.

In spite of modern weaponry, Max prefers the nimbleness of the saber that has never failed him. Reaching inside the limo for his trusty sidearm, Max clips the sword onto his wide belt. In slow deliberate finger motions, he removes his designer shades, revealing his marbled grey and yellow, cat-like eyes. The entourage likewise loses their shades in shirt pockets to vainly comb their hair, adjust their ties, and straighten their suits in perfect, choreographic motion.

In exaggerated moves and excess skin flapping at his sides, Max slithers closer to the gate, grunting the distance as he scans the crowd of citizens. The elite guards encapsulate Max and carefully staying outside his wide swings, while maintaining a safe distance from Brutus as few men have come between the pair and living to tell. With Max partially blocking the starship's access ramp, the evening guards hurriedly slip reinforced stools beneath his highness's descending rump. Each of the day guards nods respectfully and disperses into the crowd.

At first, he and Brutus merely exchange uncomfortable glances. Max brushes his head to side, grunting at Brutus as if expecting his number one to speak his mind. Brutus tips his head at the vertically raised limo. Understanding Max's preference for his native Hotonese tongue, Brutus minimizes words.

"You are late I see. Highly unusual."

Max scowls, twisting his head away much farther than humanly possible. His eyes focus upon the fresh graffiti painted across the Atlantis's port bow. Max grunts in odious displeasure, as his entourage smirks silently at 'The Angel' brushed over the starship's pristine finish. Max turns back to Brutus, saliva spewing from his slimy lips. His head swings from side to side, slinging drool into the immediate crowd. Men and women shed their soiled shirts and blouses in disgust as Max growls, eyes narrowing upon his number one.

Brutus breathes deep. Slipping paint-stained hands further inside his large pants pockets, he shrugs his shoulders, sheepishly.

Max's six-man entourage fidgets at the escalating tension between the pair. A nervous guard appears unable to contain himself. "We couldn't get around those blasted fuel trucks. They had the road shut down."

"And military vehicles kept squeezing past, down the mountain," another guard says.

Brutus turns away from Max, to face the younger, more gullible entourage with a forced puzzled gaze. He takes a deep breath, trying not to look suspicious. "What the hell's going on? The military stormed out of here like a second Spanish inquisition."

The guards chuckle amongst themselves. A guard steps forward as their spokesperson. By the man's large over-biting upper jaw and bronze complexion, Brutus instantly recognizes him as a Mayabite, a descendant of the lost Mayan tribe known to interpret any language spoken by man. "You didn't hear, Brutus? That Serin Gray woman showed up at the Cos this evening, released a good half of the inmates. Rumor has it they are all heading here, to Jake's Mountain. Anything that can fly or drive is on its way to intercept her."

Brutus suddenly feels as though he is center stage in a circus with the whole world staring down his throat. He glances back at Max's interrogating eyes and back at the Mayabite. At Max huffing, he struggles for an appropriate reply. "Have they … caught … anyone?"

"Not yet, but they are homing in on the patient implants as we speak."

Brutus gulps, staring at his feet. *Implants?*

The guard's eyes widen. Their two-ways' break squelch and pipe an update through their wireless earplugs. "They found a second panel van broken down on Logan," a guard says, fingers pressed against his ear. "Gravel embedded in the tires match those at the Cos."

"They're heading this way," another guard yells, rubbing his hands together. "Oh boy, we'll be ready for her *this* time."

The entourage jumps about, giddy with anticipation. Perspiration seeps from Brutus's every pore. He feels like a caged rat. He calmly nods at the Max. "We'll nail her *this* time."

Max rubs his chin, watching Brutus swallow at his rabid fear. Though Brutus tries to mimic the guards' euphoria, Max stares right through his façade. Max's marbled eyes tighten on his number one.

Brutus casts his self-incriminating eyes away from Max, toward the crowd of citizens, pretending to spot something off in the distance. All but Max fall for the trick. He takes another deep breath and tips his head toward Max. "I hear there are trees outside the perimeter. You know, before digitalization."

The guards peer at Brutus as if he has gone crazy. No one returns from outside the perimeter. How could he say such stupid things and to Max of all people?

"Long before you was this," Max snarls. "Today, no more. Never see you one. Never you will."

Years of fierce devotion and servitude allow Brutus to tolerate Max's criticism, but at this close proximity and Max's foul stench closing up his throat, he begins to doubt his allegiance. His heart throbs at the comm-device vibrating in his pocket. *Serin. Hope lives.* Brutus raises his voice to mask the buzzing as he fumbles for the mute button. "But I hear beyond the perimeter—"

"Never go out there do I. Neither you."

Everyone's eyes pong between the pair. No one dares intervention as Brutus scowls at Max. "I was just saying—"

Max raises his voice, unaccustomed to anyone questioning him, and most certainly not his number one. "Say you what?"

"I've never been ... I would never."

"Best you not," Max growls. "Trouble plenty out there."

"Mutated things linger out there," one guard says. "Flesh-eating monsters."

"That's why they built the wall," says another. "To protect us."

Brutus turns his head to approaching babble. He spots Andorf pushing his way through the crowd, rubbing his butt. *Andorf? What is with that God-awful coat?*

Andorf grumbles, charging ahead, oblivious to the gauntlet ahead. Max slips off the stools and slithers closer to Brutus, completely blocking Andorf's passage through the entry gate. Andorf draws the coat closed, hiding the dangling wires. He stops and grins sarcastically at the guards, then at Max. The crowd closes in as Andorf steals center stage from Brutus.

"Matte Kudasi!" Max growls.

Andorf grins up at the towering beast. "No understandy Asia-speak, pal."

"Wait—you—here," Max yells, in a tongue sharp as the jeweled sword he proudly wears at his side.

Even under the weight of Max's piercing eyes, he does not flinch. He squints at the countdown timer's magenta lights reflecting off the blade's highly polished handle and without thought, casts open palms at Max. "Whoa, down boy."

Brutus finds it difficult to maintain his straight face watching Max stare cross-eyed at Andorf. Max grunts and growls, but Andorf stands his ground.

Andorf grins. "That temper will be your demise."

The crowd gasps at Andorf's rash words. The elite guards exchange confused glances while the youngest guard dances about, unable to contain himself. The guards break into awkward laughter until Max drowns them out with his own sinister chortle. Red-faced, keeping a cautious eye on Max, Andorf chuckles.

Max grunts much louder. His tightening face portrays nothing but hate. Hate for weakness. Hate for opposition. Hate for the small one standing before him. Brutus feels anger brewing deep within the towering creature. He sees Andorf clenching hold of his trembling hands, sweat beading on his face and wonders how much longer Andorf can hold out.

Brutus spots Max's whitening knuckles gathering around the saber. Max's laughter wanes and his elite guards back away into the crowd, knocking citizens down like dominos. The mammoth sword rings as it escapes its scabbard. All gasp. Sucking air between his teeth, Andorf squeezes his eyes tightly shut.

Brutus, foreseeing Andorf's blood spilling on his fresh clothes, steps aside and shoves Andorf through the open gate, beyond harm's swath. Andorf stands a few feet up the ramp, squinting long and hard at Max before jogging up the entry ramp toward the starship. Brutus begins to sweat, thinking about the conflict Andorf just created between the he and his mentor.

The saber clinks as its drops into the holster. Max growls, fist frozen fractions of an inch shy of Brutus's undaunted face. "Fetch him back you will."

Brutus bows. "I know that one well, Max-san. He is but the favored one on my watch list."

Max snorts. "Watch list? Assigned by whom?"

"Rica. Rica herself."

The elite guards display shocked faces. "Twice removed daughter of Sir Ian Khan?" one asks.

"Queen bee of the Toxidian ruling class, Emerica Khan?" asks another.

Brutus grins. Leaning into Max, he cups his mouth with one hand. "In a hanging chair she sleeps, Max-san. Like a jack, one eye open."

"Ah! Nothing know you—these Toxidians you do." Max snorts, rubbing depressions in his upper forehead. "Important not, your little man."

"But I hear he is tight with Serin Gray, reason Ms. Rica has me tailing him."

Recoiling his threatening hand, Max pauses as if evaluating the evolving situation. He snarls at the nearest of his elite guards, pointing at the gate. "Go you there. Watch little man. Now!"

The confused guard scampers up the ramp after Andorf, pausing at Brutus's conflicting hand gestures. Judging by the way he stood up to Max, Andorf will have little trouble dealing with the ensuing guard. Returning attention to Max, Brutus worries about the more volatile second act yet to come.

Max's temperament softens. He surveys the many ridges overlooking the launch site, where renegades gather at sunrise to remember their taken family and friends. To Brutus's dismay, he grunts out a nearly comprehensible sentence above the voices of the swelling crowds. "Next morning alas, we hear songs no more."

Brutus nods. "Without the starship, what will the renegade choir threaten?"

"Shout—I hear well," Max yells, as the crowds pack in.

With Max and Brutus behaving more cordially, the five remaining elite guards jabber amongst themselves. They soon quiet at the sight of rushing waves of boisterous citizens. Their jolly faces morph to panic, hands resting on their holsters as though fretting an impending gate rush. The elite guards wave and shout at Max and Brutus, but it is only when they step back into them, do the large men recognize the heightening situation.

The crowd edges forward, at first like ripples, then growing into large and larger waves. Cheering intensifies at each wave front, building to a human tsunami, approaching the front line in a steady wave. The front line parts and Serin steps out toting a devilish grin, surrounded by dozens of her armed comrades.

Brutus grimaces, knowing Andorf's prequel was but a warm-up for the real battle to come. Poised at ground zero, he steadies himself, readying for round two with Serin. He knows that even with Serin's armed comrades, the odds are stacked against her. Max and his select few could easily eliminate them, and with the militia's pending return, Serin's confrontation seems little more than a futile gesture. "Here we go," he mumbles, gritting his teeth.

"Everyone sporting a weapon follows me," Serin calls out.

Riley needs no second invitation. He steps ahead of Serin, proudly assuming a role of bodyguard. With armed comrades protecting her rear and cheering citizens flanking both sides, she halts directly in front of Max. She pushes Riley aside to face the giant. Hers and Max's fixated eyes engage. Max glares as if considering Serin a mere blemish on the pavement. He flashes evil eyes to one side to catch his number one smiling fondly at Serin. He growls at Brutus. "Girlfriend yours—gets by not."

"She had better chill," the Mayabite says. "If she knows what's good for her."

Max nods. Without shifting an eye off his prey, he grabs his nearest guard by the tie and grunts out demands. "Central Command—call you will. Treasure of theirs we have."

The guard unclips his two-way, but freezes at cold metal brushing against his temple. Francis cocks the revolver. "Don't even try."

The other guards go for their weapons and find their holsters empty. After a brief scuffle, the guards are lying face flat against the pavement, hands held behind their backs.

The crowd ceases cheering at Max's snarl and crazed grin. He drools like Pavlov's lead dog at the dinner bell, eyes ablaze in anger, hot blood pumping through his veins. With trusty Brutus at his side, Max acts without threat. After all, the pair has faced much greater odds together. The immediate line of citizens backs away at each of his loud grunts. Even cocky Riley trembles until Serin squeezes his hand in reassurance.

Brutus scowls at the sight of Serin and Riley holding hands.

Max growls at Brutus's jealous face. "Problem yours. Deal with her you must."

Serin yells at the beast as if there were no tomorrow. "Out of my way, you stinking baboon."

Brutus spins a double take. Never before has he seen Serin so combative, not with him nor any other man, let alone the beast now before her. With Max unfazed by dozens of weapons trained upon him, Brutus stands at Max's side, unsure what to do next.

To the crowd's gasp, Serin takes a bold step toward Max, pausing well inside his swipe zone. Gagging at his foul stench, she glares at Max's sunken gray and yellow eyes, bald head, and ratty goatee. Her eyes narrow. Face twitching, she winds up for her well-rehearsed pitch. "Anata wa zo no yo ni ido suru. Anata wa roba no yona nio."

All but Max and the Myabite guard appear confused. Judging by Max's contorting face, Serin may have missed the verbiage, but her content was right on target. The Mayabite guard sits up, laughing like a hyena. "She said he moves like an elephant and smells of a donkey."

Max grunts at Brutus. He looks back at Serin and whacks her with the back of his humongous hand as if swatting a mosquito. Serin flies backwards into Riley's arms. Brutus growls in mixed jealousy and rage.

Max turns to Brutus, his most devout disciple, and his overly confident expression morphs to concern. He grabs for his trusty saber with his massive left arm only to find it missing. Max's phasor pistol emits a high-pitch whine, charging in his hand. In seconds, the phasor is primed and discharged at Brutus's head. Brutus drops to his knees. He feels the heat of the beam passing between his raised arms, singeing the thinning hairs on his head.

The Mayabite scrambles to his feet. He leaps at Francis and grabs the revolver from his hand. In Latino dance moves, the elite guard spins around and presses his gun into the middle of Brutus's back. Max's saber high above his head, Brutus freezes.

The elite guard swallows. "Lower the sword slowly, Mister Brutus. No fast moves. Don't make me have to shoot you."

Brutus lowers the heavy saber onto the pavement in front of Max as though offering a gift. Maintaining eye contact with the saber, Brutus grits his teeth at Max's wicked laugh. He know Max with a pair of charged phasor pistols could drop the line of citizens in a wide spray, clearing the pavement in a sweeping thirty-foot arc.

Rising, Brutus feels the guard's pistol pressing hard against his lower back. His mouth knots, as if pleading for mercy. At Max's nod, the guard cocks his weapon and aims it at Brutus's head.

A hand grabs for the gun from behind and the crowd cheers. The guard turns to see Andorf Johnson wrestling the gun from his grip. Andorf fires a punch into the stocky man's chest without damage. With a good fifty pounds advantage, the Mayabite guard easily pushes Andorf aside. Andorf again grabs at the elite guard's gun.

The guard shifts gun hands and swings. Andorf takes a blow to his cheek and shakes it off. A second blow sends his head spinning in a rotating motion. Staggering away from the guard, he collapses onto the pavement. The guard re-aims his cocked weapon at Andorf's head.

One by one, the other guards work loose from their restraints and secure their weapons from the untrained renegades. Weapons drawn, they encircle Serin and her comrades.

Serin lurches forward and kicks the Mayabite in the ass. She leans back as he swings the pistol at her head. Lying on the pavement, Andorf growls at the guard. He jumps to his feet, grabs the Mayabite's shoulder and lays into him, with everything he's got. The guard flies into Max, knocking one of the charging phasor pistols from his humongous hands.

Citizens rush forward, turning on the guards. Within seconds, all five elite guards find themselves fastened securely to the chain-link fence with their ties. Brutus scoops Max's saber and holds it dead center in front of him. Max's second phasor whines as it nears full charge. Max aims at the crowd right through Brutus.

At the phasor's click, Brutus rotates the large saber and grasps it by the sharp edges, flat blade toward Max. The sword burns Brutus's fingers as it safely deflects the photon stream away from him and the citizens. Max cycles the phasor for third charge.

Grinning at his master, Brutus grabs the sword in his charred, bleeding hands by its proper handle. Eyes ablaze in fury, Brutus holds Max's saber high above in his able hands, ready to strike. In one glorious moment, he vents years of pent-up frustration through one loud scream. "Serin's not my girlfriend, you bloody bastard. She's my wife!" With the roar of a lion and one mighty stroke, Brutus drops the blade, slicing his master's head off as if chopping an onion.

"Serin falls to her knees, tears streaming down her cheeks. She throws both hands to the sky. "That makes seven. Thank you! Thank you!"

CHAPTER 35

The Cavalry Arrives

The gathering crowd gawks at Max's enormous head teetering on his equally enormous torso. After leaning left and then right, it detaches and smashes onto the pavement with a SPLAT. Purplish goo percolates out torso as it falls limp against the chain-link fence behind. The immediate crowd hold their noses at the horrendous stench of Max's bubbling torso, eyes widening at each eruption of purple goo oozing out the dangling neck. Many leave to give up their dinners.

"Didn't I tell you guys?" the Mayabite yells. "The beast was some kind of bug. He wasn't even human."

Max's head wobbles past the gate, leaving a trail of goo behind. Hissing and snarling, it encircles Serin, coming to rest at her feet, shriveled to the size of a football. Serin readies her foot to punt until hundreds of legs appear beneath the severed head. The head charges at Serin, opened mouth.

Serin takes a step back. "Field goal," she yells, recoiling her leg. On contact, Max's head arcs over his bubbling torso, clears the fence behind, and splatters on the pavement twenty feet below. Serin turns to the jubilant crowd. She yells out to the sea of waving hands fanning across the parking area. "May this be the last we see of this bloody empire." For a moment, her screams are lost to the electrified citizens. Then they begin to chant repetitively.

"No more bloody empire."

Serin marvels at the crowd's unified voices. She peers at the guards in their underwear, hands tied behind their backs and the five dark suits overlaying the gooey lavender mess staining the base of the ramp. A man in the crowd tosses his shirt. With a thankful nod, Serin peels off her goo-stained blouse, wipes her face on it, tosses him the souvenir, and slips on the strangers t-shirt.

A distant rumbling steals attention from Serin's firm, bare breasts. The ardent crowd turns and rushes the entry gate, though Brutus stands hunched over, pointing the sword outward at the crowd. He appears paralyzed in thought of no longer serving a master. Riley struggles with Max's heavy saber, but Brutus refuses to relinquish his firm grip. Serin snaps fingers in Brutus's face without luck. Then she caresses his sweaty cheek, bringing him back to reality.

"Let's roll, big guy. The Atlantis is now ours."

"Et tu, Brute?" Riley calls out.

Brutus drops the saber. He raises his hands at the frenzied crowds and everyone magically stops. Riley struggles with the heavy sword and tosses it over the fence as countless hands lift the fence and roll Max's gooey corpse underneath, off the elevated pavement. The crowds cheer at the body squashing onto the ground, reuniting head, body, and sword. Cheers escalate when renegades wipe their gooey hands on the guards' discarded clothes.

Serin's face sharpens to the fringe of panic. She tugs on Brutus's arm. "Andorf! What's happened to Andorf?"

"You mean that guy in the old lady's coat who rescued Brutus?" Francis asks. "I saw him running up the access ramp heading for the Atlantis. He was mumbling something about having agents listening to him."

Brutus laughs. "The wimp actually saved my life. You should have seen how he had Max wound up, growling, all pissed off. Max was all primed when you arrived to light his fuse. That bastard! No one pushes my wife around like that."

"I was betting my life on it." Serin throws arms around Brutus's hefty shoulders and plants a wet one on his lips. She and Brutus turn beet red at the crowds cheering them on. Serin breaks away, wincing at her applauding comrades. "Ten of you stay here. Everyone else up the ramp. Move it!"

Brutus steps aside, outstretched arms holding back the crowd as Serin's comrades and their spouses run up the ramp with their worldly belongings. Serin pulls marked up drawings from Brutus's rear pocket and distributes them and hand-held tattoo printers amongst her crew.

"Accept only mating couples bearing one month's clothing rations," Serin says. "Send me the exceptions. Greg, you follow me. Greg?"

Francis extracts a guard's eartap, wipes it on his shirt, and plops it in his ear, as do four others. His eyes widen. "They're amassing troops on Speedway."

"We haven't much time. Hurry!" Serin says. "Get everyone aboard, lines three wide. And someone find my brother." Serin runs through the gate and up the long access ramp. Riley darts ahead, clearing most everyone out of her way. Outside the starship's upper portal, she grabs hold of his arm. "Find Andorf. He'll be wearing some old lady's coat."

"Huh?"

Serin waves him through the starship's upper hatch. Jostled by hemorrhaging crowds, she scans the pavement below for her brother. A Brutus-size gypsy hands her a wireless microphone linked to the starship's external speakers. She smiles at the gypsy, knowing they have pre-boarded the Atlantis by the thousands. They were the ones who have assembled the Atlantis piece by piece. The gypsies know the starship inside and out. They have smuggled necessities aboard the massive starship for months, preparing for this very moment.

The mic squeals. "Listen up people. We can only take mating couples with one month's clothing ration."

Serin fingers a discrepancy in her crinkled ship drawings. "The A-deck. Why such large quarters?"

"For guests numbering three and beyond," the gypsy says.

"No. This first cabin. It's huge and why all the private amenities?"

The man chuckles amongst his fellow gypsies' whispering voices, quite amused by her naivety. "We built that cabin to contain the beast. With Max eliminated, it's now yours, precious wife of Brutus."

"Gypsy starship, gypsy rules," his friend says, blinking nervously. "You keep your spoils."

Rolling hidden eyes, Serin spots Francis at the bottom of the ramp, yelling at her through cupped hands. "No arm tattoos, no entry," she tells the gypsy before pushing her way down the ramp. At the entry gate she turns away many singles trying to edge past. "Can't you do any better?" she yells at her frazzled crew. "Hasn't anyone found Greg?"

Singles scramble to pair with acceptable mates of the opposite sex, amongst the frenzied masses rushing the gate. Brutus finds himself separated from Serin by the sheer mass of compacting bodies. He pushes back, but cannot fight the numbers of citizens lining up beyond sight. "I can't control them all," he yells, above the deafening crowd.

Serin pulls Francis's pistol from his belt. She fires three rounds in the air and for an instant, the world atop the mountain plateau grinds to a halt.

Brutus shakes his head at her. "You shouldn't have done that. If the military wasn't on their way, they certainly are now."

Serin grabs the wrist of a young girl slithering past alone. A man twice the late teen's age takes hold of her other hand. "She's with me," he says, holding out both their wrists for inking.

As her arm is tattooed, the girl grins at Brutus, then Serin. "I could have done worse." The girl grabs the man's hand and within seconds, blends into the chaotic exodus ascending the bowing metal ramp.

"He's spoken for," Serin yells at the girl. "Bitch," she adds, to Brutus's chagrin. "Hurry, everyone. Keep moving. Everyone, keep moving."

Hands up, shaking his head, Brutus forces his way past the endless sea of bodies. "I'm heading to the lower hatch, load citizens from there."

Francis and two others jog across the parking lot after Brutus. They catch up with him at the aft gate, thumbing through dozens of skeleton keys. "Is Serin always this bossy?"

Brutus snickers. "You caught her on a good day." He drops padlocks, swings the heavy iron gate aside, and leads his crew of three down winding flights of rickety stairs to the starship's lower entry portal. Flipping panel switches, the steps and stern portal hatch are brightly illuminated and wielding a 76 mm extractor tool from the utility cabinet, he unzips the hatch bolts and swings the starship's lower outer hatch cover aside. Seconds later, the inner hatch releases and swings inward.

Blood drains from Francis face. He grabs hold of Brutus's large shoulder. "I hate to say this, but we've got no tattoo imprinters."

The corrugated metal steps overhead bow and ring in crazed rhapsody of citizens streaming downward. Brutus cringes with thought of the crack-filled step supports welded by a low government bidder. He digs deep in his pockets. "Here! Use these indelible markers. Get everyone aboard. We'll sort things out later."

No citizen complains of butt grabs as the four lift them and their bags through the bowel portal, a good three feet off the ground. Safely inside, citizens help pull the next set of passengers aboard. A pair of women slip past Brutus while he argues with two gay men.

Francis grabs the women's arms. "Mating couples only."

"That's absurd," one woman yells.

To her partner's dismay, the taller woman locks arms with the gay guys. "Why not a foursome?"

The guys smirk at the second woman contorting her face at the more open-minded girlfriend. "Out of the question. I'd rather be—"

One of the gay men grins. "Left behind?"

Brutus scribbles 'A-4' on each of their arms and directs them toward the hatch. "A-Deck," the tall gal yells. Her partner flashes soured looks, as the foursome are butt-shoved inside.

One young man is not so fortunate. He stumbles past the line, chin in chest, dragging his worldly belongings. "Look at that poor guy," says a girl barely twenty, waiting in line with her boyfriend.

The boyfriend shrugs. Inching closer to the portal, he slips an arm around his gal's waist. "Oh, he'll be okay, Amy. He'll go back to his family and—"

"Nothing of the sort, Roj. Look at his face. He has nowhere to go."

Amy exits the line, grabs the stranger's arm. The young man pulls away at the boyfriend's angry scowl.

"We can be a threesome," Amy says.

The stranger pauses. Roger grabs at her, unwilling to lose his spot in the progressing line. "Look, Amy, you've done some crazy things but ... hell, we don't even know this guy."

"Desperate times," she says, smiling at the lost young man. She throws out her hand. "I'm Amy."

The young man steps closer, reaching to shake their hands and finds only hers. "Friends call me Gandy."

Amy shakes his hand and pulls him into the line. "Glad to meet you, Gandy. This here is Roger."

"But baby," Roger yells, tugging her along with the progressing line.

Amy stands her ground, refusing to advance with the line. "If Gandy can't go then neither can I."

Those directly behind cut the line while Roger stands fuming, scratching his fury chin. "Gandalf, hmm. That's an odd name. Fabricated, I suppose."

Amy extends her arm to Brutus. "Make it a threesome."

Brutus scribes Amy's arm. Amy pulls Roger's and Gandalf's wrists closer and in seconds, the trio wear similar A-3 letters. She flashes hers at Roger, then Gandy. "The A-level, see? We've got a much larger cabin. Come on, Roj, it'll be fun." Their voices dwindle as the three disappear through the lower portal.

With but a few left in line, Francis runs up the steps. He barely makes it to the asphalt pavement when he turns around and flies down the poorly welded steps, screaming at the top of his lungs. "Seal the hatch, Brutus! The cavalry has arrived."

Steps below him tear loose from their welded side rails. Francis grabs hold of the handrails and rides the collapsing staircase head first, toward the concrete landing. At the last moment, Francis grabs hold of a stationary support arm and swings himself feet first onto the concrete base. He bolts for the portal as steps behind him collapse like citizens reviewing their tax bills, pausing long enough to catch a breath. "Copters—everywhere—rounding up citizens." He discards his earpiece. "They must have changed radio frequencies."

With help from those inside, Brutus secures the inner and outer hatch covers. The four pull themselves up and around the missing steps onto the parking lot asphalt. With his 76 mm extractor in hand and bullets buzzing past their heads, Brutus and crew burn a path across the asphalt, screaming.

"Up the ramp, Serin! Get your butt up that ramp."

Serin scans a last time for Greg. With neoprene bullets ricocheting off the ramp, she runs for the ramp, pushing her way through the crowd. A man directly in front of Serin drops to his knees, agonizing in pain. Citizens around her begin to drop like flies. She leans down to help the injured, but Francis pushes her through the starship's upper portal, taking multiple hits on his back and shoulders. He rolls inside and collapses.

Brutus traverses the ramp many times, scooping the injured as if they were sacks of flour. Rubber bullets ricochet off him and the starship's inner walls as he hands the last man off and dives inside. Snaking his way to the hatch, he tears at the sight of militia swarming the parking lot like angry bees, destroying tents, grabbing citizens, and dragging them away at gunpoint. At the sound of helmeted troops in their cleated boots racing up the ramp, Brutus struggles to seal the starship. Fingers of the troops slip inside, preventing him from closing the heavy outer hatch door.

Gypsies appear from nowhere, offering cans of partially dehydrogenated whip cream containing multi-colored sprinkles, each labeled NOT TO BE USED EXTERNALLY. Grinning at Brutus, they spray the fragrant foam on intrusive fingers, and within seconds, the troops scream profanities and retract their fingers. Brutus twists locking hatch handles, knowing the outer hatch can only be opened from the inside. Huddled together, many twitch at each dull pounding on the thick outer hatch cover. The pounding lessens to Brutus securing the inner hatch cover.

Serin gazes at grim faces surrounding her, splattered about the floor. “Now the hard part.”

“How can you say that?” one injured man yells. “Look at us. We’re badly torn up, don’t you think?”

Brutus lifts the man’s shirt to examine the man’s bleeding back. He chuckles. “Merely flesh wounds. They’re using rubber bullets.”

The man sits up, staring at Serin and Brutus. “We’re all expendable, tools of the statist bi-party regime. Hear them out there clawing on our hatch? They won’t stop until they’ve broken through.”

Brutus snarls at the man. “They won’t dare damage this ship. It would push back the critical launch window. The whole mission would be scrubbed.” His bleeding hand wipes Serin’s tearful cheeks. “Don’t worry about your brother. He’ll be fine.”

Serin rises to her feet, hands grabbing at Brutus. “I know. It’s time to find Poo.”

CHAPTER 36
Reunited

Hordes of citizens crowd the starship's passageways. Everywhere Serin turns, chattering mouths confront her. Sharing her anxiety, Brutus nudges her into a nook, hard-pressed against the cold wall. Watching everyone shuffle past, she has second thoughts about her little uprising, if everyday citizens are up to all the challenges before them.

A passing gypsy, escorting a line of bound and gagged dignitaries, pauses to acknowledge them. "I would say this is the last of these bastards, but we cannot find the last four agents."

Brutus examines the hemp rope running through the captive's belt loops. "The others must be hiding in one of the conference rooms. Say, where are you heading with this slime?"

"Figure I'd flush them outside, let the citizens left behind deal with them."

"The lower waste ejection port may not be accessible. Wait, I'll go with you." Brutus winks at Serin and disappears down the aft stairs with his fellow gypsy and string of captives in tow.

*

In a nearby conference room, Andorf addresses his own gathering of agents and one elite guard. Staring down at the bound and gagged captives, he circumnavigates the table several times, yelling at them. His angry words spill into the hallway.

Riley pokes his head through the open door for a closer look. He smiles at the five captives bound to chairs, wires erratically wrapped around their chests. To Andorf's dismay, Riley walks the table, tugging at the wires securing explosive assemblies to the captive's chests.

"If it were me, I would have run your wires directly into the detonators. Those six stage sequences are prone to failure." Riley smiles at Andorf. "I assume this is *your* handiwork?"

The hostages gulp, watching the barefoot, pimple-face lad scrutinizing each of their faces as he surpasses a second lap around the table. Andorf sneers at Riley. "The assemblies were stuffed in a fiber box. That's how I saw the damn things wired."

Riley leans over an agent's shoulders. "Whoever it was, they were pulling your leg. These devices never would have detonated, not wired like this." He offers Andorf an open palm. "Glad to meet you. I'm Riley."

Andorf looks at his rigging and then at Riley before shaking the young lad's hand. "Uh, I'm Andorf. I take it you're part of Serin's uprising?"

Riley's eyes widen. "Indeed I am. Why Serin and I ..." He pauses at Andorf's eyes, boring into him.

"Is that so?" Andorf smirks, suspecting Riley to be Serin's third lover.

Riley's eyes narrow. "Serin's married you know—to Brutus."

Serin appears, bearing a heartwarming smile. "I thought that was you, Riley. I see you've found Andorf."

Riley peers at the ugly old lady's coat draped over the fifth chair. He looks at Andorf and grins. "So you're *that* Andorf. The other husband."

"One and the same." Serin reaches over and plants a big one on Andorf.

Riley scratches at a growth festering on his chin. "Ah, this makes sense now. Andorf here was the decoy while you and Brutus—"

"Now wait a minute," Andorf yells, staring daggers after pushing Serin away. "Don't tell me I was a pawn in your little espionage game."

Serin rubs Andorf's cheek. "Don't think of it like that, sweetie. You were a key element. We couldn't have pulled this off without you." She grins at the captives. "I see you've been busy, Poo."

Fuming, Andorf's eyes narrow on Riley. Riley judiciously steps away. "What happened to the big guy?"

"Brutus? He's on a garbage run. Looks like we have another load. Riley, can you take this rubbish and that stupid coat down below? If you hurry, you can catch him."

"Okay, but you know Kaylis. She'll be worried sick about me."

Serin cringes at the mention of Riley's emotional wife. She darts for the door. "Andorf, watch for Brutus. He won't be long."

As Riley secures the captives' hands, Andorf secretly stashes the bomb assemblies under the conference table. He slips the tattered old coat over the guard's shoulders and steps outside to watch Riley marching the group through the crowded hallway towards the aft stairs.

After a few minutes, Brutus appears with his gypsy friend. To the gypsy's dismay, Andorf shoves Brutus into the conference room. "So, this is what you and Serin have been planning all this time? What else have you two been scheming behind my back? Was this whole triad relationship a sham?"

Ready to intervene, Brutus's friend charges inside. "I'll handle this," Brutus says, wedging between his friend and Andorf. At Brutus's nod, the gypsy disappears.

"Handle this?" Andorf yells. "Are you still manipulating me?"

Brutus directs Andorf into a corner, away from the open door. "You can't blame me, Poo. This was *your* idea."

Face reddening, Andorf stares Brutus down. "What the hell are you talking about? How was stealing the Empire's grand prize any of my idea?"

"It was *you* who planted the seed in Serin's head. All that jive about taking power back from the Empire. That was your idea, wasn't it?"

"Well, I—"

"Then you and her brother broke in the Archives' building. That's why the agents took him in the middle of the night. Didn't you think for once they were using him as bait to catch Serin?"

"But we walked right in. I mean after we un-boarded the—"

"You got her all worked up over her missing brother. And your obsession with those extremist political parties and planted those images of analog trees in her head. Why you practically told her whom to rescue, where to go, and what to do. Serin merely worked out the details."

Andorf stares across the room, bewildered. "But everything I did was to find Gregory. I swear! You've got to believe me."

"Come Poo, let's take a walk." Brutus land a heavy arm on Andorf's shoulder and leads him down a series of narrow winding corridors to an atrium where they wait their turn on the floating steps. Stepping onto ascending steps, each grab hold of T-handles, rising from between their feet. At the last of seven floors, they sidestep onto the A-level before the steps level out and descend. Andorf follows Brutus through more seemingly endless corridors, whining. "I can't believe I was involved in any of this."

"More than you imagine."

"But everyone's laughing at me. Even that Riley kid calls me a distraction."

"And a good one, Poo." Brutus snickers. "While The Empire was preoccupied with you, they dropped the ball. We *had* to keep you in the dark. Can you imagine what would've happened if they had scooped you up? I heard their interrogation techniques were quite painful."

Andorf cringes.

Brutus smirks at Andorf's confused face. "You must admit, that bit with the Bogus Boat People was pure genius."

"You mean Brett was a—?"

"A double agent."

"A dead double agent. I shot him at close range."

"Nothing of the sort. He was already dead when you found him. Those thugs were trying to frame you. If your tail hadn't intervened, you would've been—"

"Don't tell me," Andorf says. "A tall skinny man? Dark trench coat? One hides behind news rags?"

Brutus nods. "Malcolm."

Andorf's hands catch his drooping head. "I suspected, but—"

"Don't you see? You made all the pieces in the plan fit together. You were the lubricant."

"Lies! Nothing but lies," Andorf yells.

"Consider them half-truths. We kept the Empire interested in you, but not enough to have them scoop you up."

Andorf gulps. "And the bugs back in my condo?"

"Luckily, we caught most of them in time," Brutus says. "Our inside man, Riley, was pulling a Watergate. You know, overwriting the recordings with his wife's ranting. Who wants to hear any of that?"

"Next, you'll tell me that the night guard at the Archives' was there to—"

"Hurry you on," Brutus says.

"The copters. What about all those turbo copters?"

"Now, *they* were real. You could have made things easier by asking Serin about her information. Until they took notice of her, she had access to the master database. Everything in the Archives' was there in her files."

"But I didn't know her then. Gregory never told me."

"And what you said to Max at the gate nearly got you killed."

"I read your thoughts. I knew you were about to save me."

Brutus raises a brow. "Of course."

Andorf freezes. "You know Aunt Bonnie never filed our marriage papers. Serin snatched her papers."

"Don't worry, Poo. Every part of our triad has been real. From the moment Serin sang to us in the park, it's all been real."

"Then promise me this, big guy."

"What Andorf?"

"Don't tell anyone else about me being your pawn."

Brutus pats Andorf's shoulder. "Our little secret."

"And no more tricks, big guy."

Walking off, Brutus grins.

CHAPTER 37

A Rough Beginning

Loudspeakers ring throughout the starship to the captain's voice. "Welcome aboard the Atlantis, my fellow hijackers." The captain chuckles. "Or shall I call her 'The Angel'? Wherever you have parked yourselves, it will not be safe during takeoff. Please stash your possessions in secured bins and get your tails down to the G-level auditorium. Consider this is your twenty … no, make this your nineteen-minute warning. Expedience is required."

Andorf and Brutus spot Serin at the end of the hallway, running in and out of the last doorway. "Over here," she yells. "We've been upgraded."

Jaw dropping, Andorf enters the enormous room where giant knickknacks are everywhere he turns. Pictures tossed here and there reveal the intended resident. "We've inherited Max's place."

Brutus steps inside. "You keep your spoils."

Serin shakes her fist and then, like her husbands, wanders about, awed by the gargantuan suite and all the special amenities.

Andorf fiddles with the size 22 shoe inserter amongst many oversized gadgets. "We certainly did well."

"Our things are next door. I haven't—" Serin pauses to salivate inside the super-sized bathroom.

"Fifteen minute warning," cabin speakers blasts. "Everyone report to the G-level Auditorium."

With the hallway nearly impassable, Brutus shuffles Serin and Andorf into Max's private elevator, wide enough to house a grown stallion. In seconds, they exit onto G-level between the captain's bridge and the stage end of a seven thousand-seat auditorium. Brutus rounds the stage ahead of the others, claiming the wider aisle seat. Serin sits alongside. Andorf plunks down next to her. Serin grins at the pair. "I'm keeping Max's private bathroom."

Complaints arise as the large room packs in from the rear. Many citizens switch seats only to find them with similar defects. Brutus rushes past the many citizens in the aisles arguing with their seats. He exits behind the stage, heading to the bridge for a word with the captain. Returning to his seat, the auditorium's speakers again crackle.

"Folks, this is your captain. I have been informed of your unpleasant seating. Though your seats may seem uncomfortable now, you will appreciate how they lean forward when you experience takeoff. I apologize for the temporary discomfort." The captain clears his throat. "I believe a round of applause is overdue. Let us thank Serin Gray and Brutus Bittner for their tireless efforts in pulling off our little caper."

At Serin's whisking hands, Brutus returns to the bridge. After a moment, the captain is back at the microphone. "And let's not forget Andorf Johnson, whose antique silverware financed much of this operation."

From the bridge, Brutus hears thunderous applause, whistles and cheers. His smile vaporizes at the sight of the bridge crew's horrified faces focusing on displayed images of soldiers accumulating around the upper hatch. "My God! They're breaking out pry bars."

Captain Thom skips pre-checks and activates the stepped auto-sequence. Forehead sweat pooling on his jumpsuit, he lifts the microphone from its cradle and catches his breath. His voice quickens as he keys the mic. "Quiet everyone. Quiet! I need everyone securely strapped in their seats. Share seats if you must. The situation outside has escalated. We shall be departing much sooner than expected."

On the auditorium displays, Captain Thom watches passengers playing musical seats. "Tighten those straps. After our brakes release, we'll be accelerating down Jake's mountain at a pretty good clip. When our thrusters fire, positive G-forces will press you hard in your seats. I mean really hard. Most of you will pass out. Others will wish they had passed out. And use those headrests, folks. Let's not make this more painful than it needs to be. Things will be intense. As I said, most of you will pass out. Hell, I may even—"

Cameras follow a Whippet 600D angling for the starship. Both frontal viewport windows vibrate as the two-man copter backs away, spins clockwise ninety degrees to land, skids straddling the outside pair of six iron rails. Grabbing his mic, Sergeant Ginzbug snarls up at the bridge. Speakers mounted beneath the cab squeal. His voice is loud enough for everyone in the bridge to hear every single word.

"Troops, I regret to inform you there shall be no gunplay this evening. I know many of you were looking for a little action, but we have strict orders from the general not to damage that starship. With the exception of perhaps the ship's captain, *everyone* and I do mean everyone is to be taken alive. Am I perfectly clear? Everyone got that? Now get your weapons on those windows, soldiers."

Brutus and the bridge crew watch soldiers crawl up flatcars cradling the Atlantis, resembling baby spiders emerging from their mother's egg sack. The captain gulps. His voice jitters as he again keys the microphone.

"Folks, as I said, we'll be rolling downhill at a pretty good clip. At a critical point nearing the valley floor, our engines will kick in, thrusting us even harder into our seats. Those who have not passed out will have second opportunity. Your seats will correct to a more comfortable reclining pitch as we climb the next hill."

The captain crosses his fingers, lips vibrating in silent prayer, gazing upward. "The railcar clamps should release before we run out of vertical track. Expect a whole lot of shaking as we struggle to reach escape velocity. With good fortune, we shall awaken to a glorious last sunrise and a mild headache. I assure you, both will quickly pass."

With dozens of rifles training upon the bridge viewports, Captain Thom drops the microphone to raise both hands.

*

Passengers read fear in the captain's words. Pressing hard into their seats until passing out lacks certain appeal, even to Serin. She hears much jabbering, sees many holding hands, crying from rows behind. She jerks away from Andorf's squeezing grip to rub the color back into her hand. Mounting complaints are everywhere.

"What happens when the army breaks in?"

"What if those clamp things don't release?"

"What's he mean by our last sunrise?"

"I hate headaches."

Raised brow amid the chaos, Andorf turns to Serin. "You could have told me about stealing my family heirloom. You know how much that silver was worth?"

Serin smirks. "Under the circumstances, I didn't think you'd mind. It would have been too heavy to bring along." Andorf stares, lost for words. He begins to speak out until Serin shoulder bumps him. "You should be grateful, knowing it went for something useful instead of just sitting in that drawer, collecting dust. Besides, you could have been arrested for holding that much silver."

"I cringe at the thought of my family silver melting down." Andorf sneers. "Seven generations of Johnsons ate from that silverware. It was in my family for over two centuries."

"Now it served two purposes in its lifetime. Look at all the smiling faces, Poo."

"Oh, so now *you're* calling me Poo?" Andorf takes a moment to scan the crowd. "Is this what you call smiling? Everyone looks pretty damn scared to death, including me."

Serin scans the crowd. She clenches her teeth. "I'm not looking forward to all this either, but it's better than prison. Hell, I'm wanted for counter-subversive activities. Brutus … he'd be charged with murder."

Andorf winces with thought of Brett's slumping corpse. "I know the feeling." He sees Riley across the aisle, throwing thumbs up and everyone else lost in their own worlds. "These passengers are in for a harsh awakening. They have no idea how their lives are about to change, how dependent they've become, living off their sparse government feedings."

Lips trembling, Serin falls against the front-leaning headrest and wipes tears accumulating on her warming cheeks. "One minute I was in the van with Greg. Then next, I was herding cats up the entry ramp. I lost him in that—circus out there." She pauses long enough to sniff. "How could Greg leave me again?"

Andorf wipes her cheeks. "From what I've heard about the Cos, you should be glad he's no longer in that wretched place."

Serin sniffs her runny nose. "I am—I do. I know Greg's no longer a guinea pig destined to become ingredients of someone's power cell."

Andorf envisions his best friend strapped to complex machinery, needles poking him from all sides, injecting him with aluminized paraffin and bovine growth hormones. "No, not Gregory!"

Serin shivers at Andorf's colorful images planted in her thoughts. "Quit that, Andorf. I know Greg was your best friend, but you have no idea what I'm going through. Why can't you—"

"Ten minute warning," crackles from the auditorium speakers.

*

Both viewports vibrate as the bridge illuminates in sapphire blue. All drop to the bridge floor. Brutus gulps at the focused beam entering the bridge. He has witnessed first-hand what damage that bright spot does to organic materials such as human skin. Hard-pressed into nooks, Brutus and the crew cover their eyes from the intense beam tracing the bridge from a vantage point above. Emitting a mechanical high-pitched snapping sound, the beam sweeps harmlessly side-to-side across switchgear, control panels, and radio equipment. As the beam dissipates, the first mate raises a lone finger, but quickly retracts it at the sickening smell of burnt flesh.

"Ye—ow!" he screams, leaning against a seat to examine his charred, smoking digit. "They melted my bird finger."

A raw metal taste saturates the small cabin. Blood spurts from the shortened tip of the first mate's longest finger at each beat of his heart. The navigator grabs a barf bag and ducks around the corner. The first mate clamps his charred finger shut with two fingers from his other hand while the radioman scavenges through the medic tin. After shaking an orange powder into a bag, the radioman shoves the first mate's bleeding stub inside. As the powder morphs to bright red, the first mate screams into his arm and passes out. The radioman wraps the bleeding stub in multiple layers of bandages. The navigator returns, stumbling closer. After one look at the bright red appendage, he grabs another bag and disappears.

The radioman eases the first mate into a front seat while the captain wedges reflective foam against the viewports. Brutus reads the ingredients of the orange powder aloud. "This stuff contains Magic Dust, cement mix, and freeze-dried bacon. Hell, if it can clog up your arteries, it can surely stop his bleeding."

The captain peels back a corner of the foam to see spectators in masks of disgraced politicians, taunting the soldiers. With the auto-sequence countdown approaching single digits, he engages the external speakers and keys the mic. "Will someone out there *please* remove the wheel chocks?"

Landing troop carriers take root on either side of the wide rail bed. Squadrons of soldiers swarm out like fire ants protecting a disturbed mound. They form human chains to scale the flat bed cars. Citizens by the handfuls rush the elevated roadbed only to be turned away by as many troops. Captain Thom again keys the mic. "Citizens, we need those chocks removed."

A spattering of citizens run up the steep left grade, make faces at the troops, and then run down the right grade, chased by troops. Other citizens appear and fling the wheel chocks into the mountainside's thick thorny brush.

Captain Thom engages the auditorium speakers. "Everyone strap in. We're ready to roll." With Brutus strapped into a jump seat, the captain flips a pair of large toggle switches. The brake mechanisms disengage with a loud *THUNK* and then ... nothing. Absolutely nothing.

Brutus scratches his chin, running through the starship's blueprints in his head as the captain and crew disperse clueless guesses. "We are grossly overweight. The train wheels must be rusted in place. If only we had a little—"

"Nudge?" Captain Thom keys the mic. "Folks, on the count of two, I want each and every one of you to lean forward. On the count of four, everyone leans back into their seats. Everyone got that? Forward on two, back on four. Please remain secured in your seats while doing so."

"Here we go. One and *two*." Everyone leans forward.

"Three and *four*." All lean back.

"Again, folks. Let's do it again. One and *two*." Again, everyone leans forward.

"And three and *four*." All lean back and ... nothing!

The captain's appears lost. "What the hell's going on, Brutus? Why aren't we moving?" He points to the displays showing troops swarming from all sides. "If we don't get this bucket rolling soon—"

The first mate suddenly awakens, clasping his bandaged finger. "Why not fire up the engines, captain? That should give us a little nudge."

Brutus snorts. He pulls a panel behind his jump seat and checks test points. "Won't work. Our engines won't fire until all railcar clamps release and that can't happen without a sixty-degree attitude. There's no way to reach the compass mechanism from within the starship."

The captain glances at the displays. "We'd better do something in a hurry. The army is nearly through the outer hatch and I hear them pecking away out there on our frontal viewports."

"Use the force field generators?" the navigator says, out of a corner of his mouth.

Captain Thom stares down his radioman. "Force field?"

"All spaceships have them. Go ahead, captain, energize them."

The first mate chuckles. "You've seen too many old space flicks."

The radioman sneers at the others. "Yeah. Yeah. Next you'll tell me there's no such thing as phasor pistols."

The navigator reappears, wiping his face. "Oh *those* things exist alright. At least before they began showing up in elementary schools. The government confiscated every last one of them."

"I doubt we'll need them in space," the captain says. "But then again, I've never ventured beyond the moons of Saturn."

Brutus lifts his head from the control wiring. "My old buddy, Rob Fous, runs Titan Moon Base Operation. Why, I haven't seen him in …"

The captain grimaces. "I'd stay away from his kid sister Vickie. A bitter woman if there ever was one. She made my life a living hell when I was stationed there repairing her relay satellites."

Brutus's heart races at the name. "You've never seen her soft side."

*

Auditorium passengers are becoming restless. Andorf unstraps and rises, stretching his aching legs. "Where do you think you're going, mister?" Serin yells.

"I was about to check on—"

"Sit your ass down, Poo. Brutus can take care of himself."

Looking around, Andorf takes his sweet time complying. *No one would be here if it were not for my family heirloom.*

Serin throws her hands up in disgust. "Not that silverware bit again. Strap yourself in. You heard what the captain said. We could be rolling at any moment."

*

Sergeant Ginzbug's voice appears on the starship's main radio frequency. "Removing those wheel chocks was futile, Captain. Guava delay boards have the train wheels locked down. It would take an engineer days to bypass those lockouts and I'll be through the outer hatch in a matter of minutes. Give it up, captain. The only place you and your crew are going is to the brig."

"No wonder the starship won't budge," says Captain Thom. "Those guava circuits, whatever they are, have the train locked. No wonder we can't move." He frowns at the others. "The militia trains for these situations. Damn! We played right into their bloody hands."

At the captain's nod, the first mate keys the microphone with his good hand. "Folks, we have a bit of bad news."

"It's not all bad," the navigator says. "You hear the sergeant. He won't be shooting you after all."

"Are you kidding me?" Captain Thom yells. "I wouldn't make it three feet out the upper portal. But I'd rather be shot than return to the Cos." His crew all nod heads.

Brutus surfaces for fresh air, control modules dangling from his hands by their wiring harnesses. "Did someone mention Guava circuits? Did he mean these freshly plucked delay circuits?"

The captain toggles the brake release switch. This time two distinct thunks, but still the starship rests in place. He and the others watch Ginzbug on a display, pacing below in small circles, struggling with a limp. The upper camera auto-pivots to track the sergeant marching toward the starship. Ginzbug gazes upwards, appearing to be inspecting the private's progress with the viewport flanges, while barking out orders. The sergeant steadies himself against the nearest flatcar. He looks around, twitching.

A horrid creak grows loud enough for Brutus and the bridge crew to take notice. They feel the massive starship lurch forward, see Ginzbug hobbling down the steep grade with soldiers running behind. Columns of privates spill onto the roadbed. Unable to stop themselves, they tumble into the blackberry vine infested hillside. Outside microphones catch them hollering in pain. Dodging the wall of falling privates, soldiers follow Ginzbug, ahead of the creeping railcars.

Ginzbug spits brown goo onto the gravel roadbed. He shakes the nearest private by the shoulders and freezes. The camera auto-zooms in on the sergeant's crossed eyes before he makes a hobbled dash for his Whippet 600D. He leaps through the pilot door and reaches for the starter button just as the leading railcar butts up against the Whippet, sliding the small copter along the rails on its skids. He leaps from the passenger door onto the gravel bed and watches his Whippet's skids screeching and sparking as if it were an abandoned child's toy. At the first rail imperfection, the Whippet kilters off balance and slips off the rails to find stable footing on the steep-angled roadbed gravel, teetering above the two thousand-foot drop.

The sergeant staggers to his feet. He limps closer and grabs the door handle, but as the starship's upper wing grazes the tip of the main rotor blade and the handle slips from his grasp. Gravel beneath the skids gives way, taking the Whippet 600D for its final ride down the steep mountainside.

Soldiers gather en mass to witness their sergeant jumping up and down, swearing at the top of his lungs as his Whippet 600D tumbles end over end. All but Ginzbug appear disappointed when it finally comes to a rest among the thickets without a fireball. The sergeant unclips his handheld radio and tosses it down the hillside. One private grabs his arm. Looking over their shoulders, both men turn in tandem, entangling themselves in the thin wire of a deflated weather balloon.

Viewing the calamity outside, Brutus throws high fives at the captain and his crew. A wrapping slips from his pocket onto the floor. He hands Captain Thom the present. The captain unwraps his cherished gift, unfolding the many creases. At his nod, the first mate keys the microphone. With seasoned lips, CaptainThom blows long and hard into the hand carved shofar sending a defiant gesture blasting out every speaker aboard the Atlantis, inside and out as the starship gains momentum down the slight decline. Sergeant Ginzbug shakes a fist at the bridge creeping past as Brutus and the bridge crew strap in. Auditorium speakers crackle to the Captain's jubilant voice. "Please disregard that last announcement, folks. Everyone tighten your seat belts. You are in for the wildest ride of your lives."

*

The Atlantis barrels down the mountainside, pressing everyone hard into their seat backs. Andorf engulfs Serin's hand as both focus on the vacant aisle seat to her right. "I'm sure he's OK."

Serin squeezes his hand, flashing a half-hearted grin.

Screams wail out, louder than the clankity-clank of rail joints below, growling increasingly faster, gaining in pitch. Passengers grab their ears at the ship's fierce vibrations. The shaking lessens slightly as the starship levels out. Then the starship angles stiffly upwards. The rear burners fire full throttle and vibrations return in wicked vengeance. Steeper and steeper they ascend, pressing everyone much harder into their seats. Unprepared for such punishment, most passengers are out for the count, others are not far behind.

*

Brutus is nailed against the rear wall in his jumper seat, calling for the captain without response. Vision blurring, he appears to be the sole survivor and just barely so. With every bit of strength, Brutus drags himself forward, unclips the captain's restraints, and wrestles him onto the floor at the copilot's feet. Brutus straps himself in the captain's seat, verbalizing everything that could possibly go wrong.

Why haven't the docking clamps disengaged? With engines at full throttle, they should have released by now. In one display, he sees the upper hatch cover fly past. He feels blood draining from his face, accumulating in the rear of his skull. He squints at the instrumentation panel and sees nothing abnormal. He fights for the emergency clamp release toggle above his head, but his hand falls hard in his lap. Again, he tries, but his hand refuses movement. Giving it his all, his knee bumps a button below the panel. Warning lights, flashing ruby red, suddenly morph to emerald green. Brutus's knee relaxes.

"Good evening, captain," a voice genie speaks in a mechanical voice. "Your wish is my—"

"Siros, activate alpha gamma delta," Brutus calls out, slurring his words.

After three attempts, Siros replies, in a voice sweeter than a girl on a first date. "Hello, big guy. Controls are now voice activated."

Brutus squeezes out a sequence of words. "Monitor front camera,"

"Cannot comply," Siros says.

He repeats the command multiple times before frontal displays switch to grainy images of the three pairs of rails rushing toward him. Brutus's eyes narrow on a faint object in the background growing larger. "Bow lights on," he says, repeatedly.

The image clarifies. A warning sign zips past, too fast to read. A second sign zips past. A dashboard icon pulses red faster than his heart rate. Another hazard icon flashes bright red in unison with the first. Brutus can barely make out a third image. It too zips past too quickly to read, but the red triangle engulfing the exclamation point appears to be the third and final warning of pending rail termination. Brutus worries about the ship's weight, overloaded with passengers, many barely strapped into shared seats. He worries about the starship tearing itself apart.

He feels the engines roaring at full thrust, ship listing side to side, struggling to break free from its host. The undercarriage emits a dull scraping sound as the Atlantis pulls away, ascending under maximum G-force. Every last drop of blood draining from his brain, Brutus's heart feels as if it is about to explode. His head hits the back of the captain seat. He is out for the count.

Brutus awakens to a haunting silence and nagging headache as the captain promised. Floating several inches above his seat, his foggy eyes widen to scan the instrument panel and the captain swimming laps around the bridge. At the captain's awkward glance, Brutus unstraps and jettisons himself over the first mate to the starboard portal for a better view of the sunrise.

The first mate awakes to a flashing light. Looking back at the captain, he taps the indicator with his good hand. "Anything major, Thom? Is the circuit dead?"

Brutus grimaces. "Our outer hatch cover detached and flew off during takeoff. It's nothing we can't live without for the moment." He reaches inside the instrument panel, rips one end of a blue-striped wire loose, and the warning light returns to an emerald green. He grins at the others.

The navigator and radioman awaken, awed at the view of the sun kissing the earth off the starboard bow. The captain smirks at Brutus and his inexperienced crew on their maiden flight. He kicks off and jettisons himself into his seat. Strapping in, he directs Brutus back to the jumper seat. "Though I've witnessed this same sight a dozen times, I still find *this* sunrise breathtaking."

The crew sees passengers on the displays awakening to the radiant beauty of the sun eclipsing the planet's outline as starboard portals darken, filtering out harmful rays. Heads strain to peer out the windows at the incredible view as they float inches above their seat cushions. In the silent serenity, many play tag with items randomly floating overhead. While his crew runs through their final checks, Captain Thom keys the microphone.

"Excluding that near death experience of having our guts twisted out your throats and your current lightheadedness, I take it everyone has survived takeoff. I hope everyone caught a glimpse of that surreal Terra sunrise. Soon there will only be dots of light breaking through the dark web of space. Please remain strapped in your seats."

"What? Okay. I'm getting to that." The captain rekeys the mic. "Now a word for those playing with those items floating above your heads. When gravity returns, those large items *will* hurt you. Do your best to stay clear of those floaters when gravity returns. They become heavy real fast when our gravity generators kick in. Gravity lights are located throughout the starship. Anytime they glow yellow, you had better latch onto one of the many handrails conveniently located about the Atlantis. When those light glow red, you will find out why. So remember, green means you are free to move about the starship. Yellow means impending trouble, and red means uh-oh. Everyone clear on this? After everything we have been through, I would hate to lose anyone. Again, please remain securely strapped in those seats until those gravity lights glow bright green."

After several moments and a low frequency hum, everyone's behinds are seated firmly against their cushions. The captain and crew cringe at the screams emanating from the auditorium. Again, he keys the microphone. "It appears that our artificial gravity generators are online and functioning properly. I suggest you make your way to your cabins and get your personal things in order. You will find complementary cheese sandwiches and beverages there. For those without assigned cabins, please gather at the rear of the auditorium. Our gypsy friends will find you temporary placement and provide your meals. Enjoy this last private dinner, folks, and thank you for flying starship Atlantis. I trust your stay will be most enjoyable."

CHAPTER 38

Second Thoughts

The auditorium slowly empties. Andorf stands, eyes narrowing on Serin. "My friends, possessions … all gone. Now I'm about to spend the rest of my life in this …" He looks about the confines of the auditorium's sterile metal walls. "This metal contraption."

Serin glances at the empty aisle seat and then at Andorf and his poisoned squint. "Try losing your brother," she yells. A woman a few rows behind cries out. Serin shoots Andorf dirty looks as she fights her way through fleeing passengers to reach the sobbing woman. "I'm Serin."

The woman lifts heavy eyes to accept Serin's outstretched hand. "I know who you are, dear," the woman says, choking on tears.

Her husband nods. "We all do."

The woman wipes her runny nose on her husband's sleeve. She sniffles at the gathering crowd. "I'm sorry, Ms. Serin. When I heard someone missing her brother, everything hit me."

Serin throws an arm over the woman's shoulder, as does her husband. "It's alright, sweetie. Everyone here has left others behind." Teary eyed, the woman scans the nodding heads surrounding her.

"I left my best friend back there," Andorf says. "I'll never see him again."

Serin's evil stare has him stepping away. "He was *my* brother, dammit."

"I meant Binky." Andorf half-smiles at the surrounding faces. "My rabbit. That little guy saved my life more than once you know. Back on Earth, he's out there somewhere, scavenging food, scared to death some hawk or wild dog will make a meal of him."

"People eat their pets, when they get hungry," the husband says.

Serin reaches out to Andorf. "I'm sure someone took him in. Binky's hopping around their bedroom right now, licking their feet."

Another passenger becomes hysterical and then another.

"This must stop." Bracing against Andorf, Serin stands on a seat. "Listen up everyone, listen." She waits for the jabbering to lessen. "We, aboard the Atlantis, are the privileged few, ones who actually crawled out from under the Empire's oppressive thumb. We are the envy of those we left behind. We will journey beyond the stars. Our grandchildren of a hundred generations hence complete what we've begun today. Humanity's fate rests upon our shoulders. We cannot fail them."

The immediate crowd disperses, many wiping their eyes. Serin steps down to lead Andorf back to their seats, leaning into the awkward front-leaning seat. Andorf grins. "Guess we've survived Judgment Day."

Serin reaches into her backpack stashed beneath her seat. She tears open the Asp brand dehydrated fruit package, offering him a hardened apple chunk. "Judgment Day? That'll be what our distant successors will face when they step onto a dark, burned out world two millennia from now. They'll be the ones truly facing Judgment Day."

Andorf reads concern in her thoughts. He sees blurred images of the old man, Chester. "What troubles you, Serin? You look confused."

Serin leans back in her seat. She grabs hold of his wrist. "How do you feel about me, Andorf? I mean … would you come back from the future and warn me about things … I mean, if such a thing was possible?"

Saying nothing, Andorf raises a brow. At Serin's touch, he envisions himself an aging man behind octagon glasses warning his younger self. He shivers, seeing himself an even older man, gasping for breath, oxygen mask strapped to his face, hand reaching out to Serin. "Of course I would." He gazes deep into her brown eyes and smiles. "I'll never love another."

Serin gasps at his words. She explains what went down at the Cos and the old man predicting the seven deaths, including his own. "It *was* you, back at the Cos. You came back as Chester to warn me, didn't you? You've done this before. How many times? How many more times?"

Andorf suddenly gains a fondness for the old coffee vendor. Chester's last words become his own. "Until I won't lose you."

A stirring in the aisles has Serin and Andorf turning their heads. Sighting Brutus pushing his way through the exiting crowd, Serin leaps from her seat. She jumps into Brutus's arm and plants a juicy one on his kisser.

"We did it, big guy." She freezes. Feeling sticky wet arms, she pulls away. "Look at your clothes, Brutus. They're all ripped. You're bleeding!"

Andorf catches up. Examining Brutus, he chuckles. "Did you get a good look at her? Did you get her ID number?"

Brutus throws both hands out. "I was caught in a wiring panel when the Atlantis began its roll. I was nailed against the rear wall, rivets digging into my back. I barely made it back to the captain's seat when G-forces—"

Andorf grins at Brutus. "Uh huh, Like you really piloted this ship."

Brutus pulls up his ratty shirt. "But see where it sliced my arms?"

Serin rolls her eyes. She turns to Andorf. "I heard you've met my Uncle Steven."

"Don't you mean your Uncle Sven?"

Serin snickers. "Oh yeah, Uncle Sven. How'd you think I slipped past those dicks and agents?"

Andorf's eyes enlarge. "My patriot poster. Those were *your* eyes?"

Serin nods.

"What about Sven's wife?"

Brutus grins. "The old geezer lived alone."

"But he kept speaking of her as—"

"His little helper," Serin says. "He remembers *me* as his little helper, the little girl in the lavender blouse. That's what I wore whenever I visited. Poor Uncle Steven and his dementia. I worry about him."

"And his drinking," Andorf says. "I was really fond of the old Swede. Did I tell you about the time I barged into his place? He was ready to take me on with his broom."

Serin laughs. "Swede? Don't tell me you fell for that bogus accent? Years ago some VP shot him on a hunting trip. He could no longer work or draw a government check, so he developed a foreign accent and became another welfare Toxidian. When his memory failed, that's who he was."

Andorf grabs at a shiny metal piece dangling from Serin's necklace. "What's this? It looks important."

Serin yanks it away and twirls it in front of his face. "I downloaded the Empire's master database before I went underground. It contains petabytes of dirty little secrets and anything else you'd ever want to know about the Empire. Things we'll need to rebuild our society."

"Things the Empire would kill to protect." Brutus raises a brow at Andorf. "On more than one occasion I've been told to look the other way."

"Wait a minute," Andorf yells. "Are you implying my parent's deaths weren't an accident?"

Brutus backs away from Andorf. "Now I didn't say that. Best you drop this before it drives you crazy."

"It's on that chip!" Andorf grabs at the silicon chunk, but Brutus blocks his reach.

"I'll look it up when I have time. I promise." Serin drops the necklace down her shirt and flies out the front exit, blowing kisses. Andorf turns to give chase until Brutus snags one of his belt loops.

"Whoa there, Poo. What's your hurry?"

"What the hell's going on, Brutus? Why's Serin always running off like that? Don't tell me its best to leave her be."

Brutus chuckles. "Follow me. We've got some public relations work." Brutus leads Andorf out the back of the auditorium, through narrow winding corridors, interrupting conversations of excited citizens settling into their new digs. Many shout thanks, offer skin rubs as the pair passes their open cabin doors.

"Gosh, I feel like a celebrity," Andorf says, grinning ear to ear.

Brutus snarfs. "Enjoy it now, Poo. In a week they won't remember you."

*

Exiting Max's private elevator onto the A-level, Serin has a good ten-minute lead on her husbands. She darts out Max's door, heading for the next-door cabin. A tall woman's hand grabs her arm and drags her down the hallway, pinning Serin against an open door with her torso.

Serin peers up at the woman's face. "Don't tell me, you're having second thoughts."

"You have no idea what it's like living with guys in whom you have no sexual interest."

Peeing at the inflamed faces of the other lesbian and the two gay men, Serin pushes off the dominant woman. "Please, I have a brother."

The other woman growls. "That's different."

Serin grins. "Believe me, ladies, they're all the same."

"Not so," one of the gay men yells.

Serin backs around the tall woman, flashing dual wedding bands. "Must go! I've got two husbands."

"You go, girl! Every night a three-way," a man's voice yells.

At the two couples arguing the pros and cons of artificial insemination, Serin darts for her cabin and quickly ducks inside. A few minutes later, she pops her head out at friendlier gestures emanating down the hallway. She sees Andorf and Brutus all grins, shaking hands like hopeful candidates. She flails her arms, waving them closer. "That foursome two doors down is having issues."

Brutus grumbles. "They'll just have to work it out. We're filled way beyond capacity."

"Wait here." Serin disappears into the room. As the door shuts, Andorf and Brutus hear the odd quad down the hallway bickering, cursing at one another. Both grin uncomfortably, imagining what is taking place behind the closed door. Their own door cracks open. Serin and Brutus step aside, clearing a path.

Andorf enters. After visiting Max's quarters, everything appears compact. He slides the adjacent mirrored door aside to find his entire wardrobe hanging in the walk-in closet. His socks and briefs are neatly folded in the middle cabinet drawer, his prized collectibles strapped to shelves above. At his feet leans a rolled-up poster. A slight unroll verifies it is the patriot poster from his living room. He turns to see Serin and Brutus standing directly behind him, sporting oversized smiles.

"Didn't I tell you we'd find your things?" Brutus says.

"But you said the authorities—"

"Out here, Poo, we *are* the authorities," Serin says.

Brutus clears his throat. "Those late hours I was putting in? It took time to do all this."

"All while I was busy assembling a loyal crew," Serin says. "Ones who despised the Empire."

"And what better place to find them than the Cos?" Brutus says. "Serin had every official and militant out looking for her."

Serin laughs. "You should have seen them flying past us down Jake's Mountain like their pants were on fire. The last thing they expected was for us to be in their own panel vans heading *up* the mountain."

Brutus directs Andorf with a head tilt. "Hey, check out that top drawer again."

Andorf feels around. He finds four things hiding under his socks. "My emitters! My hologram emitters." He pokes his head out of the closest to look about the quarters. "But there's not enough room in here for these."

"Are forgetting the Atlantis has ten observation decks?" Brutus says. "They can get very dark."

Andorf re-wraps the emitters and places them back under his socks. "They'll take time to calibrate."

"Time? We'll have plenty of that."

Serin clears her throat. "I hate to burst your bubbles, guys, but with everything we've got to accomplish, I see little play time in your futures."

Andorf's mood darkens. Dropping shoes and socks, he plops onto the king-size bed. Elbows resting atop his thighs, head in upturned palms, he grabs unconsciously at a fluff of white fur floating past. He squirms at the wet nudge on his bare toes and Serin and Brutus snickering at his jerking feet.

"Cut it out, you two," Andorf yells. His brows rise at the second toe lick. Heart racing, he sits up to an excited long-eared rabbit leaping into his lap. "Binkers! You found my Binkers."

Andorf pulls Binky close to his chest. Binky chins every bit of Andorf that he can reach. Tears streaming down his cheeks, Andorf smiles at Serin and Brutus.

Sitting next to Andorf, Serin finds Brutus also in tears. "I knew you had a soft spot for that rabbit."

Brutus wipes his face on his shirt. "Who would've thought?"

Andorf's eyes glaze over. "Perhaps living in this metal contraption won't be so bad after all."

CHAPTER 39

Room With A View

Brutus yanks Serin to her feet. "Are you ready for a surprise? You too, Poo. Follow me." He leads them down the long winding passages to the rear of the A-Level and pauses outside a large room. "Another world lies beyond these doors." His palm slams a mushroomed, wall-mounted button and their hair ruffles from the air escaping the dark room. Feeling ahead with their hands, Andorf and Serin follow Brutus into the pitch-black room where pin-prickly views of space draw them toward panoramic floor to ceiling windows. Each claims a spot along the port bow, gawking at countless stars dotting the blackness like a large moth-eaten curtain. The stars appear so close, motionless, frozen in time. They bump the chilled glass, reaching out to touch.

Serin's eyes widen. "There's so many. I wonder which contain worlds such as Earth."

Andorf raises both hands over his head. Voice exciting, his hands become animated. Flailing his arms about, he emits swooshing sounds. "Or worlds with purple creatures, bulging eyes atop their enlarged pointy heads. Maybe little green men with webbed feet that liquefy and ooze across the floor."

Brutus laughs. "Get real. Those stars are so distant, we'd never reach them, not in our lifetime. Take Nero, where we're heading, some four light years away. Just getting there will take us a millennia and another millennia back to Earth. When the Atlantis returns home, Terra will be in a different location in the Milky Way."

Serin taps the glass. "I feel so small."

"Why not cryogenics?" Andorf asks. "We sleep. We dream. We reawaken at journey's end, dusting a thousand years off our clothes."

Brutus stares at Andorf as if he has lost his mind. "Freezing is only good for a hundred years. It leaves everyone sterile."

Serin rubs her itchy, expanding belly. "How will you ever keep this ship together that long, big guy?"

"I won't live forever you know. I must train technicians."

Serin turns away from the view. "How many of these observation decks did you say we have on the Atlantis?"

Brutus sits beside her for a better view of the Pleiades cluster. "Nine others, like this one. Why?"

"We'll need classrooms, lots of them. Can that game sphere of yours be reprogrammed? Can Andorf's holograph emitters be replicated?"

Rolling his eyes, Brutus glances back at Andorf. "Looks like you'll never get to play Sumatra, Poo."

"Brutus, you'll handle maintenance. Andorf, you'll recruit our workforce and match passengers with tasks." Serin pauses, watching her husbands scratching their heads. "I'll organize training. At breakfast, we'll query everyone, find what he or she does best. It's time to hone your negotiating skills, Andorf. You'll also be handling grievances."

Andorf pulls away from the window with a disgusted gaze. "It sounds like we're building another empire."

Serin follows Andorf as he paces about. "One that needs to survive the next two millennia out here in space. Our descendants *must* bring order back to a dying old world."

Brutus chuckles. "One without government suppression."

Feeling fragile, Serin returns to the window, concealing her doubtful face. She gazes back at her husbands. "What we did here was right, wasn't it? I mean … displacing all these citizens from the only world they've ever known?"

Andorf grimaces at the large A-level observation deck beginning to fill. "Not to mention the close quarters, food rationing, and shared facilities."

Brutus rubs his unshaven face. "We'll make the Atlantis our home. We'll have each other, Binky, and soon our little one. Think how lucky he'll be to have three loving parents."

"She'll have," Serin says.

The triad looks about the half-crowded room and the curious passengers drawn to the panoramic view. They relinquish their spots to mill about in the crowd. Andorf points out several expectant women with bellies much larger than Serin's. "Looks like we won't be the first."

One expecting mothers appears truly honored as the threesome step closer. The husband breaks focus on the stars to address his wife and the others, speaking in heavy German accent. "From what we have seen, I'd say we are in good hands."

Andorf grins. "Wilhelm? Wilhelm Mattigan? What the hell happened to you? I went back to your office and—"

"They never heard of me." Wilhelm shakes his head. "As you may recall, I was very paranoid that night in the restaurant. Everyone was listening." He turns to rub his wife's stomach through her stretched blouse. "Caution is in order when you have a little one on the way."

Serin's eyes focus upon Andorf. "Others should be as wise."

Andorf taps his old friend's shoulder. "But what happened, Wilhelm? Every trace of you has been—"

"Erased. That's how the Empire works, my old friend. One swipe on their devices and you never existed. Changing city names is a favored trick of the empires. They're all in cahoots with each another, you know. Serin, I heard you performed your own disappearing trick."

Serin twitches. "Getting locked away in the Cos was the last thing I wanted. When agents came snooping around at work, I grabbed what I could and went underground. Thank you for programming the temporary password, Wilhelm. That got us into the Cos."

Wilhelm nods. "I thought your whole plan was—" He pauses at the sharp jab to his ribs. "Oh, I am being quite rude. Everyone, this is my wife, Darby."

Darby turns to show off her pregnant profile. "I'm due in three weeks. Wilhelm and I are hoping to have the first space baby."

Serin stares at Darby's swelling mid-section. Odds are stacked against a third-term baby surviving such a rough takeoff. As the crowd packs in, gathering uncomfortably close, Serin reflects upon the soothsayer's words of never seeing her own babies.

"I was locked away in that dreadful Cos for two years," one man says.

"We can't thank you enough, all of you," his mate says.

After waves of thanks, the immediate crowd dwindles. One man remains, shifting eyes between Serin and the floor as if carefully choosing words. The room quiets, all eyes upon the man as he clears his throat.

"I—I'm not saying everything you've done for us, Serin, hasn't been great, but—"

Serin steps toward the bashful man. "Don't be afraid to speak. We're all friends here."

Bobbing heads and whisking hands encourage the tongue-tied man to speak his piece. "I—I think I speak for the others. I mean we're all scared. What's to become of us? What're we all supposed to be doing out here in space, so far from home?"

The man timidly shrivels within the crowd. Serin scans the faces who are waiting for answers. She doesn't know where to begin. Andorf wedges his way through the small crowd and steps ahead of Serin. "My fellow renegades. With your skills and hard work, we'll create a new society, unbound by repression from which we've narrowly escaped." He pauses to survey the nodding heads. "It is *we* who will determine our future. This is *our* ship and *we* make the rules now."

"What about those miserable food scraps we've heard about?" a woman yells, diminishing the crowd's cheers. "Those tiny cheese sandwiches were barely—"

The room quiets to a surrounding sea of frowns and a bridge of sighs. Andorf clears his throat. "Look everyone, I know things are a bit sparse right now. I'm not too thrilled about the cutbacks and communal facilities, but things will improve. We're making a few sacrifices now for our future freedom, and of course, there will be a few adjustments here and—"

"Adjustments? What kind of adjustments?"

Andorf stutters, grasping for missing words. Serin throws an arm around him and raises her voice. "Controlling our population, for instance. If we grow too fast, our rations will lessen; too slow, and we won't be able to maintain this starship. We'll take on supplies on refueling orbits around Moon Base Titan."

"What about being stuck on this ship?" another asks. "I'm terribly claustrophobic."

Andorf shivers at the memory of being stuck in the thirty-six inch concrete drainpipe with Gregory. "We'll all be way too busy to worry about such trivial things. At breakfast, we'll take names, match them with your skills. Leave them with your cabin assignments in the box as you exit the dining hall. Think about what you are good at, what you can contribute."

"What about—"

"Maintaining our ship? Brutus here will keep it running top notch, but he'll need skilled assistants." Brutus flashes a huge grin. "And we'll need citizens to handle conflicts as they occur."

Many grumble. "Something that's fair for everyone."

Serin pulls Brutus aside. "Look at Andorf. He's got all the answers."

"I knew he was good for something," Brutus whispers, taking Serin's slug on his back.

"What about fuel?" someone yells. "Will there be enough fuel to make it to that Nero place? It seems awfully far away."

Brutus's arm takes real estate next to Andorf. He takes over with details about the Atlantis. "Our current route slingshots us around Jupiter for a rendezvous with one of Saturn's outer moons. Titan has an abundance of liquid methane and other hydrocarbons pooling on its surface. As Serin said, we'll replenish our supplies and after several low-level siphoning orbits, we'll be well on our way, with inter-planetary drives powering us along."

"Doesn't the Empire have bases orbiting Saturn?" one man yells. "They'll be armed and waiting for us."

Brutus grins. "No worries, my friend. I know the buy running the satellite operation very well. After twenty years of exile, I'm sure he'll be quite glad to assist."

"His sister was one of Brutus's early love interests," Serin says, whispering in Andorf's ear. She takes his arm and leads him toward a vacant window. "This could go on for hours. He loves bragging about his baby." Her eyes drop to her midsection for a moment. "I mean the Atlantis, his first baby. Nothing happens on this starship without him knowing about it."

"What about the graffiti?" Andorf says. "I saw it painted on the side as I approached."

Serin laughs. "You mean 'The Angel'? That's what Brutus called me when we first met, before he knew better. It was his 'go ahead' signal telling me we were still on."

As if by instinct, Andorf messages her belly. He jerks his hand away after a strong kick. *Am I ready for this? What kind of father will I ...*

She returns his hand. Through his wide eyes, she peers into his soul. "You'll make a great father, Andorf. You needn't worry."

Andorf takes her in his arms, careful not to press hard against her mid-section. He breathes in the faint trace of her two-day old mountain flower perfume. "I'd be lost if anything happened to you." He begins to kiss her sweet lips when Darby and Wilhelm reappear.

Wilhelm waits for them to finish kissing before clearing his throat. "Yes, this observation room will be an interesting place to hang out. Just look at this view from the upper A-deck."

Darby squeezes her husband's hand. "Too bad we'll be losing our observation decks to training."

Wilhelm retracts his hand. "But we must keep the A-deck. I shall speak to Captain Thom about this."

Andorf glances at Serin. "It won't do any good, my old friend. It has already been decided."

Wilhelm glances at the panoramic window around them. He facetiously covers his heart. "But look at this view. Someone must—"

Darby's stern voice rises against the noisy crowd. "Wilhelm! Our baby is due in a few weeks. We have no medicines, no physicians, and no family to help. How have we lost all these critical things?"

Serin pulls on her necklace, raising the dangling chip from between breasts. "I remember scanning all sorts of strange devices in the late twentieth-century medical practice's archives."

Andorf shivers at thoughts of brightly illuminated rooms glistening with all sorts of medical devices and beeping alarms with staff in smocks rushing about doing their best to decipher complex machinery. His intense thoughts bleed into the other's thoughts.

"All those wires," Darby says. "How will we ever get them right?"

"Surely someone has seen those devices, someone who knows their purpose," Wilhelm says.

"Who in here looks that old?" Serin walks up and grabs at Brutus, yanking him away from his sermon. She coaxes him to join their party at the window. "What about those machines, the ones that make other machines? Surely we have them onboard."

Brutus grins, proudly. "Replicating printers? The Atlantis has six of them down in the bowel of the ship."

"Good," Wilhelm says. "We shall use them to build these medical devices."

Darby points at her belly. "It'd better be soon. We don't have much time, Wilhelm."

"What about labs and technicians and lots of people to train them?" Serin says.

"And teachers and story tellers?" Darby adds.

Brutus leans in and whispers in Andorf's ear. "Your days of sleeping late are over, Poo."

"Hey! Zoom the gloom everyone," Andorf says. "Tonight we enjoy our newfound freedom. We'll deal with these things in the morning."

Wilhelm stares into space, scratching his head. "Without a sunrise, how will we ever know it is morning?"

The room quiets to a Santa-looking man snaking his way through the mob. A hushing sound fans out through the room as Captain Thom and his navigator, Peter, approach Serin and company. "I didn't know we could fit this many on this A-deck." Thom chuckles. "Surely we must be violating one of the Empire's silly ordinances."

The crowd laughs and quickly quiets to the captain's maestro-like hand motions. Peter places an opened box at the captain's feet, uncorks the sole bottle of Rabbit Ridge's finest wine, and displays it to the crowd. The captain bends down, fills five small glasses, and distributes them to the immediate party, beginning with Serin.

Serin passes her glass to Brutus. "None for me." Andorf takes the second glass.

Darby winks at Serin. "Nor for me either." Wilhelm gladly accepts his wife's glass as the captain pours two more glasses.

The captain hands Peter's his glass and then taps the empty bottle a few times with his corkscrew. He removes a pouch from his pants pocket and unrolls his prized shofar from its protective leaves of cloth. After wetting his lips, he sounds long and joyous blows on the ram's horn before rewrapping the shofar and returning it to his pocket. He claims the fifth glass and holds it high above his head. "A toast for three self-less individuals. Without Serin, Brutus, Andorf, we would not be standing here now."

The honored trio takes bows to a deafening applause. With one long gulp, the captain drains his glass. "Enjoy the vino, my honored friends. From here out, sobriety is the day's order."

The other four follow suit. They lower their glasses to find the crowd around them entrenched in conversation. Captain Thom calls out, but his requests go unheard. He removes the shofar, and after one long hard blow, the room quiets. He strokes his well-trimmed beard, awaiting all eyes to refocus upon him.

"I take it no one here suffers from phobias as we have little time to address such trivial matters. Sacrifices shall be made, tough decisions to be cast. Boarding this ship and leaving everything and everyone behind was but your first. But putting this matter aside, it seems we have a pressing issue that needs addressing."

The captain pauses, scanning for stray eyes. "In short time we will be traveling well beyond humankind's furthest endeavor. Departing Titan base in seven hundred plus days, we will enter unexplored space. I have heard much talk about strange things going on outside these windows. Rumors are flying about the Atlantis faster than the speed of light. If only we could travel as fast, we would be back home within a decade."

Thom again scans the many faces, expecting questions but hearing none. He sees only detached faces. With things about to unravel, he appears to ponder how best to drive home his point.

"These rumors, stories," he says, after clearing his throat. "Ones of space pirates and phantom ships are just … stories. They are mere figments of overactive imaginations conceived for pure entertainment."

"But what about the alien fortresses, beyond Saturn," one shouts, anonymously "I've heard—"

"Believe me, there are no space pirates lurking behind the distant moons of Uranus, and there certainly are no phantom ships out there ready to take us down to Neptune's realm. The only Neptune we shall see on our voyage is the planet that we will use to boomerang ourselves out of this solar system. So rest assured, my fellow hijackers, anything you may have heard to the contrary should be considered pure poppycock. I would bet my life on this."

Captain Thom uncrosses his fingers, takes his wine bottle, and with his navigator, disappears amongst the crowd.

CHAPTER 40

The Next Morning

While passengers slept in the first morning after the launch, gypsies converted the G-level auditorium into a large dining hall and prepared the first official meal of day one. The triad arrives well ahead of the dinner crowd. They select carbene sporks and pass segmented trays beneath a quad dispenser nozzle. Sparse portions of carrots nubs, mixed greens, bread pudding, and an undetermined meat substitute blob into the appropriate quartered sections. Serin smiles at the vegetarian selection and finds a seat. Andorf and Brutus stand watching their undetermined meat substitute congeal to a solid before their disbelieving eyes.

Brutus holds his tray under the dispenser a second time, but nothing drops. "How can I possibly survive on this … crap?"

Andorf also goes for second helpings without success. He taps the chute, hoping to clear the jam, but nothing drops.

Brutus watches Andorf stuff his pockets with carrots. "Rabbit food, no insult intended."

Andorf stares dumbfounded at his remaining items. "None taken."

Brutus picks at his greens and pokes at the simulated meat item. "I knew we'd be eating light, but sheez, Binky eats better than this."

"Go grab a second tray, big guy," Serin says. "But just *this* time."

Andorf takes a seat beside her. He reaches for her carrots and gets his hand slapped. "For Binkers," he says, rubbing his hand.

Brutus presses into the seat across from Serin with his second helping. He slides both trays well beyond reach of Andorf's scavenging digits. The men choke down their veggies and meat substitute and move on to the more appetizing fluffy dessert when Andorf spots a small girl, emptying her tray's contents into a satchel. Gulping down the chewy dessert, he points at the girl with his head. "See that little girl over there?"

The others turn their heads to only adults forming a line. Serin covers her tray with both hands. "Don't you think about it, Andorf. You're not stealing my carrots."

"She was all by herself, at the dispenser. I swear."

Brutus pulls his trays closer. "Perhaps she's the phantom my fellow gypsies speak of. The one that leaves only crumbs behind."

Speakers about the dining room sound to the captain's voice. "Serin Gray to the bridge. Serin Gray, report to the bridge please."

Serin chomps on her dried-out bread pudding. "What now? I'm tiring of all the surprises."

The triad eases their trays and sporks through the sanitizer feed and arrives next door to radioman Pol greeting them outside the bridge. "They're here, Captain."

Serin steps inside to see navigator Peter seated at his instrument panel in the rear of the chamber with Captain Thom and first mate Murray, hovering above. Peter drags his index finger across the large octagon screen. "See that pair of blips?"

Serin scratches her head. "I see a couple blinking blue dots, if that's what you mean."

Casting a worried face, Captain Thom grabs Serin's arm, pulls her closer. "Those two blips appear to be starships, much like the Atlantis. It seems the Empire has still has a few aces up its sleeve."

Brutus homes in on the screen, staring hard at the troubling display and Serin's fingers running across the display, tracing the strobing blips. "They've been gaining on us so they must not be as heavily loaded."

Serin leaps at Brutus, scratching angrily at his hairy arms. "I thought you were handling all of this, big guy." She pause to eye the navigator. "How long? How long until they catch us?"

Peter rubs his chin for a good minute, studying the display. "A matter of hours."

The captain grimaces. "They must have launched shortly after our departure."

Serin paws at the captain, hyperventilating. "Can't we go any faster, Thom?"

The captain smirks. "We can't afford to waste precious fuel. Besides, everything is automated."

Serin runs through the day's events, analyzing everything leading up to their escape. All eyes are upon her as she paces the bridge, waving hands back and forth, mumbling aloud. "They'll board from the rear, head straight to the bridge." She halts in front of Brutus, ready to tear him a new one. "You told me there'd be no way this could happen. There was only the Atlantis, and what, now there are two others?"

Andorf has never seen her so worked up, not cool-headed, rational Serin. One by one, he scans the crew's calm demeanor, sharing her anxiety. Serin likewise scans the five detached faces before focusing on Andorf's perplexed gaze. *What is going on here, Andorf? Help me out.* At Andorf's shoulder pump, she turns to yell at the others.

"What's wrong with everyone?"

The crew stares off in the distance, unwilling to crack even a grin. Brutus appears red-faced as though he swallowed Aunt Bonnie's mashed potato pie. Serin nuzzles against him, batting her eyelashes.

At Brutus's snort, Thom and crew break into hard laughter. Pol raises the radio's volume and clicks the microphone three times. A familiar face appears on the radio screen as the voice breaks on the speaker. "Hey there big sis." <PHIST>

"Greg?" Serin yells.

Andorf grabs the microphone from Pol's hand. "Gregory? You're safe?"

Serin wrestles the mic from Andorf's grasp. She keys the button. "Is that really you?"

"None other." <PHIST>

Serin jumps into Brutus's arms, giving him a bear hug. Andorf flashes him an unseen thumbs up and retrieves the dangling microphone. "I can't wait to see you again, buddy."

Gregory laughs. "We're running with a skeleton crew aboard the Phoenix. Think you could spare a few passengers?" <PHIST>

Serin pulls away from Brutus. "I was wondering how we would feed and house the hundreds of unplanned passengers."

"We'll rendezvous at Titan, link our ships there," Brutus says.

"That'll be two years from now," Captain Thom says. "Until then, we must ration supplies."

Serin jabs Brutus's protruding belly "Some of us could stand to lose a few pounds." All but Brutus laugh.

Andorf leans into Brutus. "I've heard rumors of other ships, but—"

Brutus grins. "Did you really think we could retrieve enough Genghis from Nero with but one starship? The Phoenix and the Mayflower were docked on adjacent ridges, behind the overgrowth on the hidden side of Jake's Mountain. They took in our stragglers. I'll see about linking our ships."

"Always hedge your bets," Captain Thom says.

Serin brushes Brutus's cheek. "After all these years you still surprise me." Everyone cheers her on as she plants one on Brutus. She detaches from Brutus long enough to nibble playfully on Andorf's ear lobe. "Mind if I spend some private time with Brutus?" She whispers.

Chills run up Andorf's spine. "Not one tiny bit, long as you remember where you left off." *Besides, Binkers will be in there taking notes.*

Serin giggles at Binky's reference. She takes Andorf's index finger and presses it against his moist ear lobe. "Hold my place, lover." She grabs Brutus's hefty arm and leads him out the bridge door. "Come, big guy. You've yet to open *your* surprise."

Captain Thom grins. "Guess it's time for you to explore the ship, Andorf."

Andorf grabs the microphone. "Explore hell. Gregory and I have months of catching up."

Look for

WINDS OF DARKNESS

Gary McConville
Lagomorph Publishing LLC
http://www.lagopub.com

The author may be found at gmcconville@lagopub.com

Gary McConville lives in Roswell, Georgia with his wife, Nancy, and their dog, cats, and a current count of twelve penned rabbits. All of the estranged rescue pets came with unspoken tales of past lives.

Lagomorph Publishing LLC
http://www.lagopub.com

“Lest we judge a culture by the treatment of its pets.” Andorf ‘2048